He thought he'd done the right thing, but the consequences were more than he could pay…

They brought Grayson back into Costanzo's office and pressed him into a chair facing the desk. He sat stiffly, gripped with apprehension. Chauffeur parked in his usual position, behind and right. Gonzo sat port side, gun in lap.

Costanzo sat supreme, perched in his high-back leather chair, hands folded on his desk. Solomon about to dispense justice. "I'm afraid you're going to get it hard, Mr. Bolt." Costanzo had that fatherly tone of *this will hurt me more than you.* "Did you ever stop to think that there's only one way of being dead, but many ways of dying?"

Grayson felt something cold touch his spine, all the way down. "I don't follow."

"Take your man Stockard. He killed two of your beloved family members, wife and eldest son. Isn't that right?"

A strangling tightness gripped Grayson's throat. "That—that's right."

"Wouldn't you say a part of you died too?"

"What's your *point?*" Grayson's voice erupted in suppressed panic.

"You don't have to die to feel dead. I'm going to kill your other son. That'll be your punishment."

Chauffeur let out a long sigh. "Aaah."

The blood drained from Grayson's face. Just like that. Most people held the basic principle that no man should be punished for the deed of another. Costanzo was not one of them. Grayson would be cut right to the bone, and his son would be the sharpest knife Costanzo could use. Costanzo had spelled out the thought in invisible brushstrokes. It was there and Grayson had tried not to see it.

Costanzo continued as though his words had no great significance. "It'll be tough, I know. But look at it this way." His face twisted into a cruel grin. "You've already lost one son, so you know what to expect."

A tax attorney with integrity…a powerful mobster determined to bend his will…

Grayson Bolt isn't about to compromise his integrity to help a notorious crime boss escape the cross-hairs of the IRS. But there's a steep price to pay for defying The Man—Grayson's beloved wife and older son.

There's only one way for Grayson to prevent his younger son, Jim, an innocent golf prodigy, from also being taken out: play a dangerous game of cat and mouse. And what will Jim be forced to do when the woman he loves gets ensnarled in a web of betrayal and deceit?

THE
DEVIL
ORDERS
TAKEOUT

BILL A. BRIER

A Black Opal Books Publication

GENRE: MYSTERY/CRIME THRILLER

THE DEVIL ORDERS TAKEOUT
Copyright © 2017 by Bill A. Brier
Cover Design by Tammy Seidick
All cover art copyright © 2017
All Rights Reserved
Print ISBN: 978-1-626946-07-1

First Publication: APRIL 2017

Published by Black Opal Books **http://www.blackopalbooks.com**

THE DEVIL ORDERS TAKEOUT

PART I

"Let the devil catch you but by a single hair,
and you are his forever."
~ *Gotthold Ephraim Lessing*

CHAPTER 1

The sun sat low in the sky by the time Grayson Bolt finally stored the last of the luggage in the back of the Mercedes. His black suitcase looked stodgy next to Sandra's playful leopard print, complete with pink nametag. As usual, hers was stuffed near to bursting, while his held the bare essentials: underwear, toothbrush, and socks.

Their luggage habits reflected their personalities. Sandra had always been spontaneous and energetic, while Grayson had been cool, practical, and driven. Even now, minutes before departing on their first real anniversary celebration in years—a last-minute trip to Olive Garden didn't count—his mind was already running over everything he'd need to do when he got back to the office: finish the Henderson tax file, look into the Colbenson case. Tax season was almost upon him and—

Shut up, he commanded himself. *This weekend isn't about work. This weekend is about Sandra.*

Hard to believe someone as gorgeous and amazing as Sandra had agreed to marry him—and had actually stuck with him for all these years despite his long office hours.

"Is everything there?" Sandra called from the doorway.

"Yep!" Grayson hollered back, watching as she dashed to the car all bundled up in a puffy white coat at least two sizes too big. Even though she hadn't bothered to put on any makeup for the drive and had thrown her dark hair up into a messy bun, Grayson still felt his temperature rise the longer he watched her. She was stunning, with endless brown eyes that sucked him in and a crooked smile that made his heart slug faster.

She opened the passenger door and gasped in delight, pulling out a bouquet of twelve perfect red roses. "Grayson! They're beautiful!"

"I just hope they survive the ride," he replied. "Maybe you should tuck them in the back, next to the gun."

Sandra buried her nose in the bouquet, breathing in its scent. "They're so romantic," she said, planting a kiss on his lips. "You've earned a surprise for later."

Grayson grinned and started the engine. *My God, she's something.*

Sandra reached behind her and laid down the bouquet before turning back to him and batting her sparkling eyes. "I saw champagne but no bearskin rug. Will I have to send you out in the snow to wrestle a grizzly?"

"Grrr."

As Grayson headed north on Interstate 87, Sandra applied lip gloss, snapped the visor mirror shut, and dropped the gloss into her purse. "Darn," she said, rummaging inside. "I left my driving glasses in my car."

"You could always wear your prescription ski goggles."

"Wouldn't I look cute?" Sandra flipped the mirror open again and peered in. She tugged the skin at the corner of one eye. "Look at this," she said, turning to him. "Crow's feet, and I'm not even forty. Should I get my eyes done?"

He glanced at her. "Forget it. You're beautiful."

"Men are lucky. Look at you, years older and—"

"Don't remind me. I hate thinking of the big five-o."

She closed the visor. "That's okay. I like your gray." She stroked the hair above his ear. "It matches your sexy gray eyes."

"Careful or I'll start hunting for that bearskin."

Sandra smiled. "We've got the whole weekend without the kids. And please, let's agree, no golf talk. I hear it every day from Troy."

He raised two fingers. "Scout's honor. He can pester grandma and his little brother for two days."

An hour later they turned west onto Route 28, a peaceful mountain road recently plowed. A blue sky replaced earlier clouds, and the sun reflected off the snow. Grayson rubbed his temples as a dull throb began to build behind his eyes. "Sweetheart, I'm getting a migraine. We've got to stop."

"I have Tylenol," Sandra offered, reaching for her purse.

"That won't help. I need to close my eyes. Maybe we should find a hotel for the night."

"Oh, honey, we're only an hour from the lodge. I'll drive."

"You don't have your glasses."

"I'll be fine. Pull over."

With the seat and mirrors adjusted, Sandra swung the car onto the road while Grayson leaned back and closed his eyes. He pictured the thickly wooded route of aspen and poplar as she maneuvered the car through the turns and imagined the stream rising and falling on the left where the road dropped off sharply. The car thumped-thumped-thumped, and his eyes shot open. Sandra had drifted onto the shoulder.

"Sorry, honey. I was turning up the heater," she explained with a guilty smile.

They rounded a bend and Sandra screamed. A pale horse lay in the narrow road, legs kicking. Sandra slammed on the brakes.

Grayson gasped and braced his hands on the dash.

She turned the wheel, and the car veered sideways in the slush.

My God! It's either the horse or the cliff.

They skidded toward the cliff. He grabbed the wheel, yanked it the other way. The car's rear-end whipped around, just missing the horse's thrashing hooves.

Sandra pulled over and stopped the car. "Oh, my God!" She put a hand to her chest. "I didn't see it until—"

"That's okay, you didn't hit it." *Of all the times to have a headache.* He glanced out the rear window. The horse wore a saddle and was struggling on an icy patch where trees arched over the pavement. "I've got to help that animal off the road and search for the rider." He took her hands. "Everything will be okay."

He climbed out of the car and leaned against it for a moment. A sharp pain stabbed behind one eye.

The horse had wriggled up onto a knee at the edge of the ice. The poor thing panted heavily, its eyes wild as it swung its head back and forth. Grayson worried that it might regain its footing only to run off and get hit by a car or tumble over the cliff.

He ran the short distance to the animal. "Easy, boy. Easy."

The horse was struggling to get to its feet, head bobbing. It got up onto both knees. Grayson took the reins and stepped back. The horse tottered to its feet with a loud nicker. Grayson stroked the animal. "Good fella. Good fella."

"Help! Is somebody up there?" A child's frightened cry came from the steep ravine below.

Grayson swung around. "Hello?"

"Yes, yes! Down here!"

He moved to the cliff's edge and looked over the side. About ten feet down and maybe sixty feet above a rocky stream, a young girl wearing a blue riding helmet was caught in a thicket of hemlock, their roots protruding from the cliff like shaggy paws.

Icy panic squeezed at Grayson's throat, but he forced it down, calling out, "Everything will be all right. What's your name, sweetheart?"

"My horse fell on the ice!"

"I know, honey. He's fine, I have him right here. What's your name?"

"Kim," she answered.

Grayson looked at the horse. He wished he could use its reins to secure the girl and pull her up, but they were too short. "Don't worry, Kim, we'll get you out of there."

He could remove the horse's reins, hold one end, and toss the other to Kim. That would ensure she didn't slip from her fragile perch and plunge into the stream, and it would also give him time to use his cell phone to call for help.

"What's your horse's name?" he asked.

"Dakota."

"Okay, Kim. I'm going to toss you Dakota's reins."

"No!" she yelled. "Use his lead rope, that's better."

"I've got it," Sandra said.

Grayson turned to see her removing the rope from the saddle. He took it and peered back down at Kim. She was on her stomach, her hands clinging to the thicket.

"Tie the rope to Dakota's saddle and throw me the other end," she called. "He'll pull me up."

Grayson tossed her the rope, and she managed to hitch the loop under her arms. Then he swiftly tied the other end to the saddle horn.

"Let's go, Dakota," Grayson coaxed.

He stood by the gelding, tugging the reins, his temples pounding. Dakota's feet danced in place, but he refused to move. Grayson grabbed the bridle and yanked hard. The horse took two steps back, the rope snapped taut, and then he stopped.

Sandra, lying on her stomach at the edge of the cliff, looked over. "No, keep going!"

Grayson gave a hard jerk on the bridle, and the horse backed up a little more. "Good boy, easy…easy."

"Hold on, you're doing fine," Sandra shouted down to Kim.

Grayson heard an engine rev and looked over Dakota's back to see a battered green pickup round the bend and barrel toward him in the small turnout. The horse's ears twitched as he pranced nervously. The driver hit the brakes, and the pickup's rear end swept near the horse, stirring slush and spitting gravel.

Grayson gripped the bridle firmly to keep the panicked horse from bolting. The pickup's dented door swung open and a leather-faced man in a crumpled cowboy hat jumped out.

"What the hell ya doing with my granddaughter's horse?"

Grayson detected a drunken slur.

The man charged at him, clawing for the reins like a maniac, his glassy eyes raging. "Where's my—"

The horse jerked its head up, snorted, and swung its hindquarters around, hitting Grayson's side and almost knocking him to the ground. The man staggered, and Grayson shouted, "Hey! Get the hell—there's a girl down there. Back off!"

"Don't tell me what to do!" The man lurched for the reins.

The two struggled, each trying to control Dakota.

"Goddammit, you're scaring the horse," Grayson yelled. "We're rescuing a—"

"Aaahhhh!" Kim cried.

"Stop the horse!" Sandra shouted. "The rope slipped off one arm."

"That's my granddaughter!" the man hollered as Dakota neighed and pranced. "Gimme those reins!"

Grayson, almost blinded by his migraine, saw in horror the steel-shod hooves flash above him and chop downward like sledgehammers. One hoof caught him in a glancing and painful blow on the shoulder, knocking him into the slush, as the reins slipped from his hands.

The man lunged for them, missed, slipped, and fell.

The horse reared onto its hind legs, and the rope's empty loop sailed up from below and into the air.

"Oh my God!" Sandra shrieked. "She's gone!"

CHAPTER 2

Grayson and Sandra watched the ambulance maneuver up the snow-covered gravel road from the creek below them. It carried the body of young Kim, who an hour before had plunged into the frigid rock-filled waters to her death.

The police told Grayson and Sandra to wait by the squad car while they took the grandfather's statement.

The two hardly spoke, still numb over the girl's death. Ten minutes later, one of the officers climbed up from the stream, paused a moment, and put a hand on one knee to catch his breath. He was a good thirty pounds heavier than Grayson, who, at six-one, tipped in at a solid one-ninety.

Grayson watched nervously as the officer approached his Mercedes. After peering inside, he bent down to inspect the front end. He stood, arched his back, and started toward Grayson and Sandra with a stern, no nonsense face. Grayson's mouth twisted, and he said under his breath, "I'll do the talking. I don't want you getting cited for not wearing your glasses."

The policeman took their driver's licenses, his dark eyes checking each closely. "Long Island," he said. "You folks are a ways from home. By the looks of your gear, you plan on doing some skiin' and shootin'."

"Not at the same time," Grayson said, then immediately wished he hadn't tried being humorous.

The cop gave him a cold stare. "I didn't think so." He tossed his head toward the car. "That Perazzi in the back seat. Factory choke?"

Grayson nodded. "Nothing fancy. I only shoot skeet. We were on our way to Miller's lodge. It's not far—"

"I know where it is."

Grayson spotted the crazy grandfather talking with another officer. The man pointed up the hillside, then to Grayson's car.

"That poor girl," Sandra said. It's awful, it's just—" She shuddered. "Is that man her grandfather? That's what he yelled."

The officer nodded. "Gus Stockard. He's a local. I'd like to hear from you two what happened." He put their licenses in his shirt pocket and took out a notebook and pen.

Sandra peered at the ground. Grayson started, "I drove around a bend and saw the horse on its back, struggling on the road. I stopped and—"

"You say the horse was lying on the road?"

"That's right. I had to swerve to avoid hitting it."

"I see." The officer clicked his pen and began writing. "Go on."

"I pulled over and ran to the horse." Grayson told him all that followed.

The officer stopped writing and turned to Sandra. "You've been awfully quiet, Mrs. Bolt. I saw a bottle of champagne in your car."

"It's our anniversary."

"So you decided to celebrate up here in the Catskills, drink some bubbly, get in a little skiin', some skeet shootin'?"

"That's right," Grayson said.

The officer turned to him with a scowl. "I wasn't asking you, Mr. Bolt."

"Yes," Sandra said. "We come here often. They know us up at the lodge."

"Your husband said that you came upon the horse lying in the road."

"That's right. He was trying to get up from an ice patch that he must have slipped on."

"Then what happened?"

Sandra cleared her throat. "My husband slammed on the brakes, and we skidded past the horse."

"Your car didn't hit the horse?"

"It certainly did not."

He squinted at her. "You sure?"

She held his stare. "Positive."

He peered at his notes and paged back. "That's right, your husband stated, 'I had to swerve to avoid hitting it.' That's what you said, isn't it, Mr. Bolt?"

Heat rose to Grayson's face. "That's correct."

The officer put away his notebook and pen. "That's interesting, because Mr. Stockard has a different version of events. He said that you—" He pointed to Sandra. "—were driving and struck the horse with your car."

Sandra's eyes flicked wide. Grayson shook his head, protesting. "He wasn't even here. How would he know? And did you happen to notice he's been drinking?"

"He lives right up there and saw everything." The officer pointed up the hill. "Sorry to spoil your anniversary, ma'am, but I'm going to have to take you both down to the station." He whistled and hailed his partner over.

"Wait a minute," Grayson burst. "He's lying. You looked at my car. Did you see any sign of—"

The officer opened the rear door of his police car. "Get in."

Grayson and Sandra looked at each other but climbed inside. Stockard appeared and pressed his face, twisted and hateful, against Grayson's window. "Bastard murderers," he yelled. "Don't think you're rid of me. She was all I had left and ya took her away. I'll get even. I'll get good and even."

A cold knot gripped Grayson's heart. He turned to Sandra, her mouth agape, threw his arms around her, and the car took off.

CHAPTER 3

T hree ladies," announced the chubby-faced Newark police chief. Foley laid down his cards and worked an ivory toothpick in his mouth. "And what do you know—a pair of treys." Flashing a grin broader than the poker table, he added, "I guess that's a full house."

The tan-faced golf pro tossed down his cards. "Lucky bastard." He rose to leave.

"He'd rather be lucky than good," Grayson quipped, scooping up the cards. He hosted a monthly poker game with a few regulars at the private Knickerbocker Club on New York's Fifth Avenue. He wasn't the sharpest player at the table, but the game provided a good way to unwind, and he never lost more than pocket change. Over the years, he'd accumulated a faithful group of guys, most of them professional acquaintances from law firms or fellow golfers.

Others stubbed out their cigars, got up, and reached for their coats.

Grayson signaled Police Chief Foley to stick around for a nightcap. He wanted to express thanks for the chief getting him off the hook with the police, and also to tell him about his chat with Mario Costanzo. They ordered brandy and retreated to comfortable lounge chairs.

"Costanzo called again," Grayson said.

The chief's eyebrows rode up.

"Said to name a price," Grayson added. "He's desperate."

"He's also a mobster. You'd best avoid him like a Bronx alley. Let him find another tax lawyer dumb enough to hook up with his kind."

"I told him emphatically that I'm not interested." A waiter dropped off their drinks. "I didn't get a chance to thank you the other day for getting me off the hook with the Catskill police."

"They couldn't have held you, even if I hadn't known the chief. Not without evidence."

"I admitted at the station that I wasn't driving. With an eye witness, I didn't feel comfortable lying."

"What eye witness?"

"The little girl's wacko grandfather, Stockard. A cop told me he lives up on the ridge within sight of the road. He told the cops he saw Sandra hit the horse. Said he heard tires squeal and looked down. Later he admitted that he only assumed the horse was hit. Saw it sprawled out and me getting out of the car on the passenger side. After your call, the cops were nice enough to us. Said that Stockard's a known drunk and troublemaker. They gave Sandra a warning about driving without her glasses. Not a peep to me about lying."

"A goddamn shame about the little girl."

"Stockard's threats made it all the more grisly. He screamed something about getting even."

"Think he was serious?"

"From the look in his eyes, damn serious."

"I think you should report him, then. It's against the law to threaten someone. What exactly did he say?"

"Oh, nothing that would hold up in court. It was all vague and said in the heat of the moment. I don't think the police would take it seriously."

"I take it seriously. And I think you should, too."

✒✒✒

Grayson knocked off work early the next afternoon to take Sandra to dinner. She deserved it after what she'd been through. Not quite the weekend he'd planned.

"Cab, Mr. Bolt?" Ahmad, the doorman, asked, rolling a coin across his knuckles.

"Penn Station right away. Wait—make that Flower Madness, on West Fourteenth." Flowers always brightened Sandra's spirits.

Ahmad dashed to the curb, arms waving. "Late again, Mr. Bolt?"

"If I'm not late, I'm not working hard enough." Grayson slipped Ahmad a tip and hopped into the cab.

If flowers lifted Sandra's mood, work lifted Grayson's. He'd spent the morning solving a client's complex tax problem. The client, a Puerto Rican, had invested his family's savings in a Jersey scrap metal business but had been advised by his brother-in-law that cheating the tax system was the American way. Fortunately for the immigrant, Grayson had found a loophole even more arcane than the man's phony tax form. But Grayson's fee would have left the man's checkbook low enough for him to kiss the ground without stooping, so he took the case pro bono.

Concern for others was something Grayson learned from his father. As a boy, Grayson could hit a golf ball farther, hurl a baseball faster, and think quicker than any of his peers. His father drilled into him that others hadn't had the advantages he had. And to keep his head on straight, Grayson received only a modest allowance as a kid, had to pay his own way through college, and spent two hours every week volunteering at the local food shelf.

The challenge of winning, especially under pressure, excited him far more than money. But he liked money too, and rich people getting leaned on by the IRS paid cheerfully for his expertise. Anyone gambling on the crap tables of the legal system ran to Grayson, and nobody threw hotter dice.

The taxi turned onto West Fourteen Street, pulled over, and dropped Grayson off. "Wait here," he told the driver. "I'll be back." He sidestepped a group of businessmen entering a Turkish deli and dashed into the flower shop.

"Mr. Bolt, what a surprise." Nagina, the owner, frowned. "Did you phone in an order?"

"No, I'm here spur of the moment." He took a deep breath, savoring the thick, sweet fragrance of exotic tiger lilies and classic roses.

"And how's your mother? Enjoying her visit?"

"She was only here a couple days. She's back in Florida now. Listen, I'm taking Sandra out to dinner and I'd like to surprise her with something."

"Roses, of course. Maybe I throw in some orchids. They whisper elegance." She pointed to a photograph of herself with President Clinton. "He was here, you know. Fifteen years ago." In a hushed tone she added, "The flowers were for—"

"I know, Hillary." Grayson had heard the story many times, and often thought to say, "Don't bet on it."

Nagina handed him the bouquet filled with romantic reds and a hint of passionate orange.

"They're beautiful," Grayson said. "Slap an extra twenty on the bill."

The cabbie dropped Grayson at Penn Station. Forty minutes later, he jumped off the train at Westbury, Long Island, loped through the parking lot with his briefcase and flowers, and climbed into his car.

He smiled, thinking back to when he'd first laid eyes on Sandra at a UN luncheon. An interpreter with curly black hair, full arching eyebrows, and enough sex appeal to stampede an assembly of ambassadors, she still had a figure that belonged in a Ferrari.

He turned onto his street where his ten-year-old son Troy swung a golf club in the front yard. As Grayson parked and climbed out of his car, Troy ran to him. "Hey, Dad, you shoulda seen me at practice. I changed my grip like you showed me and didn't hook one shot."

"Fantastic!" Grayson ruffled the boy's hair. "And your chipping, did you work on that like I told you?"

"I was gonna but ran out of balls."

"You want to play like a pro, right?"

"Yeah," Troy said, picking up a golf towel from the ground.

Grayson ruffled the boy's hair again. "Then listen to your coach, okay?"

"Hey, Dad," Jim hollered, scampering from the house, "make Troy give me back my Nintendo."

"Tell him to stop coming into my room," Troy said, wiping grass off his club.

Grayson tugged the bill of eight-year-old Jim's baseball cap. "Hey, sport, stay out of your brother's room. Troy, give him his Nintendo."

"Troy!" Sandra yelled from the porch, her face stern. "I told you to get in here, now! You too, Jim." She shooed them into the house and hurried to Grayson.

"What's the problem?"

She crossed her arms tightly. "He was here. I saw his pickup."

Grayson's heart clawed its way into his throat. "You mean Stockard's?"

She nodded rapidly. "It was green, with a dent in the door. It crept by no more than ten minutes ago."

Grayson's gaze swept up and down the street, but by now Stockard had disappeared. His stomach twisted, both from fear and from rage. This was the third time the bereaved grandfather had driven by their home, and he was always long gone by the time Grayson returned, leaving no trace behind but Sandra's lingering fear. The worst part was Grayson's utter inability to do anything about it. Driving by a person's house was hardly reason to have somebody arrested.

Grayson feared that, by the time he had evidence of criminal intent, it might be too late.

ℰℐℰℐ

Grayson and Sandra stayed in that evening and ordered Chinese food. Grayson couldn't stop himself from continually stepping outside to look up and down the street for Stockard. The man was never around—only the troublesome whiff of his presence.

Sandra wiped off the table. "Sweetheart, we need to do something about that man. After all, he did threaten us."

She tried to sound practical, but there was an undercurrent of fear in her voice that Grayson recognized all too painfully. He recalled Stockard's words. *I'll get even. I'll get good and even*. What would make them even? With growing worries, he thought of his two sons.

"I'll have him investigated, maybe seek a restraining order," he said. "Meanwhile, let's keep the kids inside." He took her hands and tried a comforting smile. "Some anniversary, huh?"

She brushed the hair back from his ear. "I never got to give you the surprise I promised."

"What did I miss out on?"

"I was going to get you that Rolex I saw you try on in the lodge gift shop the last time we were there."

"This nightmare will be over soon, and we'll celebrate our anniversary in Hawaii. You can surprise me there." He kissed her cheek and strolled into the family room where the boys were doing homework. "Hey, guys, I have to talk to you about something. But first, have either of you seen a green pickup around the neighborhood recently?"

They both said no.

"Troy, how about when you were swinging your clubs in the front yard?"

Troy shook his head. "Is there a serial killer stalking the neighborhood?"

"Maybe a rapist," Jim said. "I saw on the news—"

"Nothing like that," Grayson said, trying to laugh, but unable to make it work. "The grandfather of the little girl who was killed is upset, and your mother saw his pickup around. So we don't want you outside playing for a while."

"What's the big deal?" Troy asked.

"No big deal, but until I find out more about him, we need to play it cool."

Troy scowled, kicking at the carpet.

"Okay, you can play outside, but confine your practice to the back yard."

"But my clubs are right by—"

"Troy! You heard me."

"Fine," Troy muttered. "But this is stupid. Nothing is going to happen, anyway."

CHAPTER 4

The next morning, Grayson was in court when his secretary, Elizabeth, marched into his office, carrying mail, the *Wall Street Journal,* and the *New York Times*. The office was a Manhattan loft located on trendy Great Jones Street. An original Salvador Dali hung over an imported black leather couch. Elizabeth placed the bundle on the credenza under the window and flipped the antique desk calendar to the correct date.

As she pulled Grayson's door shut, a gruff voice startled her from behind.

"Good morning," growled a round-faced stranger, standing in her office. The gentleman was on the heavier side, though the tailoring on his double-breasted suit almost concealed the fact. His dark eyes were set deep into his skull and his thick black hair was perfectly coiffed.

Elizabeth patted her hair and eased in behind her desk. "Good morning, may I help you?"

"I need to speak to Mr. Bolt," he said, his voice hard.

"I'm afraid he had an early court date. Do you have an appointment?"

He glanced at his watch. "It's no longer early. When's he expected?"

She regarded him while he chewed the inside of his cheeks. "Why don't you leave me your name and number?"

"The name's Costanzo, and my number's that chair." He threw a side nod. "Tell me the minute he gets in." He withdrew a paperback from his hip pocket and sat down.

Twenty minutes later the man's cell phone rang. He put the

book in his lap and wrestled a phone from his coat, smiling as he looked down at it. "Hi, Ma. How you feeling? They feed you a good breakfast?"

Grayson's phone line lit up, indicating he was in his office. He had entered through the side door. Elizabeth eased out of her chair and slipped inside. "A Mr. Costanzo's here to see you."

Grayson nearly dropped the case file he was holding. "What?"

"He's very persistent."

"I've already told him I won't take his case. Get rid of him."

Elizabeth returned to her desk, trying to devise a tactful way to blow the man off. She waited until Costanzo had finished his call, then spoke up, "You know, Mr. Bolt is *very* busy. I'll tell him you were here."

"Here and waiting," he said, his nose buried in his book.

Her phone buzzed. She turned her chair away from the man. "Right away," she said softly and hung up. She stepped quietly to a cabinet, withdrew a file, and entered Grayson's office, closing the door behind her. She handed him the file. "Mr. Costanzo refuses—"

The door opened behind her.

∽∾∽

Grayson looked up from writing to see the man standing in the doorway. His eyes were cold, black, and not particularly friendly. The man clumped over to the desk. "I'm Mario Costanzo." He glanced at Elizabeth and jerked his head at the door, a gesture that he seemed used to. He turned back to Grayson. "I'll only take a minute."

Words seemed to generate from deep in his throat, giving his voice a hardness you could etch with a laser.

Elizabeth stared at Grayson with her mouth open.

He tossed his pen onto the desk. "It's all right, Elizabeth," he told her, and she retreated to the other room. "Okay, Mr. Costanzo. One minute."

Grayson gestured to a chair and didn't try to wipe the impatience off his face.

Costanzo sat down and bent forward. "Mr. Bolt, I'd like you to reconsider your decision."

Grayson shook his head. "Look, I've already explained, I have a strict policy to maintain a low profile. It's something my clients require. To represent you would be a violation of that policy."

"I want to make you an offer."

"*Mr.* Costanzo," Grayson said, with an edge, "you'll only get yourself out of breath. I've told you, I'm not—"

Costanzo raised his hand, reached into a breast pocket of his fine blue suit, and withdrew an envelope. A thick envelope. He placed it on Grayson's desk and gave it a light tap. "For two minutes of your time. That's all I ask. I want nothing for nothing."

Grayson glanced at the bulging envelope and knew it must be crammed with cash. Maybe twenty grand.

"You already know the basic details of my situation," Costanzo said, "so I won't spend time discussing them now."

Grayson nodded and brushed a piece of lint from his sleeve.

"I have four tax experts working on my case, and they're failing me. I'm not a lawyer, but I know—" He tapped his temple. "—*know*, there's a way out of this."

Grayson picked up a pen and drummed it on a legal pad. Costanzo was right. He simply hadn't found a lawyer good enough.

Costanzo rubbed his hands together like men do when they're nervous and want something. "Here's my offer. You review my case and tell me how my lawyers can beat these bastards. That's it. You deal only with me. No one will know of your involvement. That I promise."

Grayson eyed the envelope again. Tempting. He wasn't going to lie to himself about that. He might already be a successful lawyer, but anyone could find use for a $20,000 surprise bonus. *And,* he rationalized, *it's not like you haven't helped sketchy characters before.* But those clients were different. Those clients were business owners trying to save as much of their income as possible. They weren't mob bosses trying to outsmart the FBI. They weren't alleged criminals accused of assassinating their rivals, running prostitution rings, and distributing hard drugs to poor neighborhoods. Was that the kind of client he wanted to help?

Chief Foley was right. Best to stay away from this hood, no matter how many Ben Franklins he offered. Grayson stood and shook his head. "Sorry, can't do that."

Costanzo leaped to his feet. "It'll be our secret." His mouth twitched. "You look at my case. If it's hopeless—" He shrugged. "—so be it. Your job's done. I'll pay anything. The sky's the limit."

Grayson walked around his desk, picked up the envelope, and handed it to Costanzo. "That's not something I can do." He placed a hand on Costanzo's shoulder and ushered him toward the door. "Goodbye, Mr. Costanzo."

Costanzo jerked away from Grayson's touch. "You just made the biggest mistake of your life, Mr. hotshot lawyer." He stormed from the office, knocking the files off Elizabeth's desk as he swept by, and slammed the door behind him.

"Goodness," Elizabeth murmured as she knelt to gather the papers. "What an unpleasant man."

"That he is," Grayson said, bending down to help her.

"He seemed awfully upset," she added, nervousness creeping into her voice.

"Don't worry," Grayson assured her. "He's just a lot of hot air."

But inside, he wasn't so sure.

CHAPTER 5

The next day, Grayson walked into his office and saw an envelope without a return address on top of his pile of mail. Inside, a single playing card: the ace of spades.

"That son of a bitch!" he spat as the import of the card struck home.

He picked up the phone and dialed private detective Harold Wilson, a friend and former head of the Pinkerton Detective Agency.

"Someone named Stockard is getting personal with me, and I need him investigated, pronto, Hal," Grayson explained. "The bastard's stalking my family, even sent me an ace of spades."

"The death card," Hal stated sagely. "That's a strong smoke signal. You're smart to have him checked out. Give me the particulars and twenty-four hours."

Hal was true to his word. A day later, Grayson's secretary buzzed. "Detective Wilson's on line one."

Grayson picked up. "Well, manage to learn anything?"

"Your boy's a doozy."

"Let's hear it."

"I'm sending a detailed email attachment, but here's the highlights. Let's see, he was booted out of the army as a sergeant. Has a few drunk and disorderly convictions. Did some hard time. He's currently holding down a job with the traffic engineering department."

"What'd he do time for?"

"Killing his son. Seems a few years back his daughter-in-law phoned him and pleaded for help. The son was chasing her through the house. Stockard, who'd been drinking, hauled his ass over there, and by now the son was clobbering the wife pretty bad. Stockard dragged him off, but the daughter-in-law had a change of heart and started fighting him. That must have really pissed Stockard off, because he threw her down the stairs, which caused a miscarriage."

"My God, where was Kim during all of this?"

"With the daughter-in-law's parents."

"What about the son?"

"Stockard choked him to death. Must be strong as a bear. A couple years later his wife and daughter-in-law died in an automobile accident. Subsequently, the maternal grandparents gained custody of Kim. Stockard, the paternal grandparent, was granted monthly visitation privileges."

"I see." *So little Kim was visiting Stockard the day she died.* "That's it?"

"That's the meat and potatoes of it. If he's harassing you, I suggest filing a restraining order."

"Yeah, that sounds like the best plan," Grayson agreed. He was about to say so long when a thought popped into his head. "Say, do me a favor and find out what you can on Mario Costanzo." Since turning the mobster down, and then being threatened by him, Grayson felt not just alarmed, but frightened.

"There's a lot to know. You want I should start with baby pictures?"

"A brief email will be fine. I just want a handle on the guy."

☙❧

The following morning, Grayson stayed home and called his assistant, Thompson. "I'm not coming in for a few days. With all that's been happening with this Stockard psycho, I want to keep close to my family."

"No problem. I'll hold down the fort."

Grayson hung up, checked his computer, and saw an email from Detective Wilson. The subject line said *Mario Costanzo.* Grayson scanned it. Costanzo was into loan sharking, gam-

bling, prostitution, narcotics, identity theft—cyber and otherwise—and murder. No personal vices except sports betting.
Expected to be indicted for tax fraud.

That's one nasty character. Grayson headed downstairs and
saw Troy watching cartoons. "Hey, bub, why aren't you ready
for school?"

"No school, Dad. It's teacher's day."

Grayson thought a minute. "I have the day off, too. What
do you say we get in a round?"

An hour later, they were on the driving range, preparing to
warm up.

"I want to watch you hit a few," Grayson said.

He yanked out a club from Troy's bag and reached in for
his glove. When he pulled it out, a golf ball fell onto the concrete. He caught it on the bounce, looked at it, and sucked in a
surprised breath. It had the ace of spades stamped on it. "Troy,
where did you get this ball?"

"I got a whole bunch. They all have the same cool picture."

"Where'd they come from?"

"Some old man."

"What man?"

"Never saw him before. Yesterday, I was over there putting
and he came up and gave 'em to me. Said I deserved them.
Neat, huh?"

CHAPTER 6

Grayson headed north on I-87 into the mountains toward Stockard's house. Before filing a restraining order, he wanted to assess Stockard in person. Maybe he could reason with him, maybe not. Either way, he wanted to know whether this bastard planned to simply harass or actually attempt serious harm.

He turned onto Stockard's snow-covered gravel drive, parked, and stepped from the car under a sky of yellow haze. The air was cold, windy, and sharp as needles. He spotted Stockard in the barn and treaded inside, wondering if he should have brought his gun.

"I want to talk to you," he said firmly.

Stockard gave him a side-glance when the car door closed but ignored him now while he fed Dakota and another horse. The man stood lanky, with a dust-colored mustache and leathery, sun-stained face and forehead ending at a hat line where the skin glowed white. Faded jeans hung off his narrow hips and were tucked into snakeskin cowboy boots. Probably somewhere in his sixties. Hard to tell with his type.

Stockard threw down his pitchfork and strode past Grayson and out of the barn. "Follow me," he said, throwing the words over his shoulder.

Grayson trailed behind, gripping his collar against the cold. Stockard scuffed toward the house like a caged animal that had paced out the short distance many times.

The ranch-style house perched on a plot of high ground with large shade trees and a vast view of the valley and road below.

Stockard clomped up the porch. "Come in," he said, without looking back.

Near the front door, an American flag fluttered and snapped in the wind. Inside, the living room was small and dark, filled with wooden furniture. Its stench reminded Grayson of early morning in a saloon. Stained brown cushions covered a pine couch, and a female wrestling magazine sat on a cluttered coffee table with carved legs.

Stockard gestured for Grayson to sit by the window in an oak armchair. The curtains had brown splatters. Probably tobacco spittle. Beyond the fireplace, a hallway led off to the back. The house was like Stockard himself, spooky and prone to dark recesses. The old man pressed his shoulder against the stone fireplace and tugged a fat cigar from a fur-lined waistcoat pocket. "You wanna talk. Talk."

Awkwardly, Grayson cleared his throat. "First, I want you to know that not a day passes when Mrs. Bolt and I don't grieve for your granddaughter. But so help me, God—" He held up his hand as though swearing. "—Sandra did not hit Dakota with the car. He'd already fallen onto the road. We stopped and tried to help. As for Kim—" He took a breath and released it. "It was a tragic accident." *And if it weren't for your idiocy, it wouldn't have happened.*

Stockard looked down at his unlit cigar and stroked it with his thumb but said nothing. His free hand scraped, scraped against whisker stubble. He looked at Grayson. "Have ya seen combat, Mr. Bolt?" He bit off the end of his cigar and spit it onto the floor, missing the fireplace.

"What?"

"You heard me." Stockard struck a match on the fireplace and short-puffed the cigar. He threw the match into the blaze and hooked a slab-sized thumb under his thick leather belt. "Ever been on the battlefield?"

"South China Sea. But what the hell does—"

"Navy! I said battlefield, not a fuckin' boat."

Grayson's face grew hot.

Stockard blew out a huge puff of smoke that billowed like a ship's gun. "Tell ya what I done." He jammed the cigar into his mouth. "I done real fightin'. Vietnam. Two tours. Leveled thirteen villages in six days. Killed more gooks than you got brains."

Grayson's face grew even hotter. "What do you want from me, Stockard?"

"Whatsamatter, don't wanna talk about fightin'?" Stockard smoothed a finger down each side of a drooping mustache. "How 'bout dyin'? That's somethin' you know about. To die fightin' fer your country—well, that's dyin' ya can't blame anyone for except maybe piss-ass gooks, and hell, ya can't blame them for doin' their job. Another kind of dyin' is up close and personal. My son died two years ago when—"

"I know about your son. What's your point?"

"Ah, lawyer-man's been snooping." Stockard's lips drew back from yellow teeth. "You see, we have a little different situation here." He flicked a tubular ash onto his boot that blew away as he strutted up to Grayson and leaned into his face, the searing cigar tip inches from Grayson's nose. "The way I see it, if ya hadn't come along, Kim would still be alive."

Struggling to hold his temper, Grayson knocked Stockard's hand away. "That's absurd and you know it. We were trying to save the poor child's life."

Stockard straightened. "You and the missus will be held accountable. An' jus' gettin' even don't settle the score."

Any feelings of sympathy evaporated from Grayson's mind as hot anger took over. He got to his feet, prepared to give Stockard a hard shove. But Stockard stepped back.

"Don't fuck with me, Stockard, and don't ever approach my son again." Grayson jabbed his finger into Stockard's chest. "I'm not a piss-ass gook, and if you harass my family, you'll get real fighting, close and personal. If you want something, tell me, because mailing death cards and giving my son golf balls won't get you shit."

Stockard laughed in his face.

Grayson turned and headed out the door, and Stockard followed him down the steps. "You'll get yours, big shot. Because if ya hadn't messed with Dakota after hittin' him with your car, he woulda picked his self up from the road and come home. I woulda found Kim and had her rescued proper. Not by a fuckin' yahoo with a rope, trying to cover up his missus's sins and be a hero." He spat and hurled his cigar. It bounced and sputtered at Grayson's feet.

Grayson yanked his car door open and climbed in, slammed the door and hit the engine with a roar. "You stay away from my family," Grayson repeated, voice strained. "I'm filing a restraining order against you, you understand? If you come near us again, they'll throw your sorry ass in jail."

Stockard's mouth twisted into an obscene sneer, as though he was laughing at a private joke. He sauntered over and gripped the chrome windowsill with strapping hands. Grayson imagined them around Stockard's son's throat. The man bent down. Blood vessels pulsed in his temples. "You don't scare me, tough guy. I'll see that you suffer plenty." His voice was little more than the icy whisper of an obscene phone caller.

A cold knot twisted around Grayson's heart, the same one that he'd felt when Stockard put his face to the police car window.

"Remember," Stockard hissed, "you and the missus dealt your own hand." A smile played at the corner of his lips. "I'll bet she loves tickling your zipper and getting put to bed wet." He banged his palm on the car's roof. "See ya around, lawyer-man."

Grayson stomped on the gas, spitting snow and gravel. He gripped the wheel hard to keep his hands from shaking. He'd need more than a restraining order to feel safe from this monster.

CHAPTER 7

At eight a.m. sharp, the doorbell rang, and Grayson scrambled down the stairs. "I'll get it."

He opened the door to reveal a trim middle-aged man with a snappy mustache and thick wavy hair. "Good morning, Mr. Bolt," the man said, flashing a badge. "I'm Fred Belton. Chief Foley sent me."

"Come in. Foley fill you in on everything?"

"Yes, sir. I'm to accompany your wife and children when off the premises."

"Are you armed?"

"Armed and experienced, sir. Former secret service."

For the next three days, Fred accompanied Sandra when she ran errands and drove the boys to and from school. Both the bodyguard and Sandra stayed with Troy at golf practice and Jim at baseball workouts. No one saw or heard from Stockard.

On the fourth day, Grayson worked from home. He planned to pick Troy up from school and take him to his golf practice. Maybe they'd even get in nine holes together.

⌘

Sandra yelled upstairs to Grayson in his office that it was time to pick up Troy. Five minutes later, when her husband still hadn't emerged, she climbed the stairs to see what was taking him so long. She found him on the phone, talking business. She pointed to her watch, and he nodded but continued his conversation.

Fred and I will go, she mouthed, and he again nodded distractedly, turning back to his call.

She rolled up to Troy's school under a dull, gunmetal sky. He came running when she beeped, hopping in the backseat behind the bodyguard. "Hi, Fred. Mom, I thought Dad was picking me up."

"He was held up on the phone."

"Gee."

She glanced back at him. His head hung down. "He'll meet you at the course later, sweetie. You'll still get to play golf with him."

His face brightened. "Great! I'll be all warmed up. You should play with us sometime, Mom."

"I'd like that, but Canadians don't grow up learning to play golf."

"That's okay, Dad's a good golf partner."

She gazed at him in the mirror and smiled. "You really like playing golf with your dad, don't you?"

"For *sure*. Especially when I beat him on a hole."

"Beating your dad's important, huh?"

"Sure. I try to beat everybody. That's what counts."

Sandra pursed her lips. She disliked that Grayson stressed winning so much with the boys. Grayson's dad had been that way with him, but she believed there were more important values, such as simply taking pleasure in the activity. "Can you enjoy playing if you don't win?"

"Mom, the only reason to play is to win."

She sighed. There was no point arguing. "Well, sweetheart, I wish you luck beating your dad."

"I can hit my driver over a hundred yards. Well, almost. But on a short hole, if I get on the green, and my putter's really smokin', I'll get a birdie and maybe beat him. Dad's as good as Tiger Woods ever was. So if I can beat Dad, I can—"

WHAM!

Fred's airbag exploded, and Sandra's seat belt cinched against her chest. Her head jerked right. Blurred images swished before her eyes: cars, storefronts, a bus. A silver SUV came at her from the other side, tires screeching, horn blaring—

BAM!

Then there was nothing.

CHAPTER 8

Clouds drifted across the pale blue sky like barges, and shadows hung from ancient oaks like curtains. The mourners walked from their cars up the cemetery's grassy rise in groups of two and three, or clusters of four and five. The women dressed in overcoats. The men wore suits or sport coats.

They had come from a Requiem Mass at St. Mary's Cathedral, with its gothic columns reaching to God for grace, and gathered around the gravesite surrounded by tulips.

Grayson stood between Chief Foley and his mother, who was holding Jim's hand. Jim stared at the coffin stoically. He hadn't shed any tears, not when he first heard the news and not now, during the funeral. Sandra's mother worked a rosary between her fingers. A priest faced the gathering, his back to the twin graves. Grayson cast his eyes beyond the parked cars to a small dirt road that veered off into an apple orchard and thought of Troy. Troy liked apple pie, but Grayson couldn't recall if he himself did.

Dreamily, he began humming, "Don't sit under the apple tree with anyone else but me, anyone else—"

"Grayson!" his mother said under her breath, elbowing his side.

He stopped humming and thought of the sun, fat and powerful, burning the back of his neck. Sweat erupted from his pores, and he swabbed his face with a handkerchief.

The priest was still speaking. "…and may their souls rest in peace." He sprinkled holy water onto the caskets draped in a cascade of trumpet-shaped flowers.

Grayson stared at the coffins, and all of a sudden he saw Sandra and Troy's lifeless bodies inside. Their faces were powdered and made up by the mortician to look like they were simply sleeping, but Grayson could see the sadness at the corners of their mouths, the grief of being cheated out of life.

"Oh, my God," he murmured.

Chief Foley leaned toward him and whispered, "What's wrong?"

Grayson felt panic welling up inside him, threatening to erupt. "I can't do this. I can't *do* this!" Heads turned his way, but he didn't care. "This isn't right! It should have happened to *me*, not to them! My life is nothing without Sandra!"

Chief Foley put his hand on Grayson's arm. "Grayson, listen to me. You have a son, Jim. *He's* your life now."

Grayson shook his head, jerking away from Foley's touch. "You don't understand. I should have protected them! Should have—Oh, *God*!"

His internal fortitude gave way, and he buried his eyes in his sleeve as sobs wracked his body. He didn't care what anyone else thought. He just needed to release the pain that had been steadily building ever since he got the phone call from the police station. Yet the more he wept, the more pain flooded over his heart, as if he was drowning in a sea of black despair.

He felt a small hand grasp his own, and he looked down. Jim stared up at him with wide, solemn eyes. "It'll be okay, Dad," he whispered. "We've still got each other."

Grayson dropped to his knees and hugged him, burying his face in Jim's shoulder. His son was right. They still had each other. And he'd be damned if he'd let anything threaten them ever again.

෧෨෧

Five days later, Grayson sat slumped at his desk, holding a framed photo in his hands. In the picture, a younger and happier version of himself embraced his two sons, and Sandra looked on adoringly. It was his family as it was supposed to be: innocent and happy—something that would never be possible again.

His phone rang, jarring him out of his thoughts. He grabbed for it and heard Chief Foley's familiar voice. "How you holding up, pal?"

"I…um…I saw the psychiatrist you recommended."

"Yeah, and?"

"He asked what I thought about my outburst at the funeral, I guess to see if I was a nut case."

"What did you tell him?"

"That I saw their bodies in the coffins. That I really wanted God to take me. That I believed in Him." Grayson relayed the awkward session as he made his way to the bar, phone in hand. "I told him that God had talked to me when I was ten. The doc said I had obsessive delusions brought on by guilt." He plunked ice into a glass and mixed a scotch and soda. "Guilt or no guilt, I should have been the one in that car, not Sandra."

The chief took in a long breath. "What about Jim? How's he doing?"

Grayson sipped his scotch. "He's in Florida with my mother. She thought a few days away from here would be good for him." He peered into his drink. "I feel terrible about Fred."

"He was a fine man, but a bodyguard knows his life is always on the line."

"I've been thinking about something, and I don't want you to think I'm off my rocker again, but I believe Stockard caused the accident."

"Grayson, when a car gets hit broadside by two others, from two different directions, that's an accident. Sandra must have run a red light."

"Sandra was always a careful driver, especially with the kids in the car. Stockard blames me for his granddaughter's death. He sent me the ace of spades and gave Troy golf balls with that fucking image stamped on them, and when I went to his house he repeated his threat quite emphatically."

"I'll be retiring, so I can't help, but talk to the locals, and they'll investigate."

"That won't work. No evidence, no witnesses. It's my word against Stockard's."

"You never know what the cops could turn up. Give them a try."

Grayson sipped his drink. He'd give something else a try.

CHAPTER 9

The next afternoon at his desk, Grayson's chest felt caved in, compressed by an invisible force. It happened every time he thought about how he'd stayed on the phone, rather than picking Troy up from school. No client was that important. No matter how severe their problem. He stood, walked to the French doors and looked across the yard to Troy's putting green for several moments, before lumbering back to the desk and taking from his pocket the ace of spades that Stockard had mailed to him. He looked at it a long time. Stockard wasn't through yet. He wouldn't stop until he finished the job by killing Jim. "I'll get even. I'll get good and even."

Yet, could he go through with it? Could he execute Stockard because of blind vengeance? He shook his head. The whole idea was foolish. He had to let the police deal with him.

He picked up the phone. He'd call the police right now. Ask them to start an investigation. He'd—

His eyes fell onto the framed picture on his desk. It was the last formal portrait his family had taken together. They were all sitting on the front steps outside the house, autumn leaves bursting into color around them. Sandra wore her favorite blue sweater. Leaning against her was Jim, his collar crooked. Grayson sat next to Sandra, one arm around her and the other around Troy.

Grayson's hand tightened around the phone as hot anger seared through him. Because of Stockard, there would never be any more family portraits. Because of Stockard, he could never again hold Sandra or ruffle Troy's hair. Because of Stockard, half his family was dead.

Grayson slammed the phone down.

ೲ

At exactly five p.m., Grayson put on his coat and left the house under a darkening sky. He climbed into a limo and was driven eight minutes to an airfield, where he boarded a Piper Cheyenne turboprop. Seventeen minutes later, he landed near Short Hills, New Jersey, and slid behind the wheel of a waiting Mercedes.

At five forty-five he stepped into suite 407 of the Hyatt Hotel. He switched on two table lamps and closed the curtains. Fifteen minutes later a rap came at the door.

Costanzo toddled in, looking even more haggard than at their meeting in Grayson's office. *If you're a gangster, talking to the IRS must take a toll.*

"Mr. Costanzo, thank you for coming." Grayson gestured to a chair. "Please."

Costanzo removed his coat, sat down, and crossed his legs. Grayson took a seat opposite him.

"I read about your personal tragedy," Costanzo said. "Life's so precious, yet fragile. And to think, a stupid car accident."

Grayson coughed into his fist. "It wasn't an accident. My wife and son were murdered." The man showed not a flicker of emotion, though Grayson wouldn't have been surprised with a shrug. "I know the killer. He somehow caused the—the accident."

Costanzo rubbed his eye. "Caused it?"

Grayson told him about Kim's death and Stockard's threats.

Costanzo's dark eyes narrowed. "How could he manage such a thing?"

"I don't know, but he did." Grayson took the ace of spades card from his pocket and handed it to him. "It came in the mail two days before the car crash."

Costanzo returned the card. "Why are you telling me this?"

"Because he's the reason I'll handle your tax matter exactly as you wanted."

Costanzo pinched the loose skin at his Adam's apple while the wheels in his head seemed to turn. "You've come up with a figure, have you?"

"No figure."

A stiff smile moved the corners of Costanzo's lips.

"I want your help. You see—"

"Hold on a minute." Costanzo leaned forward and gave Grayson a hard look. "Sometimes people get fucked over and think they deserve justice. They see movies and they get nutty ideas. They think the police are incompetent, bumbling keystone cops. They might even think there's a Godfather who magically creates justice. Do you have fucked up ideas like that?"

"Not exactly."

Costanzo let out something between a snort and a laugh. He stood and reached for his coat.

Grayson got to his feet. "You haven't heard what I want."

"You're a nice man. Bad things have happened to you, now go home and forget it. If you'd like to discuss a reasonable fee for your services, perhaps we have something to talk about. If not, we're done."

Grayson was getting squeezed. He'd squeeze back. "Fifty million. As you once said, I want nothing for nothing."

"I also said a reasonable fee."

"And that the sky's the limit."

"That was before, this is now."

"Let's stop playing games. I won't ask you to kill anyone. That'll be my job."

Costanzo snorted again. "When we last talked, you were too good to get your hands dirty helping a client like me. Now you're talking about murdering someone in cold blood. What happened to your integrity, Mr. high-and-mighty-lawyer?"

Grayson took a deep breath. "Things change."

CHAPTER 10

Grayson scanned the airport terminal, watching for Jim. The boy had stayed in Florida with Grayson's mother all week, which Grayson had, at first, thought was for the best—it got him out of the house and away from the memories. But now, he wanted his son back with him, and, based on how quickly Jim had agreed, it seemed his son wanted that, too.

"Boo!"

Grayson flinched and turned around.

"Ha-ha, I scared you," Jim said, laughing and jumping up and down.

"Hey, there's my boy." Grayson knelt down, ruffled Jim's shaggy blond hair, and pinched his pink cheeks. "Looks like you brought back some Florida sunshine."

"I'm hungry. All they gave me on the plane was a bag of crummy peanuts."

"How about we eat at the miniature golf course and play a round?"

Jim's face lit up even brighter. "Yeah! That'll be fun."

After they finished their hotdogs, Jim ran over and picked out putters and balls. He hit first, and Grayson watched his ball roll through the windmill arms and heard it rattle into the hole.

"Wow!" Grayson said. "A hole in one."

"Yeah!" Jim hopped up and down. "Troy used to get mad at me when I did that. His ball always hit the thingy. He…" Jim's voice trailed off abruptly.

Grayson put his arm across Jim's shoulders and tugged him close. "You miss Troy, don't you?"

"It's not fair!" Tears sprang from Jim's eyes. "Why did he and Mom have to die?"

"Let's sit down." Grayson led Jim to a bench next to one of the putting greens. "You're right, it isn't fair."

Jim scuffed his foot across the ground, and tears ran down his cheeks. "Why did it have to happen to them? Why not someone else?"

"Only God knows that."

"Does God know everything?"

"Yep. Everything." Grayson's jaw tightened. When he was ten, God told him that he'd grow up to win the Global Golf Championship, but God had evidently changed his mind. After that, Grayson had transferred his hopes to Troy. Obviously, that was also out of the picture. "We don't know why God does the things he does. But when bad things happen, it's okay to cry."

"Do you still cry?"

"Sometimes. I cry less now, but it still hurts inside."

Jim wiped his cheeks with his fingers. "Me too."

"All we can do is continue living our lives."

Jim thought about that for a moment. "Come on, Dad." He hopped up and pulled Grayson with him. "It's your turn."

They returned to the tee, and Grayson hit his ball, which bounced off the windmill. He took three more strokes to make the hole.

"I won that one, Dad," Jim said with a grin, running to the next tee.

A flame began to flicker at the back of Grayson's eyes, a small, weak, smoky flame. His heart tapped a little dance. Jim's talent was obvious. But was it enough to win the global?

CHAPTER 11

At his house? Are you nuts?" Grayson sputtered into the phone.

He was standing at a phone booth outside a gas station a few miles from his house, the payphone Costanzo had ordered him to wait at when he called the day before. Grayson hadn't known what to expect when he arrived, but he *had* expected Costanzo to be on the line. Instead, it was a voice he didn't recognize, laying out a plan that seemed utterly insane.

"That's how it's goin' down," the voice growled. "You got a problem with that?"

"That's bullshit," Grayson shot back. "Why do I need you if I do it at his house?"

"Listen, you fuckin' amateur, if you don't like it, we'll hang up, and I'll tell The Man you don't want his help."

A lump swelled in Grayson's throat. This was no good. He couldn't do it himself. He *was* an amateur, and amateurs made mistakes. Let the professionals with killing experience manage the sticky details. Grayson's plan was for Costanzo's people to kidnap Stockard and take him to an isolated location. They'd give Grayson a gun, he'd kill Stockard, and they'd dispose of the gun and body. It had seemed simple when he'd thought it up, but now doubts were filling his mind. He nibbled at his lower lip. Maybe he should hang up and forget it.

"I haven't got all day, dickhead."

Grayson ran a hand through his hair. He had to do this to protect Jim. But alone, and mistake-free? Fuck! "What do I do?"

"That's better. You'll be picked up around the corner of the mini-market on Glenoak Road, two miles west of the 87. Park a little ways down the street, out of sight from the road. To-night, one o'clock."

"One in the morning?"

"No, fuck-face, we're doing this in broad daylight with bells on."

Grayson felt woozy. "That soon, huh?"

"Do you want this job done or not?"

"Okay. Who am I meeting?"

Click. The phone went dead. Grayson's breath felt cut off, and trepidation thrust an icy finger into his heart. *My God!* To-night. He would kill Stockard tonight.

He got back into his car, gripping the wheel so tight his knuckles turned white as he headed home. Fear pooled into his stomach, so strong it was almost sickening. As buildings blurred past him, a timid voice drifted through his mind. *You don't have to do this*, it told him. *You can still back out. Go to the police. They'll handle it.*

Part of him really wanted to listen to that voice, to pull a U-turn, and make a beeline for the nearest police station. What was he thinking, trying to pull off a murder like this? He had no idea what he was doing. And even with Costanzo's men, the whole thing was dangerous as hell. Besides, did he really want to get involved with the mob?

More importantly, did he even want to kill a human being?

He turned into his driveway, walked through the door, and headed straight for his den. He needed a drink—badly. He poured a shot of scotch with shaking hands, gulped it down, and then poured another.

He sat down and frowned at his desk, rolled a pencil slowly across its surface beneath the palm of his hand. Staring at the ceiling, he gnawed a fingernail then ran a hand through his hair. He fished the playing card from his pocket then shoved it back almost before he looked at it. He chewed his lower lip. Finally, he shook himself. Stockard wasn't human. Grayson had to destroy that monster once and for all.

CHAPTER 12

By six o'clock that evening, Grayson had already thrown up twice. After a shower, he dressed in khakis and a tan shirt and put gloves in the pockets of his wool coat. He sat in his den and downed two scotches. The ticking grandfather clock against the wall told him it wasn't even seven. He couldn't just hang around another four hours until leaving to kill Stockard. Go to a restaurant? Not with his queasy stomach. A movie sounded good. Maybe an R rated, since Jim wasn't with him. He was spending the night at Elizabeth's watching *The Lion King*.

At ten o'clock, he returned home, hardly aware of the movie he'd seen. Both Jim and the housekeeper were in bed. While mixing a drink, Grayson realized his clothes were all wrong. They should be dark and free of loose fibers. He finished his drink, changed clothes, and managed to keep down a few spoonfuls of yogurt.

Finally, eleven o'clock rolled around, and he left the house in black jeans, a black shirt, and a black nylon jacket. Two hours later, he turned off highway 87 to Glenoak Road, headed west two miles, and turned right at the mini-market. Clouds masked the moon, leaving the sky dark as northern seas. Good. Stockard's property had plenty of trees but no concealing shrubs.

Grayson cruised slowly past the market. A neon light flickered under the awning. No cars or people anywhere. He parked about fifty yards from the corner, where the car couldn't be seen from the main road, and reached into his jacket for his gloves. Shit! They were still in his overcoat at the house. He'd have to be careful not to touch anything. He stepped out of the car into the cold, zipped up his jacket, and made his way toward the corner. Out of sight from the road, he stood behind a tree.

It was five past one. He jammed his hands into his pockets and shifted from foot to foot, hoping to get warm. The only sounds were the constant buzz of the neon sign and an occasional passing car. He thought about his phone conversation with Costanzo's goon. Sounded like a hood: gruff and nasty. And what was that he called Costanzo, The Man?

A black Lincoln edged around the corner, and Grayson slipped back into darker shadows. The car approached, revealing the dim outlines of a driver and passenger. A sharp twinge hit his gut. He had expected only one man. He stepped into the street and the car jerked to a stop. When he approached the driver's window, it lowered with a hum. The man inside gave him a cold-eyed look and a nod. "In back."

Grayson returned the look without the nod and climbed in. He'd wait for his companions to explain the plan, but the goons only chatted idly with each other. About last night's football, and how The Man had scored over a million dollars, but lost almost as much when Surge Michaelson clobbered Nick Nelson in a golf match. They liked reruns of TV's *America's Most Wanted*. Maybe saw old friends.

After forty-five minutes, Grayson had finally had enough. "Would you guys mind telling me the game plan?"

The driver's mouth twisted contemptuously. "What do you think the game plan is?"

Grayson's jaw tightened. "Look, you guys have your instructions. Now are we going to play I've-got-a-secret or talk business?"

"Testy, testy," the driver said, then turned and winked at his partner.

The partner's cell phone rang, and he tugged it from his pocket. "It's me, boss…Uh-huh…Uh-huh…I'll have the midget bring him in." He hung up and said to the driver, "We got a problem with Snake. One of the midget's boys. The Man wants to handle it personally."

They were on a lighted highway now, and Grayson could make out their features. The driver was swarthy, with an apish slope of his broad shoulders. He had a face only a gangster's mother could love, flat and pockmarked with divots like a par three tee box. The other one, the long-necked and long-faced one with the phone, turned back to Grayson. A vertical cleft in his chin made his face appear longer yet. Dark brown eyes sat deep within his expressionless face.

"Asshole," he said. "I'll ask you a question."

Grayson had recognized the rusty voice as the one from the payphone. He figured the guy had more than just a streak of ruthlessness in his nature. "Who the fuck are you that The Man would want us to help kill someone?"

"Take that up with your boss," Grayson snapped. "I'm not doing this dance after every question. Why at his house?"

"Because that's where he'll be when you stab his ass," the driver said.

Grayson's mouth dropped open. "What? I'm not stabbing anyone. You're supposed to give me a gun."

Longface twisted toward the driver. "Gonzo, turn the car around."

"Wait a minute!" Grayson tapped the driver's shoulder. "Keep driving and give me a goddamn gun like you're supposed to."

"You best keep your nose out of the weapons business," the driver said, scowling.

Grayson's lips quivered with anger. "And if I don't?"

"I'll blow it for you. Right through the back of your head."

"Listen, dickhead," Longface said, "if you want to call the plays, you can carry the ball. The Man said specifically you're to use this." He swung his arm around and thrust a gray blade in Grayson's face. "Take it."

Grayson found himself holding a crude ten-inch piece of sheet metal shaped like a knife. Soiled cloth was taped around one end to serve as a handle.

"I'm supposed to use this…this knife?" Grayson cradled it in both hands like a Samurai warrior. He hoped they were joking.

"Hey, he catches on quick," the driver said.

"It's not a knife, numb-nuts," Longface said. "In the killing business, it's called a shank."

"Yeah," the driver added. "You're gonna shank your man, Stockard." He chuckled, his shoulders bouncing.

Longface aimed a dark stare at Grayson as if sizing up his nerve. "If you don't have the balls, we can turn around."

Grayson returned his look. "Keep driving."

The driver turned west onto Highway 28. Grayson placed the shank on the seat. *Okay, so that's the way it's going to be. Stockard gets it with a shank.* He looked at Longface, his weapons benefactor. "What's your name? I know his." He nodded to the driver. "It's Gonzo."

"Chauffeur," the man said, not looking back.

Grayson felt his insides eating at him. He looked out the window into darkness, focusing on the humorous idea that Chauffeur should be driving. Stockard popped into his mind and his stomach did a flip-flop before settling into a dull knot.

At two-twenty, the Lincoln passed the spot where the horse had fallen. A mile up, they turned off Highway 28 onto Stockard's road. Chauffeur put his forearm across the seatback, turned to Grayson, and laid out the plan in grisly detail. He finished by saying, "In a minute, we'll turn out the lights and ease up to the house. We'll get out without slamming the doors and enter through the rear porch. Once we're inside—"

"Are we going to break a window or something?"

Chauffeur switched on his cold-eyed look. "Now don't you think breaking a window just might wake up your soon-to-be-dead Stockard?"

"We'll use this." Gonzo turned around and held up a key.

CHAPTER 13

Grayson pressed his lips together, desperately trying to conceal his unease. The moment had arrived: he would break into a man's house and commit murder. A part of him wanted to break down and beg Costanzo's men to take him back home, but he forced the panic down. He'd gone too far to turn back now.

Gonzo unlocked Stockard's back door and slipped inside. Chauffeur and Grayson followed. Chauffeur took out his phone, which supplied enough light to move around without bumping into things. They stood bunched together on the rear porch beside a washing machine crowded with cleaning supplies. A deflated wading pool sat crumpled in the corner. Chauffeur removed his shoes and signaled others to do the same. Grayson bent over, set down the shank, and slipped off his Italian loafers, wondering how Gonzo had obtained the key.

Chauffeur led the way into the kitchen. Grayson took up the rear. The sink was on the left under a window. On the right, the refrigerator hummed. They moved past a table in the middle of the room. Just ahead, in the darkness, would be the living room, the grungy curtains, and the armchair Grayson had sat in. Right now, he could see that only in his mind.

Chauffeur and Gonzo turned right at a hallway. Careful not to rustle his nylon jacket, Grayson shifted the shank to his left hand. He opened and closed his right fist several times, then switched the shank back.

The three crept down the narrow hallway like shadows, past a closed door on the right, a bathroom to the left. Chauffeur and Gonzo stopped short of an open door on the right. Chauffeur turned to shine his light at Grayson and made a stabbing motion. Grayson showed him the shank. Chauffeur turned the phone off.

The plan was for Grayson to stay just outside the door while Chauffeur and Gonzo went into the room. Chauffeur would creep up next to the bed, gun raised. Gonzo would stand by the door, count to five, switch on the room light, and Grayson would enter. Chauffeur's gun would be pressed in Stockard's face. After Chauffeur roused Stockard to his feet, his and Gonzo's job would be done. Then, Grayson would step close, ask Stockard a few questions, get a few answers, and give him a thank-you-shank in the gut.

Chauffeur and Gonzo entered the room. Seconds later the lights came on and Grayson stepped in, shank behind his back. Chauffeur had Stockard almost on his feet. The man breathed with a mix of wheezes and gasps, his dazed eyes still trying to focus.

Grayson moved in front of Stockard. Close and personal. Close enough to see the terror in Stockard's eyes. Grayson's legs felt shaky, but he forced himself to stay cool, squeezing the shank's handle still held behind his back. "How'd you do it?"

Stockard's eyes bulged with terror.

"Tell me," Grayson spat through clenched teeth. "How did you kill my wife and son?"

Stockard's lips trembled.

"Talk, now!"

"Ah…um…" Strangled sounds came out of Stockard's mouth, but no intelligible words.

Chauffeur stepped forward. "This will help him open his trap." He backhanded Stockard across the face with his gun. Teeth and blood flew from the old man's mouth.

Stockard's hand shot to his face. "St—stop!" he cried. "Jesus Christ! Wha—what da ya wanna know?"

Gonzo spoke up. "You were already asked twice, dipshit."

"I didn't—" He glanced at Chauffeur, who drew back his gun. "—okay! I did it."

Grayson now had the shank pressed against his thigh. "How?"

Stockard stared at his bloodied hand then at Chauffeur. He wet his lips. "I—I rigged the traffic light in her direction to be green when it sh—shoulda been red. She entered the intersection against cross traffic."

Chauffeur scoffed. "How the fuck'd you do that?"

"I—" Stockard's eyes fixed on Chauffeur's gun. "I work for the traffic engineering department."

Grayson recalled Wilson telling him that. Stockard looked at him then back at the gun. "I s—stood at the corner's control box and worked the controller on the electronic board. At j— just the right time, I turned the signal green in both directions."

"I don't fucking believe you," Chauffeur said, threatening that backhand again.

Stockard's arms went up. "S—she drove through that intersection every day, taking the kid golfing." He swallowed with a loud gulping sound. "It—it took me three days at the controller before the timing was j—just right."

For one long instant, Grayson felt the entire room freeze, as if it would never change: Chauffeur's gun. Stockard's face. The shank against his thigh.

"Holy fucking shit," Gonzo burst. He got behind Stockard. "Do it now!"

Grayson raised the shank waist level, eyes locked onto Stockard's.

"*Now*, dickface," Gonzo yelled and gave Stockard a hard shove.

Stockard lurched forward and Grayson's free hand shot up to stop him. Stockard's mouth opened around Grayson's index finger. Jaws clamped down. Grayson screamed, "YAHH-ah-a-hhh," and thrust the shank into Stockard's gut. Stockard thrashed against him, and Grayson stabbed him a second and a third time, each thrust more frenzied than the last. Finally, Stockard's eyes rolled and he slumped to the floor with a long groan.

Grayson dropped the shank next to Stockard's body, where it was quickly submerged in the blood still spurting from all of

Stockard's wounds. Grayson looked at his bloody hand and clutched it with the other.

"All right, the job's done," Chauffeur said, coolly.

"Hold on," Grayson said, feeling faint. He bent down and pried his finger from Stockard's mouth.

"Hey, dumbshit," Gonzo said. "You wanna leave your business card, too?" He pulled out his handkerchief and wiped Grayson's fingerprints from the shank's handle. The pungent smell of blood and human excrement felt suffocating.

Stockard moaned, stirring feebly.

"Hey, he ain't dead yet," Chauffeur growled.

"Let me fix that," Gonzo said. He lifted his foot and gave one hard stomp onto Stockard's throat, then a kick to his skull, then another. And another. Grayson flinched as bones crunched and splintered.

By the time Gonzo finished, Stockard's head was nearly unrecognizable, a crumbled puddle of mush. Gray brain matter peeked out of white bone. Teeth were scattered everywhere, while the lower jaw remained intact, grotesquely showcasing half of Stockard's tongue. The other half had been sliced off and buried somewhere under the pile of bone splinters. One eyeball hung from its socket, while the other had rolled against his shoulder and stared into space.

Grayson felt like he was going to faint.

My God, what have I done?

CHAPTER 14

Two weeks had passed since Stockard's killing, and Grayson couldn't shake the residual terror that comes after you wake up from a particularly nasty nightmare. He'd learned from Wilson that Chauffeur had worked for The Man over fifteen years, starting as a driver—hence the moniker. Gonzo was The Man's godson and carried water for Chauffeur. He earned his name as a juvenile and, like Chauffeur, was a "made" member of the crime family. They had both carried out a laundry list of crimes, including murders.

Grayson sat on a cold park bench under a harsh, gray sky. He watched a young couple with two small boys bundled in coats and earmuffs feed breadcrumbs to ducks, and his mind drifted back to his own two boys and the time they all ice fished in Canada. Jim had angled a rainbow trout, and when he yanked it from the hole, it flopped onto the ice. He had picked it up and held it for everyone to see. It glistened pink and magenta in the low sun while it spawned a profusion of eggs into Jim's tiny hands.

Grayson was smiling when he heard the crunching sounds of footsteps on the frozen grass. His smile vanished when he looked up and saw Costanzo and Chauffeur approaching from their car. He hadn't seen Costanzo since their meeting in the hotel, and it worried him not knowing what this get-together was about.

Costanzo extended his gloved hand, and they shook. "Good morning, Mr. Bolt. My apologies for being late. I was visiting my mother, who's not feeling so good these days."

"My sympathies."

"She's a tough bird." Costanzo gestured that they walk. Chauffeur trailed behind, his long neck stuffed inside his black leather trench coat, looking like a high-paid assassin. "Too bad about your finger. My doctor sew it back okay?"

Grayson held up the bandaged finger. "Hopefully good as new. Won't know about feeling or mobility for a few weeks."

"It's a good thing you thought to retrieve it from Stockard's mouth. Aside from the benefit of having it back, of course."

Grayson turned to him. "What's the other good thing?"

"One you should appreciate. The police believe they've apprehended Stockard's killer."

Grayson pulled up short and searched Costanzo's face.

"If they had your finger, they'd have fingered you." Costanzo smiled. "Funny, play of words, huh?" He rubbed his arms. "Let's keep moving."

But they did have Grayson's blood in Stockard's mouth. Fortunately, thanks to Gonzo's skull crushing goodbye, they'd probably figure all the blood was Stockard's.

"Anyway," Costanzo said, "the shank found on the floor was made by ex-con Ellis Washington," Costanzo explained. "He's the one going down for the killing."

Grayson tucked both hands into his coat pocket. "That doesn't prove he killed Stockard."

"The police seem to think so, and it will be in your best interest not to disabuse them of that belief."

"I don't know about this. I mean, an innocent man being convicted for a—" Grayson glanced around and lowered his voice. "—for a murder I committed. He'll rot in prison."

Costanzo's mouth curled into a wry smile. "Nothing for you to worry about. Besides, once in jail, he won't live long enough to rot." His cell phone rang. He reached into his pocket, began talking with the caller, and walked away.

Chauffeur edged up to Grayson. His voice had a dark edge, which suited the day's gloom. "I know your kind, Bolt. You're a smartass who won't stay upright long because you think you can play by your own rules and are too fucking dumb to know better. The Man told you, but I'll tell you again in case you're forgetful. He wants Washington put away, so save the violin for someone else. Have a nice day, shithead."

Someone whistled. Costanzo stood by his car, waving for Chauffeur. "It's the midget. Get your ass over here, fast!"

CHAPTER 15

Chauffeur sat curbside behind the wheel of a Lincoln at JFK, the heater on, and wishing he were home in bed. He had just pulled up when Misha, aka, the midget, a mid-level operator who ran The Man's West Coast identity theft division, opened the back door. Huddled behind him were Snake, his wife and five-year-old kid.

"Hop in," the midget told them, then he climbed in front.

Chauffeur pulled away from the curb and headed toward the George Washington Bridge, and away from the rising sun.

Snake worked for the midget. Quick on his feet, he could talk his way out of just about anything. But he had made the mistake of forgetting to take his cell phone along on his family's Hawaiian vacation. In fact, he'd left it in a car he'd used for a job the day before his flight, and the midget found it the next morning. Chauffeur had ordered Misha to meet the family upon their return to LAX and immediately escort them to New Jersey, where they were to meet The Man.

Chauffeur glanced at them through the mirror and smirked. *They look like fuckin' pumpkins in their Hawaiian getup. Must be freezing their asses off.* Snake, wearing his usual snakeskin hat, belt, and shoes, had a sunburned forehead, and his nose was already peeling. Thinking he was about to get a promotion, the self-satisfied prick sat grinning like a moron. But he knew better than to ask questions. The little girl slept while the wife's eyes flitted around like a frightened bird's. She had good reason to be anxious.

The Lincoln turned into an alley and pulled up beside a new white Caddie parked in front of a warehouse.

"You stay here with the kid," Chauffeur told the midget. "You two, Mom and Dad, come with me."

Chauffeur opened a sheet metal door and led them into the musty, dimly lit, and nearly empty warehouse. An early crimson sky showed through the windows near the high ceiling. The Man and Gonzo sat in chairs behind a long folding table. On it rested four folded hands and one cardboard box.

Chauffeur threw a thumb toward two chairs facing the table, then dropped into one beside The Man.

The woman sat stiffly, hands in her lap. Snake took on a relaxed pose—arms folded, feet crossed.

"You two have a nice vacation?" The Man asked.

"Yes, sir," the woman replied coolly.

"It was very nice, Mr. Costanzo," Snake said. "Just wonderful."

Chauffeur shook his head. *The dumb fuck has no clue what's coming.*

"Do you know why you're here, Snake?" The Man asked.

"Misha told me I was to be transferred, but didn't say where, just that I was being promoted." He smiled, his chest swelling. "Oh, and that you wanted to tell me—uh, tell us—about it personally."

The Man took out a phone from his breast pocket. "Is this yours?"

The wife's Hawaiian sunburn immediately drained from her face.

"It—it looks like—" Snake said.

"It's his," Chauffeur droned, leaning back in a slouch.

The Man slowly turned the phone end over end on the table.

Snake swallowed hard. "I forgot it when we left for vacation."

"So I'm told," The Man said. "You left it in the BMW after your last run. Misha called your wife to let you know he had it."

Chauffeur smirked. *For once the midget did the right thing and followed his suspicions.*

Snake nodded.

"Right now the phone can't be used," The Man said. "Requires a password." He took a minute thumbing keys. "Your password's hard to crack. What is it?"

"Um…the password?"

"You heard right, dickhead," Chauffeur snapped.

"Capital L, star, V, lower case a, star, n, star, n."

"That's right. I forgot to capitalize lv." He tapped keys. "Here's an interesting text exchange between you two."

The wife threw a hand to her mouth and gasped.

The Man snickered, but didn't look up. "From *Ann*: 'The F called again.'" He looked at her and cocked his head then went on, "Then *Snake* answers: 'We'll talk tonight.' Then another from *Ann*, two days later: 'Two Fs came to the house. Offered a deal we should take.'"

The Man stood, reached in the box, and took out a hammer. He put the phone on the floor, bashed it to bits, then scooped up a few tiny parts, and approached the woman.

"Open your mouth," he ordered. She burst into tears. He grabbed a fistful of hair and jerked her head back. "Open your fucking mouth!"

"Please, Mr. Costanzo, she didn't—" Snake said.

Chauffeur slapped his palm on the table. "Shut the fuck up!"

Her mouth opened, and The Man stuffed the pieces inside. "Now swallow."

She gagged then gulped.

"Look at that," Gonzo said. "She swallowed her words."

She gagged again, lowered her head, and retched.

"What a shame," The Man said, stepping back. "And on your pretty Hawaiian dress. Take it off."

Her eyes bulged.

"Now!"

She shook her head and took in rapid breaths of air.

"Mr. Costanzo," Snake whined.

Annoyed, Chauffeur whipped out his gun. "One more peep and you're gonna swallow a bullet."

Ann wriggled out of her dress and it dropped to the floor, revealing a lacy blue bra and panties.

The Man yanked her bra off. "Give me your underpants."

She threw a hand to her slobbering mouth, bent over, slipped them off, then clutched her arms around her front. Silent tears streamed down her face.

The Man took the panties, sniffed them, looked at them thoughtfully, then stuffed them in his pocket and paced back to the box. He pulled out two ropes that he threw to Gonzo. "Put her on her back and tie her arms around this post." He patted the post, then turned to Snake. "Anything you want to say before the fun begins?"

"I swear, I wasn't gonna let her do it. That's the God's truth."

"But you admit, she wanted to rat us out to the feds."

"Na, she was just scared, that's all. Come on, Mr. Costanzo."

The dimwit took The Man for an idiot. Chauffeur backhanded his gun across Snake's face, and blood flew. "Mind your manners, asshole."

Snake grabbed his face and crumpled to the floor.

The Man again reached into the box, pulled out a roll of tape and two jars—one small, one large. He went to Ann, lying on her back, tied up, and crying. "Snake, get over here."

Chauffeur kicked him in the side. "He didn't mean next week."

Snake stumbled to his feet and went over.

The Man handed him the tape and his wife's underpants. "Tape these in her mouth. But don't seal it completely."

Snake's hands shook like he had fuckin' palsy.

"Now hold out both hands." The Man removed the small jar's cap and poured a thick watery substance into Snake's palms. "Smear that on her face."

"What is it?" Snake asked and sniffed.

"Never mind," Chauffeur said. "Just do what you're told." Chauffeur had concocted a savory mixture of meat juice and honey, which he was proud of.

Snake obeyed.

"Get it into her nose and mouth," The Man ordered.

After Snake complied, The Man gave him the large jar and told him to open it.

Snake twisted the lid off. "Jesus Christ!" he burst and flung the lid. "Fuckin' fire ants."

"Hold the jar down hard over her face."

Snake broke into tears.

"Now!"

Chauffeur pushed his gun against Snake's head. "Or I'll do it standing over your dead body."

Snake shook his head desperately. "I—I can't."

The Man shrugged. "No big deal. We'll just bring the little girl in here, and Chauffeur can do everything to her instead. Gonzo, go grab—"

"No!" Snake howled. "I'll—I'll do it."

Snake turned his head away and pressed the jar against his wife's face. She squirmed, and her screams were like echoes from the bottom of a well.

"Tap the jar," The Man said. "Get 'em all out."

Snake did so then flung the jar and frantically brushed ants from his hands and arms.

"Look at 'em go for the eyes," Gonzo said. "They're fuckin' hungry."

"You see what happens when people fuck with me?" The Man said and took out a gun. He pointed it between Snake's eyes. "So long, you stinking piece of shit." He pulled the trigger. Snake's head exploded, blood flew, and he fell onto his back.

"You still want to take out the kid?" Chauffeur said.

"We'll let the midget do it."

CHAPTER 16

Grayson and Chief Foley had just slid into a booth at the Knickerbocker Club, their poker playground. Grayson had ordered a stiff glass of scotch, which wasn't his first stiff drink for the day, but he wasn't going to think about that. Since killing Stockard, he felt no relief, no gladness, no sensations at all. Just hollowness. Now with the weight of it bearing down, he could neither eat nor sleep. He needed something. Someone to talk to. Anything to help him snap out of it.

"How is it living the life of luxury?" he asked.

"Feels damn strange not being chief. Jersey's no place to retire and sit on your ass."

"You're too pretty to retire."

"That's why I'm taking my gold watch and moving to LA."

Grayson shifted in his chair. "Listen, Chief, there's a couple of things I need to tell you. First, I—"

An arm came between them, holding a tray of drinks. "Jack Daniels, up. Walker black with a twist." The waiter placed them down and left.

Grayson hoisted his scotch. "To a lifelong friendship." They touched glasses and sipped. Grayson tried again. "I…um…I took a piece of that Costanzo case."

The chief's eye's widened. "I don't fucking believe it!" He thumped his drink onto the table, and it splashed. "Didn't I warn you? Didn't I tell you to stay away from him? He's like a leaf that blows from one gutter to another, a killer who'll do it without thinking. Christ, he'll do it instead of thinking." Foley shook drink splashes from his sleeve.

Grayson peered into his drink and made an effort to smile.

He was having second thoughts about confessing murder to an honest policeman, even a retired one. And he certainly wasn't going to say anything about Costanzo's help. He trusted the chief's confidence, but not his conscience. How might he react?

"You said there were a couple of things. What's the other one?" The chief lowered his head to look into Grayson's downcast eyes. "Come on. No more tantrums, I promise."

Grayson pursed his lips.

"We've been pals a long time, so spit it out."

"I'm…" Grayson put a finger in his drink and swirled the ice cubes. "I'm not sure you're the person—"

"The person you should confide in?"

Grayson nodded.

"You saved my life. Don't you think that counts for something?"

"We were at war."

"Horseshit! A dozen men stood on deck, and only one jumped in to save me."

"I was young and foolish." Grayson pushed his drink aside. "Okay, this is it. I…um…I killed Stockard."

The chief didn't blink. He had probably learned to control his expressions a long time ago.

"He confessed to killing Sandra and Troy by manipulating the traffic light, so, um, I killed him."

"I read about the murder. He was stabbed, head crushed like an eggshell. Never figured you had a hand in it."

"Not a hand, a finger." Grayson raised the bandaged finger. "Stockard bit it off just before I stabbed him."

The chief took in a sharp breath.

"It's sewn back on." Grayson didn't want to mention Costanzo, but he didn't like the chief thinking he could stomp a man's head. "It was someone else who gave Stockard the broken egg treatment."

"Someone helped you?"

"When in a bear trap, you don't want to chew off your own leg."

"God, I wish you had let the police do their job. They might have found out about the traffic light manipulation. And by the way, how the hell he'd do it?"

Grayson shrugged.

The chief took a gulp of his drink. "That's a dark hole you've jumped into."

"Nights are the worst. Can't tell if I'm awake or asleep. I see Stockard's terrified face and hesitate, but stab him anyway. Then remorse drives me mad. I try to remind myself that he killed Sandra and Troy. After that I heave my guts."

The chief tossed down the rest of his drink and wiped his mouth with the back of his hand. "This is a big deal, Grayson."

"I know."

"I might be retired, but I've got responsibility still. I've got my conscience."

"I know." Maybe he shouldn't have burdened his friend with a confession.

"I'm not saying the bastard didn't deserve it. He completely deserved it. But murder is murder. You've put me in a difficult position."

"And I'm sorry, really sorry. I just—I just couldn't keep it to myself. I had to confide in someone, and you're the best friend I've got. I know you need to do what you think is right. And whatever it is, I won't fault you for it. But—please, Chief, look at it my way. As a husband and father."

The chief let out a long breath. "What are you planning to do now?"

"I don't know. Another guy was arrested for the crime. He's no angel, but I can't let him rot in prison for my sin. I'll do something." He looked straight into his friend's eyes. "You have to know, if I had to do it all over again, I'd make the same choice."

Foley reached out and gave Grayson's shoulder a squeeze with a sad smile. "I understand. I probably would, too."

∽❧∾

Grayson got to wondering on the way home why Costanzo wanted Washington to take the fall for Stockard's murder.

Costanzo had somehow got hold of Washington's shank and made sure it was the murder weapon. But if he wanted Washington dead, why not simply have him killed?

Grayson called Wilson and asked him to check into it. A few days later, Wilson called back. "I've got that rundown on Washington."

"And Costanzo's connection?"

"He's connected, all right. Washington was locked up for five years on a first-offense armed robbery conviction before getting paroled. He's now charged with first-degree murder of your boy Stockard." Wilson chuckled. "Knowing Stockard's charming nature, I'm sure it was warranted."

"What have they got?"

"A jailhouse witness who'll testify that Stockard assaulted Washington in prison, but Washington's lawyer has a different story. He says it's true that the two were in the same prison, but in different cellblocks, and there's no evidence they knew each other or ever came in contact."

"There must be some evidence against Washington."

"Fingerprints."

"What?"

"His fingerprints were under the shank's cloth handle."

That explained Costanzo's insistence on using the knife. "What's Costanzo's involvement?"

"That's where it gets interesting. Made-men and the police believe that while in prison, Washington iced a made-man but was never charged for lack of evidence. In Costanzo's big-shot role as Don, he was expected to seek retribution and have Washington taken out.

But Costanzo had a problem. The police knew he was expected to kill Washington. So rather than ordering the hit and becoming a suspect, Costanzo shifted responsibility for retribution to the State by framing Washington for Stockard's sad demise."

Grayson swallowed hard. This was getting too close to home. He tried to keep his voice from shaking as he asked, "If that's true, who killed Stockard?"

"Wasn't able to find out. But I could keep digging."

"That won't be necessary," Grayson said, maybe too quickly. "Thanks for your help."

Grayson hung up, relieved to have cut Wilson free before he unearthed too much. As it stood, with the probability of Washington being convicted, Grayson could maybe have the good fortune of continuing to sleep in his own bed.

He padded into his den and mixed a scotch and soda, drained the drink, and thought well enough of it to mix a second before the ice melted. As he settled in at his desk and sorted through the day's mail, a letter from the New York County Court caught his eye. Opening it, he found a jury summons to appear Monday morning, eight o'clock.

CHAPTER 17

"All rise," the bailiff directed. "The honorable Judge Wendy S. Welcome presiding. Case number 87270, the State of New York versus Ellis P. Washington."

Grayson Bolt, juror seven, second row, end seat, stood beside eleven other sworn citizens. The bailiff told them to be seated, and the judge gave instructions while Grayson struggled to control his rage.

Costanzo had somehow yanked strings to get Grayson on the jury to assure a conviction. Now that he knew Washington had indeed committed murder, just not this murder, Grayson had no objections to him being convicted and put away. But he resented being the hangman. Even one-twelfth of one.

The judge finished her remarks and the prosecutor, Clayton Morrison, stood and buttoned his coat. A tall African American with shoulders that disappeared around the corner, he strode to the jury box with an easy grace and scanned the faces of his prime audience with eyes so black they were like the tinted windows of a sleek limousine. His face transformed into a smile wider than his back.

"Good morning, jurors." His voice was velvet-edged. He explained how they would find the defendant, Ellis Washington, guilty beyond reasonable doubt of maliciously stabbing and killing Gus Stockard on the night of October third. They would learn that the defendant made the weapon, and that he had motive and no alibi.

The defense told the jurors that Washington was innocent and had never been charged with a violent crime. In fact, the crime for which he had been incarcerated, armed robbery, was committed with a toy gun, and there existed not one shred of evidence placing him at the murder scene.

The trial was expected to last two or three days. On the morning of the second day, the defense put Washington on the stand. Coal-skinned and awkward, the man had curly black hair and a thick mustache that drooped over his lips. He wore baggy gray pants, a matching wrinkled coat, and an electric blue tie. Drops of moisture clung to his forehead. He said lots of yes sirs and no sirs, the no sirs usually accompanied by rapid headshakes. One of his "no sirs" grabbed Grayson's attention, the one in response to the question: "Have you ever killed anyone?" Maybe it was Washington's eyes that shone large and honest, or the certain headshake, or the body posture, or…Grayson didn't know what it was, but something made him believe Washington was telling the truth.

Grayson glanced at Chauffeur sitting in the back of the courtroom. He'd been there throughout the trial, giving him all the dirty looks he had in stock. Now the man met his gaze with a hostile stare.

At four-thirty, the jurors were excused and told to return the next morning at nine-thirty. Grayson arrived home, clomped into his den, and had a drink. He couldn't shake the feeling that Washington was telling the truth about never killing anyone. If so, this trial was a travesty without the least justification. He picked up the phone and punched in Wilson's number.

At ten o'clock that night, Wilson's knock came at the door. He had just visited Washington in jail. The accused told him that he'd never killed a made-man in prison, that the story was made up to protect the killer, who was himself a made-man. And since the authorities never knew who the real killer was, Washington—who never saw the inside of a high school—was pleased as a birthday boy with his exalted status.

Two days later, the judge finished reading the jury their instructions, and they retired to the jury room. The first order of business was to elect a foreperson. They chose a middle-aged mother of five with hair piled in a beehive. After being elected, she pronounced, "I know how this will turn out, but I'll keep an open mind."

Ken, who was only old enough to have voted last year, and whose shirt pocket held an iPod, suggested they take a vote and perhaps "wrap this thing up."

Two others spoke up, preferring some discussion. "Shouldn't we kick things around a bit?" Eric, the retired accountant, suggested. The forewoman agreed.

For half an hour, everyone kicked it around: Washington was guilty because he made the weapon. His fingerprints were on it and nobody else's. He had motive, was already a convicted felon—God knows, he just got out of prison. And did you see those cold eyes?

The forewoman stood, her large breasts tugging her pink blouse apart between buttons. "It seems we're all in agreement here. Why don't we take a vote? All those for guilty raise your hands."

Everyone's hand—everyone's except Grayson's—shot up straight as flagsticks. Not one bent elbow, and twenty-two eyes locked onto Grayson. He had told Foley that he would not let Washington rot in prison, for his sin. He couldn't go back on his word. Not now. But dare he risk being tied in a gunnysack and thrown into the East River? Without allowing himself to think further, he blurted, "But there's no evidence."

The thirty-something plumber threw down his pencil. "Oh, for God's sake!"

"There's always someone," Joyce, a crossing guard, muttered while chomping on a stick of gum.

"All right, now," the forewoman said. "Let's not get into a dither. Everyone has a right to express their opinion."

"Thank you, ma'am," Grayson said, nodding at her. "Washington admitted making the shank for protection while in prison, but said he gave it away when he left. To me that sounds—"

"What's he going to say, for crying out loud?" the bald man next to the woman in the wheelchair retorted.

"That's a *pret-ty* weak defense," the woman at the far end added, studying her nails. "I don't buy it."

This was going to be a tough sell. Grayson would try a different tactic. "It would be like one of us owning a gun. The gun's stolen and then used in the commission of a crime. Ownership of the gun is not proof of who committed the criminal act."

"Are you a lawyer or something?" the woman in the wheelchair said, adjusting her cushion.

The gray-haired insurance man placed his palms on the table. "That may be true, but the fact is Washington had a grudge against the guy from their prison days. He made the shank and stabbed Stockard with it. Case closed."

There followed several comments of agreement.

The plumber stood. "Everyone for guilty, raise your hand." He raised his, and talking stopped. People looked at one another. Ken's hand rose tentatively, then another's, then everyone's except Grayson's. He sat, lips pressed firm, hands folded on the table. Wetness formed on his brow, but he ignored it. He had to think of something.

"Are you going to hold out and make this a hung jury?" the insurance man asked. "If you are, tell us now so Ms. Forewoman here—" He jerked a thumb at her. "—can tell the judge and send us home."

A drop of sweat fell on Grayson's bandaged finger. He stared at it.

"Well?" the forewoman said. "The man's right. What's it going to be?"

Grayson muttered, hardly above a whisper, "He's innocent."

"What was that?" asked someone across the room.

"He needs to speak up," another said sharply.

Grayson pursed his lips. He'd have to concoct a story.

"Okay, that's it," the forewoman said. She stood and headed to the door. Her hand grasped the knob.

"I know for a fact that he's innocent," Grayson said calmly.

All heads swiveled to Grayson.

"How the hell would you know, old man?" Ken demanded.

"Because," he wiped his brow with a handkerchief, "because I know who the killer is."

The room was quiet as the shank plunging through Stockard's gut. Grayson folded his hands on the table. "Stockard's sixteen-year-old stepdaughter killed him." Grayson waited several long moments to let the idea sink in, while he tried to think of what to make up next. "Stockard had been molesting the girl for eleven years. Almost every night of those eleven years, Stockard would go into her bedroom, have his way with her, and whisper to her that if she ever told anyone, he would cut her mother's stomach out and make the girl eat it."

Jurors gasped, and several threw hands to their mouths. "I'm going to be sick," Joyce murmured.

"Should we take a break?" Grayson asked. He hated lying, but it was the only way to save Washington.

"Come on, finish the story," the plumber said. "She'll be all right."

Joyce lowered her hand and nodded. "Go ahead."

"A year ago, the stepdaughter ran away to the city and became a street prostitute. She was arrested not long after but refused to give her real name for fear of being returned to her stepfather, so was remanded to a nunnery in the Bronx. She learned through the Internet that her mother had died. So, she went back to her house, removed the key from the ledge, went inside, took the knife from where she knew Stockard kept it, and stabbed him in the stomach."

"My God," Joyce said. "The same way he had threatened to kill her mother."

"Wait a minute," Ken said. "How do you know all this?"

Everyone looked at Grayson.

"She told me," Grayson said calmly.

All eyes widened at once.

"She was shocked that an innocent man would be convicted of a crime she committed. She secretly took all our pictures that first day in the courtroom and used the Web to learn some of our identities. After discovering that I'm a lawyer, she came into my office and told me her story. She gave me permission to tell you, but only if necessary, and without disclosing her name."

The room felt as if all the oxygen had been sucked out of it, and nobody said a word.

"I think it's time we took a new poll," the forewoman said finally. "All in favor of not guilty, raise your hands."

All twelve jurors put their hands high in the air.

"Then, it's agreed." The forewoman's gaze wandered from face to face. "What's said in the jury room stays in the jury room."

Everyone looked at each other and nodded.

Grayson let out a silent sigh of relief—then he thought of Costanzo.

ം∽ം

"Please rise," the bailiff directed.

The judge marched in, took her chair, and everyone followed suit. She asked the forewoman if the jury had reached a verdict.

"Not guilty."

Chauffeur bounded from his chair and glared at Grayson with such a withering look, Grayson felt a chill down to his toes. Then Chauffeur turned and stomped out of the courtroom.

CHAPTER 18

Grayson left the courtroom, feeling like his insides had been carved out. Through swirling rain, he scurried to his car and drove aimlessly. A hard, angry, hammer of a pulse beat in his temples. Would The Man really throw him into the East River?

He drove through the Lincoln Tunnel and out of New York. The rain pounded the car as if it was trying to get in. The defroster of his ninety thousand dollar Mercedes didn't work, and he kept wiping the windshield with his sleeve. He was trapped, knew why, and made himself admit it. He'd invited something evil into his life, and he had to do the only thing he could: face Costanzo and hope for a miracle.

Grayson wheeled up to Costanzo's front gate in New Jersey's exclusive Short Hills Estates. The property served as both residence and office. Grayson rolled down his window and shouted through pelting rain into a metal box. Two minutes later, he stood before The Man, water dripping from his coat.

Costanzo sat at his desk, a muscle quivering in his jaw. Chauffeur occupied a side chair just behind Grayson's right shoulder.

"You want to explain?" Costanzo asked calmly. His face looked gray as rotten meat.

"Well—" Grayson cleared his throat noisily. "The jury—"

"Stop!" Costanzo slammed both palms on his desk, and the sound reverberated throughout the room. Absolute silence fell. From the way Costanzo's cheeks were moving, he was biting them on the inside. "Let's pretend," he said, eyes narrow, "that your balls are laying here on my desk, and I'm holding a hammer. Now, as you were saying."

Grayson heard Chauffeur stir and shot him a barbed glance over his shoulder. His eyes flitted around the wall of celebrity golf photos behind Costanzo and out the window at leaves battered with rain. He drew in a long breath. "The verdict was mine." With no expression in his voice, he added, "That's it."

"You son of a bitch!" Costanzo bucked from his chair and threw his phone, striking Grayson's shoulder. Chauffeur sprang to his feet like an attack dog. Costanzo hand-signaled him down and stormed around his mammoth desk, nostrils flaring like sails.

Grayson stared ahead, contemplating the temperature of the East River.

"Did you think you were on that jury to serve justice? You were to serve me, you dumb fuck." After several long moments, a dangerous smile tipped his face. He drew in a long, hissing breath, then the smile began to pull in around the edges. He shook his finger and a little laugh spurted out of him. "You failed me. I relied on you, and you failed me." His voice became somber, like a chagrined father about to teach a willful child the errors of his ways before the walloping. "How long would I last if I tolerated failure? The people I depend on? I simply can't do it, regardless of the person or the cost. The whole system is based upon prompt reward and swift punishment."

"I understand," Grayson said. And feeling like an unrepentant child who masks his fear with defiance, he added, "But I'm not your people. We had a business agreement and we both delivered. No more IRS, no more Stockard."

"This goes beyond any business agreement." Costanzo strutted to the window and peered out. "I made it clear what I expected and you defied me."

"But the fact is—" Grayson knew it was foolish to say it. "—Washington never killed—"

"Enough!" Costanzo's voice cracked like a whip, and he whirled around, nostrils again flaring. He inhaled deeply, then lifted his chin and ambled back to his desk. His face told nothing of his thoughts. He whisked his hand in a brief gesture of finality.

Chauffeur was on his feet and at Grayson's side. His fingers clutched the front of Grayson's shirt, and the tendons on the back of his hand looked sharp. Gonzo rushed in through a side door, gripped Grayson's arm, and put a gun to his head. "Do you feel a sneeze coming on? A real loud sneeze?"

Chauffeur jerked a thumb over his shoulder. "Let's go." The two footmen pinwheeled Grayson around and marched him to the door.

CHAPTER 19

H old up," Costanzo said.
Grayson stopped in the doorway. Goosebumps broke out on his arms, and a rush of relief swept through his mind and body.

"We'll do this differently."

They brought Grayson back into Costanzo's office and pressed him into a chair facing the desk. He sat stiffly, gripped with apprehension. Chauffeur parked in his usual position, behind and right. Gonzo sat port side, gun in lap.

Costanzo sat supreme, perched in his high-back leather chair, hands folded on his desk. Solomon about to dispense justice. "I'm afraid you're going to get it hard, Mr. Bolt." Costanzo had that fatherly tone of *this will hurt me more than you.* "Did you ever stop to think that there's only one way of being dead, but many ways of dying?"

Grayson felt something cold touch his spine, all the way down. "I don't follow."

"Take your man Stockard. He killed two of your beloved family members, wife and eldest son. Isn't that right?"

A strangling tightness gripped Grayson's throat. "That— that's right."

"Wouldn't you say a part of you died too?"

"What's your *point?*" Grayson's voice erupted in suppressed panic.

"You don't have to die to feel dead. I'm going to kill your other son. That'll be your punishment."

Chauffeur let out a long sigh. "Aaah."

The blood drained from Grayson's face. Just like that. Most

people held the basic principle that no man should be punished for the deed of another. Costanzo was not one of them. Grayson would be cut right to the bone, and his son would be the sharpest knife Costanzo could use. Costanzo had spelled out the thought in invisible brushstrokes. It was there and Grayson had tried not to see it.

Costanzo continued as though his words had no great significance. "It'll be tough, I know. But look at it this way." His face twisted into a cruel grin. "You've already lost one son, so you know what to expect."

Chauffeur and Gonzo snickered.

"You can't!" Grayson could barely get the words out. "Kill me. Right now. End this whole business."

Costanzo shook his head and made a soft sound with his lips.

Grayson couldn't let this happen. Not Jim, too. He'd throw himself across the desk and tear at Costanzo's throat. Wait! Those golf pictures on the wall—Costanzo and John Weekly playing together. And that conversation between Gonzo and Chauffeur on the way to Stockard's house. They talked about how The Man bets on football.

And golf.

That flicker! That smoky flame in the back of his mind at the miniature golf course with Jim. Without knowing what he was going to say, he blurted, "If you kill my son, you'll throw away a fortune."

Costanzo cocked an eyebrow, leaned back and locked his hands behind his head. "Is that so?"

"My son, he's a golfer. A gifted golfer who will become the world's greatest." Grayson ran a hand through his hair. "You could make millions off his long career."

Costanzo studied him. "How old is he?"

"The kid's eight," Chauffeur put in.

Grayson shot him a hateful glance.

Leering back at him, Chauffeur added, "And he gets out of school at two-fifty."

Grayson's blood turned to ice.

Costanzo flapped a lazy wrist. "Get outta here, Bolt. You're puttin' me on."

"He's won every tournament he's entered." Another made-up story. Grayson glanced back at Chauffeur, who turned to The Man and shrugged.

The Man rubbed his knuckles. "So how am I supposed to make millions off this kid?"

"Bet on kiddy golf?" Chauffeur chimed in.

Costanzo rocked in his chair and howled.

"It's a long-term investment that costs you nothing," Grayson said, yanking out a handkerchief and dabbing his brow. "I continue to work with the boy, manage him, hire coaches, and of course, cover the entire overhead. In a few years, he'll be playing the Junior Amateur. People bet on that, and—and he'll win. After that, there's the US Amateur. He'll win that too." He stuffed the damp handkerchief back into his pocket. "That automatically qualifies him for the Global. And he'll win that too." The fearful strain had left him, and he felt a bizarre excitement. He stood, and Costanzo made an *it's okay* hand gesture to Chauffeur. "Look at it this way," Grayson went on, "Tiger Woods is finished. He was great in his time—" Grayson glanced up at the picture of Costanzo and John Weekly. "—and Weekly, of course. But look at the future. Golf is entering a new era, ready for an upstart, someone young and exciting." He didn't try to hide a smile. "Think of the sensation. A great-looking kid who's played golf since he was four, learned from his dad, able to cream a golf ball over three hundred yards, lands them perfectly on the green. Put a putter in his hands and—"

Costanzo raised his hands. "All right, I got it." He pressed a finger against his pursed lips, picked up a pen, clicked it several times, then dropped it on the desk, and got up. There was silence. He paced to the window and gazed out. The silence grew deeper.

"Shall we get to it, boss?" Chauffeur asked.

Grayson's stomach sank. *Don't kill Jim.*

Costanzo's fingers twitched behind his back. Did that mean yes or no?

The rain stopped. A strong sun broke through the clouds and streaked through the window. The Man turned, and his face gave off a yellowish sheen. He smiled. "I like that, a long-term investment. Like owning a racehorse. The kid does well, he may live longer than a racehorse." He chortled, rubbed his hands together, and strode back to his desk. "Okay, Mister Lucky, you've got a deal. The kid's got a temporary reprieve. Now get the fuck outta here."

A great wave of relief rolled over Grayson's body. He turned to leave, then stopped. *Temporary reprieve. That's no good.* "Mr. Costanzo, my son's…shall we say?…commitment, ends when he wins the Global."

The corners of Costanzo's mouth drooped while he thought. "Fair enough. He gets one chance. He loses, or fails to play, by, say, his twenty-first birthday—" The Man pointed two fingers to his head and pressed his thumb down.

Chauffeur accompanied Grayson to the door. "You won't always be so lucky, fuck-face. You don't walk out of things like this more than once. Next time you're carried."

ოჴო

Chauffeur sank into a chair and patted the bulge under his coat. "You shoulda had me take him out."

"Business before pleasure," Costanzo replied. "First, I make money, if that's possible. But no matter, it'll be fun watching Bolt sweat it out for the next decade or more."

Chauffeur watched The Man's eyes fill with the same antic-ipation the cat must feel for the canary. "The dumb fuck has no more understanding of what's in for him than he has of the reason why. And puttin' him on that jury pissed him off royal-ly."

"He'll be more than pissed when I finish with him. Too fucking good to take my business. I can still see that smirk of his." The Man's face hardened. "Made me grovel like I was scum."

A fate worse than death, if there ever was one. Chauffeur stood up to leave.

"Hey, get the midget to take out Washington. It's not the way I wanted it done, but fuck it."

"But he's supposed to return to LA tonight."

"LA can fuckin' wait. Give him whatever hardware he needs."

Chauffeur ambled downstairs to hunt for the midget. Misha wasn't a real midget, but he and The Man enjoyed calling him one. Especially to his face. He ran the outdated LA identity theft detail and, compared to what The Man was pulling in through his cyber-crime division, it barely made pocket change.

But Misha had been at it a long time, and it kept him busy between pulling takeout duty. He never balked at a job, had rust in his blood, and was crafty enough to steal the gold fillings out of your teeth while you slept.

Chauffeur found him stretched over the pool table trying to reach the cue ball—difficult, considering that, even wearing elevator shoes, his height only matched the length of the five-foot-long pool table.

"Hey, Misha, let's go outside for some fresh air."

Misha hit a banking shot that sank two balls. "And just when I was winning."

"Of course, you're winning. You're playing with yourself, numb nuts."

Misha climbed off the table and tossed his cue on top of it. He was whip-thin and in need of a haircut. He wore it slicked back, just off his high bony shoulders. He followed Chauffeur outside, and they strolled past the pool along a gravel path into the garden. Chauffeur pulled out smokes and offered the pack to Misha.

"You know I never touch those things."

"That's right, stunts your growth."

Misha wrinkled his face like a hurt Chihuahua. "You know I don't like those jokes, Chauffeur."

Chauffeur chuckled. "Just bustin' your nuggets a little." He threw an arm over Misha's shoulder. "The Man was impressed with your idea of adding hospitals to the operation. Hire people who can get personal information that makes us money."

Chauffeur rubbed his knuckles on Misha's head. "You keep that Jew brain working."

"I try to be creative. You know, always thinking."

"Good, because the boss has something new for you to think about. It's on the takeout menu."

CHAPTER 20

A week after Costanzo granted Jim's reprieve, Grayson sat in the Florida sunshine, eating lunch at Disney World with Jim, and listening to a band across the street. He felt like his old self: invigorated, motivated, and determined. Life once again had purpose. He would make Jim into a world-class golfer who would win the Global by age twenty-one.

Grayson thought about how his dad had taken him there in 1965 for his tenth birthday, and he could almost smell the boundless flowers in bloom. He had rubbed shoulders with the world's best golfers and never forgot watching Jack Nicklaus clobber Arnold Palmer by nine shots. When Nicklaus dropped that final putt, Grayson had a mental vision from God. He turned to his dad. "Dad, God just told me that I'm coming back someday and winning this tournament."

Grayson never forgot that vision. He continued on to become a sub-par golfer. At age eighteen, he made it to the semifinals in the US Amateur but lacked the intestinal fortitude to become a professional. All his life, he suffered a nervous stomach, and although mentally he thrived under stress, he had the crippling habit of—when it really mattered—interrupting his back swing by heaving onto his golf shoes.

He cursed his condition until Troy was born, then he conferred his vision of winning the Global onto him. With that came exhilaration. The excitement he once held for himself, then for Troy, was now resuscitated by his deal with Costanzo. Jim's win would also be his win. Troy's win.

Grayson and Jim had spent Christmas with Grayson's

mother in Palm Beach, and they took this Disney excursion before returning to New York.

Grayson set down his hamburger. "Jim, I was thinking. How about you and me playing some golf? You know, like Troy and I used to."

"Gosh, I don't know, Dad. What about my baseball? Hey, look! There's the seven dwarfs. Are they real dwarfs, or just little kids?"

"That would be interesting to look up. But anyway, you can still play baseball. The thing is, I had a vision that—"

"What's a vision?"

"A vision is like, uh…well, a vision is when God tells you something. My vision said that you're going to become the world's greatest golfer."

"Wow! God said that?" Jim stuffed fries into his mouth.

"That's right." Grayson would count on God's infinite flexibility regarding the script change. After all, He was the first to deviate.

Jim's blue eyes sparkled with excitement. "What else did God say about me, Dad?"

"Well, that's about it. Except maybe one other thing—"

"What's that? What was the other thing, Dad?"

"It was pretty remarkable."

"Better than saying I'm going to be the world's greatest golfer?"

Grayson gripped Jim's shoulders and looked him in the eye. "Son, you're going to win the greatest golf tournament in the world—the Global."

The son who had never played more than miniature golf was about to become a real golfer. Grayson knew that Jim had both the athletic and mental ability to succeed. But to compete in the professional ranks, to play in the Global—to win the Global—Jim had to take on a regimen of rigorous training and discipline.

Grayson would provide some of the training and all of the discipline. In time, Jim would develop other interests, become distracted by external influences, and perhaps lose sight of the goal. But like a football lineman clearing a path for the ball carrier, Grayson would block any and all distractions that might hinder that all-precious touchdown.

Step one: get Jim onto the driving range.

CHAPTER 21

It was early still. The sun had just cut itself on a sharp hill and bled into the valley. December was cold in New York, early mornings the coldest. The air assaulted like buckshot, ears become brittle, and grass crunched under footsteps.

Jim had trudged twenty yards from the car on his way to the practice tee when he slipped and fell. "It's too damn early to play golf," he whined.

"Get up," Grayson said, "and stop swearing."

Since losing his mother and brother, Jim had taken up swearing. Grayson tried not to scold him too severely.

Jim reached the tee box and dumped his clubs on the ground. They clinked like piano keys.

"We'll start with a short iron," Grayson said. "Pull out your wedge."

"What's a wedge?"

"It has an 'S' stamped on the bottom."

Jim picked up his bag. "I want to use this one. It's bigger."

"That's a driver. It comes later."

"Which one hits the ball farther?"

"The driver, but—"

"I want to hit with the driver." Jim started to pull it from the bag.

"Oh, for Christ sake." Grayson yanked out the wedge. "Here, and no arguments."

Jim looked at the ground, arms at his side.

"Goddammit, Jim, take the fucking wedge."

Jim reached out and took it, eyes still on the ground.

"Okay," Grayson said, trying to sound calm. This was not

the way he wanted to start Jim's golf experience. "Sorry about the swearing. Now go ahead and take a swing."

"There's no ball."

"You'll get it in a minute. Let's see you swing."

Jim swung.

"Very good." Grayson moved Jim's hands together, interlocking his little fingers. "There you go. Try again."

"I don't like holding the thing this way."

"It's not a baseball bat. You'll get used to it."

"I like my way better."

Grayson exhaled. "Okay, let's compromise. Hold it your way, but with your hands together."

Jim made a couple more swings, and Grayson put a ball down. "Go ahead and hit it."

"Why do I have to play golf?"

"Come on, keep your head down and take a big swing."

Grayson stepped aside and watched Jim take a stance, looking every bit like a golfer. Jim placed the clubface behind the ball and swung it so far back it practically wrapped around his neck before whipping that great distance to the ball. It took off high and straight. Grayson's heart soared to the races. "Not bad, not bad at all."

"Can I go now?"

"Here, hit another one," Grayson said eagerly. He couldn't put a ball on the ground fast enough.

Jim just stood there.

"Come on, come on."

"Do I have to?"

"Yes. Hit away."

Jim set up as before, took that big swing, and hit a grounder to the right. Before Grayson could say "four," Jim threw his club onto the ground.

"I hate golf!" he yelled and ran toward home.

"Jim, come back here!" Grayson called, but Jim kept running. Grayson chased after him, easily catching up on his longer legs. He grabbed Jim's arm and jerked him to a stop. Jim tried to pull away, but Grayson held firm. "What's gotten into you?"

"I told you, I hate golf!" Jim yelled.

"You never used to," Grayson said, trying to keep his voice calm. "You liked playing miniature golf with Troy."

"That's not the same!" Jim's eyes filled with tears. "Besides, I'm different than Troy, so you can stop trying to make me be like him."

Grief stabbed through Grayson's heart. "Be like Troy?" He sank to his knees and grasped the boy's shoulders firmly. "Jim, listen to me. I loved Troy the way he was, and I love you the way you are."

"You guys always played golf together," Jim said. His voice softer, he added, "I thought I wasn't—wasn't good enough."

"That's not true. I just felt you weren't interested until God spoke to me."

Jim's face brightened. "Oh, yeah, that I'd win the Global. Okay, I guess I'll play golf. But I still hate playing in the cold."

CHAPTER 22

Nine years had slipped off the calendar when Grayson stepped from the cab at the Knickerbocker Club. He was meeting Chief Foley for dinner and felt nervous about what he was going to ask of him.

"Hey, you old fart, I hardly recognize you," Grayson said, entering the lobby and grasping the chief's hand. "I'll bet there's not a strand of hair under that Yankee cap." He tugged the bill. "Let's have a drink in the lounge."

"It doesn't have to be only one."

They sat at a back table and Grayson ordered. "What are you doing in LA besides chasing starlets?"

"Playing poker. Do pretty well at it too."

"And I thought you were just lucky."

"I plan to take a crack at the World Series of Poker Tournament. Pick up some cash and win a fancy gold bracelet." Foley shook his head. "I do miss police work, though. Tell me how Jim's doing. I read he captured the Junior Amateur title and was voted Golf Digest Amateur Player of the Year. And hey, what's this I hear of him putting with his eyes closed?"

The chief's interest warmed Grayson's heart. "He shows off sometimes. Claims he has the image locked in his mind like a photograph. The US Amateur is up next. He wins that, he qualifies for the Global."

Their drinks arrived, and the chief raised a toast. "To Jim's success."

"Hear, hear."

They clinked glasses.

"Jim was just getting into golf when I retired. As I recall, he hated it."

Grayson chuckled. The old man even remembered way back then. "Our first day of practice was at dawn, and he hated the cold. I agreed to later practice times and winters in Florida. I also threw in a horse for motivation."

"A horse?"

"And last year, a car."

The chief sipped and ran a finger across his lips. "You've done a hell of a lot to get that boy to love golf and to keep him motivated."

Grayson picked up his scotch and shrugged.

"Don't be modest. From what I've read, you've spent a great deal of time coaching him."

"A personal coach does the heavy lifting, but Jim's the workhorse." Grayson sipped his scotch and put the glass down. "I don't know if Jim was born with his special talent, or God saw fit to save his life and bestow it upon him later."

The chief cocked his head. "Save his life?"

"There's more to Jim's golf than you know." Grayson had never told Foley about his deal with Costanzo, but to gain his favor, he had to be upfront with him.

After hearing Grayson out, the chief sat quietly, fingers stroking the side of his glass. "I'm going to be blunt. What you're saying sounds off the wall. I'm supposed to believe that Costanzo's going to kill Jim if he loses the Global?"

"I'm not making this up. Every word's the truth."

"You made up seeing Sandra and Troy at their funeral."

Grayson *saw* them in their coffins. "That was a delusion brought on by guilt. The doctor even said so. Besides, that was a long time ago. You can't compare it to this."

The chief picked up his glass and peered into it. "I could understand Costanzo killing Jim to punish you. It's like him to play you as the reluctant virgin, but putting it off doesn't...well, it just doesn't make sense." He threw down his drink.

"We made a deal, that's why."

"Well, okay, if you say so." The chief swirled the ice cubes in his empty glass. "You've always had a thing about the Global."

And Grayson had a damn good reason. "Listen, Chief, I swear, everything I've told you is true. And believe me, Jim *will* win the Global."

The chief held up his glass and looked around. "We need a refill. I remember once saying that you'd jumped into a dark hole. It turns out to be deep, too."

Grayson puffed up his cheeks and blew out. "When Jim wins the Global, this nightmare's over. I hope I can trust Costanzo to keep his word and not—um—"

"If that was the agreement, he'll stick to it. He's pretty well known for that, and proud of it."

A waiter appeared, placed two drinks down and left.

"Jim graduates from high school soon. He'll compete in the US Amateur, then start college at Berkeley."

"Why there?"

"Because Berkeley has the best hard-ass golf coach in the country. If Jim wins the Amateur, he'll need someone of that caliber to keep his head on straight and prepare him for the Global."

"No telling what mischief he could get into. Berkeley students are known to be independent."

"I have people to handle that. But here's the thing, if anything happens to me, I'd like you to, um…" He looked down, embarrassed. This was the hard part. He'd already asked the chief for so much.

"To care for Jim? Hey." Foley gently shook Grayson's arm. "Be careful and you'll be fine." He raised his drink to his lips. "But just the same, you can count on me." He sipped and winked. "Even from the grave."

CHAPTER 23

Grayson sat on a bench, shielding his eyes against the sky's yellow haze, and watched his seventeen-year-old son prepare for work.

Jim finished stretching, then tossed off his warm-up jacket. He yanked a club from his bag like a plumber grabs a wrench. His sinewy six-foot-two-inch frame straightened tall, legs spread. A towering figure, looking to clobber the ball to Timbuktu—maybe into orbit. The club moved so fast it became a blur, and the ball shot like a missile to parts so distant you'd pack a lunch to walk there.

"Hey, Dad, come here," Jim called. Grayson paced over. "After this, I want to putt for an hour, then how about you and me going to Glen Creek and playing a round? Winner picks the restaurant for dinner. You can play from the senior tees."

"I'll senior tee you, wise guy. You're on, but I get two strokes a side."

Grayson returned to the bench. No sooner had he sat down than he felt a hard tap on his shoulder. He turned to see Chauffeur but didn't bother to act surprised, though, in fact, he was.

The henchman looked mousier, but mean as ever. "The Man wants you to join him for a beer on the patio."

It had been several years since Grayson had seen either Chauffeur or Costanzo. But just to let Grayson know he was still in The Man's heart and mind, every June first—Jim's birthday—Grayson opened his mail to find the joker playing card. The Man had kept tabs on Jim's tournaments and bet heavily on them. Detective Wilson had informed Grayson long ago that Costanzo had one weakness that twice nearly ruined him: seven-figure gambling. He once had to mortgage his house to pay more than four million dollars he lost betting on one of Super Bowl's biggest upsets. With thirty-five seconds left in the game, Eli Manning, of the twelve-point underdog New York Giants, lofted a touchdown pass that stole the game from the New England Patriots and put Costanzo into a three-day rage.

Grayson trudged to the patio to talk to a man he despised. More than despised—hated. Costanzo was watching golfers hit off the first tee. He looked older, grayer, a little hunched. He also had a suspicious line at the corner of his mouth.

"Sit down, Bolt. I ordered you a beer." The suspicious line became an unsettling smile.

Grayson remembered the days when it was Mr. Bolt. "Good morning, Mr. Costanzo." They shook hands.

"My mother needed a break from the old folks home, so I thought a field trip out to Long Island might be nice."

"I'm sure she appreciates the outing."

"She's sleeping right now." Costanzo took a swig of beer. "I've got to hand it to you, Bolt. You've done a hell of a job with that kid of yours. I thought you were blowin' smoke up my ass about all those tournaments he was going to win." Grayson's beer arrived. Costanzo picked his up and nodded. "To Jim. May he continue to—" He double-clicked his tongue. "—make me money."

The toast didn't settle well for Grayson. Tension knotted his stomach, and he wondered what Costanzo's real purpose was in coming out to Long Island. "You have something you want to talk about?"

Costanzo's face darkened. "Right to the point, isn't that right, Bolt?"

Grayson smiled with tight lips.

"You won't like what I'm going to say." Costanzo looked at him and raised an eyebrow. "But you're going to follow my advice, anyway."

Grayson's grip tightened around his icy mug.

"Next week's the US Amateur, and I don't, repeat, don't, want Jim to win." Costanzo took a long drink of beer, as though to allow time for the message to jolt Grayson's nervous system.

Grayson stiffened so hard he could feel muscles strain throughout his body. "Why would you want him to lose that all-important tournament? For Christ's sake, that's the one he must win to qualify for the Global."

"I have my reasons," Costanzo said with a sly grin. "Don't worry. He can win next year." He raised the beer to his lips and added, "I promise." Beer sluiced over his lower lip and he swallowed. He put the mug down with a clank, dabbed a napkin to his lips, and broke into a satisfied grin.

Grayson opened his mouth. Chauffeur, sitting near, reached over and clutched Grayson's shirt, yanked him close enough to kiss, and hissed, "The Man isn't talking to exercise his lungs. He insists."

Grayson jerked away. "Fuck off!" He turned to Costanzo. "You can't expect my son to do *that*."

Costanzo's grin faded like a blind date at the door. His face took on a purplish poisoned color and his voice dripped with contempt. "Bolt, never tell me what I can or can't expect. And remember, fucking up has consequences." He pushed his chair back, stood, and strode off.

Chauffeur reached for his mug and drained it, got up, and scrubbed his lips with the back of his hand. He threw some bills on the table and bent down into Grayson's face. "Go ahead, asshole, fuck up. The earth's full of losers," he said in a thick, clogged voice.

Grayson pushed his chair back and leaped to his feet. He jutted his chin into Chauffeur's long face. "And there's plenty of room for flunkies and yes men."

Chauffeur grabbed him by his collar and dragged him in close. "Tough talk from a guy whose son is on the line," he hissed.

Grayson's breath caught.

"That's what I thought." Chauffeur shoved him back. "Remember that next time you think about giving me lip." He turned and left.

Seething, Grayson watched him go. But he didn't dare reply. Too much was at stake.

ೞೞ

Chauffeur caught up with The Man, as he ambled toward the car, while smiling to himself. The Man loved giving Bolt the screws. "The fuck doesn't know whether to piss standing or sitting down. He needs to get used to the kid losing."

"Don't count on it," Costanzo said. "The twisted fuck's gonna go through hell and come out the other side as stubborn as he's always been. Just watch."

CHAPTER 24

Grayson sat watching players practice on the putting green of Pennsylvania's Oakmont Country Club. The club was hosting this year's US Amateur Championship. Grayson felt like crying and put his head down. Costanzo never believed Jim would win the Global. He only agreed to the deal for the sadistic pleasure of having Grayson's balls in the wringer for years before finally giving Jim the coup de grace.

After two days of play, Jim had advanced to the final series, where each of the sixty-four players would battle each other separately.

"Come on, Dad, I tee off next," Jim said, striding up.

Grayson had not yet told Jim he'd have to lose the tournament, hoping he wouldn't have to. Hoping for an early elimination. Hoping to let destiny take its course. After all, as Costanzo had said, there was always next year.

Competition continued, and as play unfolded, destiny's course turned to disaster. The sky was dull gray, but Jim lit up the course mistake free, splitting fairways and landing approaches close to the hole. And the few that weren't close would still find the cup one putt later. Including tough breakers from twenty, thirty feet.

He won Friday's quarterfinal, and Saturday's semifinals. His final thirty-six-hole match was against Richie Kelly, a twenty-year-old Carolinian known to be a fierce competitor.

Grayson still held off speaking to Jim. If the boy was ahead after the first eighteen holes, he'd have no choice but to order him to lose. *Order* him? Would he even listen? Such a thought would go against everything Grayson had drilled into his head since he was eight. Losing was a dirty word. Winning was everything.

At eight o'clock Sunday morning, with temperatures heading into the nineties and record high humidity, Jim and Richie teed off on the first of thirty-six holes to determine this year's US Amateur Champion.

After nine holes, Kelly was burning up the course with four birdies, putting Jim four down. Jim only managed to win a few of the next nine holes. The final afternoon's eighteen holes would start at two o'clock with Jim seven down.

Jim and Grayson ate lunch in the clubhouse, with Jim jabbering on with unbounded confidence about the final round. How he would win this hole and that hole. And coming into the final hole, he and Kelly would be tied, then he'd clobber him for the win.

"It's broiling and humid out there, Dad, and I'm going to beat his ass. I'll pressure him 'til he melts like Gramma's chocolates." Jim took a rare pause to gulp down a bite of hamburger, hardly chewing it before he swallowed, and then picked up where he'd left off. "This is it. I win, and we're going to the Global. I can feel it!"

Grayson sensed something he couldn't control. He faked a cough, excused himself, and escaped to the restroom. An unsettling passion welled, his eyes moistened. He wanted to hold Jim in his arms and press into him the love and pride he felt. But how could he?

He had to walk this dark path of wanting Jim to win and needing him to lose. He returned to the table reassuring himself that, even with Jim's optimism, he had an impossible chance of winning.

"Are you all right, Dad?"

Grayson smiled and nodded, unable to muster a convincing lie.

Jim popped a last fry into his mouth. "You haven't commented on my great plan. What do you think?"

Grayson put his hand on Jim's shoulder. "I believe you, son."

Jim put on a big smile. "Thanks, Dad. Let's go. It's time for me to whip Kelly's ass."

They stepped from the clubhouse restaurant into a sun, large and blazing. Humidity made people hot in the middle and wet around the edges. They slogged through the lumpy air to the first tee, and Grayson watched Kelly warm up, looking fresh as the grass he trimmed with his practice swings.

Grayson joined the gallery and watched Jim roll his ball into every hole. Astonishingly, when they reached the eighteenth tee, the two competitors were tied.

Kelly pulled out an iron for the short par four. A wise choice. *Nobody* used a driver on this treacherous hole. That club offered a high percentage of failure. If not hit perfectly—that is, sending the ball two hundred yards absolutely straight, then hooking sharply left—the ball would either sail into the woods, onto a bunker, or out of bounds.

But Jim was to hit first, and he yanked out his driver.

Grayson's heart crumbled, then soared. There was hope!

Jim stepped up to the ball, and Grayson closed his eyes, waiting to hear the familiar *whack*, followed by a groan from the crowd.

Grayson heard the whack, but not the groan. Never had he listened to such long silence. Then, as if on cue, a roar erupted that could be heard all the way to Costanzo's ears. Grayson opened his eyes. Jim's shot had missed the bunker, avoided the trees, and had curved onto the green, three hundred-thirteen yards away. Scoring an eagle, Jim won the hole—and the tournament.

CHAPTER 25

Grayson rode in air-conditioned discomfort, looking out at the dim blue sky through the windshield of his Mercedes. With a nervous pain in his empty stomach, he was on his way to Costanzo's home for a final farewell. By allowing Jim to win the tournament, he'd defied Costanzo a second time. He'd talked his way out of being killed the first time, but his luck couldn't possibly hold this long.

Grayson had called Thompson first, quickly explaining that if he turned up missing, that meant he was dead. "Don't ask questions," he ordered. "Just notify Foley. He'll take care of Jim."

"For God's sake, Grayson," Thompson protested. "You can't be serious!"

"I'm damn serious. Just do as I say." Grayson hung up. If he was going down, it wouldn't be alone. He wore one of his perfectly tailored suits with a pocket just right for his .38. He'd never been frisked when entering Costanzo's house before, so hopefully no one would bother to do so now.

But Chauffeur did bother. He greeted him at the door with metal-detector eyes. "Hands against the wall, asshole."

Maybe he was going down alone.

Grayson again stood before Costanzo. But there were no preliminaries like before, no asking for explanations of why, no throwing the telephone. Costanzo immediately launched into a rant about the ghastly consequences that befell other recalcitrants, and the threat of what could—what should—be done to him and his son. But Grayson had figured if he, and or, Costanzo died, there would be no reason for Jim to be killed.

In the middle of the rant, though, he abruptly stopped and smiled, a thin forgiving smile. Grayson felt like a little boy who had stuffed his fingers in his ears on the Fourth of July only to discover that the firecracker was a dud. Costanzo became the epitome of fatherly compassion. He stood, arms wide, with a huge grin on his face, as though about to hug a favorite nephew. Though the hug never came, a new note in his voice did. "Mr. Bolt, I forgive you." He shook his finger. "But you did cost me money. And you tried to enter my home with a concealed weapon." The finger wagged again. "Naughty, naughty."

Grayson tried to figure out what the change of attitude was all about, now back to being Mr. Bolt.

"Don't worry, Mr. Bolt," Costanzo said, surprisingly friendly. "You and your son are safe. After all, you're both worth more to me alive than dead." Long chortle. "So relax. The Global is coming up soon. Jim will compete, and when he wins, I make a few million, and we go our separate ways. That okay with you, my friend?" He didn't wait for an answer but put his hands on Grayson's face and gently slapped it. "Now get outta here."

Grayson felt so relieved, he almost thanked him. Instead, he nodded and turned to leave.

At the door, Chauffeur smiled tightly. "You're swimming through razorblades, dickhead, and are about to get something no one ever gets."

"What's that?"

"A third chance. But don't bother asking for the gun. We'll find uses for it."

Grayson picked a speck of lint off Chauffeur's lapel. "You'd better get back to your master. His shoes need licking."

❡❡❡

The Man bent over with laughter. "Didn't I tell ya, didn't I tell ya?" he crowed. "I *knew* the son of a bitch couldn't let the kid lose."

"You set him up brilliantly, boss. How much did you win?"

"A million four." The Man stopped laughing and all mirth drained from his face. "Get the midget on the horn. Bolt's about to get the surprise of his life."

CHAPTER 26

Kamal Datar never wanted to be a gangster. He wasn't brought up for that occupation. He was supposed to finish college at UCLA and settle down to a respectable life. That's what his father had expected of him.

But that was on hold. Currently, he worked for Misha in the identity theft business, a job once held by Snake. He had just finished his Beverly Hills collection run and was on his way to Misha's office, located in Hollywood above a small equity theater.

With Eminem blasting from a CD, he stopped his red Jaguar at a signal, peered into the mirror, and brushed his thin black mustache. He thought it made his twenty-five-year-old baby face look masculine.

From Sunset Boulevard, he turned onto Las Palmas and swung into a parking lot. He popped the trunk and grabbed three plastic bags he'd collected that morning from gardeners at three locations. They contained bank records, credit card receipts, and other forms of useful identity information the gardeners had scrounged from trash bins.

He crossed the street, skipped up some stairs, and scuffled into an outer office that might have been taken for reception. But this wasn't that kind of office. The place was dark and colorless. No pretty pictures. No signs saying *This is a smoke free environment.* With the bags slung over his shoulder, he trudged down a hallway sporting a lone light fixture last dusted around the time of Reagan's first term.

He stepped into an empty room, tossed the bags onto a table for others to sort through, and clumped into Misha's office at the end of the hall. Kamal sat at a conference table-sized desk. At least it looked that way with him sitting at it. The Jersey bigwigs called him the midget—a moniker Kamal would never dare use.

Misha scribbled notes while holding a hamburger. Loose skin gave his face the wrinkled scowl of an old man.

"Where is everybody?" Kamal asked.

"Lunch. Where the fuck do you think?"

"You should get out and enjoy the fresh air," Kamal said. "At least open a window." He reached for a French fry from a bag on the desk.

Misha slapped his hand. "Don't they teach manners in India? Ask."

"Sir, may I have a—"

"No. Sit your smart ass down. I keep the place shut up to prevent fuckfaces like yourself from breaking in." Misha bit into his hamburger. "What's on your schedule tomorrow?"

"I've got four gardeners to pick up from the Westside. I also need to see a nurse's aide at Hollywood Presbyterian Hospital who texted me about a possible score."

"I hope it's better than what your jerk-off janitor came up with."

"Give him credit. He got both a social and credit card number."

"Yeah, of a goddamn US Senator." Misha opened his desk drawer, took out an envelope with Kamal's name on it, and tossed it onto the desk. "Clear tomorrow's schedule. We're leaving town."

Kamal picked up the envelope and peeked inside. Air tickets to Palm Beach, Florida. "A paid vacation?"

"You wish. Don't bother packing sunscreen."

Kamal looked closer at the ticket. "Returning the same night?"

"A business trip. In and out."

"What kind of business?"

"You'll find out. Meet me at LAX two hours before flight time."

◆◆◆

At nine o'clock the next morning, Kamal drove south along the 405 freeway toward the airport. He'd never taken a business trip with Misha and felt anxious, not knowing what it was about. Content with his new position in the outfit, he had no aspirations for further advancement or learning online hacking, even if it were offered. Soon he would have enough money to quit, return to college, and be respectable.

Kamal wondered if Misha's boss, that mucky-muck with the ridiculous name, Chauffeur, had ordered this trip. Kamal wished it didn't include him.

Misha was waiting for him at the terminal. They checked in and ambled down the corridor to the gate. "What's this all about, Misha?"

"You don't get paid per question. In this business, we do what the fuck we're told."

Kamal felt a sharp twinge of apprehension.

"The Man tells my boss to do something, he tells me to do something, I tell you to do something, and so on. That's how it works."

Kamal's apprehension ratcheted up. He was the last of the *so on's*. Perspiration beaded on his brown forehead.

Misha stopped at an entrance that said *First Class Lounge.* "I'll see you when we land. Your gate is straight ahead."

Kamal looked at his ticket: *Coach.*

"Hey," the midget said, "I need leg room."

The plane landed at nine p.m., and they slogged to Avis Car Rental. "Kamal, we'll use your credit card," Misha said. "I'll reimburse you."

Kamal hesitated.

"Come on, come on, we don't have all night."

Kamal surrendered his card and signed for the rental, a Toyota Prius. Misha ordered him to get into the driver's side, and Kamal didn't argue. He turned north onto I-95 while Misha studied his phone's GPS.

"Go straight a couple of miles and swing left on Okeecho-bee Boulevard. We're close."

"Close to what?"

"Our business location." Misha turned off the radio. "How can you listen to that rap crap?"

"What business?"

"There's a woman with a bad heart. We're going to fix her up."

"Fix her up!" Some primeval instinct made Kamal wary. He looked at Misha. "What does *that* mean?"

"Turn left past the golf course."

Kamal made the turn. "What does fix her up mean? And why the hell am I here?"

"Look for a sign, *Shore Meadows*." A minute later: "There it is. Drive past, turn around. And don't park under the fuckin' street lamp."

"I don't like this, Misha."

Misha looked at his watch. "We're early, so take deep breaths and relax."

"Are you going to kill this woman?"

"Call it whatever the fuck you want."

"I don't want any part of this, goddammit." Kamal's breath was quick and shallow. He looked across the street at the low, L-shaped building tucked in among lush foliage. "What is this place?"

"A joint for old rich people. It holds only six or seven gee-zers. The staff's off for the night, except for a nurse in the rear and a security guy at the front desk."

Kamal's worry had turned to fear. "You really are going to kill her, aren't you?"

"Shut up and listen. The guard's going to open the door, and I'll give him a nice thick envelope." He patted his coat pocket. "He'll say a room number and then take a five-minute piss."

Kamal's heart pounded against his ribcage. He was being used for cover. Misha made sure the car wasn't under his name, and he probably managed a phony ID for his plane tick-et. Kamal took a deep breath. "So your plan is for me to wait here while you go in and kill some woman?"

Misha looked as if struck with a sudden gas pain. "Use your fucking head. Why would I need you to sit in the car and play with your dick? You'll stand guard outside the room." His face became a warning. "And don't fuckin' argue."

Kamal's heart was now slamming around like crazy.

Ten minutes later, they climbed out of the car and paced to the building's entrance. The guard opened the door, took the envelope from Misha, and whispered, "Babbling Brook," then disappeared.

Misha looked at Kamal and held up his hand, fingers spread. "Five minutes, let's go."

They scooted down a polished hallway with wall sconces spilling soft yellow light and stopped at a room named *Babbling Brook.* "Change of plans, Kamal. You're gonna bust your cherry."

Horror swept over Kamal, and he had an urge to flee. "Oh, no. Not me."

"Oh yes—you. But don't worry, you'll only have to do it once. Use a pillow, and it'll be easy."

"This isn't the ride I signed up for." Kamal turned and took a step. "I'm off this train."

Misha grabbed his arm. His lips curled back and showed a set of small, sharp-edged teeth. "Listen, dickhead, if I have to do it for you, I leave the car rental receipt as a calling card."

Kamal thought a moment as anger battled his fear. He looked up and down the hallway, then reached for the door handle. Misha stood at the door while Kamal slipped inside. The room was large, lit only with glowing blue night-lights. He heard running water. In the corner was a three-foot high waterfall, and flower arrangements were everywhere. A bed lay straight ahead. In it, a figure appeared to be sleeping. He stepped quietly to the head of the bed. A nightstand held a glass of water and a dozen bottles of pills.

He looked down at the woman's face. It was deeply lined, the cheeks hollow and pasty white. Her hair, thin and silver, spread across the fringed pillowcase like a fan. Her chest was covered in yellow-laced pajamas and moved slowly up and down. She looked very thin and very old. Maybe ninety. He wondered how much longer she'd live before dying naturally. It would be a hell of a thing to stop a beating heart. Time was running out. His eyes scanned the room. On a table lay an extra blanket and pillow. He grabbed the pillow.

He shook the woman's bony shoulder, bent over and whispered, "Psst, wake up." Her eyes popped open. "Don't move. I'm not going to kill you." She gasped. "We just need to pretend." Her mouth trembled. He held the pillow up, and she began whimpering. "Don't worry, it's okay." She shook her head wildly. "I'm only going to place it near your face. When I leave, wait ten minutes before calling for help, or I'll have to come back and really kill you." Her eyes went wild. "Tell people that someone tried to smother you but it just didn't work."

Her body flinched. She clutched her chest and took a sharp intake of breath.

"Hey, are you okay?" He grabbed her hand. Her trembling fingers gripped tight, then relaxed. She became still—frozen still—her eyes staring, mouth locked open.

"Wait! Don't die." He grabbed both shoulders and shook hard. "Oh, no." He took her wrist and felt for a pulse, let it drop, and glanced at the door. He chewed his bottom lip a minute, then put the pillow back on the table and straightened her covers. He bounded three steps to the door, opened it, and stepped into the hallway. "All done, let's go," he said to Misha.

Misha's beady eyes squinted suspiciously. "Hold on a minute." He disappeared inside a few moments and returned. He slapped Kamal on the back. "Good Job."

☙❧

The moon's whiteness shone through the bedroom curtains onto Grayson's bed as he crawled under the covers. Two hours later, he spiraled upward from sleep, awakened by the ringing telephone, which took him several gropings to find in the dark. He managed a drowsy, "Hello?"

"Hey, Bolt, it's your buddy, Chauffeur." The voice squeezed out sharp and flat like sheet metal. Or a shank. "Too bad about your mother. Old age, I guess. The Man sends his condolences." The phone clicked, like the cocking of a revolver.

CHAPTER 27

Grayson sat at his desk with a scotch and soda, his mind reeling over his mother's death. He should have realized Costanzo would never let an act of transgression go unpunished. For two weeks, Grayson had thought of ripping out Costanzo's heart and watching it beat in the gutter. He'd thought of it in the car, here at home, at his mother's funeral—especially at his mother's funeral.

But the clock was racing, and he didn't have time for that. He would have Wilson investigate. His mother would rest forever, along with Sandra and Troy, in a bitter part of his heart. But now it was time to get back to focusing on Jim winning the Global.

On the positive side—if you could call it that—Costanzo probably considered things even between them, freeing Grayson to deal with other worries. In a few weeks, Jim would be moving to Berkeley, city of drugs, liberals, perverts, and other corrupting influences. Grayson would periodically dispatch another high-paid assistant from the office, "hooknose" Gillfillen, to monitor Jim's off-campus activities. A small part of him recoiled for having to be so underhanded, but it was necessary to keep Jim safe. And keeping him safe was the only thing that mattered.

Grayson would not, could not, let anything interfere with Jim's chance of winning the Global. To paraphrase one-time presidential aspirant Barry Goldwater: *Extremism in the defense of winning the Global was no vice.*

PART II

CHAPTER 28

In Berkeley, California, the Monday morning air felt so cold and hard, you could bite it. The sun's reddish glow reached up from the hills like a fan, and rain clouds, their dark bellies barely lit, pushed in from over the bay. UC student Heather Morrison was in the last leg of a speed-skating workout. She pumped through the tree-lined bike path of graceful curves and angled slopes, striving for a personal best. *Stay focused*, she told herself. *No mistakes.*

She winged through the tunnel, icy air blasting her face and eyes. In full throttle now, she sped into a wooded forest of dank redwoods and pine. Above, a squirrel sat on a branch, dropping pinecone flakes that fluttered like confetti. She vaulted the path's root-raised concrete gap and an in-line wheel clipped the edge, pitching her forward, arms looping wildly to regain balance.

Recovering, she crouched low along a series of S-curves then burst through a streamside canopy, scattering finches into thick dogwood and willow. She pushed hard through the last bend, attacking the grueling quarter-mile incline that paralleled the old road. A cramp gripped her right calf but she wouldn't let up. Neither would the cold.

She glanced at her pink sports watch: eighteen more seconds and it'd be a record. She bore down, thrusting into the final downhill straightaway, thighs bulging with each vigorous push. Ahead, dangerously close to one side, a group of cyclists with numbers pinned to their backs were strapping on helmets. She tensed, fought to regain rhythm and shot past. *Only a few more yards. Don't let up.*

She peeked at the time and, from nowhere, a rollerblader lingered across her path.

"Ahhh!"

They crashed. The guy flew airborne, and she bounced onto her back, becoming a speed bump for an oncoming cyclist.

Thump-thump.

Her right foot took the hit. Pain spread up her leg like cracked glass, and the horror of it filled her with panic. A broken foot meant no more tennis. Hand in her scholarship at the door. Hairdressing school's down the street.

The stricken rollerblader only appeared shaken. "I—I didn't see you. Are you all right?"

Heather had seen only a blur. She wore her Brainsaver helmet, but was dazed and in no mood to be nice. "No, goddammit! I'm not all right." She tried to sit up. "Ah, my foot!"

"You shouldn't move," the guy said and reached in his pocket. "I'll call nine-one-one."

"They've already been called," a woman nearby said.

Heather lay back down and tried to take off her helmet.

"Let me help," the guy said.

He unhitched the strap, and she lifted her head. He removed the helmet, took off his jacket, and placed it under her head.

She wanted to scream at him, but instead she thanked him and closed her eyes. She felt the person gently brush hair from her forehead.

"You'll be fine," he said. "What's your name?"

"I'm sorry, but I don't feel like talking." Pin-size drops of rain sprinkled her face.

"Yeah, yeah, I understand. I'll wait with you for the ambulance."

She opened her eyes. "I'm Heather Morrison."

The guy smiled. "My name's Jim. Jim Bolt."

જ∙જ

Linda Meyers, one of Heather's four roommates, picked her up from the Alta Bates Medical Center on Ashby Avenue. Heather stretched her freshly plastered foot across the car's rear seat, her head against the frigid window. Rain poured in gusty slants, hammering the Honda's rusty roof and blurring Berkeley's nearby hills.

They turned left onto College Avenue and splashed through downtown, wipers drumming. People scurried to lunch counters and cafés. Heather stared droopy-eyed out the window. The weather would cancel tennis practice. But it didn't matter. Not for her. Tired eyes drifted closed behind a curtain of dull throbs. Her eyes popped open. "Oh my God! Linda, the contest—tonight's the contest."

"You rest, darlin'," Linda said. "You've got lots of time." She honked her horn. "Move it or milk it, asshole."

At twenty-nine, a decade older than Heather, Linda was an apple-faced university senior majoring in psychology. She had short legs, a large chest, and a larger laugh. She wore arm bracelets like wind chimes—the noisier the better. One look at her eyes and you knew she could call you more dirty words than you'd find in a dozen middle school lavatories.

The car zipped past the all-night pizza parlor, turned onto Russell Street, and motored into a tree-lined neighborhood where once grandiose homes were now carved into apartments. Houses that were spared renovation remained with peeling wallpaper, rickety staircases, and indifferent college students.

Linda spotted a rare parking space outside their still intact, two-story, four-bedroom rental. "Lookie there, darlin'." She shook her finger, and silver bracelets jangled. "It's our lucky day." She glanced at Heather in the mirror. "Sorry, did I say lucky?"

"Just get me inside," Heather moaned, hoping she was up to concentrating on tonight's contest, which would be a cryptogram. If not, she was doomed.

CHAPTER 29

Jim put his jacket back on and watched the ambulance pull away. Man, was that girl hot, with that cute little face inside her fancy helmet and the blonde hair falling over her shoulders.

He rolled over to a bench in fits and starts, collapsed onto it, and raised a pant leg. His knee was scraped and hurt like hell.

Carlos, Jim's golf team buddy, came charging up on rollerblades and skidded into a three-hundred-sixty-degree stop on the wet cement. "Hey, dude, you wipe out already?" They had planned for Carlos to give Jim his first ever rollerblading lesson, but he was a little late now.

"Some girl came tearing out of nowhere and crashed into me."

"Bummer." Carlos stared at Jim's knee. "Shit, it's all swollen. Gonna need ice. You'd better forget the lesson and get home. I'll pick you up for practice. Be sure the coach doesn't find out you've been rollerblading, or he'll ream your ass."

Jim groaned. "Right. And my ass is too precious for that. I'll go home and lick my wounds." He now lived in a hillside penthouse overlooking the San Francisco Bay. Drove a new BMW, had his own credit card, and signed his own checks—on his dad's checking account. And best of all, he was free. Free to do what he wanted, when he wanted, and with whom he wanted. At least as long as Dad didn't find out and Jim kept practicing golf. Life could be worse.

After arriving home, he iced his knee and spent the rest of the morning listening to the rain, studying, and playing Tomb

Raider on his computer. He removed the icepack, did twenty squats, and determined the knee was good. To celebrate, he heated up a frozen chicken rice bowl and thought of that girl who'd crashed into him. *God, talk about hot. Heather…Mor…Mor…Morrison. That's it. Wonder how bad her foot was hurt.*

After eating, he googled her and managed to find her Facebook profile. She'd included a landline on her "personal info" page, and he reverse searched it to find her address. She lived close, on Russell Street. He looked out the window. The rain had stopped, leaving the sky with patches of grayish blue, but to the north loomed mottled coal-black clouds. He did a few more squats and glanced at his watch. He could go see Heather, just to make sure she was all right, and still be back in time for Carlos.

Her neighborhood was a lot older than where he lived in the hills. Crap, anything built before last year was older than where he lived. He parked in front of a large two-story home, ignoring the red no-parking designation, and bounded up the walk and onto the porch. The door was wide enough to fit a truck through. He rang the bell, which was more like a buzzer.

In a minute, the door opened. It was Heather. Jim's heart banged against his ribs. She hobbled a step on her crutches and thumped a shoulder against the jam. A foot in white plaster with red toenails poked out from the door. The sun blasted her eyes, and she raised a hand to block it. God, was she cute! Hers were the most beautiful eyes he'd ever seen on a girl. Pools of blue water. Those eyes narrowed as she recognized him.

He shuffled his feet, not sure how to begin. "I'm—I'm sorry I caused your—" He glanced at her cast. "—your broken foot." Her yellow sweatshirt read *Berkeley* in blue letters. He swallowed. "Are you—are you a student?"

"I'm sorry. What was your name?"

Man, her blonde hair was awesome. It wasn't the dirty kind, but the kind that looked clean and bright. It was pretty enough that he didn't mind she'd forgotten his name. "I'm Jim. I go to Berkeley too."

She adjusted her stance with a hop, her mouth refusing to melt into a smile. "I appreciate the apology, Jiem, but it was really more my fault than yours."

He loved the way she pronounced his name. Her lips were puffy and sexy. He imagined kissing them. "Let's just call it even." Maybe she'd be cool with that. Even smile.

"Thanks for trying to be nice, but I've got problems more serious than this broken foot. I have to go."

Her foot swung into darkness, clear of the slamming door.

She was class. Pure class. And the way her body moved. Magic. She had magic. And Jim was totally under her spell.

CHAPTER 30

After brushing Jim off at the front door, Heather hobbled into the living room and back onto the couch, letting her crutches drop onto the hardwood floor. She stuffed a pillow under her cast. Soon the cryptogram would arrive on Linda's computer. She tensed at the thought. If she didn't win the contest, she'd be out of school, with or without her tennis scholarship.

A year earlier, her mother had gotten sick and lost her job. Obamacare was no help, and she also lost her health insurance. She lived in Visalia, a few hours south, where Heather had grown up.

Heather had helped her financially by teaching ice-skating part time at Berkeley Iceland, but her meager earnings hadn't been enough to support them both, and she racked up six months of credit card debt on three cards.

Her mother eventually moved to Ireland to be cared for by her sister. Heather had already lost her car to the bank and was now two months behind on her rent. Getting kicked out loomed like a water balloon full almost to the bursting.

Back in elementary school, her mother had given her a subscription to a monthly mag that had started her on the path that could lead her out of this financial nightmare. Dell's Puzzle Magazine was jam-packed with riddles, puzzles, brainteasers, and cryptograms, and Heather always figured them out. That was her talent.

Three weeks ago, her mother had written her about an Internet puzzle contest that offered a winner-take-all, ten-thousand-dollar grand prize. Included with her mother's note was a check for the hundred-dollar entrance fee and a thumbs-up sticker.

Heather had solved all the early round puzzles, and if she got the final cryptogram by the deadline tonight, she would win the big one. But the cryptogram was going to be the toughest yet. Would she be able to figure it out?

She had to. She just had to.

 భువం

Heather finished the leftover meatloaf Linda had heated for her and hobbled to her corner room off the kitchen to lie down and veg. The space was small, but it had bright yellow walls that usually cheered her up. Her mother had made the pukey green window curtains that Heather finally learned to live with.

There were three more bedrooms upstairs. Linda lived in the one overlooking the street. She had lived in the house longer than any of the housemates. When she was not in school or studying, she taught dog training and performed phone-sex for distant patrons with dirty minds and clean credit. Heather admired her saucy manner and enjoyed the homey expressions she had picked up from a southern grandmother. Linda was also a fantastic liar. Whenever Heather needed a cover story, Linda could always come up with a good one. The girl had saved Heather's butt a few times.

Brad, the *stoner* and only non-student, lived upstairs in the back. He would stockpile dirty dishes for days before hauling them down in a laundry basket. Two sisters, who were hardly ever there, shared the fourth bedroom.

Darkness fell early, and, with it, came the storm, hard and slanting, like a curtain of crystal beads. Heather was lying on her bed with her foot on a pillow when Linda came bouncing in and blowing on her recently painted blue fingernails.

"You've got an hour until your cryptogram arrives, Ms. Big Brain. My computer's warmed up." Linda straightened the covers, adjusted pillows, and jangled her bracelets in Heather's ears. "This should make you comfy, dumplin'."

"Thanks for the huge help. And for letting me use your computer."

"No problemo," Linda said, starting to hang up Heather's clothes. "When you win all that money you'll get yours fixed. Meanwhile, you keep resting while I go upstairs and wash my hair."

Rain hammered against the window, and the table lamp flickered. A torrent of water battered through the drainpipe behind Heather's head, a reminder of the freight trains that rolled across the plains back home in Visalia and those rainy Sundays with Mother when they went to early Mass before serving breakfast to the homeless.

Drowsy and lulled by the rain, Heather started drifting off. She heard the door latch and jolted up from the pillow. "Linda!"

Linda stopped in the doorway and turned back. "Yes?"

"When the cryptogram arrives, please print it and bring it down right away."

"Lickety-split. Do you want a pain pill? Got some of Brad's Vicodin."

Heather shook her head. "God, no. I need a clear head. This…this will be a major problem to…" Her eyes felt heavy.

"I'll go wash my hair and bring down the crypto thing the second it gets here."

"They only allow two hours to work on it. So…so make sure you…"

෨෧෨

An hour later, Linda swept into Heather's room, waving a printout, bracelets jingling. Her blow-dried hair spread across her shoulders, bouncing with each stride. "Up and at it, Sleeping Beauty. You've got two hours to save your sweet ass."

Heather had been asleep, one of those light sleeps that was merely assumed. She rubbed a crick in her neck. Linda placed the computer printout between her lips and helped Heather sit up.

The downpour surged and battered against the window.

"I don't know how you sleep with that god-awful racket," Linda grouched. "Never seen such a storm."

Heather snatched the paper from Linda's lips, glanced at it, turned a stiff neck to the clock, and reached for her pencil and paper.

Plopping into a chair, Linda grabbed an apple from a bowl on the table. "So this is the ball-buster of ball-busters."

Heather's eyes darted around the jumbled letters. "Oh, man. It's a non-spaced substitution cipher."

"Which means?"

"Look."

WGJTAQNAHNJUGAUESTALWNCLHLAPLDDTLWN.

"Each of those letters replaces another letter. I have to figure out all the originals."

"That will actually say something?"

"Yep, and it's super hard with no spaces between words. An Internet auto-solver couldn't even do it." After a minute of full attention, Heather shook her head. "I don't know about this."

Linda finished her apple, stood, and tossed the core in a wastebasket. "Okay, Einstein, I'll be upstairs when you're done." She left, and lightning flashed through the window, flooding the room with brightness. The table lamp flickered again, and the house rumbled with the echo of thunder.

Heather pressed her lips together, trying to ignore the thunder crashing outside. She had to concentrate. Her eyes flicked to the different letters stuffed into the cypher, and doubt filled her mind. How would she ever solve this? It was impossible!

Nothing's impossible, she encouraged herself. *You're just not looking at it right. You can do this.*

She stared at the cypher again then tried another tactic, working backward. Ten minutes passed, then twenty, then forty. Ideas were considered and discarded. But Heather refused to give up. Eventually, an idea was analyzed without being discarded—an idea that showed real promise. Heather felt a tiny flame of hope growing inside her, a hope that increased the further she progressed with the idea. Finally, the flame had burst into a full-fledged inferno. She'd figured it out!

CHAPTER 31

eather grabbed her cell phone. "Linda, I've got it! Hurry down."

Linda flew into the room, and they hugged like high school cheerleaders.

"It really, really sucked," Heather said. "Cryptograms with few words and no spaces are the hardest they come. This one didn't even have any common words like a, I, and, the, at. See." Heather handed over the paper.

Cryptogram:

WGJTAQNAHNJUGAUESTAWNCLHLAPLDDTLWN.

Decipher:

GOD INVENTED CONCUBINAGE, SATAN MARRIAGE.

Linda beamed like a proud big sister. "Girl, you *are* a genius."

Heather looked at the clock. "We've got six minutes. Hurry up and—"

Lightning flashed, and the room lights flickered once, twice. The two stared at each other and froze. A deafening clap of thunder, and it got blacker than the outdoors. Heather's heart jolted within her chest, then bumped like a rollercoaster halted mid-descent.

"Oh no, not now."

"Don't panic," Linda said, sounding panicky. "The power will come back on. It will, it *will.*"

"Does God hate me or what?" Heather cried.

"I'll get a flashlight." A minute later, "*Shit!*" Heather listened to Linda scuffle into the room. "Brad has the fucking thing. We've still got five minutes. I'm gonna take the answer up to my room and light a candle. I'll be ready to type it in when the power comes back on. You stay here."

Linda's bracelets jingled off into darkness. Heather plopped against the pillows and gripped the comforter. The wind groaned and scratched behind her head like a shivering animal trying to get in.

A flash of light knifed through the window and Heather drew the comforter to her chin and counted. One, two, three, four, five—boom! She jolted.

Too anxious to stay in bed, she fumbled for her crutches and hobbled into the kitchen. She maneuvered around the table and chairs, hopped to the living room's arched entrance and peered into blackness. The pounding rain, the wind, the thunder—she was in a tin can.

Anxious to reach the stairs across the living room void, she supported herself on one crutch and thrust the other into darkness. She tapped and hopped along, the dark leaning against her. She dropped her crutch and caught the back of the couch. *Damn! Should have grabbed my cell phone and used its light.* On her hands and knees, she groped for the crutch and tried to guess how much time had lapsed since Linda went upstairs. Three or four minutes. The dread thickened. Maybe only two minutes left. "Linda, are you ready?"

Thunder boomed and drowned out any possible answer. She clambered to her feet and hopped near the stairs by the front door. She cupped her hands to her mouth—"LINDA!"

She heard Linda rush through the hallway. "I'm right here. Everything's set. We've only got about one—" The front door swung open, knocking Heather onto the floor.

"What the fuck!" cried a voice.

Scrambling down the darkened stairs, Linda yelled, "Heather, are you all right?"

"What the hell's going on?" the voice croaked.

"Brad, is that you?" Linda called, accidentally kicking Heather.

Heather yelped. "What hap—"

The kitchen and entry became a blaze of light. Heather and Linda locked eyes.

"Quick, the computer," Heather yelled.

Linda flew up the stairs and disappeared down the hallway.

Brad reached to help Heather up. "Are you okay?"

Heather caught a whiff of marijuana, waved him back, and clawed to her feet. She hollered up the stairs, "Linda, did we make it?"

After a moment the hall light clicked on, then footsteps and jangling bracelets approached.

Heather saw her, head down and solemn. "Oh, no. Please, don't say it."

Linda shook her head.

CHAPTER 32

The morning after his collision with Heather, Jim sat at his kitchen table, chomping granola cereal, peering out at the Golden Gate Bridge, and thinking of Heather. *Man, she's so goddamn hot.* Especially standing there in her doorway with that cutesy little expression on her face—though not a happy one. It sure would have been fun to kiss. And, God, her voice. The way she added that extra *e* to his name was sexy as hell. He checked his watch. He absolutely *had* to see her again.

There was just enough time before biology class to swing by the flower shop at the bottom of the hill and get her a bouquet. A real nice one. He dressed fast, and twenty-five minutes later he squealed up in front of her house.

He grabbed the bunch of roses and jumped from the car. A woman, a real plumper with long black hair that fanned out like straw, came down the steps of the house. Her coat swished by her knees because of her *don't screw with me* walk.

"Good morning," he said in his friendliest voice.

She stopped. "Well, hello, handsome. This is what I call the start of a good day. Prince Charming pulls up to my house in a fancy sports car and gives me flowers. What have I done to deserve all this?"

"Sorry to disappoint you, ma'am. You see my name's—"

"Jim and you don't rollerblade worth a shit."

Jim grinned. "So Heather told you about me."

"Nothing good, so you can put your face back to normal. Hate to tell you this, but if you're into her—and, from the way you're panting, I think you are—forget it." She reached for the flowers. "I'll see that she gets these."

Jim yanked his arm back. "I'd like to give them to her myself."

"Look, I'll be straight with you, lover-boy. You've picked a bad time to get your hormones racing. For one thing, Heather's in bed resting, and for another —" She shook her head. "It really doesn't concern you. I'll convey your love." She snatched the flowers, turned, and tramped into the house.

Jim wasn't going to get turned away so easily. He'd wait until the woman left and try again. A minute later the woman came back outside and scowled at him.

Jim raised his hands. "Okay, I got it. It's a bad time. But please tell Heather I'll come back." He turned and started for his car.

"Wait a minute."

Jim turned around, ready for an argument.

"Why are you so persistent?"

That caught him off guard. "Since I caused her foot injury, I feel an obligation, you know, a moral one, to…to do something."

"The flowers filled that bill. Why do you want to see her?"

Jim swallowed hard, trying to think. "She told me she's got some serious problems, and, well, maybe I can help."

"That could be a heavy load to carry for someone you don't even know."

"I'm used to carrying heavy loads."

"Not in that flashy set of wheels your daddy must've given you."

Jim's face heated up. "I earned that car." And he did, the way he saw it. Sacrificed like hell growing up under *Daddy's* thumb. "Forget it. I don't know why I'm talking to you."

"Huffy, huffy. Let's get back to your helping Heather. What's the real reason? You want to get into her pants?"

Jim's face felt totally hot. "Let's just drop the whole thing, okay?" He turned to leave, stopped and thought a moment, then turned back. "Okay. I'll tell you why I want to help her, and you can go ahead and laugh. It's because I've—" How was he going to put this? "Because she's goddamn cute and I like her." He started for his car, wishing he'd thought of something better to say.

"You got ten thousand dollars?"

CHAPTER 33

During a decade of playing golf, Jim had racked up eighteen tournament victories, made dozens of eagles, scores of birdies, sixteen holes-in-one, but had never been in love.

Until now.

Two months and two weeks after their fateful meeting on the bike path, Heather was back on both feet, and she and Jim sat holding hands under an umbrella. They were doing lunch at Jim's favorite health food café, *The Block's End,* on Euclid Avenue, located on the north side of campus, just down the hill from his apartment. The street was crammed with restaurants and outdoor cafés, offering food well suited for Jim's health food diet, with names like *Brewed Awakening* and *Asiana Garden Vegetarian.* The place had lots of shade trees and a cool breeze that smelled like eucalyptus. Heather wore a blue UC Berkeley sweater and a pair of gold tennis ball earrings Jim had surprised her with for their two-month anniversary.

An elderly couple with a small, well-groomed poodle occupied the table near a space heater. The dog slept curled in the man's lap. Next to the low ironwork fence separating the sidewalk, a hooknose man in wire-rimmed glasses sat facing them, hunched over with coffee and a newspaper.

A waitress delivered Jim and Heather's food and drinks. Heather shook ketchup onto her veggie burger. "I'm really excited about your tournament this weekend. Can't wait to meet your dad."

"Yeah, yeah, that's right." The mention of his dad turned Jim's mood to crap.

"When does he get in?"

"Friday, day after tomorrow. Don't worry, you'll like each other."

"I wasn't worried." She swirled her lemonade with a straw. "Should I be?"

Jim shook his head. "Of course not." Bullshit. She wasn't going to like him. Andrea hadn't. She had been his high school crush until she broke up with him because she didn't like his dad's—or his obsession with golf. "He wants us to pop in for dinner at the Claremont Hotel, where he's staying."

"Woo-hoo, steak. Sorry, but veggie burgers *are* getting kind of old." She looked up from under her golden eyebrows. "You never talk about your dad."

"I've told him all about you." He took a bite of his falafel.

Heather sipped her drink. "Did you tell him I beat you in strip poker?"

"Poker's something you guys have in common."

"You mean our kind?"

He grinned. "I did clue him in that you're on the tennis team and smart enough to win ten thousand dollars by doing a…what'd you call it?"

"A cryptogram. And if it wasn't for my mother telling me about the contest, I wouldn't even be here right now."

Jim shifted in his chair and studied the contents of his falafel. "I hadn't heard that part of the story."

"I almost didn't even win."

Jim dabbed a finger in the tahini sauce and tasted it. "No kidding?"

"There was a power outage, and I was fifty-five seconds late getting my answer in. Linda hadn't wanted me to tell anyone this, but I don't see why I can't tell you. The next day Linda called the contest people and twisted their arms. I don't know exactly how she did it, but she did it. She's totally awesome."

"Yeah, yeah, I'll say." After he'd given Linda a ten thousand dollar check, she had made up a fake letterhead with the name of the contest sponsors and mailed it to Heather along with a ten grand money order.

Tricking Heather was a total bummer, and Jim's stomach tightened just thinking about it. Still, it seemed unavoidable since she probably wouldn't have accepted an honest offer. But she was going to be really pissed about being lied to. He'd lay the truth on her. But after sex. She was always in a good mood after sex. He bit into his falafel. "You said your mother. Where's she live?"

"Ireland." Heather reached over and wiped tahini off Jim's upper lip with her finger then licked it. "She's pretty bad off with migraines that the doctors can't do anything about." Heather bit into her veggie burger. "She's a great mom, though. But I think she let me get away with too much. I never made my bed and didn't even know how to clean house until Linda taught me." She laughed. "Mom's a goody-goody. Not in a bad way, but she'll fight for a cause or help anyone with a story."

"Dad takes on legal cases for free once in a while, but most of his clients are super rich."

"Nice to know at least something about your dad. Money's never been important to Mom and me."

"Hey, you guys want to sign a petition?" a girl said, holding a clipboard. "It's to erect a statue of Mario Savio in the free speech area. He led the free speech movement back in '64."

Heather held out her hand. "Sure, I'll sign."

"Me too," Jim chirped.

After the girl left, Jim pursed his lips. "1964 was the year Arnold Archer won the Global by six strokes."

"Is that a big deal?"

"Yeah, yeah, it's a big deal. The Global is the primo golf tournament. The one I'm going to win. I could tell you lots of stuff about the Global."

Heather took his hand and looked at him with those amazing blue eyes. "You've mentioned the Global before. I love that you're passionate about your golf."

"Really?"

"Uh-huh." She dropped her fork, reached down to pick it up, and found a coin.

"What's that?"

"A peso. Maybe it'll give me good luck. I've never been to Mexico."

"That would make a cool ball marker on the green."

"Then you take it. It'll be your lucky ball marker."

Jim put it in his pocket. "Thanks."

"I played golf in high school," she said. "Could hit the ball far but not very straight. I was a good putter, though. Everyone said I had an eye for reading greens and would make a great caddy. Anyway, I think it's wonderful that you have all this intensity." She ran her finger down his chest. "I also appreciate your intensity in other areas. And just so you know, I'll be there rooting for you when you win the Global."

The old couple stood and buttoned their coats. Their poodle trotted over and sniffed at Jim's pants cuffs. He reached to pat its head and got a handful of spit.

"Let's go," Heather said. "I need to get home and start working on an English lit paper."

"Home?" The words dragged Jim's face down like a double dose of gravity. "What do you mean? I thought we'd go to my place." He leaned into her ear. "And I'd run my tongue over your luscious body." He pulled back. The hooknose man was peering at them over his newspaper.

"Sounds yummy, but not today, honey bunny. My assignment's due tomorrow and I haven't even started it." She puckered and put a lipstick spot on his forehead. "I promise, tomorrow night." She got up. "We'll have lots and lots of time."

"Let's meet here, say five o'clock. It'll be our last night before Dad arrives." Tomorrow, that was when he'd fess up about the money.

"After dinner we'll start off with strip poker. Maybe I'll lose a sock or two. Then romance." She blew him a kiss and ran off.

CHAPTER 34

Grayson had just lined up his putt on the ninth green and was about to hit when Thompson's cell phone rang. Grayson looked at him and growled.

Thompson raised his hand. "Hold on, it's Gillfillen. Hello…uh-huh…he's right here." He handed Grayson the phone. "He wants to talk to you."

"What is it, Gill?"

"Jim and that Heather Morrison girl just finished lunch together."

"Stay on them. I want to know everything they're up to."

"Um…"

"Um, what?"

"They went separate ways."

"Figure it out!" Grayson hung up and tossed Thompson his phone, then missed an easy three-foot putt. He threw the putter to his caddy and trudged off toward the clubhouse, Thompson at his heels.

"What are the love birds up to?" Thompson asked.

"It's not important what they're up to, because whatever it is, it's not golf." Grayson glanced at his watch. "Right now it's noon, California time, three days before Jim's tournament, and, instead of practicing, he and his girlfriend will probably spend the rest of the day goddamn rollerblading." Grayson's face heated up. "She's *exactly* the kind of distraction I've feared."

"What are you going to do?"

"I'm going to end that goddamn relationship."

"*You're* going to end it?"

"You don't think Jim would, do you? Even if he agreed to, I wouldn't believe him. With me here in New York, he thinks he can do whatever he damn well pleases."

"How you gonna do it?"

"By yanking his ass out of there."

⌘

Grayson wasn't back in his office ten minutes when Elizabeth approached his desk. "I'm glad you're sitting down," she said, "because you're about to blow your top."

"My top's already been blown off today. What is it?"

She handed him a folder. "Jim's last month's credit card receipts along with his bank statement and canceled checks. On top is the doozy."

Grayson opened the folder and felt his head explode. "Ten thousand dollars!" Stunned, he looked at Elizabeth and wailed, "Who the hell's Linda Meyers?"

CHAPTER 35

eather smiled as she watched Jim strip off his underwear. "I guess that ends the poker game," she said, having lost all of two shoes and one sock. She stood up. "Come with me, lover boy." She led him by the hand into his bedroom.

Jim had already arranged everything with dim lights, candles, and roses. Amazing roses. They filled the room with color and sweet fragrance. Glistening city lights and diamond-like sparkles from the bay reflected through the bedroom's glass wall.

Heather steered him toward the bed and pranced to the CD player to cue up Michael Bublé's "The Way You Look Tonight." She put on Jim's cowboy hat from the dresser, and with a racy cowgirl smile, planted her feet apart. The music started, and so did she, dragging one foot toward the other, then away. She lazily rotated her hips while unbuttoning her white blouse and letting it drop to the floor.

Jim's eyes swelled, and his tongue stuck out like Pluto's.

She almost laughed at the view but, instead, raised her arms and swayed gently to the music, did a few breezy twirls and unzipped her jeans. Slid them down, slow and inviting. Kicked them into the air, turned around, and reached for her bra clasp, paused, and gazed over her shoulder at Pluto, whose tongue was now to the floor. The bra fell, and she bent over and wiggled her booty.

"God*damn*, you've got a bitchin' ass."

She turned to him. "Glad you like it, pardner." She strutted easily to the bed, put her hands on her knees and circled her hips in a leisurely figure eight. Slowly she slipped off her pink lace panties and twirled them until they sailed off somewhere.

Jim's eyes gleamed with eagerness, and he spread his arms. "Get over here, littl' doggie."

She dropped the cowboy hat over his saddle horn. "Looks like someone's ready for round up," she said with a giggle, jumping into his arms.

He took her hand, raised it to his lips, and kissed the palm. "They say you only fall in love once, but that's not true. I fall in love every time I look at you."

She flung away the hat and wrapped her arms around him, then snuggled close, her breasts tight against his deliciously firm chest. "It's like magic when we cuddle. Makes my lips tingle."

He stirred the curls behind her ear, and she gazed into his awesome bright eyes. They sparkled with anticipation. He lowered his head and hot breath touched her ear. His wet tongue circled inside and she quivered. Their lips moved closer and touched. She slipped her fingers through his wavy blond hair while their tongues flitted like butterflies, here, then there. His tongue slid in and out between her lips, and her bones began to melt. She ran her palms down his back and pulled him close. The breeze stirred loose wisps of hair around his face, and he brushed them back impatiently.

Blood pounded in her ears. "Oh, Jiem," was all she could say between labored breaths. She gasped when he slid his splayed hands beneath her hips.

When seized by feelings too intense to contain, she bit her lower lip to hold back screams of heaven, made stronger when she felt deep inside her the staccato spasm of his release. She didn't know if it was seconds, minutes, or eons that they lay in a state of complete collapse.

Jim moved first. He propped himself on one elbow. "Baby, that was incredible," he said, still breathing unevenly. He glided his fingers along her cheek. "I love your smile."

"You're the reason for my smile."

He swung on top of her and brushed the hair from her face. "It seems that my whole life was meant to be with you."

She squirmed. "I'm losing circulation."

He rolled off her. "I've got a cramp in my foot."

After showering together, they put on white bathrobes that Jim had purchased at Barneys. He'd had the pockets embroidered, his with golf balls, hers with tennis balls. He drifted into the kitchen to prepare tea. Minutes later, she found him standing with his hands behind his back and grinning.

"Close your eyes," he said.

She smiled, obeying.

"Okay, now you can look."

"Oh my, what's that?"

He handed her an envelope with *Delightful Travels* embossed on the corner. "Happy birthday."

"My birthday isn't for days." She tore it open. "Mexico! I've always wanted to go to Mexico."

"Seven-day cruise. We'll spend spring break south of de border."

She bounced on her toes "This'll be perfect."

Jim poured their tea, and they took it into the living room. Heather wanted to talk about his golf. She'd tried a few times before, but he always said there wasn't much to tell and changed the subject. He didn't talk much about his parents either, only that his mother had died when he was young and his father had raised him.

They sat on the couch, and she took his arm and snuggled close. "You've never told me how you got into golf. How old were you?"

"Eight. I learned at my dad's country club."

"How fun. What was it like?"

"My dad coached me, taught me the fundamentals, things like that."

"Uh-huh." She sipped her tea. "Go on."

"I practiced a lot, and Dad drilled into me stuff like proper attitude."

"And that is?"

"Never give up and always win."

"Always *try* to win."

Jim shook his head. "Dad doesn't believe in that word.

Every golf shot is do-or-die. If I screwed up, I always heard about it."

She pressed her lips together. "Uh-huh, go on."

"Winter golf in New York is the pits." He shivered. "So in December and January I lived with my grandmother in Florida. Dad hired golf coaches to work with me."

"What about school?"

"Private tutors."

"Ooh, impressive."

"They were good. Really knew how to teach."

Heather curled her legs under her. "When did you start dreaming of going professional?"

"It was never a dream, always a goal. A goal being quantifiable."

She nodded. "I see."

"The goal was decided…well, kinda by my dad, but by me too. I'm not a professional yet, but I'll be playing in the Global this year."

"Wait a minute. This *year*? You said you wanted to win the Global, but I never imagined—"

He grinned. "I qualified by winning the US Amateur last year."

Heather opened her mouth, then closed it.

"It's all part of the plan."

"Whoa." She swung her feet onto the floor. "Part of what plan?"

"We have everything planned out. That is, Dad and me."

"How did all this *planning* come about?"

"It's a long story. Sure you want to hear?"

She sipped more tea. "Every detail."

"I had an older brother, Troy. He was going to be the golfer."

"Was?"

"Yeah. He started at age six, but died in a car accident with my mother. The next thing I knew, I was learning to play golf."

Heather shook her head. "What do you mean, the next thing?"

"I started a few days later…uh, maybe weeks later, I can't remember, but it was Christmastime. I know because my dad took me to Disney World and told me I was going—" He hesitated. "Well, he said I was going to start playing golf."

"That's it, just like that?"

Jim scratched his head. "The truth is…this will sound weird. My dad said I was ordained to become the world's greatest golfer."

"And you believed him?"

Jim shrugged. "I was a kid. Made sense to me." His brow furrowed as he thought. "And anyway, even if he was wrong, I still turned into a pretty good golfer. So it really doesn't matter why I started golfing. All that matters is winning the Global."

"That can't be all that matters," Heather insisted. "I mean— what about *me*?"

Jim laughed, rolling his eyes. "Well, of course, *you* matter."

"More than golf?" Heather asked, gazing up at him. She feared his answer.

Jim never broke her gaze. "Definitely more than golf. You matter more than anything else in the world."

∽∾∽∾

Around midnight, they left Jim's apartment building under a sky that glared white. The faraway wash of the surf licked at the fog that was creeping in, gray and wet. They lowered their heads into their coats, locked arms, and toddled down the hill to Heather's car parked at The Block's End Café. For five minutes they kissed goodnight, then Heather headed home. She would have stayed at Jim's place like usual but he needed to meet his dad early the next morning.

As she drove, she thought about Jim's bizarre childhood. Losing his mother and brother so tragically must've hurt, big-time. And his father—telling Jim he was ordained to become the world's greatest golfer? Meeting Bolt Senior tomorrow might be an interesting experience.

Heather climbed into bed, thinking of another kind of experience. The pregnant kind. The first time she and Jim hooked up, a month after they'd started, they fell asleep with Jim in-side her. The condom had slid off, and now her period was late. As tempting as it was to devolve into full-fledged panic, she kept herself calm by reminding herself of what Jim had told her. '*You matter more than anything else in the world.*' Whatever happened, at least they'd get through it together.

❦❦❦

Jim welcomed the walk back up the hill. A fuzzy moon got lost somewhere in the fog as he took his time getting home. He never liked thinking about his mom and Troy, but he was glad he'd told Heather about how important golf was to him after they died. He still worried about whether she'd like his dad. Even more, he worried she'd be mad at him for the sneaky way he donated the ten thousand dollars to her relief fund. There just hadn't been enough time to tell her tonight.

All at once an icy thought to hold. If his dad's secretary hadn't yet thrown up a red flag about the check he'd written, she soon would. Drawing funds from his dad's account was a bad idea. Should've sold some stocks his Grandma had given him and started his own account. But everything happened so fast. Meeting Heather, falling in love—

Dread scraped his nerves like steel wool.

He arrived at his penthouse, locked the door behind him, and fell onto the couch, only to bounce back up again a minute later. He was too wired to go to bed. There were too many things on his mind. Instead, he paced the living room, mind awhirl.

His eyes fell onto the golf clubs tucked into the corner, and he scowled as he remembered all the grueling days that he'd lugged them around throughout his childhood. He'd never thought there was anything unusual about his training until Heather had started asking questions. But the more he thought about it, the stranger it seemed. He'd gone to tournaments in-stead of vacations. While his school buddies were playing football and joining the Math Club, he'd spent every free hour on the course or at the driving range. His dad hadn't even cared what his grades were in school, as long as he kept winning championships.

He's just a proud parent, Jim argued to himself. *Any parent would want their kid to succeed.*

And then there was Troy. Winning the Global was as much for Troy and his dad as it was for Jim. He couldn't let either of them down.

He trudged into his bedroom, which still smelled like roses—and Heather. She always smelled so fresh and sweet. He breathed in the air, enjoying the memories that flooded him: her smile. Her eyes. Her skin. Her taste.

He'd meant it when he told her that she was more important to him than golf. After he won the Global, he'd have a lot more time to spend with Heather. A lot more time.

CHAPTER 36

Jim and Heather got off the elevator hand in hand and headed to Suite 404. Heather gave Jim a wink, and he returned a thin smile. "Here goes," he said and knocked.

Heather watched him rub his free hand along his pant leg.

The door swung open. "Hello, Jim," Mr. Bolt said, holding a glass and smiling. "And you must be Heather. Come in." He gestured them inside.

Heather scanned the costly suite and gave Jim an approving nod.

"Can I offer you two a drink before we go downstairs?"

"Sure, Dad," Jim said as he and Heather sat on the sofa. Mr. Bolt paced to the mini-bar, looked at Heather, and raised his glass. "Jim knows I'm a scotch man. Many people these days prefer wine, and I agree it has its place."

Heather was struck by the similarity of the two men. Both stood tall and solid with graceful body movements and smooth hand motions. They each had gentle voices, though Grayson's was deeper.

"What'll it be for you two?" he asked.

"Oh, a Diet Coke—or regular—would be fine, thank you," Heather said.

"Diet Coke it'll be," he said.

"Water for me," Jim said.

Heather sat straight, hands folded in her lap. Great tailoring on that suit. Nice shade of dark blue. A lot like new denim, but not. He was no Adam Levine, but not a bad trim job on the hair, and those eyes could belong to Adam. She tried to picture Jim with parted hair.

Mr. Bolt placed their drinks before them on the coffee table.

"Thank you, Mr. Bolt," Heather said. "How was your flight from New York?"

"My father was Mr. Bolt," he said, his tone even. "Call me Grayson." He settled into a stuffed chair. "I spent my flight time working." He sipped his drink.

"I flew to Atlanta once," Heather said. "I spent the time working, too, but it was just a research paper."

"The sun's in your eyes, Jim," Grayson said, and got up to close the curtain.

"Thanks, Dad." Jim whispered to Heather, "When did you go there?"

"High school, Tennis Nationals," she said softly. "Grayson, this is a wonderful suite." Her gaze flitted around the room. "The Claremont has such character."

"Years ago I played college baseball," Grayson said, sitting back down. "Harvard, actually. Played here once or twice. My mother came to watch. She loved this hotel."

"I guess we're all excited about Jim's tournament," Heather said and patted his leg.

Grayson's face fell sober and he turned to his son. "Jim, tell me what to expect at our match this weekend."

Heather lifted her eyes. *Our* match? She listened to twenty minutes of golf talk before Grayson stood and suggested going to dinner. He left for the restroom. Jim grabbed Heather's coat and held it open. "I'll try to cut things short with my dad."

"Fine with me," she said, relieved to get out of there. Maybe dinner conversation would be more interesting.

Once seated, a maitre d' with a white mustache and large menus stepped out from the shadows and bowed. Grayson ordered drinks. Scotch-and-soda, Diet Coke, and water. Heather could have used a beer, but worried that since she was under twenty-one, Grayson might not be big on the idea.

Prompted by his father, Jim continued to discuss, in detail, the course he would be playing for the next two days: yardages of each hole, kinds of grass, firmness of greens, opponents' strengths and weaknesses, and how the course compared with the Brentwood Country Club where Jim would compete in the Global.

As the evening wore on, Heather felt benched—and pissed about it. She gave Jim the hard-eye, hoping he'd get the message to include her or at least change the subject. When that failed, she broke into the conversation with what she thought was an intelligent question. "You two seemed concerned about Jim's opponents. In golf, why does that matter?"

They both looked at her blankly.

Oops, had she stepped over the line into sacred ground? "I mean, in other sports, like tennis, a player's actions are usually based on what the opponent does. But in golf—"

Jim opened his mouth to speak but Grayson touched his arm. "It has to do with strategy," he said, then turned back to Jim and acted as if she had disappeared into the ether.

Following the main course, Jim finally got around to acknowledging Heather's presence. "You know, Dad, Heather's a math major and is on the varsity tennis team."

"Math?" Grayson said. "That's an unusual major for a woman."

"For some, I guess," Heather said, as the waiter delivered chocolate mousse desserts all around and a drink for Grayson. "I've always liked analytical problems."

"Really now?" Grayson sipped his brandy. "You must be very bright."

Her cheeks burned, and she hoped they didn't look like cherries.

"Jim's mother was intelligent," Grayson went on. "We met at the UN. She was an interpreter, Canadian born. She taught Jim French."

Jim cleared his throat. "I've forgotten most of it."

"Her work required social skills," Grayson said. "That's not to say there's anything wrong with mathematics." He took another sip. "What exactly do you expect to do with it, Heather?"

"I—I don't know. I suppose, um—"

"Tennis is a fine sport," Grayson said. "I heard you mention high school. Tell me, did your father get you started?"

Heather rubbed her palms under the table. "No…uh, I never knew my father."

Grayson cocked his head. "You don't say."

"I was born in Ireland but grew up in central California. I learned to play tennis at the Y."

"Ah, I thought I detected a touch of Irish. Where in Ireland?"

"A small town just outside Dublin. My mother moved back not long ago."

"What town would that be?"

"Kildare, it's near—"

"Do you have family here?"

"Um, no, my mother's all I have," she said, adding quickly, "and an aunt who lives with my mother."

"You've managed to do quite well for yourself, young lady. Getting into Berkeley and making the tennis team are no small accomplishments. Given your lack of serious coaching, you must be quite talented."

The tablecloth began to ripple, stirred by the rhythm of Heather's bouncing knee. "I had an excellent high school coach." Her face felt hot behind her forced smile. "That made up for other deficiencies." She spooned out a bite of mousse, hoping the attention would shift back to Jim's golf.

After dinner, Jim and Heather said goodnight to Grayson and took the Tunnel Road through town to Heather's house. The silence between them hung like the outside mist. That was, until Jim made the mistake of asking why she was so quiet.

"I'm not quiet. But if I were, what's wrong with it?"

Jim shrugged. "Nothing, I suppose."

She didn't say anything for a full minute, but felt like exploding. "Do I have to talk every second to keep you happy?"

He reached for her hand. "I'm happy. Are you happy?"

She twisted away and cupped her elbows with her hands. "Don't touch me!"

Jim's thumbs tapped the steering wheel.

She had to say something. She turned to him. "I wouldn't call that a fun evening."

Jim blinked. "What do you mean? You were happy about the restaurant and had the steak you'd been wanting. Especially since you're so tired of *veggie burgers*."

"I've never complained about eating at that pasture you call a restaurant."

"Pasture!" He shot her a glance. "Protein shakes are a lot healthier than the artery clogging crap you go for. And *you* call yourself an athlete."

That did it! "You're so full of shit. Is this obsessive diet of yours another of your dad's '*plans*'?" She made finger quotes in the air. "Like playing in the Global?"

Jim tightened his grip on the wheel like the seat belts tightened across their chests when his foot hit the brakes like a brick. He screeched to the curb and wheeled on her. "Playing in the Global was *my* plan. *I* qualified. My dad had nothing to do with it."

"Your dad had everything to do with it, and you know it!"

"Even if he did, so what? He gave up a lot for me. And at least I live my life without bullshit. You can't even manage your own finan—Oh, forget it." He stood on the accelerator and squealed from the curb.

"What's that supposed to mean?"

"I said forget it."

Heather clenched her teeth and looked away. After a few blocks of gloomy silence, her adrenalin subsided. "Look, I don't know your dad very well, but he was rude—and so were you—to shut me out all evening. You could've at least stood up for me."

"Stood up? And what do you mean, shut out?"

"Come on!" Her adrenalin kicked in again. "I even tried to join your exclusive golf conversation and was treated like I was stupid. And the same thing with tennis. 'Tennis is a *fine sport*.' What bullshit."

"You're overreacting. Tennis *is* a fine sport. A great sport."

She folded her arms. "Right. And that crap about comparing my being a math major to your mother's career. What the fuck was that about?"

"You don't understand my dad."

"Look, we shouldn't get into this now. You have a golf match tomorrow, so let's drop it." She stared out the window. Grayson was a dickhead. His big smile could snap into a frown just like that. And dammit, she hated herself for feeling cowed by him.

The car rolled to the curb. "You don't have to get out," Heather said.

He touched her leg. "Are you all right?"

"I'll see you tomorrow." She opened the door, forced a smile, and marched off.

CHAPTER 37

Jim drove away, gnawing his lower lip. Old fears were stirred. Heather had every right to feel left out. He hit the steering wheel with his fist. He shouldn't have argued with her. All during dinner, his stomach was in knots. He should have *known* his dad was going to be like that. He was always either dismissive, condescending, or downright rude to every girl Jim ever brought to the house. And what did Jim do during dinner? Exactly what his father had wanted him to do. Ignore Heather and talk to him about golf.

Jim wanted to include her, made one feeble attempt, but, other than that, he just sat there feeling embarrassed and ashamed. And then in the car, Jim defended him. Even worse, when Heather pulled away from him, all the tension and anger built up inside, turned him into an erupting volcano. Fortunately, he only vented a little steam. And damn it to hell, he had to have that talk with her about the money. No more hiding and pretending all was just great.

⁂

He woke up the next morning still feeling crappy for not being nicer to Heather at dinner. Should've known something like that would happen. He could never be himself around girls with his dad there. He'd take Heather to breakfast before the tournament started and try to make up. He dressed in his golf clothes and drove to her house.

He rang the buzzer, but no one answered. He peered through the door's peephole. It looked like someone was standing way back in the room, but he wasn't sure. He pressed the buzzer again, and finally the door opened.

"Oh, it's you," Heather said, throwing a shoulder against the doorjamb just like the first time he came over. God, she looked awesome, even with her little pout. She probably made him sweat it out on purpose, kept him wondering if she was home. "Don't you have a tournament this morning?"

"Look, I'm really sorry about last night. You were right to be pissed. I was, like, really nervous and just wasn't myself. Can I make it up to you with breakfast?"

"You did ignore me, you know?"

"You're right, and I'll never do it again." And he meant it.

One side of her mouth curled up. "Promise?"

"Cross my heart."

She smiled. "Then kiss me."

∾∾∾

They walked under a cold, cloudy sky to College Avenue. Being the first customers at the Golden Bear Café, they settled into a booth near the back and ordered oatmeal, scrambled eggs, and biscuits. Jim helped out with Heather's share.

He piled the strawberry jam onto a biscuit. "We shouldn't have these fights," he said, "especially if either one of us has a tournament the next day."

Heather reached across the table and held his hand. "I'm sorry, honey. I overreacted. I do that sometimes."

"Na, I was stupid. You were right to get upset. I should've—" He looked up and panic punched him in the chest.

"What's wrong?"

"There's my dad." His voice felt horse.

"Your dad?" Heather swung around. "What's he doing here?"

"Tracked me down, I guess."

Grayson stood in the doorway, scanning the restaurant. He spotted Jim and stormed over, brushing a waitress with his shoulder. "What the *hell* are you doing here?" he snarled.

"Having breakfast."

Heather stared at her hands wrapped around her coffee mug.

"Get your ass in the car. You've got a goddamn tournament to play."

"My tee time's not until—" *No sense arguing with Dad when he's a douchebag.* "Fine!" Jim tossed some bills onto the table and slid from the booth. "Sorry, Heather. See you later."

She grabbed his hand. "Good luck," she said softly.

⌘⌘⌘

The limo eased into the lot at the Orinda Country Club. Grayson had said little to Jim on the way, commenting only that he had damn well better get his mind back on golf.

"You go on ahead, son," Grayson said, patting Jim's leg. "I'll catch up with you later on the driving range." Jim got out, and Grayson flipped on his cell phone and dialed.

"Thompson here."

"I'm at the golf course. Gillfillen told me where Jim and his girlfriend were having breakfast. I rousted him a good one."

"How's he doing?"

"He's pretty shaken."

"That's what you wanted. How'd dinner go last night with Heather?"

"I think I succeeded in being a condescending prick."

"That should have been easy."

"This is no joke. And it's sure as hell no fun. It was a mistake sending Jim here to Berkeley."

"You think he's frazzled enough to play poorly?"

"I hope so. It'll make it easier to justify yanking him out of here. This is no time to be indecisive. Jim's leaving town—alone. He'll spend two of the next three weeks concentrating one hundred percent on the Global."

"I called the talent agency and gave them Heather's phone number."

"That's sure to stir up the pot."

"She's going to be one pissed-off young lady."

CHAPTER 38

Heather stood at the sink, scooping chocolate mocha ice cream into a dish. She had spent the day at the tournament under a cloudy sky, watching Jim, careful to stay away from that lunatic, Grayson.

Brad, who still spent most of his time stoned, breezed into the kitchen, reeking of pot.

"Hey, Brad, how's it going?"

"Breathing deep, breathing easy," he said and nodded for about five seconds.

Brad was a longtime friend of Linda's who she'd said was handy as a back pocket on a shirt. He tried repairing the front fender of Heather's car, all the result of a misunderstanding at a right turn, by slapping on Bondo Body Filler like he applied butter to toast at his day job at Denny's.

He dipped a weed-stained finger into Heather's ice cream container. "How'd your boyfriend do in the golf tournament?"

"Okay." Heather crammed the lid back onto the container and put it into the fridge. Brad was a moocher who would have accepted a bowl, if offered. "The tournament's only partly over. We're behind UCLA, but tomorrow our boys will kick butt."

"*All right*!" Brad slid out a chair and plopped down. "You've got one hell of a boyfriend there, Heather girl. Wanna toke?" He offered her a joint from his coat pocket. "It's good shit."

"Not tonight. I've got to get up early and root for my man."

"That's cool." He rubbed his nose, which always poked into things.

Heather didn't like the quizzical stare he aimed at her. "Something wrong?"

"No…no, nothing's wrong." He pocketed the joint. "It's just that your boyfriend's one generous dude."

Heather slid the spoon from between her lips and inspected a glossy mound of chocolate ice cream. She glanced at Brad, at the flickering emotion in his eyes. He was scheming down inside himself. "What do you mean, 'generous dude'?"

"Forget it." He started to get up. "I gotta get outta here and meet a friend."

Heather placed a firm hand on his shoulder. "Hold up, Brad boy. What do you mean, Jim's one generous dude?"

"Hey, it's none of my business."

"It is now. Spit it out."

"Can I get a beer?"

"Later. Talk."

Brad leaned his chair onto its hind legs and took out a pack of cigarettes. He spread his arms. "Mother, may I?"

Heather threw a nod toward the rear porch off the kitchen, the designated smoking area. Brad got up and shuffled over. He tapped out a cigarette and lit up. Heather relaxed against the doorjamb. "Let's hear it."

Brad drew in several rapid puffs, as if sucking oxygen. He studied the smoldering cylinder. "You know all that money you won?"

Something in Heather's chest contracted. She stared at him coolly. "What're you talking about?"

"Hey, I don't give a flying fuck. I just know the money didn't come from any puzzle contest." He paused to suck in a lungful of smoke from his cigarette.

Heather folded her arms tightly. "You'd better start explaining, right now."

Visibly enjoying his sense of power, Brad said, "I want a goddamn brew."

He handed Heather his cigarette and walked to the fridge. Drop him on the moon and, within five minutes, he'd find beer. He never had any of his own, so he rummaged around for one of Linda's.

Returning to the porch, he popped the can open and snatched back his smoke. He put his back against the wall, crossed one foot over the other, and stretched his stuff. "The money train went from your lover boy to Linda, to you."

Heather's throat tightened. "You're lying."

Brad shrugged and sucked in a deep drag. His words came out with oozes of smoke. "My friend works at Linda's bank and verified a large deposit she made." He blew a smoke ring. "It was drawn on Jim Bolt's account. Ten grand, I'm told."

Without a sound, Heather tottered to the kitchen and sank into a chair. After several moments, she managed, "Linda told you?"

He laughed and brushed a finger at a smoky eye. "Are you kidding? She doesn't even know I know."

"I do now, you son of a bitch!" Linda barged in from the darkened dining room, bracelets clanking like jailer's keys. A damp towel covered one shoulder, and her hair looked like that of a pissed off wet cat. "I'm going to kick your ass so hard you'll wear it for a collar."

Brad skittered out the rear door.

Heather shot Linda an icy glance. "What was that about?"

"I was afraid something like this could happen someday." Linda sat down. "I'll explain everything."

She told Heather about how Jim had put up the money and how she had concocted the story about winning the contest. Heather paced the kitchen floor, listening and trying to keep her anger in check. When Linda finished, Heather said nothing, just stormed into her room, and slammed the door. So that was it, she'd been played for a fool.

Jim's dishonesty hurt the most. Okay, maybe the two of them didn't think she would take the money, and that's why Jim gave it to—

Blood rushed to her face as she realized how much he knew about her tight financial circumstances. She felt both humiliated and angry—but mostly angry. She reached for the phone and began dialing Jim's number, then glanced at the clock. Eleven-thirty.

She pondered a moment and hung up. He'd be asleep by

now after having dinner with his dad. She'd wait until she saw him tomorrow.

About to get into bed, she glanced at her desk. *Damn!* She picked up the pregnancy test, read the instructions, and sighed. She couldn't do it now. There'd been enough bad news for one day. She put the kit down and crawled under the covers.

☙❧

Heather got up the next morning with mixed feelings about Jim. It was wrong of him to play games with her, and the idea that he kept the secret this long meant they had serious trust issues. On the other hand, he did give her ten thousand dollars. So he got points for that.

She shuffled to the kitchen and peered out the window at dark rain clouds spilling over the mountains. Jim would be happy competing against rival UCLA in a downpour. He had said the wetter the better when playing against Southern California wusses.

She reheated yesterday's coffee and splashed it into a cup. Confronting Jim before he teed off sounded good, and she chuckled at the wicked thought. But she couldn't do it. If he missed a putt, his dad would kill him. She'd watch him play first and talk later.

After dressing quickly, she grabbed her umbrella and keys and headed for the door. Her phone rang. *Shit!* She dug it out of her purse. "Hello?"

"Is this Heather Morrison?" The female voice had an especially syrupy southern accent.

"Yes, who's this?" Heather glanced at her watch.

"Patty. I'm trying to get a hold of Jimmy. We're *real* good friends."

Heat crept up into Heather's face "I *see*."

"I understand you know him."

"You could say that."

"Well, I wonder if you might have his phone number. I lost it somewhere and need to talk to him."

Her face got hotter. "You mean he gave it to you?"

"That's right. It was in my purse, but—"

"Can I ask where you know Jim from?" Heather tried to keep the snark out of her voice, but it wasn't working.

"We met recently at a golf tournament in Palo Alto when his team played Stanford. I worked the registration desk. He's a real good golfer. Anyway, I'm having a birthday party, and that's why I need his number."

Heather pursed her lips. "So you want to invite him to your birthday party?"

"Uh-huh."

"Fine, here's his number." Heather gave it to her and added, "I'm sure *Jimmy* will have a wonderful time seeing you again. By the way, how'd you get my name and number?"

"Well, I tried to call Jimmy's golf coach but I got the tennis coach by mistake, and he didn't know Jimmy's number but he said you knew him, and—"

"I got the picture." Heather banged the phone down and stormed from the house.

Fifteen minutes later, she roared into the parking lot of the Orinda Country Club, wipers thumping. She got out of the car, slammed the door, and marched to the putting green. Jim wasn't there.

She glanced at her watch. A few minutes to nine—his starting time. Hurrying to the first tee through the light rain, she wished she'd grabbed her umbrella from the car. She scanned the area but didn't see him. Maybe he'd teed off already. Or he could be in the clubhouse. She'd check.

On her way, the public address system crackled. "Next up, hitting for Cal, Jim Bolt." She rushed back to the tee, and there he stood under the trees, talking to his dad. Working her way through a small crowd, she made it to the ropes. Jim started toward the tee box and didn't see her. He pulled a ball and tee from his pocket and bent over. She waved her arms and jumped up and down. Water spritzed from her hair. He caught sight of her and straightened with a quizzical look. She watched him glance at the officials, hesitate, then come toward her.

Frazzled and furious, she would let him have it: the money, the secrets, and don't forget Patty.

Jim approached within a few feet. She opened her mouth to spring it all on him then saw Grayson looking at her from across the tee box, water dripping from his fedora. Their eyes locked for an instant before he looked away. Blood roared through her veins and seemed to freeze the image of Grayson's eyes in her head. She turned to Jim, his forehead creased, and she felt like reaching across the ropes to hug him. Her lips parted and she sputtered, "Sorry I'm late—Good luck!" Without waiting for a response, she whirled and dashed off. She didn't feel like watching him play, not today—maybe not ever again.

❦❦❦

That afternoon, Heather faced that fear she could no longer avoid.

She slogged into the bathroom, peed into a collection cup, and set it on the sink. If she were the type to chew her nails, she'd be gnawing away by now. The test was supposed to be ninety-nine percent accurate. She picked up the stick and dipped it into the liquid then withdrew it and waited. Fifteen seconds, thirty seconds, a minute passed. A faint line began to appear on the stick, and when the line turned into a plus sign, her breath caught in her throat. She dropped the stick like a hot match, threw her hands to her face, and sobbed.

CHAPTER 39

Grayson and Jim climbed into the limo, and Grayson told the driver to drop Jim off at his apartment before heading to the airport. They rolled out of the Orinda Country Club parking lot and past the lake to the main highway. Jim had made his last putt, and Grayson wasted no time pulling him away from his teammates, who were heading to the coach's post-tournament meeting.

Jim had played poorly. Drives sailed everywhere but where they should have. Iron shots plunked into sand and putts rolled past holes or stopped inexcusably short. He'd scored a final round 77, five over par, capping previous rounds of 75 and 74. Grayson had the solid justification that he wanted to get Jim out of town—and away from Heather.

The limo entered the tunnel on Highway 24, and Grayson turned to Jim. "Your class finals are over on Tuesday. That right?"

"In the morning. Afterward, I'll pound away on the driving range until—"

"Until nothing," Grayson snapped. "Have you forgotten that the Global is only three weeks away? Wednesday night, you're flying home to New York. Thursday, you and I are going to England to do some serious work on your game. God knows you need it."

"*England?*" Jim gasped. "I have plans. Heather and I are going to Mexico."

"*Were* going to Mexico."

"But it's her birthday present."

"How many fairways did you hit today?"

Jim's face scrunched. "Thirteen."

"Make that twelve. How many greens?"

"Um—"

"Come on."

Jim peered out the window. "I hit eight greens."

"That's the first thing you've got right all day." Grayson snapped his fingers in Jim's ear. "I hope you're listening to me. I don't know where your mind was, but it sure as hell wasn't on the course."

Jim stared down, not replying. The car turned onto Ridge Road.

"It's high time you got your head out of your ass and back on the ball." Moments later, Grayson placed a gentle hand on Jim's leg. "I know you've gone through a lot of changes the past few months, changes that are difficult for someone your age. Believe me, son, I'm doing this for your own good." He squeezed Jim's leg. "We'll have a great time abroad. Play some wonderful courses. We'll go up to Scotland and play St. Andrews. It'll be good for you. You'll see I'm right." Grayson smiled, confident that Jim would come around. "Coach McAlister will be joining us. He'll get you back in the groove."

Jim made a face that Grayson pretended not to notice.

"Don't worry, you'll have lots of time for those other things." Grayson patted Jim's arm and looked out the window. "After the Global. Heather will understand." They reached Jim's apartment. "Pull up here, driver. Son, you bone up for those finals. Don't screw those up, too. I'll be in touch tomorrow."

Jim got out of the car without a word, and the limo slid from the curb on its way to the airport. Grayson spotted Gillfillen angling his Ford into a parking spot across the street. The man brushed his hooked nose with a finger and nodded.

Grayson tugged his phone from his pocket and called the office.

"Thompson," he barked. "The tournament's over, and I'm returning tonight on the redeye. I just left Gillfillen, and he's going to continue keeping an eye on Jim. Don't forget our meeting tomorrow morning. In the office, eight o'clock."

"Right-o, I'll be there."

Grayson opened his briefcase and thumbed through a medical report emailed to him that morning. "Call Doctor Cox. I want him there at the meeting. Tell him to bring along his specialist, Doctor…" Grayson flipped pages. "…Doctor Di-Marco."

"Who's he?"

"Never mind. Just make damn sure he's there."

"Will do."

"One more thing."

"Yes?"

"Be sure DiMarco has a passport."

"A what?"

"You heard me. He and I will be traveling."

Grayson snapped the phone closed and pulled a handkerchief from his pocket. He wiped his forehead. Jim *would* win the Global. His life depended on it. Grayson leaned his head against the backrest. *Please, God, don't let my boy hate me.* He wished that with his whole heart, body, and what remained of his soul.

CHAPTER 40

Kamal wanted nothing more than to continue in the identity theft business by supervising gardeners and hospital workers—and to save money. Then he'd quit and go to college, be respectable, and please his father. He never wanted to tail some New York dude and his kid, and damn sure never wanted to frighten an old woman to death. But here he was, in a car with Misha on a stakeout a few doors down from the kid's apartment. He and Misha had kept tabs on the old man since he hit town and spent the day at a goddamn golf course. Chasing a ball around without kicking it hardly seemed like a sport.

Misha yanked out his phone and punched keys. "Chauffeur," he said, "the tournament's over, and your man Bolt just dropped his kid off at his fancy apartment. And guess what? Bolt must be keeping tabs on the kid. Some hooknose guy's sitting in a Ford, eyeing the building. Why don't I recruit the fuck as a double agent? You'll learn everything both the kid and Bolt are up to and I can get back to fucking LA."

Misha hung up and slipped on dark glasses.

"What's the plan?" Kamal asked.

"Let's get out, and maybe you'll learn something." They crossed the street to the sidewalk. "We're gonna walk casual-like past that Ford. Keep your eyes straight ahead." They stopped a few car lengths past the Ford. Misha snorted. "I'll play it hard and soft. He's a fuckin' amateur."

"How can you tell? He's just sitting in his car."

"Experience, dipshit. Amateurs wear fucking ties. Plus, he was too busy picking his big nose to bother noticing us walk past."

Kamal realized the midget had been watching the man secretly through his dark glasses. Plus, he didn't have to stoop to see through the window.

"I'll deal with him," Misha said. "You keep your mouth shut. Let's go."

Kamal stepped back. "Maybe I should just wait here."

"You want to learn, or not?"

This time, Misha had no credit card receipts to threaten him with. But then it was never wise to piss off the midget. "Do I have to?"

Misha lifted his shades and looked up at him, hard.

Kamal swept his arm out with a flourish. "After you."

They treaded back to the Ford and stopped at the passenger door. Misha drew his gun. The guy was looking away toward the youngster's apartment with his hands in his lap. Misha banged the car's top with his gun. The dude bolted upright, as if something sharp had come through the bottom of his seat. Kamal stifled a laugh.

Misha jabbed a finger at the door lock, but the guy didn't move. "Stop scratching your nuggets and open the goddamn door, fuckface. Now!"

The man pressed buttons like the car was on fire. The locks clicked, and Misha signaled Kamal to get in the rear.

"Wha—wha—" the man babbled.

"Shut the fuck up and listen," Misha said, sliding in next to him. He took off his dark glasses and put his scary eyes to work. "I'm going to ask questions, and you're going to answer. Am I clear?"

The man gave an energetic nod then looked back at Kamal, who offered a weak smile.

"Don't worry about him," Misha said. "He's in training. Now, am I correct to surmise that you work for Grayson Bolt?"

The man did more nodding.

"Are you keeping tabs on his son?"

The man's nod slowed, and his forehead scrunched.

"Good." Misha's eyes softened. "You look like a nice guy. What's your name?"

The man cleared his throat. "Dennis. Uh, Dennis Gillfillen."

"Mr. Gillfillen, I work for someone named Costanzo. He's from New Jersey. Maybe you've heard of him."

"I—I—"

"That's okay. Here's the thing. Mr. Costanzo has a business relationship with your boss, Mr. Bolt, and indirectly with his son. He wants to know everything that you learn about what's going on with those two. Do you follow me?"

Gillfillen adjusted his wire-rimmed glasses. "I believe so."

"Then we're all set." Misha patted Gillfillen's knee and withdrew a card, snatched a pen from Gillfillen's white pocket protector and scribbled a phone number. "Report everything you learn to Mr. Chauffeur at this number." He handed over the card. "You're officially on the payroll, Mr. Gillfillen, and at the same salary you're receiving from Mr. Bolt."

"Um…hold on a minute." Gillfillen brushed a hand through his hair. "I feel like I'm being…uh…being asked to betray Mr. Bolt."

"Not at all, Dennis boy. First, you're not lying or deceiving Mr. Bolt, only telling us what you tell him. No one will know. Second—" Misha's eyes got hard again. "—I'm not asking. I'm just being polite."

Gillfillen ran his tongue across his lips. "How long must I—must I continue this, um, this arrangement?"

"We'll let you know." Misha opened his door and crawled out.

Kamal reached over and patted Gillfillen's shoulder. "You'll be okay. Just do what you're told."

Misha stuck his head back in the car. "Mr. Chauffeur will be expecting to hear from you daily." He slammed the door.

CHAPTER 41

Jim stomped into his apartment and threw his hat across the room. This was totally fucked! He trudged to the fridge for a bottle of water. He was mad, and not just at his dad. His whole life was screwed up. Never should have promised Heather that trip to Mexico. Big mistake with the Global being so close. Dad was right. He needed to totally concentrate on golf. Nothing else.

To clear his mind, he played an hour of Tomb Raider on his computer. That helped him feel better. Then he made a peanut butter and jelly sandwich and ate it staring out at the bay. Getting away would be good, though practicing in the cold UK sucked. But then, it might force him to work harder.

He tried to reach Heather by phone, but she didn't answer. She always forgot her damn phone. He'd see her later and explain about the money and that their trip had to be canceled. They'd do Mexico in the summer. She'd understand. He put a knuckle to his mouth and gnawed. He'd tell her in a way that kept his dad out of it.

Putting everything that way would technically be a lie, but the lie and the truth weren't too far apart. The plan was good, and he felt better. Mostly.

⁊⁊⁊

Late that afternoon, Jim wheeled into the Alameda South Shore Center Mall. He jumped from his car and zipped up his coat.

The rain had stopped, and it felt like winter on a New York

golf course. Perfect weather for shopping.

Jim strode into the mall, past Applebee's, and into a shop lined with sparkling display cases. He nodded to a security guard, inhaled the fragrance of high cost, and checked out the jewelry. He'd buy Heather an awesome birthday present she'd really like.

An older saleswoman with red lips and rosy cheeks, probably in her forties, approached "Welcome to Zales. May I help you?"

"Just looking, thanks." Lots of spendy stuff to choose from. Silver necklaces, gold earrings, diamond studded watches—stuff more for someone like his grandmother.

Overwhelmed, he scanned the store for their youngest saleswoman and spotted a clerk with black hair and pale white skin. He glided over and hung out for a while, waiting for her to finish serving an old rich-looking woman. When the customer left, Jim stepped forward. "Excuse me, I'd like to buy a birthday present for my...um...girlfriend, but I don't know what to get."

The clerk smiled. "How much would you like to spend on it?"

He frowned. "I hadn't thought about that. But it can be expensive."

"What does she like?"

Jim shrugged. "I don't know. She plays tennis."

Five minutes later, the sales woman handed him a bag containing a small silver box with a pink bow. This would definitely make it up to Heather.

CHAPTER 42

Heather tapped lightly on the door. She'd heard Linda come in from teaching her dog-training class.

"Who is it?" Linda said.

"It's me. You busy?"

The door swung open. "Just got back from—Jesus Christ! You look like something the cat dragged in."

"Don't say it." Heather folded her arms and brushed past Linda into the room. It smelled of jasmine incense that glowed under a picture of Gandhi. She plunked down in a chair by the door. "I'm pregnant."

Linda drew in a breath. "Oh, that. Sperm, it takes just one to hit a homer."

Heather put her head in her hands. "I don't know what to do."

"I imagine motherhood isn't on your bucket list."

Heather sighed and looked up. "I'm worried about how this will affect Jim. I can deal with postponing school, but he doesn't—"

The phone rang, and Linda raised her hand. The answering machine clicked on. Linda put a finger to her lips, picked up the receiver, and covered the mouthpiece. She listened a few moments and replaced the receiver. Sitting on the bed, she smiled a grimace of a smile, clearly distracted. "Jim doesn't know—about the pregnancy, I mean?"

Heather shook her head and pretended not to notice Linda's uptightness. "I don't know how well he did in the tournament and haven't talked to him about the money. I wasn't exactly doing the happy dance after getting a call from some girl he's clearly chummy with." She filled her cheeks with air and blew. "I'm not going to tell Jim yet. I want to be absolutely—"

"Psst—Linda—you in there?" came Brad's raspy whisper outside the door. "Gillfillen's trying to get hold of you—"

Linda shot up from the bed.

"He wants to know what she's—"

Before Brad could say more, Linda lunged for the door and tripped over Heather's foot, crashing into the doorknob. Blood spurted from her nose. "Shit!" She flung the door open, and it bumped against Heather's knee. Without looking at Heather, but at Brad standing in the doorway, she yelled, *"Heather,* are you all right?"

"I'm fine," Heather said, uncertain what was going on. "But you're hurt."

Linda's face was covered with blood. "The first aid kit," she said through bloody fingers. "It's in the kitchen." She waved for Heather to go.

When Heather returned, Brad was nowhere around. Linda sat at her desk holding a towel to her face. "What a freaky fucking thing to happen," she said. "My nose may be broken."

"Here, let me help."

Linda waved her back.

"What was that about with Brad?"

"About an idiot whose brain's the size of a marble. He's getting his car to take me to emergency. Help me downstairs."

Outside, the moon was just rising, a thick white sliver, like a slice of cantaloupe. As Heather was helping Linda into Brad's car, Jim strolled up from across the street. He looked at Linda holding a bloody towel to her face. "What happened to you?"

"Heather will tell you." Linda slammed the door and the car growled off into the night.

CHAPTER 43

Jim and Heather tramped into her room. He fell into a chair and, for something to do with his hands, grabbed an apple from a bowl. This was the moment of truth. Double truth. *Surprise! We're not going to Mexico. And by the way, about all that money you won...*

He tossed the apple in the air and caught it. "I have stuff to say, but first, tell me what happened to Linda."

Heather leaned her back against the bed's headboard and crossed her legs. "We were in her room talking. Not about anything special—just, you know, talking." She brushed her hair behind an ear. "Anyway, Brad came to the door and whispered about some Gillfillen guy trying to reach her. Linda rushed like mad for the door and tripped over my foot, hitting her nose on the doorknob. She definitely didn't want me to hear what Brad was going to say."

"Who's Gillfillen?"

"No clue."

"Probably their drug dealer. Oh, yeah, before I forget." He put the apple down, stood up, and removed from his pocket the small silver box with a pink bow and placed it on her desk.

"For me?"

"For later. We need to talk first."

"I imagine we do."

He didn't like the tone of that, but he pushed on. "Sorry about breakfast this morning. Dad can be really scary when he's mad."

"Tell me about it. And by the way, I'll never set foot in that restaurant again."

"Like the joke about the couple who had sex on the restaurant table and said they'd never go there again."

"That's so funny I should've laughed."

"Okay, look. I'll admit I'm nervous. Here's the thing: you didn't win the puzzle contest. I gave Linda the ten thousand dollars."

She pursed her lips and nodded. "So, you lied to me."

Jim blinked. "That's your reaction? I lied to you. That's all?"

"That seems to be the issue—" Her face suddenly got red. "—*that*, and how you knew I needed the goddamn money!"

Exactly the tone he had expected.

"Did you get your *daddy* to pull strings and snoop into my finances?"

"God, no! How could you think that?"

"Then how?"

"Linda told me."

"Linda! Nice of her to leave that part out."

"But it's not like you think. I came to your house to give you flowers, and Linda—"

Heather waved her hand. "I know the rest of the story. Forget it."

"You do?"

"Linda told me last night. And believe me, I was *so* not happy." She sighed. "Although I'm glad you finally came out with the truth."

"I've been wanting to tell you, but kept putting it off." He climbed onto the bed and kissed her. "I'm sorry. Forgive me?"

A small smile played on her lips. "Okay." The smile dropped. "But I want you to promise to never lie to me again, no matter what."

"I don't think it was technically a lie, but I promise."

"Lying includes deceptions."

He raised his hands. "You're right." He hopped off the bed and flopped back into his chair. "There's one more thing to talk about, and that's my golf. I played like crap this weekend and need to bear down and work harder on my game."

Her forehead wrinkled. "Honey, I get it."

"I've decided I need to get away. You know, no distractions, just work, work, work."

"Where would you go? You've got school."

Jim swallowed. "To England."

Her eyes bulged. "England!"

He picked up the apple and kneaded it with both hands like dough. "Um, yeah, yeah, during Easter break."

"But wait a minute. We're supposed to go to—"

"I know, babe, we'll have to put off Mexico. You understand."

For several seconds her chest heaved and her eyes shot fire. She rocketed off the bed and grabbed the silver box from the desk, shook her arm at him, and yelled, "You think *this* makes up for Mexico?" She hurled the box at him. He ducked, and it hit the wall.

He put the apple on the desk and backed up a few yards. "Well, I—"

"Don't you dare say *I*. This was your father's idea, and you know it." She put the apple in the bowl. "And aren't you cute? Acting like he had nothing to do with it. Your father has everything to do with everything."

Jim clenched his jaw and cocked a brow at her.

She cocked one back.

He raised his hands in surrender. "There's no point talking about this anymore right now."

"Then why don't you just leave?"

"All right. I will. Take your present and throw it in the trash if you want to." He opened the door.

"Fine! I will."

Jim reached the curb when he heard the front door open. He turned to see Heather. "And by the way, Patty invited you to her birthday party." She slammed the door.

Patty? Who the hell's Patty?

CHAPTER 44

Heather paced her room like a schoolgirl hoping to be asked out to the prom. She was expecting Jim's call any minute.

She had spoken to him only once before he left for England, and ever since, they'd been emailing each other. She apologized for being selfish and agreed that Jim needed to focus one hundred percent on his golf. He said he was sorry for not being straight with her about how his dad had arranged everything.

She craved his arms around her. And the hot sex, that was something she always liked, but with him it was more. A lot more. She missed touching his firm body and the things he said to her in bed.

The phone rang. She hurried to it and picked up.

"How's my girl?" came the voice of her guy.

"Suffering. You're ten minutes late."

"Sorry, we're in a restaurant."

"You're forgiven. How's it going?"

"I'm practicing my butt off. Did you open your birthday present?"

"It's not my birthday yet. Besides, I'm waiting for you. I love looking at the box. It reminds me how much I love you. It has a dent where it hit the wall."

"Uh-oh. Hope nothing's broken. Just kidding. I love you, too, babe. I just returned to London with my coach after two days in Scotland. Dad had to take off on some business. When he comes back, we'll head out to New York and then I'll continue home to you."

"I can't wait. I got my old job back at Berkeley Iceland. I've been super busy."

"How's your mom? Headaches any better?"

"Afraid not." Talking to her on the phone last week tore at Heather's heart.

"Damn."

"It looks bad. I'll tell you all about it when I see you."

"You okay? Is there anything I can do?"

"I'm fine, sweetie. Thanks. The only thing you can do is come home as soon as you can."

✞✞✞

The next afternoon was really hot. Heat waves shimmered off the court. Heather finished the last of a grueling practice session and looked forward to kicking back.

She had just opened her car trunk and tossed in her tennis gear when a voice came from behind.

"Excuse me." It was a man's voice, tight and hard.

Startled, she turned to see some guy in a suit. He pushed his wire-rimmed glasses up on his large curved nose. "Are you Heather Morrison?"

He attempted a friendly smile that looked kind of weird, like he was nervous. "Yes, I'm Heather."

"My name's Gillfillen. I'm an associate of Grayson Bolt."

Heather narrowed her eyes. "*Ye—es*," she said cautiously. Where had she heard that name?

"Mr. Bolt would like to meet with you. He's in the lounge down the street at the Claremont. If you would follow me in your car, I'll—"

"Wait a minute. Grayson's in England."

"I assure you, Ms. Morrison, he's at the Claremont, waiting for you."

"That's impossible. I just talked to his son yesterday, and they're bo—Huh?" Heather's mouth stuck open. She remembered Jim mentioning his dad was on a business trip somewhere. "W—why's he in Berkeley? And what's he want me for?"

"All your questions will be answered. Please, just follow me. It won't take long."

She got into her car with a churning stomach. *Maybe I'm being kidnapped. That's ridiculous, I'm in my own car. Is Jim at the Claremont, too? The man didn't say.*

At the hotel, Heather's door opened and a valet handed her a ticket. Gillfillen stood in front of the hotel's large glass doors. He opened them, led her through the lobby into the lounge, and disappeared. Grayson rose from his seat at a back table and waved.

Heather swallowed hard.

"Thank you for meeting with me, Heather." Grayson gestured for her to sit. "I know this must seem strange." He looked haggard, his face yellow as an old cloth, though his clothes appeared fresh as the flowers on the table.

"Where's Jim? Why do you want to see me?"

"I'll explain everything, Heather. Would you like a drink? Something to eat?"

"I'm fine," she said, before realizing she was thirsty.

"Very well." He slid his drink to the side. "I'll come right to the point. I know you're pregnant."

Her mouth sprang open before she could stop it, and her hand went to her throat. Everything around Grayson's face went hazy.

"I also know your mother's ill, and—" Grayson raised a thick brow. "—expected to pass away. You wish you could do something to make her well but know that's impossible. You've reconciled yourself to what will sadly happen. Are you with me so far?"

She stared, unable to believe his words. A thousand pins pricked her body. Words shot from her mouth with a life of their own. "I don't understand. Why aren't you in England with Jim? Jim's in England, isn't he? Where is he?"

"Easy, Heather. Jim's in England, and everything's fine. He doesn't know I'm here—and never will."

Sweat dripped from her underarms. "You're saying that he…that I…what are you saying? I don't understand."

Grayson interlocked his fingers on the table. "As I've said, you're pregnant and your mother's terminally ill. I can fix both."

Heather told herself to breathe and get a grip. "How did you find out about my mother—about the pregnancy?"

He shook his head. "What's important is that I can help."

Again she swallowed hard. "How—" Her throat caught. "How will you do that?"

"You know that your mother has a primary brain tumor. What you don't know is that there are two—*two*—brain surgeons in the world able to perform the kind of operation that could save her life. The operation requires a multidisciplinary medical team and could take twelve hours. As you can imagine, this potentially lifesaving procedure is quite expensive."

Heather's mind raced to understand what he was getting at. Her throat raw, she rasped, "Go on."

"I could pay for the operation and all related expenses." He leaned back, picked up his drink, and sipped.

Heather licked her salty lips. "You'd do this because— because I'm Jim's girlfriend?"

Grayson put his drink down, peered inside, and swirled the ice cubes with his finger. He looked at Heather with faded eyes. "No, Heather. Jim's *ex*-girlfriend."

CHAPTER 45

W hat?" Heather sucked in a breath. Grayson knew she was pregnant, knew her mother was terminally ill, and now—

Grayson sighed. "Jim will not return to Berkeley, and you—" He cleared his throat. "—you'll never see him again."

"But—" Heather croaked, the protest lifeless on her parched tongue.

"I'm sorry, Heather, no buts. Your relationship with Jim—particularly since you're pregnant—would be a serious, even fatal, handicap to his career. I can't let that happen. If you're willing to play ball and handle this the way I ask, everyone wins."

Tears flooded her eyes. She parted her lips and made a halfhearted attempt to lick them.

"You're to write Jim a letter—not an email—a letter, breaking off the relationship. Your pregnancy, of course, will be terminated." He picked up his drink, caught her eye for an instant, and turned away. "That's been arranged. Afterward, you'll fly to Ireland to care for your mother, who will be treated for her condition and, God willing, recover." He sat back. "I'm sorry, but it has to be this way."

Heather exhaled, feeling bruised and beaten. Her mouth tasted sour. She asked for a glass of water. For more than a minute, she sat with her head down. Her water arrived, and she gulped, as if to wash down all the insults her mind screamed at Grayson.

She set the glass on the table, straightened her back, and tried to keep her chin from quivering. "Let's see if I have this right. You believe my relationship with Jim will jeopardize his golf career."

Grayson picked up his glass. "Correct."

"And you want me to break up with him?"

He held the drink to his lips. "I'm afraid so."

"If I do that, you'll pay for my mother's medical needs and arrange for my abortion. Am I on track?"

His eyelids closed slowly, like curtains. "On track." He sipped.

"I suppose I'm to say it's my idea."

"That's right. And you may keep the bracelet."

Heather jolted.

"Diamonds are a wonderful remembrance."

He must be referring to the unopened birthday gift on her nightstand.

"I know it must feel terrible, but look at it this way: You've only been seeing Jim for a couple of months. It's not even really that serious between you two. You'll bounce back."

Heather sank into her seat. After a moment, she glared at him. Her heart pumped with a strange violence through her veins. "I'll tell you what, *Mister* Bolt. I don't know how you learned everything about my mother or my supposed pregnancy, but you can take your proposition and shove it up your smug ass." She stood. "We'll see what your son has to say about your charming offer."

She reached across the table and, hoping her hand wouldn't shake, snatched up her glass. She swigged the remaining water and slammed the glass onto the table.

Straightening her shoulders, she scowled at Grayson and marched for the door. Asshole! She'd find another way to save Mom.

She reached the valet station and felt a hand touch her shoulder. Whirling, she saw Gillfillen. "Get away from me!"

"Please, Heather, give me a few minutes, and I'll tell you everything you want to know." He motioned to a bench beyond the valet station.

Lulled by Gillfillen's deferential tone, she decided to get a few answers. She turned, stomped to the bench, and spun around. "How the fuck did he know about my mother?"

Gillfillen motioned that they sit down. "You gave it all away."

Heather's mouth dropped. "Huh?"

"That's right. You told him your mother moved back to Ireland—Kildare. He wondered why, found out her name and where she lived. He also got hold of her medical records."

"How the hell'd he do *that*?"

"His own doctor managed it."

Heather shook her head. "He's pathological."

"Let's just say he knows what he wants and has the determination and resources to get it."

"Does he assume my mother would go along with his scheme? We're Catholic. She'd never consent to my having an abortion."

"She'll never know, but she's thrilled about her operation."

"*What*?" Heather shouted.

"It's scheduled for next week. She has a round-trip air ticket to New York. First class, actually."

"I can't believe this!" Heather thought a moment. "Did the doctor meet my mother?"

"Oh, sure. Grayson and the specialist flew to her home yesterday—or was it the day before? Anyway, the doctor had her charts, X-rays, the works. He explained everything to her, told her that if the operation went well, she'd be up and around in no time. As you can imagine, she's quite excited."

"Up and around in no time, huh?" Heather laughed, a mirthless laugh, got up, and paced in a small circle. Her pulse banged against her temples. "I can't believe this is happening. Of course I want to save my mother's life, but there's got to be another way. It feels—" She stopped circling. "—it feels monstrous."

"Look, Heather, when it comes to Jim's golf, Grayson can be…well, let's just say…insistent. Even if you don't agree, he'll go to Jim and make him end it."

"Then why doesn't he?"

"He'd rather you do it. But if he did, and Jim went against him, Jim could kiss off any financial assistance to his education, and his chance of playing professional golf would be zilch."

Heather plopped back down on the bench. "This is the sickest goddamn thing I've ever heard."

"Sick or not, Grayson holds all the cards."

"Is this an all-or-none deal? Do I have to have the abortion?"

"Absolutely. Grayson would consider your having Jim's child as an unacceptable bonding. Of course, you're never to see Jim again."

Tears welled in her eyes, and she turned away from him. Her gaze caught the sparkling chandelier across the hotel drive, and she stared at it. Then, as if by crystal magic, it all came together.

Gillfillen, of course! She turned to him. He was the one Brad talked about outside Linda's door when she practically killed herself trying to hush Brad. The knowledge of it all passed before her eyes. In Grayson's attempt to separate her from Jim, he used Gillfillen to make traitors of her friends.

She clenched her fists. What a shit. What a set of shits.

ↄ∂ↄ

That night, Heather sat at her desk and wrote the letter to Jim, just the way Grayson had demanded. Writing it tore her heart to pieces. Halfway through, she stopped and crumpled the letter, not wanting Jim to see tear splotches. She started over, her new diamond bracelet skidding across the paper. Jim's birthday present.

> *Hi, Jim,* she began, moving her tongue along her lips as she wrote. *I've come to the hardest decision of my life. I'm breaking up with you and moving back to Ireland where I'll take care of Mom and go to school. They say love conquers all, but that's not true when it has to compete with golf. Golf will always be number one in your life. I couldn't live with myself if you promised to give it up. So I've decided now is the time to say good-*

bye. I won't be coming back to the US, and please don't try to contact me. I'm so, so sorry.

She finished with a PS. *I opened your birthday gift. I want to thank you from the bottom of my heart. The diamond tennis bracelet is the most beautiful gift anyone has ever given me. I'll wear it forever.*

She threw down her pen, quickly folded the letter, and stuffed it into an envelope. She would stop by school tomorrow and mail it. Now she'd crawl into bed and cry herself to sleep.

☙❧☙

Gray rain clouds floated over the hills like wings while a nippy breeze wafted in off the bay. Heather made a final visit to school where she mailed Jim's letter full of lies and posted a notice on the communal bulletin board. Speaking to no one, she left the university for the last time.

With a hurting heart, she drove to the bike path and parked near the spot where she and Jim had collided on rollerblades. The salt air smelled of redwood and pine. The leaning picket fence wrapped in white honeysuckle stood nearby, backlit by a squatty red sun in a rim of light. Through the branches of large evergreens, the city shone on the bay. The buildings sparkled brighter even than the gleaming water that surrounded them. She sat a long time. She loved Jim so much. He was good and strong and funny and smart and loved her back. *No one else will ever be like Jim.*

She wondered about Grayson, and that strange look that flashed in his eyes at the hotel when he said her pregnancy would be terminated. There was sadness in their depths, but dim and far back. It just peeked out at her for a second.

The sun crept below the pines, and darkness edged in from all sides. How much was Jim like his father? Could he be that crazy driven? It seemed so. Yet, he was sensitive and sweet. Someday, maybe…

CHAPTER 46

Grayson returned to London's Dorchester Hotel in late afternoon, haggard and rumpled. His last days in Berkeley had been spent making medical arrangements for the two Morrison women—Heather's abortion in San Francisco and her mother's brain operation in New York. He wasn't a monster, no matter how Heather judged him. The cluster of dividing cells wasn't really his grandchild, he told himself. It was tissue. Someday he'd have grandchildren, and if they never swung a golf club, he'd be just as happy. He never would have imagined that, day in and day out, year after year, he'd be living with the horror of his son being murdered. Jim's winning the Global was the only way out.

He checked in and tried to relax with a sauna and massage, then dressed in gray slacks and a blue sports coat. He took the elevator down to the front desk. "Any mail for me, Suite 810?"

The clerk checked, and there was nothing. "How about for my son, Suite 808?"

The man looked. "A letter, sir."

That would be from Heather. "Please hold it for him." Tightness gripped Grayson's chest and caused a pain at the base of his throat.

He strolled into the lobby and settled into a dark leather armchair that offered an outside view of the entrance with its bubbling fountain. The sky was gunmetal gray, and it had started to sprinkle. Beside him sat a table holding a tall cloisonné vase bursting with an array of exotic cut flowers. A silver-haired man with an aging violet face snoozed peacefully in a stuffed chair with his head against an Ali Baba oil jar large enough to hold a tiger. Grayson doubted he'd live to such a ripe age. Not with Costanzo clawing at him. He checked his watch, crossed his legs, and unfolded the *New York Times*. Jim would arrive soon.

Twenty minutes later, Grayson glanced up to see Jim jump from a limousine. He fished out a few tees and balls from his pocket and handed them to the driver. He shook hands with Coach McAlister, who would continue on to the airport and return home to Scotland. Jim bounced in through the large doors.

"Right on time," Grayson said, getting up from his chair. He gestured toward the bar, beyond the front desk. "Let's have a drink and celebrate your hard work."

They neared the counter, where the clerk was studying his register. Grayson coughed, and the man glanced up and saw Jim.

"Oh, Mr. Jim Bolt. A letter arrived for you."

Jim scrunched his brow in surprise. Glancing at the envelope, his eyes lit up like the chandelier above his head. "It's from Heather!" He ripped the letter open. A dark cloud tore across his face.

Grayson grabbed his arm. "Jim, what is it?" He guided him to a chair, sat him down, and scanned the letter. "Let's get you upstairs to your room."

Once they reached the suite, Jim paced frantically. "I don't believe this. It can't be happening." He grabbed the phone and pressed zero. "Long distance, please…thank you." He hung up and started dialing.

Grayson drifted into the bathroom, gazed in the mirror, and adjusted his tie. His face looked lurid as a worn golf towel. The last seventy-two hours had brought on a heaviness that centered in his chest like an old wound that ached on a rainy day. Seeing his son collapse after reading Heather's farewell letter left him feeling shameful. He had orchestrated this heartbreaking scenario.

Ten years of doing everything possible to prepare Jim for the Global and free him from Costanzo's death threat. He hated causing Jim such suffering, but it was unavoidable.

"Goddammit!" Jim spat, from the other room. "Her phone's disconnected."

A knock came at the door, and Grayson opened it.

"Mr. Bolt?" said a pleasant-faced man with a gray mustache and black bag. He was short, fiftyish, hair parted down the middle. "You called for a doctor?"

"Please come in."

Jim sat in the corner staring at the letter, his face a mask of tears. Grayson lumbered over to him. "Jim, I know this must feel like a terrible tragedy."

"How could she do this?" Jim said and began sobbing. "It doesn't make sense."

Twenty minutes later, Grayson slipped out of Jim's room, leaving him tucked in bed with a strong sedative to keep him out for the night. He hoped Jim would get over his pain by pouring his heart into golf. Heather would become a memory, shredded and scattered and swept away like leaves in a stream. The Global would start in three days.

☙❧

Jim stayed in his room all the next day, alone, with Heather's letter. He didn't eat and didn't answer the phone. And when his dad knocked, he told him to go away. Didn't want to see or talk to anyone. And he sure as hell didn't want to play golf again. Ever.

He awoke the next morning to find a note under his door.

Jim, if you'd like to eat breakfast together, please give me a call. Otherwise, please be packed and ready by noon. Our flight is at three. I know you're in great pain, and rightfully so. Tragedies like this take time to heal. You and I went through a similar heartbreak after your mother and Troy were killed. We were eating hotdogs at the miniature golf course, and you began crying and got mad. You said it was unfair for people you love to die. We talked some more, and when you were ready, you grabbed your putter and ran to the tee

box. As I recall, you made a hole-in-one.
   I love you, son.

Jim fell into a chair and cried. It *wasn't* fair. Finally, he stood up, blew his nose and stepped into the shower. *Goddam you, Heather! I hate you!*

He got out of the shower, dried off, and began slapping on clothes. *Fine! If that's the way she wants it, fine. I'll show her just who she'll be missing.* He picked up the phone.

"Dad, I'm starving. Let's eat."

CHAPTER 47

Grayson sat in the clubhouse drinking coffee and watching the TV commentators.

"Hello everyone, Howie Collins here. Welcome to our CBS coverage of this year's Global championship, held at the Brentwood Country Club in Summerville, South Carolina. The course is in its full botanic beauty of magnificent pines and blooming azaleas. Not since Tiger Woods took on Phil Mickelson has a competition between two rivals been so anticipated. The question on everyone's lips: Will Bat Brady, the seasoned three-time champion from Louisiana, hold back the current U.S. Amateur champion, eighteen-year-old Jim Bolt? Let's go down to the driving range where two-time Global winner, Nick Nelson, has caught up with Bat."

"Bat, the media has stirred up quite an interest in this matchup between you and Jim Bolt. What do you think of an amateur competing at this level?"

Bat pushed up his black cowboy hat and said with a lively suntanned smile, "Jim's got the right stuff to be a contender. He adds enormous excitement to the game."

"But does he have the right stuff to compete against the world's best?"

"We'll see over the next four days, won't we?" Bat flashed his big Bat grin.

Excitement swept up Grayson's spine. After years of preparation, Jim was only four rounds away from breaking free of Costanzo's death curse. If Jim was to see his twenty-first birthday, there could be no second place.

The tournament got underway with clear skies, no wind and

a record gallery. Round one ended with Jim at three under par, settling in at fifth place, one behind Bat.

The mood in Jim's suite after round two was confident, even jubilant. Friends had dropped by to congratulate him on his superb play and enjoy free champagne. Jim and Grayson weren't interested in greeting friends *or* drinking champagne. They huddled in a bedroom reviewing the day's round. The tournament was half through and Jim stood solid on the leader board. One behind the leader, Surge Michaelson, and one ahead of Bat. But he'd made a couple of mental errors that Grayson wanted to review. They strategized the next day's round, expected to be played under a clear South Carolina sky.

Grayson's cell phone vibrated in his pocket. He stepped away and checked the screen. *Shit!* He answered. "Hello."

"Good evening, Mr. Bolt."

"Good evening, Mr. Costanzo."

"I want to congratulate you on Jim's outstanding performance today."

"Thank you. I appreciate that." Grayson needed to get back with Jim but knew that these conversations ended when Costanzo wanted them ended.

"That boy's going to do it, Bolt," Costanzo said with uncharacteristic enthusiasm. "Two more rounds and he'll trounce Bat's ass."

"He'll do his best."

"I'm counting on it."

If Jim's first two rounds were superb, the third was magical. It had rained the night before, softening the greens and allowing Jim to aim at every flagstick. He knew the greens so well, he could have putted with his eyes closed. He'd tap the ball knowing it would drop into the hole, as if it had already happened. He only needed to wait patiently for the present to catch up. He finished the round with the day's lowest score—the course's lowest score—sixty-two.

With one more round to play, Jim led Bat by six shots and the rest of the bleeding pack by a distance of eight.

CHAPTER 48

"That son-of-a-bitch can't do this to me! He's going to win that goddamn tournament and cost me a fortune. This is a fucking disaster."

The Man had been on his feet the last two hours, and Chauffeur had never seen him so shook up. His blood pressure had to be off the charts as he stomped in front of the television watching Bat get ripped to shreds.

"The kid's kicking his butt," Chauffeur said.

"He's not kicking *my* butt." The Man gave a lamp the heave-ho across the room with a crash. "It's time I kicked *his* ass."

The Man had a record of picking winning golfers, and everybody expected him to make millions betting on the Global. People also knew Jim Bolt was his wunderkind, and that The Man would lay big money on the kid to win. That perception gave The Man better odds when he placed his last minute bet on Bat, not the kid. The kid, who Grayson had claimed at age eight had won three tournaments, but in fact hadn't known a golf club from a pogo stick.

Always do the unexpected. That was The Man's lifelong philosophy, but the unexpected was tripping him up. If Jim continued making shots that had the gallery hollering to the next county, The Man could kiss a fortune goodbye. He could not allow that, especially since he was still suffering from a second near disastrous Super Bowl loss.

He hollered to Chauffeur, "Get Gillfillen over here. Now!"

Chauffeur smirked and went for the phone. *Gillfillen's gonna learn that being on The Man's payroll means a hell of a lot more than he could've imagined.*

છ૭છ૭

Gillfillen rode the elevator up to the top floor, got out, and made his way quietly down the hallway. Chauffeur and Gonzo had thrown him before The Man's feet like a Carthaginian slave. The Man then placed a heavy boot to his skull, helping him understand the importance of what he was to do.

Halfway down the hall, Gillfillen stopped and looked at a scrap of paper he was holding. It read 518. He stuffed the paper in his pocket and continued on. He stopped, dabbed his brow with a handkerchief, closed his fist, and knocked.

"Who is it?" came Jim's groggy voice.

"My name's Gillfillen. I work for your father. Please open the door."

CHAPTER 49

Jim threw on his clothes and stormed three doors down to his dad's suite.

Bang! Bang! Bang!

The door swung open. "Jim, what the *hell's* the matter with you?"

"Matter? *MATTER?*" Jim shoved Grayson's chest, launching him back. "There's several *goddamn* matters." Jim charged in and slammed the door. "Matters of importing spies to report on Heather and me. Matters of recruiting more spies with the names Linda and Brad."

Words spat into his father's face like sodden bullets.

Grayson's legs weakened like loose and tangled muscle.

"How could you do this to your own son? You forced Heather into writing me that letter and made her abort her baby I didn't even know about. You murdered my child—*your* grandchild." Jim shook his fist while Grayson worked his bent body to the front of an armchair, hand over hand. Jim trembled with anger. "I hate you, Dad. I will *always* hate you."

Grayson sank into the chair. "Who have you been talking to?"

"Someone who's been honest with me."

"Jim, please sit down. I'd like to explain."

"Why? So you can bend the truth to serve your own selfish motives?" Jim stomped to the door and turned. "If I could slit my wrist and drain your half of my blood, I'd do it!"

"Jim, please—"

Jim stormed out and returned to his room. With a shaky hand he picked up the phone and called a taxi. He threw fistfuls of clothes into a suitcase, then stomped down to the lobby and outside. A moment later, a cab pulled up. The driver placed Jim's suitcase in the trunk, and Jim collapsed in the backseat.

"Let's get the hell away from here," he said. "Anywhere, I don't care. The countryside." He squeezed his eyes closed, trying to make sense of everything. His nerves had unraveled from sturdy cords to frazzled threads. His breaths were ragged and shallow, and his heart pounded like it wanted out.

The driver peered into the mirror. He had thick eyebrows, brown skin and a puffy face. "You all right back there?"

Jim stared out the window. "Please, just drive."

To think, all this time he was being used to gratify his dad's selfish needs. He dropped his head into his hands. His shoulders shook, and tears ran between his fingers. A dam inside had burst, releasing a flood of pain. He longed for Heather. He could find her. Ask if she still wanted him. But why should she? Who knew what vicious lies his father had told her. She must hate them both.

The driver cleared his throat, then asked, "Do you need a hospital?"

"I'm—" Jim drew in short hiccup-like breaths. "—fine." Heat rushed through him, first warm, then hot. "Driver, pull over." He scrambled out and stood by the road. The morning breeze cooled him down. A horse grazed just beyond a fence. The sun's low rays lengthened its shadow up to his feet.

Jim opened his wallet. "How much?"

"You're getting out here?"

"I'll be okay. You can go."

The driver checked the meter. "Fourteen-fifty."

Jim handed over a twenty. "Keep the change." He turned and started off.

"Hey, your suitcase." The driver scurried to the trunk.

"Which way to town?" Jim asked.

"You're heading toward it. It's not far."

Jim scanned the rural landscape. "Is there a longer route?"

The driver pointed left. "That way's about a ten mile loop back to town."

Jim grabbed his suitcase and started walking. The sprawling ranch-style estates reminded him of home on Long Island. He sniveled and blubbered along the road, sometimes on the weeded shoulder.

His dad never loved him. Never cared about his feelings. Feelings never mattered. Only golf mattered. Jim hadn't chosen to play golf, his dad had. Because Jim happened to like it, he thought playing had been his decision. It was clear now. His dad wasn't good enough to play in the pros—in the Global—so he wanted his sons to do it.

What a fool he'd been. Ordained by God to play golf? Right! And the manipulation. Making him feel guilty whenever he wasn't playing. He'd even dragged Troy's memory into his scheme. Jim pulled up a clump of grass and offered it to some horses by the fence. He had a horse once. But did he ever spend time with it without feeling guilty for taking a minute away from golf? Hell, no.

Heather never had that kind of guilt about tennis. She worked hard and got good, but she never gave a crap about being great because she enjoyed herself too much off the court.

He was through with golf. Had no reason to continue, and a shitload not to. Golf belonged to Mr. Asswipe.

An unbearable burden seemed to have lifted. His step became lighter. He would release all his birdies and eagles into the sky and enjoy a life without bullshit and pressure. The breeze swept through the blooming countryside and poured over his face.

And he laughed.

He reached the end of the neighborhood and entered a commercial district. He'd missed breakfast, and all that walking and purging had kicked up an appetite.

Wandering into a small diner, he grabbed a seat at the counter and put his suitcase at his feet.

A waitress with fat arms and a saucy smile came over. "What'll it be, young fella?" She had one of those cool southern drawls. She swept a cloth over the counter and sent the last customer's crumbs onto the floor.

He ordered oatmeal and eggs with the works.

The works included grits that he mixed with his eggs. Different, but not bad. He peered out the window across the street, and his eye caught a large blue-and-white sign over a doorway. "Talk about a new life," he mumbled.

He thought about that sign while he worked on a hunk of apple pie. Soon an idea began rolling around in his head.

He tossed some bills on the counter, picked up his suitcase, and treaded outside. He stood, staring hard at that sign. After a minute or three, he marched across the street, stopped, and let his eyes rake over the poster in the window.

He opened the door and strode inside. A square-built man with a flat nose and round face sat at a desk. His brown shirt looked pressed and tailored.

"Good morning, young man," he drawled with a friendly smile. "How can I help y'all today?" He stood and extended a thick hand.

Jim set down his suitcase and ran his hand up-and-down his pant leg. He licked his lips and pumped the man's hand. "I'd like to sign up, sir."

"Well, pull up a chair, good buddy, and welcome to the United States Army."

PART III

CHAPTER 50

Heather Morrison took a break from the poker table and made her way into the coffee shop for a cheese sandwich and Diet Coke. She tugged the hem of her blue V-neck sweater and found an empty booth. She'd made only one mistake by failing to raise a bet and force the winner to fold. Other than that, she'd played smart.

After spending three years in Ireland, Heather had just arrived in Atlantic City. She planned to spend a few weeks sharpening her American poker skills before moving to LA. After a few days of West Coast poker, she would compete in the upcoming Las Vegas World Series of Poker Tournament, hoping to catch the coveted gold bracelet. Competitions had always intrigued her. Tennis, puzzles, poker. Especially poker, a battle of the minds.

She heard an announcer on the TV behind her say the name Bat Brady, a golfer Jim had mentioned. She turned around. A golf tournament was on. Here she was, transported back to the days of good times and dark shadows.

And Jim.

❧❦❧

Chauffeur picked up the ringing phone. It was Gonzo.

"You had it right, Chaufie. The Morrison girl checked into a hotel on Route 30 and went straight to the Lucky Star. She's been playing poker five hours and building up a shitload of chips."

Chauffeur grinned. "You still on her?"

"Yeah, she's taking a break, and I've got to piss."

"Tie a knot in it until you see what she does next."

Chauffeur hung up and shook his head. "Hey, boss, you'll never guess who just returned from the dead."

Costanzo stopped writing and looked up.

"Jim Bolt's old girlfriend, Heather Morrison."

Costanzo whipped off his glasses. "What's she doing back from where-the-fuck-ever?"

"Ireland. She probably couldn't learn the fuckin' language. Get this, Gonzo said she's playing poker in *your* casino."

The Man's lips drooped. "Which one?"

"This one—Atlantic City."

The Man picked up his glasses and chewed the earpiece thoughtfully. He got up, clomped to the window, and gazed out at a gray sky. "I want to be sure she doesn't fuck up my plans to put the final screws to Bolt. Find a way to keep an eye on her. A constant eye."

CHAPTER 51

The next day, Heather sat at the same poker table, playing Texas Hold'em when a cocktail waitress with long, two-tone fingernails and a ruffled blouse placed a drink before her. "Hi, there. It's on the house."

Heather looked up from her cards.

"Diet coke, right? That's what you drank yesterday. I hadn't seen you around before. On vacation?"

"No, but I'll be here awhile." Heather tossed her cards down. "I'm out," she said to the dealer.

"Listen," the waitress said, "I'm on a lunch break. Care to join me in the coffee shop? I don't meet many single women my age. I—I don't see a ring."

Heather considered her a moment. She seemed nice. "Sure, why not? I'm Heather." She extended her hand.

"I'm Joann."

Heather gathered her chips, and they chatted their way over to the coffee shop. They had a lot in common, and Heather had no complaints about the free lunch. Both had former boyfriends in their California days, and each had gone to college, though Heather earned her degree in Ireland, majoring both in mathematics and accounting.

It was great meeting someone who'd gone through some of the same shit.

Joann finished her hamburger and picked up her Coke. "Why Atlantic City?"

Heather pushed her empty plate aside. "To get a job and play poker."

"Looks like you're doing pretty well." Joann sipped her

drink and nodded toward Heather's rack of chips on the table. "Maybe you don't need a job."

"I can't live off poker. Besides—" Heather took a swallow of Coke. "—winnings are used only for expenses. Entering tournaments, and such. I'm also supporting my family back in Ireland."

"How'd you get interested in poker?"

"I played a little with my boyfriend in college, but never studied the game until—" She leaned back while the waitress dropped off coffees and took away their plates. "I've always been good at mental gymnastics—puzzles, that sort of thing. I had a job in Ireland with a security company doing problem solving. In school, I took a class that taught—"

"What kind of problem solving?"

"Oh, figuring why something did one thing when it should've done another. I ended up quitting."

"How come?"

"I worked on alarm systems, and fooling around on my own, I designed a motion sensor that didn't go off when the neighbor's cat wandered by at four in the morning. The engineering department—all men—accused me of treading on *their* domain. Anyway, I got into poker by—Sure you want to hear this?"

"Go on, it's fascinating."

Heather sipped her coffee. "At school I took a class in statistical probability. I learned that, despite its reputation, poker's actually a sophisticated contest where knowledge of odds matters. And I'm good at figuring those odds."

"When I play blackjack, I trust my hunches whether to hit or stick."

"Hunches don't work in poker. Computers teach probability when playing hands. Hunches are for…well, there's no other word for it…amateurs."

Joann picked up her coffee and sipped. "Sounds complicated. I'll stick to blackjack."

"What do you do around here for fun?"

"Movies, tennis, swimming, stuff like that."

"I used to play tennis."

"Used to?"

"Back at Berkeley. But my school in Ireland didn't have a women's team. Which was just as well, since tennis always reminded me of my college boyfriend."

Later that afternoon, Heather had just cashed in her chips when Joann came scurrying up. "Heather, I've got terrific news. The casino manager saw us talking and asked me about you. I told him you're looking for a job and had an accounting degree. Well, guess what? He needs someone in payroll." Joann's eyes sparkled as if Heather had won a Lucky Star jackpot. "You've got an interview in the morning. It's a fantastic position."

"Joann, I...I don't know what to say. Thank you!"

ଚ୬ଚ୬

After being hired on the spot, Heather sat in the personnel office of the Lucky Star Casino, completing paper work when she heard her name. "Ms. Morrison?"

She looked up, and looming over her, stood a blow-away man bent into a question mark. "Yes."

His eyes blinked behind thick glasses. "Hi, I'm Sam Collins, your assistant."

Heather shook this curious man's hand. "Happy to meet you, Sam. Please call me Heather."

"Okay, Heather," he said tonelessly. "If you're done here, I'll take you to your office and you can meet the manager, Ernie Oz. His office is next to yours."

They climbed upstairs, down a hallway, and into Heather's office. She looked at her big desk and smiled. *Wow, the perfect place to work.*

A man came bursting in. He was well dressed with big shoulders and pudgy around the waist. With barely a foot in the door, he growled in a voice that sounded rough as sandpaper, "I'm Ernie. I don't know who you know that got you this job. But understand, *I'm* your boss." He tapped his chest. "You follow *my* orders."

Heather stopped smiling and stared at him while blood

raced up from her neck like a thermometer under a heat lamp.

"If I say get me coffee, you ask how much sugar." His eyes bulged. "Understood?"

Heather swallowed. "Will that be with or without cream?"

Sam raised a hand to conceal a grin.

Ernie glared at her. "I don't use cream." He turned and stomped out.

Heather looked at Sam, who dropped the hand but not the grin. He shrugged, and they both burst out laughing. "As you can see, your boss is a certified asshole."

CHAPTER 52

Private Buford Stoval jerked the Humvee around a pothole. "I don't know about you, Jimbo, but when I get out of this shithole, I'm gonna get drunk and married, in exactly that order."

"You won't be doing either if we hit an IED," Jim replied, tearing his eyes away from the Willis jeep they'd just passed. It was upside down and charred.

Buford looked at Jim. "You don't listen very well. The captain said the road was just cleared."

Jim had already been blown off the road a year ago in an accident that had ended up killing one of his army buddies. With only a week left in the army, he did *not* want to return home draped in Old Glory.

"Just the same, Buford, keep eyes front."

Jim turned and glanced at the other Humvee in their dusty red wake before settling back down and watching for trip wires, rebels, and any other damn thing that looked out of place.

"How 'bout you, Jimbo? Whatcha gonna do when you get out?"

"Haven't thought about it. Probably go back to school."

"Ya got a girlfriend?"

Jim shifted in his seat. "Nope. No girlfriend."

"You're a good lookin' guy—and don't take that the wrong way. Grew up in New York, went to college in Californ—i—a. Lotsa girls there. That's not to take anything away from Mississippi, 'course."

For three years, Jim had avoided talking much about himself, and especially about girlfriends. Instead, he'd smoke a cigarette and listen to his buddies spout off. Guys liked to brag. Hell, back in Berkeley, he did his share with Carlos. Jim's mind whirled back to a time long ago, and sadness gripped his chest. You could never forget the people you loved, even if you tried.

"Not to brag or anything," Buford said, "but I've had lots of girlfriends. Playin' football didn't hurt. 'Course all that ended in the twelfth grade when I met Coralee. She stole my heart. Here, I'll show you her picture." He leaned over and reached in his back pocket.

"Look out!" Jim grabbed the wheel and yanked it hard right. The Humvee veered into a ditch, bounced about twenty meters, and rolled onto the driver's side. An ear-shattering explosion came from the road. The other Humvee! "Buford, are you all right?"

"Not sure, but I think so. How 'bout you?"

"I'm fine." Jim wiped his blurry eyes with a sleeve. He had seen someone's head pop up in the ditch on the other side of the road, and now he heard loud voices. Dizzy, trying to figure out which way was up, he unbuckled himself, slid open the window, and breathed in red dust. He squirmed up through the opening, fell head first to the ground, and got up. Buford was leaning on his side against the driver's door. "Unhitch yourself, Buford," Jim called. "I'm going to pull you out."

Jim opened his door, unfastened the metal first aid kit from the side panel, and wedged it in where it would keep the door open, then hurled his upper body inside, and pulled Buford up, over, and to the ground. Jim tossed down their carbines. "Let's get those bastards."

They scrambled up to the road. A dozen rebels were jumping up and down, laughing and shouting in Arabic. They had one of Jim's unit buddies, Jeb, and the captain on the ground. A man dressed in black had a pistol pointed at the captain, who was missing an arm and raising the other one, fingers spread. "No, please—" A shot to the forehead cut him off. Jeb was shot right afterward.

"Shit!" Jim let loose with his carbine. Buford followed suit.

The air filled with gun blasts and screams, smoke and blood. Several rebels fell to the ground, while others ducked behind the flaming Humvee and fired back. Jim held the trigger until his magazine was empty then slung his carbine over his shoulder. "Let's get outta here!"

The two men ran back to their Humvee. Jim grabbed more mags and locked one in his carbine.

"Get the first aid kit," Jim said. "This way."

"Wait!" Buford said. "Camp's the other way."

"That's where they'll expect us to head."

Two men appeared on the ridge.

"Look out!" Jim yelled and shot off a burst. "Let's go."

They ran north through the ditch about three kilometers and stopped.

"We've got to get away from the road," Jim said. He pointed his carbine. "That way, over the rise."

"But we have to cross two hundred meters of open desert to get there. Besides, that's going farther north. Choppers will never find us."

"We've got to. It's our best shot. We'll make our way back after dark. Let's go."

They zigzagged across no-man's land until they crossed the rise and collapsed to their knees.

"Jesus Christ," Buford said, "your eye's swollen shut, and your forehead's bleedin' like a stuck pig."

"You don't look so pretty yourself. Check your leg."

"Holy shit!" It was soaked with blood.

"That's why you were limping." Jim ripped open Buford's pant leg, hoping there wasn't a bone sticking out. He wiped blood away with his sleeve. "It's a puncture wound. You'll be fine." He opened the first aid kit and slapped on antiseptic, gauze, and a bandage wrap.

"Give me those. I'll patch up your forehead." Buford went to work. "Does your eye hurt?"

Jim shook his head and caught sight of a boy, maybe five or six in orange pants and sitting on the dusty trail up ahead. "Look."

Buford squinted. "He's holding a little dog."

They went over to the boy. The dog's tongue was hanging out. "What's wrong with your dog?" Jim said.

"He's dead," the boy replied in a monotone.

"Where are your parents?"

He pointed. "Over there."

They were lying in the dirt. "Jesus Christ!" Jim said, hesitantly approaching the bodies.

"Fuck, man," Buford said. He turned the woman onto her stomach. Both bodies' backs were riddled with bullets.

"How'd this happen?" Jim asked the boy.

He turned around and pointed to the sky. "Airplanes."

"Ah, shit." Buford said and stomped his foot.

"Where do you live?" Jim asked.

The boy pointed up the trail.

"Come on, we'll take you home."

"You outta your fucking mind?" Buford said. "If anybody sees us, we're good as dead."

"We can't just leave him here."

"Oh, sure, we'll take him to his village, or wherever, and tell them here's an orphan, compliments of our air force."

"We'll be careful. Come on, kid."

"He's not our problem, Jim. We're going farther and farther away from camp."

The boy took Jim's hand, and they started off.

"You're fuckin' crazy, you know that? Hey, kid, no point bringin' that dead dog along." He reached for it.

The boy turned away from him.

Jim looked down at the boy. "We'll make a nice little cemetery."

"But he'll be sad all alone," the boy said.

They trekked ahead, and Jim was surprised by the memories that came to mind of a fishing trip in Canada with his dad. He had been so distressed to learn that the eggs from the fish he'd caught would never become fish themselves.

The boy led them farther and farther away from camp. They passed a mud brick house with red mortar set back from the road. It had a red dirt yard.

"This is bullshit," Buford said, his carbine held ready at his hip. But they kept on.

A few more isolated houses appeared, along with a small store that was closed.

"Where the hell is everybody?" Jim asked.

The boy let go of Jim's hand and ran to a house several meters ahead. In front was a scrawny tree with no leaves. A rope and car tire hung from a branch. The boy went inside, and Jim and Buford followed, carbines at the ready. "Anybody home?" Jim called.

No answer.

It wasn't much of a home. A big room with lots of mats. At one end was a kitchen counter with a kettle, jars of dates and beans, a basket of bread, and a goldfish in a bowl. On a table were wooden figurines and photographs. Jim picked up a wedding picture. The bride wore a red dress with fancy stitching and a matching headpiece. She smiled at the camera. The groom wore a white suit and red something or other wrapped around his head. He looked happy. Jim laid the picture down and sighed.

"Home sweet home," Buford said and began opening cabinets.

"Hey, let's show some respect and leave things alone." Jim went out back to find the boy standing before an open shed and crying, the dead dog at his feet. "What's wrong?"

"The animals are gone."

It was clear what had happened. Command knew of rebels in the area and launched an air strike. The boy's parents were just unlucky.

Afterward, the surviving rebels must have rounded up the residence, including livestock, and taken them somewhere. Buford came outside with a handful of dates.

"Hey, kid, anyone live here beside you and your mom and dad?"

The boy wiped away some tears. He'd been crying so silently, Jim hadn't even noticed. "Ahmed," he said.

"Who's he?"

The boy shrugged.

"Probably his uncle," Jim said and asked the boy, "You hungry?" He didn't say anything. "Buford, give me some dates."

Jim took them and gave the boy one. He just held it in his hand.

"Let's get the hell outta here," Buford said. "Choppers won't be looking for us this far north."

Jim peered at the red sun low in the afternoon sky. No point exposing themselves if they didn't have to. "We'll head back after dark, like we planned."

Ants had formed a single file into the dog's mouth. Jim put his arm across the boy's shoulder. "Let's bury your dog. Any other graves around here?"

The boy nodded, and Buford went back inside.

Jim found a shovel, and he and the boy buried the dog beside an earlier goldfish grave. "There," Jim said. "He won't be alone."

They went in the house. The boy climbed onto the kitchen counter, grabbed a hunk of bread, and ran out the front door.

"He's on his swing," Buford said, sitting on the floor, his back against the wall, and peering out the window.

Jim rinsed his eye with water. He hoped it was only swollen and nothing serious. Then he flopped onto the floor next to Buford. "You know what sucks the most around here?"

"Everything."

"The shit that kids go through. Losing limbs, getting raped. And now this little guy with nothing but a goldfish and an old tire. And if he's lucky, maybe an uncle."

"We've seen some heavy shit."

Jim put his head back against the wall and closed his eyes. He couldn't dare talk about what he'd seen—or what he'd done. Some things you have to forget.

"Baber!" came a voice from outside.

The men jumped to their feet.

"Ahmed! Ahmed!" the boy hollered. He jumped off his swing and into the arms of a man in a blue shirt and Panama hat.

"The uncle," Buford said. "What are we gonna do?"

"Stay here and cover me," Jim said. He left his carbine and opened the door.

The man looked at him and jerked back. "American!"

"Rebels forced us to abandon our vehicle. We found the boy on a dirt road."

The man put the boy down and talked to him in Arabic. The boy said something back. The man shook the boy's shoulders and yelled at him. The boy began crying, and Buford came up to the doorway.

"His parents are dead," Jim said. "They were shot a few kilometers south of here."

The man collapsed to his knees and wept. Jim thought it best not to say how the parents were shot. "We're real sorry for your loss, sir. Do you want to come in?"

After a minute, the man stood and pressed his palms to his eyes, then he put his arm around the boy, and they went inside. The man removed his shoes. "Please, sit," he said. "I will make tea."

Jim and Buford sat on a mat. Jim felt bad keeping his dirty boots on, but—

Out the window, a man! Jim dived for his weapon. The door flew open with a crash, and Jim fired a burst. The rebel crumpled to the ground.

"Everyone out!" Jim yelled. "Let's go."

The man scooped up the boy. "Follow me," he said, and they took off around the house, across the graveyard, and into a rocky ravine with enough brush to provide cover. They stopped and ducked down. "He must have followed me," the man said. "There'll be more coming."

Jim peered through the brush. Didn't see anyone. They'd have to make a break for it.

And then.

The faint sound of twirling rotor blades was heard in the far distance. The boy's eyes flashed. "Helicopter!"

The man gasped and pointed through the brush. Men with guns appeared on the ridge looking around. They must've heard the boy.

"No one move," Jim whispered.

A burst of gunfire ricocheted off nearby rocks.

"Our only chance is to get on that helicopter," Jim breathed. "When I say go, everyone run out in the open and wave your arms."

The whirlybird was a good kilometer away. *Keep coming. Keep coming. Faster, goddammit!*

"Ah, shit!" Buford murmured. "I knew it! He's turning back."

The rebels let loose on the chopper with their AKs.

The chopper swung back around. The pilot must have heard the ping of bullets.

"Go! Go!" Jim yelled. He stood up and fired a long burst up the ridge, eliminating three men. The chopper kept coming, guns blazing. It dropped altitude and swung toward the group on the ground.

Someone out of sight was shooting at the helicopter, and Jim's mag was empty. If the guy wasn't killed, they would be. Jim knelt and locked in a mag. He ran up the ridge, and there the man was, behind a rock, lowering his aim from the chopper to the waving group. Jim took him out with a long burst then raced for the chopper as it touched down.

A sergeant jumped out, grabbed the boy and handed him to someone, then helped everyone else in. The helicopter lifted from the ground with a stomach-dropping spin, and they soared back toward camp. The boy looked out at a view he'd probably never seen, and Jim wondered if the little guy would ever see it again.

CHAPTER 53

Chauffeur ambled into The Man's office and fell into a chair. "It's getting to be old home week. Guess who's being discharged from the army."

"George Washington."

"Grayson's kid. First the old girlfriend shows up, now we've got the golfer back on our shores from Libya, or wherever the fuck."

The Man removed his glasses and tossed his pen onto the desk. "Well, well, well. The day has finally arrived."

Chauffeur laughed. "He was a hero in Benghazi. Earned the Silver Star. Maybe they'll carve that on his tombstone."

The Man rose, sauntered to the window, and gazed across his lush backyard landscape.

Chauffeur watched, his heart racing in anticipation. *This is gonna be good.* "So, how do you want him taken out?"

The Man turned. An oily grin crept across his face. "Back in the day, I did pretty well by that kid. Maybe I should give him another chance. Think he still has the touch?"

"Na, I'd forget it. His touch has been around triggers, not golf clubs."

"Athletes come out of retirement all the time. Give him some practice, and he'll hit the ball to the moon."

"He might be all fucked up from car bombs and shit."

The Man grinned. "That would add an interesting unpredictability. The Global is coming up in three months."

Chauffeur was disappointed, but there was no arguing with The Man. "Bolt's probably shittin' in his pants, thinking the kid's about to get taken out now that he's back in the country.

He'll probably try to hide him some fucking place."

"No, he won't." The Man tramped to his desk. "I'll call him. Bolt wants that Global like a bitch in heat. I'll tell him the kid gets one more shot. He wins the Global this time or—" The Man spread his hands. "—he has an unfortunate accident."

Chauffeur stroked his long chin and thought. "Suppose the kid wants nothing to do with the old man? They squared off after Gillfillen laid out the facts of life. He might not want to play."

"He'll play." The Man put his feet up on the desk. "And it's going to be your job to guarantee it."

Chauffeur hoped he'd heard wrong.

The Man laughed. "That's right, you're going to put Humpty Dumpty back together again."

CHAPTER 54

Jim sat in the mess hall, wolfing down his last military lunch and wondering how he'd adjust to civilian life. Hopefully, one without nightmares—nightmares about dusty Benghazi roads filled with mines. About the woman with a baby. About the orphan boy. About the little girl getting—

"Sergeant Bolt!" came a voice over the intercom. "Report to the mess sergeant, on the double."

Startled, Jim jumped up and marched to the sergeant. Beside him stood a man in a dark suit, arms behind his back and rocking on his toes and heels.

"That will be all, soldier," the man said to the sergeant and turned to Jim. "I'm Colonel Green, Army Intelligence." He had a cleft chin and a long face like an AK-47 magazine. "Where can we talk privately, Sergeant?"

Jim looked around and nodded to an empty side room.

"That will do," the colonel said and led the way.

They sat across from each other. The colonel folded his black-gloved hands on the table. "Sergeant Bolt, you're up for honorable discharge, and Army Intelligence is now at liberty to disclose to you your personnel record."

"My record, sir?"

The colonel dropped his chin and regarded Jim from under heavy eyebrows. "Sergeant, before you were awarded the Silver Star, a thorough background check was conducted on you. And I mean *thorough*."

"Just for getting the Silver Star, sir?"

"More than that, Sergeant." The colonel lowered his voice. "Once certain information was uncovered, most unusual information, regulations required the work of the CID, CIA, and FBI."

Jim nodded slowly. *Where is this going?*

"When you were a boy, your father got involved with a shady underworld figure."

A knot formed in Jim's stomach.

"Your father performed legal work for this person. They later had other dealings that created unclear situations."

The knot got tighter. "What situations?"

The colonel pushed his long face close. "Situations that threatened your life."

"My life!" The words shot from Jim's mouth. His eyes searched the room.

"For some reason your father became indebted to that underworld figure who threatened your life if your golf didn't meet his expectations."

Jim's breath caught in his lungs. "What the hell does that mean? What expectations?"

"It means your father had to do what he believed necessary to keep you focused on golf and winning tournaments." The colonel slanted glances to either side. "Or someone would be ordering takeout, and you'd be the main course."

Jim's mind wheeled. *You'll win the Global...God said it.* "This doesn't make any sense."

"You'll have to sort that out with your father, son." The colonel started to get up.

Jim grabbed his arm. "Hold on. What else does the report say? Is my life still in danger?"

The colonel's eyes darkened, and he snapped his arm back. "That's all I can tell you, Sergeant. You won't be hearing from us again. Your file is sealed."

"For Christ's sake, Colonel, this is a lot to take in. At least leave me the report."

"Negative, Soldier. Army regulations prohibit turning over documents or memoranda of this nature. This one and only verbal communiqué is all military code 2870-38 allows, and only because of a threat to your life." The colonel stood and extended his gloved hand. Jim hesitated, then shook it. "Good luck, Sergeant."

Jim remained in the mess hall, trying to weigh everything. For three years he'd been shielded behind a mental barricade, never allowing himself to think of his father. Now everything was closing in like Islamic insurgents. Grayson's relentless push for him to win tournaments wasn't selfish? Not like Gillfillen had said? All that coaching and training was just to keep him alive?

Old anger turned to confusion. He felt like an actor in a school drama that he had no control over. Who was this underworld figure? *And why would he want me dead?* The questions didn't have immediate answers, but at least he knew where to find them.

ოჯოჯ

Chauffeur left the mess hall, wearing an unusually broad smile. His swift exit didn't allow more questions from Jim. When he got over being confused, he'd be left with doubts and want to hear the whole sob story. Chauffeur threw a snappy salute to the guard as he wheeled out of New York's Fort Drum's main gate. He speed-dialed his cell phone.

"Hey, boss, I don't know what you told that fort commander, but the MPs treated me like the pope."

"I didn't tell the commander squat," The Man said. "My Pentagon man handled it."

"You should've seen the kid. He practically ducked for cover when I told him he was a target. He'll double-time it to Daddy."

"Daddy will be waiting. I told Bolt that in view of his son's heroic achievements, I felt it my patriotic duty to let him tee-up once more at the Global but with the original terms."

"Brilliant, boss." *Happy days are here again.*

CHAPTER 55

Jim eased his rented Chevy Volt up the dark, winding driveway of his dad's house. A lone light shone in the upstairs den. He parked and walked up to the front door, a duffle bag slung over a shoulder.

As nervous as if he were meeting a blind date, he wet his lips and knocked.

Lights came on, and the front door opened. His father's face was older and strained. Gray hair graced his temples. Words Jim had nearly forgotten fell from his lips. "Hi, Dad."

Grayson closed his eyes for a moment, as if a great weight had been lifted. "Hello, son."

"Can I come in?" Jim asked, managing a thin smile.

"Of course." Grayson stepped aside and patted Jim's shoulder as he passed. "So, have you been making the world safe for democracy?" He shook his head. "Sorry, wrong war."

They trod into the living room, Jim tossed down his duffle bag, and they sat.

A nervous pain stabbed his stomach. He'd better get right to the point. Standing over the ball only prolonged the worry. "I've learned some awful things about your past, Dad, and I want you to fill in the blanks."

Grayson blinked. "Awful things?"

"That you're connected with an underworld figure and that my life has been threatened."

Grayson pursed his lips and got up. "Let's go into the den." He led the way and started mixing a drink. "Can I get you anything?"

"Nothing, thanks," Jim said stiffly and sat down, anxious to hear about the underworld figure—and his own life expectancy.

Grayson took his drink to a leather chair. "The person you're referring to is a mob boss named Costanzo. I don't know what exactly you've learned, but I assume it came from one of his people." He told Jim about his relationship with Costanzo: that he'd taken on his tax matter in exchange for helping Grayson to kill a man.

Jim's stomach sank. "You actually ki—killed someone?"

Grayson explained about Stockard, and how he had murdered Jim's mother and brother.

"Jesus Christ!" Jim slumped in his chair. *Murdered! My God.* He looked deeply into Grayson's drooping eyes. He wasn't being a controlling jerk all those years. He was trying to keep his only son alive. After a long moment, Jim sighed. "How'd I get picked to be involved in all this?"

"Well, Costanzo had planned to send an innocent man to jail, and made sure I was called for jury duty. I couldn't let the man be convicted."

This was hard for Jim to take in. Did he even know who his father was?

"So to punish me, Costanzo was going to kill you."

Jim all at once got a big bite of fear. "What do you mean, was?"

Grayson explained about his golf treaty proposal.

"But I withdrew from the Global. Why am I still alive?"

"Because you weren't around to be killed."

"Jesus!" Jim jumped up. "Well, I'm around now!" He ran both hands through his hair and paced. "I can't believe this."

"Don't worry. I've talked to Costanzo. You're safe."

Jim stopped and stared at Grayson. "Safe? What the hell does that mean?"

"It means you won't be killed."

"Well, I guess the news isn't all bad." Jim sank back into his chair. "How did I get so lucky?"

Grayson took a sip of his drink. "He said because you were a war hero."

That sounded fishy, but Jim would let it go. He nodded toward the fridge. "Is there a beer in there with my name on it?"

"Your name's on anything you want."

"In that case, is it okay if I bunk here a few days while I figure out what I'm going to do with my life?"

Grayson nodded toward the stairs. "Your room's where it's always been."

Jim took the beer into his room and looked around. He had forgotten the many trophies he'd won over the years. All dusted and shined. He picked up his gold US Amateur trophy and thought how good it felt when he psyched out Richie Kelly by using a driver on the eighteenth hole. He peered out the window at his old putting green, neglected and overgrown with weeds. It felt good to be home. If he hadn't received the Silver Star and had that background check, he never would have learned about the freakish events that had shaped his life.

A soft tap came at the door.

"May I come in?"

Jim wiped his eyes with a knuckle. "It's open."

Grayson stepped in and tossed Jim's duffle bag on the chair. "I thought you might need this." He sat on the bed.

Jim put his trophy down and sat beside him. "Anything else I should know?"

Grayson nodded slowly. "During the last three years, I learned a difficult truth about myself: that I was too controlling. I should have trusted you to make your own decisions. As for Heather's baby, I told myself it wasn't a human being yet, and that it was a case of you or the baby. Sometimes it's too late to apologize no matter how much you mean it." Grayson's eyes moistened.

A cold finger touched Jim's heart at the thought of Heather having to abort their child. He shook himself and stood up. "I have something for you, Dad." He rummaged through his duffle bag and pulled out a small plastic case. "This is for you. It's my Silver Star."

Grayson took the award and cradled it as if it were the Holy Shroud.

CHAPTER 56

Grayson reserved a table at D'Raymond's, Jim's favorite Italian restaurant. When they arrived, Joe, the owner, hugged Jim and congratulated him on his return from Benghazi.

"Have a seat," Joe said. "I'll send over a round on the house."

The room hadn't changed through the years. It still had the same dark-wood paneling, dimly lit booths, and Jim's signed picture above the bar when he received his US Amateur trophy.

Between talking to Chief Foley and reading Detective Wilson's email, Grayson had learned enough about Costanzo to know that once a takeout order had been given, reprieves were doubtful, regardless of the recipient's distinguished army record.

But Grayson had put in his own takeout order. He'd tracked down the best foreign assassin for hire and negotiated a deal to give Costanzo a taste of his own gun powder upon Jim's return to the US. Now, in view of Jim's temporary amnesty, Grayson had put the directive on hold.

Watching Jim wolf down his salad and bread sticks, Grayson had another worry. Veterans often struggled to cope, once back in civilian life, and he hoped that wouldn't be the case with Jim. That was one of the reasons why Grayson didn't dare tell him yet about Costanzo supposedly giving him a last chance to win the Global and rid himself of the death threat.

Grayson cleared his throat. "I served in the navy during the Vietnam War and consider myself fortunate not to have seen serious combat. I had friends who fought, and a lot of them suffered like hell when they returned home."

Jim nodded and continued chewing.

"I say that because, from what I've read, troops in Benghazi have been under a kind of pressure I can't even imagine."

Jim nodded again.

"And…um…well, I hope the army had counseling available."

Jim picked up a breadstick. "Maybe they did, but nobody I knew was offered any. Once our tour ended, we were shipped home." He broke the breadstick. "Like that."

Grayson picked at his salad. "If you ever want to talk about…well, anything…I'm here."

Jim took a slug of beer. "Thanks, Dad. Maybe sometime."

The waitress set down their lasagnas and left.

"I don't imagine you've played much golf the past few years," Grayson continued.

"Haven't swung a club." Jim tore off a piece of garlic bread and stuffed it into his mouth. "We should get out and play sometime."

Grayson dabbed a napkin to his mouth, trying to hide the thrill of hearing Jim's suggestion. "Ben Hogan won sixty-three professional tournaments. You know what happened to him then?"

Jim gulped more beer and ran his fingers across his mouth. "Um, he fought in World War Two."

"And then had a head-on collision with a Greyhound bus."

"Didn't know that."

"He had so many broken bones that nothing worked in his body. After a month, what do you think he did?"

"Sued the bus company. This lasagna's fantastic."

"He picked up a club and began swinging it."

Jim smacked his lips. "I know what you're getting at, Dad."

"May is only three months away. You could be ready if you start training now."

Jim put down his fork and scrubbed his mouth with a napkin. "If I don't win, will this Costanzo asshole try to kill me?"

Grayson clenched his teeth. "That won't happen."

"What's going to stop him?"

"That's nothing you should worry about."

Jim took another gulp of beer. "I don't worry, Dad. I can see around the fear."

ⱷⱿⱷ

It was near three in the afternoon when Grayson persuaded Howler Stemps and his Global committee to allow Jim to play in this year's championship. It took a lot of eloquent words about Jim's war heroics—plus a sizable donation to the Global's endowment fund. Grayson also arranged for Jim and himself to fly to Florida in two days and meet up with Coach McAlister.

Jim was eager to get a club in his hand so, early the next morning, Grayson took him to his country club for a practice round.

The only sounds in the deserted golf course came from pigeons still roosting in the trees. Jim hit his first shot into the thick oaks, and they treaded down the fairway. Grayson enjoyed a spring in his step, one he'd forgotten he ever had. He was filled with pride that his son wasn't frightened by Costanzo. No, Jim was a far better, braver man than that.

Jim had just found his ball when they heard them coming. At first, the sounds were faint and far away. Farther up the fairway stood a large rise where the sun's low rays made the dormant grass look golden and bright. Heads began to bob up from behind the mound and draw closer. Soon a raucous throng of people reached the crest. Someone yelled, "There he is!" And the horde charged down the hill, shouting, carrying video cameras, and waving notepads and microphones.

Jim stood by his ball, his dad at the bag, and a dozen media people swarmed up to them, everyone jabbering at once.

Neither the public nor the media had forgotten Jim. The story was just too good to let go: a boy wonder that had the Global locked up three years before, only to be struck by a surprising case of patriotism, drop out, and sign up to fight in Libya.

A small woman with a large voice thrust a microphone bearing the WBDI logo in front of Jim. "Is it true, Jim, you'll be playing in the Global this May?"

"Jim, will you finish the tournament this time?" hollered a man with a British accent.

"Will you win it, Jim?" yelled a man in back, his microphone held high.

Grayson laid down the golf bag and raised his arms like a preacher about to address his flock. "I'll tell you all, unequivocally, that Jim *will* compete in the upcoming Global, w*ill* finish all four rounds, and *he will win!*"

Shouts and applause followed the declaration, with reporters jostling each other to snag even more good sound bites for the morning news. With everybody chattering and following them around, Jim leaned next to Grayson. "Maybe I should pick up and call it quits."

Grayson had always encouraged distractions during Jim's practice. They forced him to develop a cocoon-like protection, allowing him to visualize and properly execute his shots. "Grab your club, son," he said before turning to the crowd. "Thanks everyone, you're welcome to tag along for the rest of the round. But if you could make room, the future Global champion will take his next shot."

Jim struck the ball perfectly. It took off through tree leaves, curved between branches, and landed within a club's length of the hole.

CHAPTER 57

For nearly three months, Heather had worked under Ernie in payroll, and it was time for her to move on to LA. Her plan was to start a new job and play poker—she hadn't given up on her dream of competing in the Las Vegas World Series of Poker Tournament and battling for the first place gold bracelet.

Besides, she detested Ernie. She had once entered his office and seen him scramble to put away what she recognized as a duplicate ledger, which made it obvious that he was skimming from the top.

But worse still was when she had approached his slightly ajar door with her letter of resignation and heard him talking to someone else.

"Come on, baby, put it in your mouth."

"I can't," came a woman's voice. "I just can't."

"You wanna be a Vegas cocktail waitress, this is how you punch your ticket."

Heather felt sick to her stomach and quickly returned to her office. She knew the easiest thing to do would be to just hand in her letter and be done with it, but her heart broke for the woman she'd heard with Ernie. If it hadn't been for Joann, Heather could have faced that choice, too. And, sometimes, bending to his request didn't even get you the job, particularly if the girl pretended to enjoy it. In Ernie's book, joy was reserved for himself.

It wasn't right, and the bastard couldn't keep getting away with it. It didn't take long to devise a plan that would give him something more to worry about than a case of STD.

$\mathcal{C}\mathcal{O}\mathcal{C}\mathcal{O}$

Heather shined her flashlight on the couch, moved it away from the wall, and checked the floor. She slid the couch back, removed a picture from the wall, shined her light on the empty space, and rehung the picture. She shuffled over to Ernie's grand-piano-sized desk, and there she found it—Ernie's hidden safe.

She sat cross-legged on the floor, peering at the safe's combination lock, when a key tickled at the door. The thin line of light under the door silhouetted a pair of feet. She switched off her flashlight. The lock clicked, and the door swung open. A hand reached in, and light flooded the room.

"Oh my God, Sam," Heather breathed. "You nearly gave me a heart attack. Quick, turn off that light and close the door."

"Heather, what the heck are you doing?"

"Shh! Get over here." She turned on her flashlight and showed him the safe. "Look, Ernie's skimming." She moved the light to another safe against the wall. "That's the casino's." She swung the light back. "This one's Ernie's."

"Heather, you can't—"

"Be quiet, Sam. I have to think." He shut up, but his glare burned the back of her neck. She hadn't planned on opening the safe. She'd only wanted to confirm her suspicions that Ernie had one.

The safe had a wheel pack design with a numbered dial and opening lever. The kind that had been around for more than a hundred years. Heather had never cracked a safe, but working for the security company had taught her to check out a few things. People liked to save time opening their safes by presetting the first two numbers, so she ran the dial through all possible third numbers. No good. She wiped her brow and attempted to work the various tryout combinations that manufacturers initially assigned safes. They were industry standard numbers. None she could remember worked.

"Heather, we need to leave *right now*!"

"In a minute." She stood up and rummaged through the

desk drawers. Lots of people wrote down the combination and tried to hide it somewhere convenient. She aimed her light into the far back of a side drawer and found a slip of paper with numbers scribbled on it.

"Yeow!" Sam yelped when Heather swung the safe's silver door open. Both shelves were crammed with banded hundred dollar bills.

"Tell me this is petty cash, Sam. Your cell phone has a camera, let's have it."

"It's in my office."

"For cripes sake, get it—quick." When Sam returned, Heather took a picture that included everything: the open safe, the money, and on the desk, a photo of Ernie's smiling mug. She swung the steel door closed, and the two scurried out and into Heather's office.

Sam ran a hand through his pile of red hair. "Jesus, I don't like this one bit."

"Ernie's days of abusing women around here are over, Sam." Heather flipped on her computer. "By the way, why'd you come into Ernie's office?"

"To drop off the labor report."

Heather connected a cable to Sam's phone.

"Ah, crap!" he said and fluttered his birdlike little hands nervously. "What am I supposed to do with that picture?"

"Don't have a cow. It'll be gone in a minute. I've gotta type a couple of notes while you go get a thumb drive."

Sam just stood there, drawn and bent, looking about to cry.

"Please, Sam, get the drive. No, get two."

Heather typed two notes and printed them. Sam returned, and, before erasing the phone's images, Heather downloaded the picture to both drives.

She pulled a self-sealing envelope from her drawer, inserted one thumb drive, one note, and sealed it. "Here, take this envelope and mail it to whoever owns this place."

Sam kept his hands to his side and cast her a pleading look. "Heather, you don't know for sure that Ernie skimmed. Maybe he's laundering money for The Man."

"Who?"

"The Man. He owns the place. There could be some kind of reasonable explanation."

"True," Heather said and tapped a fingernail against her front tooth. "But I doubt it. In any event, Ernie will get in trouble for lack of security. I'm counting on you to get The Man's address and mail it to him first thing tomorrow."

"No way!" Sam shook his head emphatically. "I've got a sister and two nieces to support. I can't get involved."

"You're not, Sam. Since we're mailing it, The Man won't know who tipped him off."

Sam scrunched his face and thought a minute. "What's the second drive for?"

"Back up. I'll take it with me to LA."

Sam's face fell to his ankles. "LA?"

She propped the second note on her desk. "I'm moving there, Sam. I have a six a.m. flight."

CHAPTER 58

Ernie had just entered his office when the phone rang. "Boss, get over here, we've got an emergency."

He strode to the office of his assistant, Marcus, who was standing in front of a monitor. Marcus was tall with a bull's neck and a lizard's mouth. A surveillance tape was switched on. The screen showed static, then went black.

"What the hell's this?" Ernie said.

"Hold on."

A spotlight popped on, and the shadow holding it moved to the couch and pulled it away from the wall. The light shined around the floor, then up to Ernie's golf picture. "That's my office!" he squealed.

"Fuckin' A," Marcus said. The image turned black except for a dim light at the bottom of the screen. "I think she put the light down and checked behind the picture." The spotlight wandered over to Ernie's desk.

"What the—who the fuck's that?" Ernie shrieked.

"Keep watching." The light danced around a few seconds, then a hand came into view and swung open the desk's bottom door. A woman's silhouette appeared.

"Is that Heather?" Ernie jumped from his chair and got his nose up close to the screen. "Son-of-a-bitch! That *is* Heather!"

"It ain't Grandma Moses. She opened the fuckin' safe and took a picture. Sam was with her."

Ernie threw his hands to his face. "Holy shit!" They raced from the room and down the hall to Heather's office. Ernie flung the door open—empty. A note propped on the desk said, *I quit! Asshole!!* "Why that—Follow me," Ernie snapped.

They stormed across the hall and into Sam's office. Marcus yanked Sam from his chair and threw him to the floor, breaking his glasses. Sam whimpered. Ernie told him to shut up and cough up. In less than a minute, Sam regurgitated everything.

Ernie returned to his office with the thumb drive and Heather's travel plans, feeling grateful at least that Marcus had installed a camera inside a phony smoke alarm. He had to think this through carefully. If The Man learned he'd been skimming from the casino, it was the end. *His end.* He didn't worry about Sam flapping his mouth. He probably only got involved because of a hard-on for Heather. A heart-to-heart with him about the good health of his sister's children would keep him on the reservation.

Heather was a loose end that needed tying up quickly. He sat drumming his fingers on the desk. After a minute, he picked up the phone and dialed.

"Chauffeur, it's me, Ernie. How the hell's it going?"

"What da ya want?"

"Listen, I've got a bit of a problem. Not a big problem, but a problem." Ernie got up and lumbered into his private bathroom. "You know that girl, Heather, the one you had me hire?"

"What about her?"

"Well, I hate to say it, Chauffeur." Ernie examined his teeth in the mirror. "But she ripped us off."

"What? When?"

Ernie bent his knees and smoothed his hair. "Yesterday. I just found out."

"How the fuck did you let her do that?"

Ernie straightened and laughed nervously. "Hey, I never wanted to hire the cunt."

"Cut the shit! How'd she do it?"

"She somehow got the combination to my safe."

"Where is she now?"

"That's just it, she skipped to LA."

"Oh, for chrissake! I'll have the midget get her."

"That won't be necessary, Chauffeur. You know me, I handle my own messes." He padded back into his office. "I do need one little favor, though. She'll be arriving there in a few hours, and if you could have the midget hold her at the airport, Marcus and Clarence will be right along to take her off his hands."

Chauffeur put him on hold and returned in a minute. "The Man says okay. I'll get the midget to handle it. Just one thing—"

"Sure, what's that?"

"When you get the girl, bring her around. I want to see her, personally."

Ernie switched the phone to his other ear. "Sure, sure, I can do that."

"How much did she get?"

"Jesus Christ, Chauffeur, it just happened. How the fuck do I know? Don't worry, every goddamn penny will be returned."

"If not, the dick's up your ass."

CHAPTER 59

Kamal had dropped off the day's collections and was on his way home to the Valley when his cell phone rang. The caller ID read Misha. Kamal had considered using *midget* as the ID, but if Misha ever saw it, he'd bite his head off and spit it in the gutter.

"Kamal!" Misha barked in his ear. "I need you to go to LAX right away and detain a woman flying in from Jersey."

"How come?"

"Never mind how come. I was told to do it, now I'm telling you." Misha gave Kamal all the information.

"How am I supposed to detain this woman?"

"Figure it out. Keep her by the luggage carousel. Two men from Jersey will show up on another flight shortly after she arrives and take her off your hands. Don't fuck up."

Forty minutes later Kamal pulled into the lower-level parking garage nearest the Delta terminal. He hurried inside the large glass-fronted building and checked the flight monitor. *Delta flight 22 from Atlantic City. On time. Carousel two.* He hurried over and found it deserted.

After a while travelers arrived, some with wheeled carriers. Kamal drifted among the growing number. He watched for an attractive woman traveling alone, blonde, early twenties.

A buzzer sounded and the carousel began its circular journey as luggage dropped onto it from a conveyor belt. Kamal continued to roam, trying to look inconspicuous. After all, this was an airport, and Americans often mistook him for Middle Eastern. He positioned himself where he could see everyone.

A good-looking blonde woman came scampering up in

tight jeans and tennis shoes. *Yes!* She approached the carousel, but didn't appear to see her baggage. Nothing more was coming down the chute.

He had to keep her from leaving, so he approached a couple gathering their things within earshot of her. "Did you see an elderly man with white hair and a cane on your flight from Atlantic City?" They said they hadn't. He turned to the blonde woman and asked her. She shook her head.

Kamal threw down his hands. "My dad always misses flights. Either that or the airline loses his luggage."

The woman frowned. "I think I'm in that boat."

Kamal feared she'd leave. He pointed to the chute. "You never know, some bags take longer to come out."

"I'm going to check with Delta," she said.

"I'll keep an eye on the chute for you in case more come down."

"Okay, thanks." She scooted off and returned a few minutes later. "It's not here. The airline will send it along later. Thanks for your help." She started for the sliding doors. "Good luck finding your father."

Kamal trailed a ways behind her, pivoting in a circle, eyes searching for two hood-types from Jersey. They weren't around and she'd made it outside to the curb. Shit, now what was he supposed to do? While she waited at a red light, he eased up alongside.

She looked at him, surprised. "Oh, hi again."

"I'm afraid my dad must've missed his flight. Where are you heading?"

"I'm taking the FlyAway bus to the Valley. I guess it stops somewhere out here." She looked up and down the crowded airport street.

"To the Valley? That's where I live. Listen, my dad's not here, and I've got an empty seat in my Jag." Hopefully, the car would impress her.

She frowned. "That's okay, I'll take the bus."

Kamal's cell phone rang and caller ID flashed Misha. "Hello, Mom," he answered. "What happened to Dad?" Kamal ignored Misha's protests and curses. "The hospital?...Uh-huh…Uh-huh…I see…Call me the minute…Okay, Mom. Bye."

"Is your dad all right?" Heather asked.

"They think he broke his hip. The doctor just came in, and Mom had to hang up. She was so upset she didn't think to call me earlier."

"I'm so sorry."

"I've got to run," Kamal said. "Are you sure I can't drop you off? The *SnailAway* makes a million stops and I'm going to the Valley anyway."

She thought a moment, her blue eyes searching his baby face. "Do you know where Van Nuys is?"

"Like the streets of New Delhi."

She extended her hand. "I'm Heather."

"Happy to meet you. I'm Kamal." *Damn! Shoulda given her a fake name. Too late now.*

Kamal wheeled out of the parking garage. So far, so good. No way could he keep her at the terminal, but at least she was in his car. He'd take her wherever she wanted, then tell Misha.

Soon they were northbound on the 405 freeway. Like on most Southern California spring days, the sky was bright and blue. Kamal clicked his teeth together. He talked too much when he was nervous, so he resolved not to initiate conversation. This idea worked well, because Heather seemed obligated to talk and spilled some juicy information.

She was relocating to the Valley and had no relatives or friends here, except an old college housemate from Berkeley. She had a job lined up and would be met at the FlyAway by a realtor who was going to rent her a house, and later her family would join her.

Kamal exited the freeway at Sherman Way and turned west toward Woodley. His cell phone rang.

"Hello."

"Where's the fucking girl?" Misha blasted, loud enough to be heard all the way back to the airport.

Heather's heart dropped, and so did her mouth. Had Ernie found her already?

"Wrong number, buddy." Kamal flipped the phone closed

and set it on the console. He kept his eyes glued ahead. "That's the trouble with having an easy number," he said. "I get a zillion wrong numbers."

Bullshit! "Oh, really? Let's see your number." Heather snatched the phone.

Kamal tried to wrest it away. "Hey, give that back!"

"Look out!"

Kamal slammed the brakes as a small dog ran out in front of him, and the car stopped with a thump.

CHAPTER 60

Heather dropped the phone and jumped out. She ran past a squealing dog in the street and into opposing traffic stalled at a light. The signal turned green, and she raised her arms in front of a pickup carrying pool-cleaning equipment. The driver, a bearded guy in a red tank-top, watched through tinted sunglasses as she raced around and hopped in. "Quick, get away. Some guy has a gun." She cursed herself for not keeping Kamal's phone.

The driver glanced in the mirror and stomped on the gas. He swung into the parking lane and roared ahead three blocks before forced to stop at a light. "Thanks a lot," Heather said, and jumped out.

She looked back but didn't see Kamal. Ducking into a coffee shop on the corner, she found a seat in the rear offering a view of the street and front entrance.

She was still shaking. *Where's the fucking girl?* How did Ernie track her down so fast? She tried to remember what information she'd given Kamal. Only that she had a job and was renting a house in the Valley. Nothing that could lead anyone to her. She hoped nothing had happened to Sam. She'd check with him later. Right now she needed to call the realtor and be picked up here at the restaurant, not at the FlyAway, as planned. She pulled out her cell phone and discovered the battery was dead. Damn! She'd use the restaurant's pay phone.

The realtor apologized a million times. "The current tenants have not moved out—they should have been gone three days ago—they promised—"

"Call me when it's ready." Heather slammed the phone

down. *That's great! Now what?* She stared out the window, and her old Berkeley roommate drifted into her thoughts. Didn't Linda live somewhere in the Valley? Hmm. Linda did screw her over. But damn, Heather needed a familiar face. Especially a fun one.

☙❧

Kamal jumped from his car to the blaring of horns, a wailing dog, and a woman in a walker screaming at him from the curb. He watched Heather shoot across the street and jump into a pickup. His phone rang from the car. He searched around and found it on the floor.

"What?" He stuffed a finger in his ear and heard Misha shout something about the girl. "I can't hear you," he yelled and hung up.

He hurried over to where the dog lay, a small golden-haired mutt with a sharp nose and bushy tail. Its left front leg was bent unnaturally, but there was no blood. Its howls had become plaintive whimpers. The woman with the walker yelled that there was a vet two blocks "that way" and pointed.

Kamal pulled into the Mid Valley Dog and Cat Clinic parking lot and scooped up the mutt. He would never leave a dog he'd injured abandoned in the street.

"He looks comfortable with you holding him," the perky young receptionist said. Her nametag, the shape of a dog, said Shannon. The pooch appeared normal except for a dangling rear leg. "Please follow me, and the doctor will have a look at him."

Kamal traipsed after her through a hallway that smelled like the donkey he rode to school on. Kinda nice. They entered a brightly lit examination room with a colorful wall chart that displayed a canine's internal organs.

"He's not my dog," Kamal said. "I accidentally hit him with my car. Or he hit me, I'm not sure."

"Put him down. Easy does it."

"All set." Kamal brushed his hands. "I wish the little guy a speedy recovery." He turned to leave.

"Hold on," Shannon said. "He doesn't have a collar, so you—"

Kamal raised his hands and stepped back. "Like I said, he's not my dog. Do with him whatever you want."

"No problem. I'll just need you to sign him in."

Kamal scribbled his name and left the clinic. He was on his way to the 405 freeway when his phone rang. He drew in a deep breath. "Kamal here."

"Kamal? Kamal, are you there?" a raspy voice bellowed. Misha.

"Misha, listen, it wasn't my fault that—"

"Shut up and forget the girl. She's not my problem anymore. Meet me at your house right away."

"My house? I've got a million things to do."

"A million and one. Get your ass over there. Now!"

The phone went dead.

"Bhoot-nee ka! Son-of-a-witch!" Kamal got off the freeway and turned around.

CHAPTER 61

Heather called Linda from the restaurant before ordering a hamburger and Diet Coke. She smiled, wondering if Linda still wore those jingling arm bracelets.

Heather had just paid her bill when Linda squealed up. "Omigod!" Heather shrieked. "The *same* Honda!" She opened the dented passenger door like she'd done a thousand times in Berkeley, jumped in, and they hugged.

Causing brakes to screech in both directions, Linda made a U-turn on Sherman Way. "When I heard your voice on the phone, my heart raced crazier than a sprayed roach. There in Berkeley you disappeared like a fart in a whirlwind. Nobody knew what happened to you. Campus police said you had a family emergency."

Heather had already decided she wasn't going to discuss Jim, *or* Grayson, with Linda. Linda must've told him of her pregnancy and probably got big bucks for her betrayal. That still hurt when Heather thought about it. But Linda was the big sister she never had. Was kind to her when she moved into the Berkeley house, taught her how to cook and clean, drove her around when her foot was broken, and never accepted gas money. And her laugh. Oh, her laugh could cheer anyone up. It sure felt good to Heather having a shred of normalcy back in her life. Deep down, Linda was a good person, and Heather didn't have anyone else to trust right now.

"I should have told you I was leaving," Heather said. "My mother got really sick and I was in total panic. I'm sorry."

"Is she okay now?"

"Fully recovered, thanks."

"Did you have the baby?"

"Oh…no." Heather peered out the window. "I lost it."

They rolled into the town of Sylmar, an inexpensive enclave in the San Fernando Valley. Linda rented a small one-bedroom, one-bath, 1940s bungalow there. A fat cat sat on a windowsill, watching Linda and Heather come up the walk.

Linda opened the door, and they stepped into the living room. It was so small and narrow, the cat had to back out to turn around. Linda flopped down cross-legged on a sagging couch near the front door. Her breasts and shoulders were shrouded in thick hair, and a row of turquoise bracelets covered much of her beefy forearms. A matching necklace hung from her neck.

Heather sat in a stuffed chair. And, judging from the tattered legs, it may have belonged to the cat.

They talked and drank from jug wine on a wooden coffee table propped with books that replaced a missing leg. On the end table, beneath a picture of Gandhi that Heather remembered from Linda's room in Berkeley, sat a bag of marijuana and a packet of rolling papers.

"You sounded stressed out on the phone," Linda said. "Your realtor must've really screwed up."

That wasn't the half of it. No way would Heather mention Ernie or the casino by name. "Not only do I have realtor problems," she said, "but I may have gotten myself and someone else into trouble with my old boss at the casino."

"Sounds intriguing."

"I sent the casino owner, The Man—" She rolled her eyes and made finger quotes. "—that's what they call him. Anyway, I sent him a thumb drive proving the manager was skimming from the casino."

"Whoa!"

Heather frowned. "But he might not have gotten it. At least that's what I think, because some guy tried to kidnap me at the airport."

"Kidnap? What the hell for?"

"Probably to get my backup drive."

"Where's that?"

Heather patted her jacket pocket. "I keep it with me." She didn't trust anybody. Especially Linda.

Linda offered more wine. Heather shook her head. Linda poured herself a tall one and reached for the pouch of marijuana. While Linda rolled a joint, Heather phoned the airlines and told them to deliver her luggage to Linda's house.

"What are your plans?" Linda asked.

"I'll stay in a motel tonight, stop by my new job tomorrow. Pick up a company car and decide where to stay until my house is ready."

"There's a Holiday Inn Express in North Hollywood not far away. I'll take you later. I'd invite you to crash here, but the only place to sleep would be Barney's bed here on the couch." She nodded toward the cat in the window, its eyes on Heather. "That's him. He's my lookout, except when he's eating stamps or toilet paper. He ate tinsel off the Christmas tree once. I was hoping to use the fur balls to scrub pots."

She offered the joint to Heather, who waved no.

"Did you ever get your social work license?"

"Never got my master's. Right now, I'm an out-of-work physical therapist. A pygmy with water on the brain accused me of trying to molest some bitch client who's crazier than a shithouse rat. Eventually, when I can afford it, I'll return to Berkeley for my master's. Right now I'm about as rich as I am skinny. My next paycheck goes toward a car battery." Heather got up. "Bathroom?"

તડ૦

Linda's eyes found their way to Heather's purse on the chair. She glanced at the bathroom door and tapped a red-and-blue-striped fingernail against a front tooth. Untangling her legs, she darted to the purse and pawed around inside, then stopped and rubbed an earlobe. She shrugged and started to close the flap, but noticed a slip of paper in a side pocket. She glanced at the bathroom door and pulled out a pay stub. *Lucky Star Casino, Atlantic City.* She returned it, closed the purse, and scooted back into her chair.

CHAPTER 62

Kamal felt jittery on the drive home to meet Misha. They had only met at Kamal's house once, when Misha wanted him to hide guns. Misha's voice had that same tenseness. It made Kamal wish his financial investments hadn't taken a dive. He would have been out of this business by now.

He turned off the freeway at Sepulveda Boulevard into a section of the Valley called Studio City. It was an older, tree-lined neighborhood of small, well-maintained houses. He arrived to find Misha's car in the driveway, so Kamal had to park curbside. Misha was trudging up to the front porch in his two-inch elevator shoes, plaid coat, and carrying a silver briefcase. They stepped inside and Kamal punched numbers into the security pad to deactivate the alarm. They passed through the living room and into the dining area.

"What's the deal with the Jersey guys?" Kamal asked.

Misha swung the briefcase onto the table with a grunt and a thud. "They missed their connecting flight in Chicago."

"What'd they want the girl for?"

"She stole money from their casino. They'll catch her ass, cut her tongue out, and stuff it down her throat. After that they'll get tough with her."

Kamal eyed the briefcase.

Misha gave it a tap. "I want you to nurse this baby for a while." His tone was casual. "I'm leaving town for a few days."

"Where you going?"

Misha's lips curled down. "What the fuck's it to you? Just

take care of my briefcase. I don't want it lying around."

"What's in it?" Kamal asked, knowing Misha wouldn't like that question either.

Misha waved that one aside. "Your house has a security system, and I know my documents will be in good hands. Give me a key and change your code to nine-one-one, in case you're not here and I want it."

Documents, my ass. Kamal didn't like the idea of being responsible for a briefcase probably crammed with cash. "Don't worry. I'll hide it in the hall closet and guard it with my life."

Misha's eyes locked onto Kamal's like sabers. "And don't you forget it."

CHAPTER 63

Linda's brain had calculated sums. Large sums. After dinner, she dropped Heather off at the North Holly-wood Holiday Inn Express Motel and returned home. She called information, got a number, and dialed.

"Lucky Star Casino, how may I direct your call?"

"You got a manager there?" Linda asked. "Get him on the line."

After two rings, a voice picked up. It sounded like sand in bearings. "Ernie Oz, what can I do for you?"

"Are you the manager?"

"That's right."

"A little bird told me you were looking for something."

A few seconds of silence. "Who's this?"

"It tweeted zeros and ones."

"What the hell you talkin' about?"

"You know what I'm talking about, Ernie."

There was a long pause. "Do you have it?"

"No, but we both know who does and that she's in LA. It'll cost you twenty big ones, Ernie."

"For what?"

"Her location."

"Fuck you. You're crazy."

"Twenty thousand or I hang up."

Another pause. "Ten thou. Now where the fuck is she?"

"Not so fast, Ernie. There's details."

"Such as?"

"She's in a motel. I don't know which room, but if you're there bright and early in the morning, you'll see her come out.

I'm sure if you ask nicely she'll hand over what you want."

"Give me the damn name and address."

"Don't get your pants on fire, Ernie. There'll be no rough stuff. You get your—"

"Okay, okay, where's the fucking motel?"

"You're not hearing me, Ernie."

"All right—she won't get hurt."

"At midnight tonight, have someone leave the money with the cashier at Denny's coffee shop on Sepulveda Boulevard in Sylmar. She'll go by the name Beth. In return, she'll give you the name and address of the motel. Now Ernie, if Heather gets hurt, I call The Man and tattle about your dirty little secret. Do we have a deal?"

"My assistant, Marcus, will be there." He hung up.

℃℃℃

Linda arrived at the motel the next morning at five-fifty. It had rained during the night, and steam rose from the motel's second-story roof. Thirty-two rooms were laid out in an L shape. She parked across the street with a view of the near empty parking lot. At six-ten, a beige Buick Regal splashed onto the lot and backed into a stall from where every room was visible.

Linda made out two figures inside the Buick, which did not make her happy. Ernie had mentioned only one guy, Marcus. Now the three of them were all waiting to find out which room Heather had holed herself up in.

Linda had checked with her friend at Denny's, earlier that morning. Marcus had made the drop, but she didn't trust him to forgive Heather for the inconvenience. No matter how much Linda needed the money, she didn't want Heather to get hurt. Ernie had better stick to the deal. She lit a cigarette and removed the Colt .45 from her purse. She set it on the passenger seat, took a lethal drag from her cigarette, and crossed her fingers.

CHAPTER 64

Heather awoke in Room 116 at six-thirty with an after-taste of jug wine in her mouth. She'd take a shower before going to the front desk for toothpaste.

She slipped into the same jeans and the same long-sleeved top and tennis shoes she'd worn the day before. Stepping outside, she crossed her arms and looked up at gray clouds draped low over the motel like a ragged blanket. The acrid smell of damp asphalt reminded her of the church parking lot back home where she and her mother had run a monthly rummage sale. She patted her jeans pockets to check for her room key and closed the door.

From her first-floor room at the far end of the motel, she cut across the parking lot and entered the office. Linda was coming to pick her up in a couple hours for breakfast, so she ignored the assortment of pastries, approached the desk, and requested a small packet of toiletries. She stuck a banana into her jeans pocket and headed back to her room.

⋯

Linda's heart banged so hard she could almost hear it as she watched Heather leave her room, go into the office, and then head across the parking lot again. The two men got out of the car and crouched beside it. *What the hell are they doing?* She threw her cigarette out the window.

Heather reached her door, pulled out the banana, and fished for her room key. The men took off running. Heather opened the door, and the lead man charged toward her, raised his foot, and smashed it into her back, hurling her into the room. Both men followed, and the door slammed shut.

❧❦❧

Heather found herself sprawled on the floor opposite the bed with what felt like a broken back. And she couldn't breathe. She opened and closed her mouth like a fish. Raspy rattling sounds came out her throat, but nothing flowed the other way—like air.

"Where's the fucking thumb drive, you little bitch?" a muffled voice snarled.

She couldn't move or talk but made out two blurry figures. A hand gripped her arm and yanked her to her knees. Her head bobbed violently as gulps of air rushed into her lungs.

"Where is it?" demanded the voice, cranking up the snarl.

Her breathing returned, but she couldn't see the man's face, though she recognized his husky voice. It was Marcus, Ernie's assistant.

The faint light through the curtains allowed her to recognize Clarence, Ernie's head of security. He had cold black eyes and knew how to follow orders. He held a gun at his side.

Marcus yanked her to her toes. His eyes tore into her like claws. "Quit stalling, cunt," he hissed. "I *want* the fucking drive!"

He shook her like a cat shakes a mouse.

"It's—it's in my jacket," she gasped.

Marcus dropped her and she collapsed as if her knees were hinged. He crossed the room and got the drive, then nodded to Clarence. "Do it now."

Clarence looked at Heather, his eyes unsure.

"Goddammit, Clarence, shoot!"

Clarence turned back to Heather, his eyes colder now. He raised the gun.

The door flew open with a splintering *crack* and crashed against the wall. Linda stood in the doorway, legs spread, arms extended. Both hands gripped her larger-than-life pistol.

"Drop the gun, asshole. Now!" she yelled in a voice

Heather had never heard. The room grew absolutely still. "This is a gun, jerk off," Linda said coolly, stepping into the room. "It goes boom-boom, and guys fall down. Wanna see?"

"Shoot her!" Marcus yelled.

Before Clarence could swing his gun around, two bullets found his chest. He jolted back and slammed to the floor. Marcus, standing near Linda, tried to slap the gun but missed. He caught the next two bullets, the first in the chest, second in the crotch.

"Let's get out of here," Linda cried. "Go, go!"

Heather snatched the thumb drive from the floor, grabbed her purse and jacket, and followed Linda through the door.

CHAPTER 65

The eleven-thirty newscast ended and Grayson switched off the TV. Jim had spent the last month living with him and practicing. The Global tournament was fast approaching, and Jim was acting like a goddamn irresponsible teenager. Uncommunicative, secretive—and he was smoking and drinking.

Grayson grabbed his keys and coat. He pulled into D'Raymond's parking lot next to Jim's car. The days of dragging him from restaurants, as he did in Berkeley, were gone forever. To help Jim now, he had to gain his trust.

Joe greeted Grayson with his usual big smile. "So glad to see you, my friend." His face turned grave as he added softly, "I've been driving Jim home in his car the last few nights. He's been tossing down more than just a few beers."

"Thanks, Joe." Grayson squeezed the man's shoulder and paced into the bar.

Jim was talking with Carlos, his old college golfing buddy and would-be rollerblade instructor, whom Grayson had met in Berkeley. He approached them with a warm smile and extended his hand. "Carlos, how's the world treating you?" Grayson asked, laying his other hand on Jim's shoulder.

"I'm good, Mr. Bolt. How are you?"

"Great, just great. Call me Grayson."

The bartender dropped by. "Pour me one of those," Grayson said, pointing to the men's beers. "You boys ready for another?"

"I'm good, Grayson," Carlos said.

Jim gazed into his half full glass. "I'm cap'd on, Daddy-o."

Grayson slid onto a stool. "Carlos, you're a long way from Berkeley."

"I live in New York now. Advertising. Love it, but it doesn't leave much time for golf. Can't wait to see Jim play in the Global again."

"Yo!" Jim howled. "Maybe I'll even complete all four rounds. Ha, ha."

Grayson tensed.

"Dad, did you know that Carlos went all the way through high school as an illegal alien?"

Carlos sipped his beer, face expressionless.

"He sneaked across the Mexican border with his parents and two sisters." Jim shook Carlos's arm. "How old were you? Three, four?"

"Six," Carlos said meekly.

"Six!" Jim echoed loudly.

"That says a lot for your parents," Grayson added quickly. "Wanting to make a better life for you and your sisters. That's admirable."

"He's legal now." Jim shook Carlos's arm again. "Aren't you, ol' buddy-boy? A certified American." He slid off his stool. "Gotta drain the snake."

"You okay, Carlos?" Grayson asked.

"He's just drunk."

"Was he like this in Berkeley?"

"God no. He never even drank." Carlos shook his head. "He's different."

"How do you mean?"

"We used to talk about everything. Golf. Girls. Stuff you'd only tell your best friend. Now he acts weird and tells jokes. He seems, I don't know…lost."

Two men in T-shirts were drinking at the end of the bar. The one wearing a Jets baseball cap hollered to Grayson, "Me and my friend have a disagreement. He says that guy who just left is Jim Bolt, the golfer. I bet him ten bucks he's not."

"You made a bad bet."

Carlos looked at his watch. "I've gotta run." He stood. "Tell Jim I'll catch up with him later."

Jim returned and flopped onto his stool. "I saw Carlos on the way out." He peered into his glass. "I know you want me to talk, Dad, but I'm not ready." He picked up his glass and swirled the beer. "You've probably lost confidence in me. But…well, fuck it!" He downed the rest of his drink.

"Hey, Bolt." It was the guy in the baseball cap. "My friend says you'll be playing in the Global. You got the balls not to quit this time?"

Jim bolted from the stool and Grayson grabbed his arm. "Jim, I'll handle this." He stepped over to the man. "You like to bet, don't you, big mouth? Here's a bet for you." He yanked out his wallet and slapped some bills on the bar. "Five-hundred says Bolt wins the Global."

"Whoa!" The man put up his hands. "A little steep, old man."

"Not for you." Grayson pushed the bills toward the man. "I'm laying five-hundred-to-one odds." Grayson looked to Joe, who stood near. "Hold the bet, Joe." He gestured to Jim. "Let's go home."

In the car, Jim turned to Grayson, eyes filled with uncertainty. "I'm trying, Dad. This new life is hard. Sometimes I wish Costanzo would put a bullet through my head."

An icy finger touched Grayson's heart, making it hard to breathe. "Don't ever wish that," he told his son, clutching his shoulder. "I don't know what you're going through, but I know it's hard. And I know we'll get through it. Together."

The words seemed to comfort Jim, but Grayson's sense of cold dread haunted him all the way home.

CHAPTER 66

W hat's the matter, sweet pea?" Linda said. "Aren't ya hungry?" She sat scarfing down a Denny's Grand Slam breakfast as casually as if she'd just shot a dollar in a slot machine instead of two men.

Heather pushed her plate aside and winced. Her back. She had no idea what had hit her. "How can you eat?" she whispered and leaned in close. "You just killed two people."

Linda thoroughly chewed and swallowed. "Listen, my stomach's like a fucking jumping bean right now. I've never killed anyone before, and if I'm not careful, I might someday feel guilt over those prick bastards." She tore off a chunk of Heather's toast. "Besides, it looked to me like it was either you or them."

A waitress came by and Linda touched her arm. "Honey, we'll take two coffees, black, strong, and made this year."

The waitress left.

"Maybe it was me or them," Heather said. "But—" She noticed a blood splatter on her sleeve and dabbed at it with an ice cube from her water glass. The waitress plopped two coffees onto the table and didn't appear to mind the splashes. "It just seems like we should be doing something more than eating breakfast. Won't the police be searching for us? Maybe we should call them."

Linda sopped up the last of her egg yolk with the last of Heather's toast. "Yeah," she said, "when you find a woodpecker in the salt shaker."

"Huh?"

Linda's eyes fixed on Heather's plate. "If you don't want

that bacon, I'll take it off your hands." She reached for it.

Heather's jaw clenched. "Why shouldn't we call them?"

Linda bit into the bacon. "The police will figure out they're New Jersey gangsters. They don't know who you are." She glanced at Heather and cocked a thick black eyebrow. "I assume you gave a phony name and paid cash at the motel."

"Yes, thank God." She did leave her fingerprints in the room, but since she had no record, it shouldn't matter.

"So look at it this way, two bad guys are dead."

"But there's more bad guys. The casino manager and Kamal—the guy from the airport. Plus, whoever called Kamal when he was driving me. " She nibbled crumbs of toast while Linda sipped coffee. "How do you think they found me?"

"Who the hell knows? These days anything's possible. Maybe they tracked your cell phone. Ever think of that?"

"The battery's dead, and the charger's in my luggage."

Linda wiped her mouth. "The thing to remember is this. When this hotshot, The Man, gets your letter explaining how your boss ripped off his casino, your problems are over."

"*If* he gets the letter." Heather sighed and thought of poor Sam. Ernie must've gotten to him or else his thugs wouldn't have known about the backup copy on the thumb drive. She felt like crying.

Linda crumpled her napkin. "Let's go."

They got up. "By the way," Heather said, "how did you happen to come by the motel so early?"

"Couldn't sleep and worried about you. Lucky, huh?" Linda grabbed the check and handed it to Heather. "Relax, you couldn't be safer in your mother's arms. Go play poker, win your gold bracelet, and forget this shit. Meanwhile, I've got to take Barney to the vet. He's probably clogged up with fur balls again."

They left, and Linda dropped Heather off at Van Nuys Lexus, where she'd start work the next day as accounts manager. She desperately hoped things would be calmer from now on, but she wasn't sure if that would be the case.

✐✐✐

After Heather visited her new office and completed paper-work, the manager gave her keys to a company car: a green Lexus, loaded with extras. She slid in, punched Crowne Plaza Hotel into the car's GPS, and she was off. The Commerce Casino was located in the hotel.

In less than thirty minutes, she handed her car keys to the hotel valet, checked in, bought a few clothes in a woman's shop, and called Sam from a pay phone.

"Where have you been?" came Sam's whiny voice. "I've been leaving messages on your phone. Never mind, we have a problem."

"You mailed the envelope to The Man, right, Sam?" She held her breath.

"That's just it, Ernie and Marcus got to me before I mailed it and—and holy crap, Heather, I had to give it to them."

She let her breath out so slowly it hung on her lip.

"They made me, and I had to tell them where you went. I'm sorry, Heather, but—"

"What else, Sam? What else did you tell them?"

"Well, I—I told them you had a backup drive."

Heather put a hand to her forehead. Exactly as she'd feared. She was silent a long time while her top teeth nibbled at her bottom lip. Maybe she could buy some time before Ernie sent someone else after her. "That's okay, Sam. They'll ask you if I called. Tell them yes, and that I gave the backup drive to Marcus and Clarence."

"Okay…I guess."

"I'll be in touch tomorrow."

CHAPTER 67

Heather dragged herself to her room and soaked her throbbing back in the bathtub, wondering if Ernie would believe she gave his two thugs the backup drive. Maybe, at least until he found out they were dead.

Only one person knew she was staying at the Holiday Inn Express. Linda. Who just happened to show up at exactly the right time—and with a gun. No way would Heather tell Linda where she was now.

She stepped from the tub with a plan. She'd call Sam tomorrow and get the address of The Man. Then she'd send the drive to him by overnight delivery. It was now time to put Marcus and Clarence out of her mind and stop worrying about the police. They couldn't trace her. *As for Linda, I'll deal with her when I pick up my luggage.*

She put on red lipstick, makeup, and dressed in her new fleece V-neck sweater and corduroy pants. She grabbed her purse, looked in the mirror, and took a deep breath. "Okay, California, deal 'em."

She sauntered downstairs to the chatter of the brightly lit casino, stopped at the raised entrance, and surveyed the largest gaming room she'd ever seen. The card propped on the table in her room had said the casino had three rooms with two hundred tables offering a dozen games, including Hold'em, 7-Card Stud, Razz, Pan, even Mexican Poker.

No tournaments were going on, only cash games. She stocked up on chips and grabbed a seat at a Texas Hold'em table. She had three days to prove to herself she really was good enough to win the Vegas World Series of Poker. Each player received two cards face down. Then five communal cards were dealt face up. Four betting rounds and the player with the five best cards won the hand. Heather's cards were cold for the first hour, so she kept throwing away bad hands, saving her money, knowing that, in time, cards improve.

There were two empty seats at the table, and a plump guy with a Yankee baseball cap slid in next to her. He took an ivory toothpick from his mouth, put it into a silver case, and slapped five hundred dollars onto the table. "I'll start with my usual, Oscar," he told the dealer.

Oscar slid him chips. "Good luck, Chief."

Chief! Chief of what? Police? Heather wanted to run away, but that would look suspicious. She told herself to calm down. He looked old enough to be retired, and maybe he was a fire chief.

The guy did well his first two hands. "The chief wins again," the dealer announced.

Heather watched him rake in chips and began analyzing his play.

"When ya got'em, bet'em," he said with a laugh.

After watching him a few more hands, Heather smiled to herself. She'd figured him out.

Three hands later, she got the chance she was waiting for. She was dealt two tens, face down. During the next three betting rounds, five communal cards were dealt face up— three fives, a nine, and a four. Everyone folded except Heather and the chief.

With her two tens and the communal three fives, Heather had a full house. For the chief to beat her, he had to have two of the same face cards, or the forth five.

She tossed a huge stack of chips into the pot. "Raise."

The chief peeked at his cards. He turned to Heather with a poker face. She didn't have a poker face, so she smiled back. He looked at his chips, counted out a large stack, hesitated, then turned again to Heather. This time he smiled, showing a nice set of white teeth. He shoved the chips into the pot. "Re-raise."

For a mid-limit poker game there was a hell of a lot of

money on the line. Heather peeked at her cards and then reached for her chips.

"And another re-raise," she said with the confidence of a winner—or the boldness of a bluffer—and pushed in her remaining chips.

The chief called.

She flipped over her tens. The dealer announced, "Full house, fives full of tens."

The chief flashed a half grin and threw his cards away face down. "The lady wins."

Heather scooped up her chips, and the chief leaned over. "Congratulations, young lady. You played that hand with consummate skill."

"We all get lucky sometimes."

"True, but you were more than lucky."

"If you're going to insist on complimenting me, I guess I'll have to be a lady and gracefully accept." She extended her hand. "Heather Morrison, Chief. Nice to meet you."

"Nice to meet you too, Heather. Would you be offended if an old man offered to buy you a cup of coffee?"

Heather shot him a thoughtful glance. His round face and deep green eyes looked friendly, but not too friendly. "I guess not," she said and gathered her chips. "But winner buys."

They strolled to a snack area, got coffee, and sat at a table. "Why do they call you chief?" she asked. "You don't look like an Indian chief. Were you a fire chief?" She took a sip of coffee.

"Police chief. Now that I'm retired, I play a lot of poker instead of cops and robbers, but the name stuck anyway." He sipped his coffee. "How about you?"

"I've been working in accounting." With all that had been happening, Heather wasn't keen on giving too much of her life story to anyone she just met and certainly not to a retired cop.

"That's a solid profession. No family?"

"They're back in Ireland. They'll be moving out here with me soon."

The chief looked at his watch. "Time for me to be going." He stood. "You know, you've got a real talent at poker. You should think about entering the World Series of Poker Tournament in Vegas this weekend. You might do very well."

"Thanks, Chief. I'll consider that."

⍣

Chief Foley left the casino and drove thirty minutes to his apartment at the Park La Brea Towers in the heart of Hollywood. He poured a glass of milk, pulled out his phone, and dialed.

"Grayson. Foley here. I found her."

"Where, and what can you tell me?"

"At the Commerce Casino. She's one hell of a poker player. Got into me for better than four hundred bucks."

"How'd you recognize her?"

"She looked just like her tennis picture on the link you sent. I guess your buddy Chauffeur was right. How'd he know she was in LA?"

"How the hell does he know anything? Telling me was his way of letting me know that his boss hadn't forgotten me. Did you talk to her?"

"We had coffee together."

"Did she mention Jim?"

"No, and she didn't disclose much about herself."

"Try to see more of her, will you? And if she even hints at contacting Jim, let me know. That's all he'd need, more distractions. He's got serious depression and problems with concentration. The other day, he froze in the middle of his back swing. When I called his name, he mumbled something like, 'Sorry, Jessie,' whatever the hell that means."

"If he's got shit bottled up, that can't be good. You don't think his seeing Heather might help him snap out of it?"

"Are you *nuts*? Then he'll never get his mind back on golf.

"Did you tell him about Costanzo?"

"He knows, and I promised him he has nothing to worry about."

"That's nice, but what if he loses?"

There was a long moment of silence. "That's something neither you or Jim need to worry about."

CHAPTER 68

Kamal had stashed Misha's briefcase under towels and shit up in his hall closet. He'd tried working the three-ring combination, but the sucker was not only sturdy, but tamper-proof.

It must be crammed with money, but why'd Misha leave it with him? Something had to have the midget running scared. Maybe it was connected with the soon-to-be-dead, after losing her tongue, Jersey girl.

His cell phone rang. "Hello."

"Is this Kamal?"

Sounded like that chick at the vet. "Yeah, it's me."

"I'm Shannon from the Mid Valley Dog and Cat Clinic. I'm calling to say your dog's ready to be picked up."

She must've looked up his number. "Hey, rewind our last conversation. He's not my dog."

"But you brought him in," she whined.

"And gave him to you. Goodbye."

"Wait! He's a really nice dog, a puppy, and if you don't take him the county will put him to sleep."

"Give him to the pound. I'm sure they have lots of stray dogs."

"But the pound is full. You're an Indian, right? Not the bows and arrow kind, but like Apu. You know, The Simpsons."

Kamal stifled a chuckle. "What if I am?"

"Hindus believe all life is sacred. Plus, by taking the dog, you'll have good karma."

He thought a minute. In his line of work, he could use good

karma. Besides, thinking about it, he'd like having a dog. Growing up poor in India, he had played with friendly street mutts but never dreamed of owning one. Never owned much of anything. "He's a nice dog, you say?"

Thirty minutes later, he rolled into the vet's parking lot, and a woman in a piece of shit Honda cut him off and got the last good spot. He parked in back and went inside.

"Hi, Apu," Shannon said, from behind the counter. She winked. "Just kidding. Lucky is getting his shots right now. Just to be safe." She leaned close to the window and whispered, "Don't worry, I'm not charging you."

"How did you know the dog's name?"

"Oh, I named him. He's lucky that you're his new master. Have a seat. It won't be long."

He sat across from the bitch that stole his parking place. She was flipping through a magazine and sounding like she was shaking a can of pennies. Silver and turquoise bracelets covered both her arms. At her feet was a cat in a crate.

"Having a nice day?" Kamal asked.

Her gaze rose from the magazine then lowered. "No complaints."

"I would think not since you took my parking spot."

She looked up at him and flashed an exaggerated smile. On and off, then she put her nose back in the magazine.

Kamal's jaw tightened. He snatched a pamphlet from the end table. "*Bitch.*"

She tossed her magazine onto the table and looked down at her cat. "Did you hear that, Barney? Apu's all sad that he didn't get to park where he wanted."

"Correction, Barney," Kamal said leaning toward the cat. "Not sad—pissed, because the parking spot was rightfully mine. I was there first."

An attendant came out and went to the woman. "I'll take Barney now." She picked up his crate and left.

The cat lady said to Kamal, "Sounds like you're getting a new dog. A pet is the best cure for feeling pissed. Know anything about caring for dogs?"

Kamal's tension slipped away. He was just as happy to stop

hassling with the woman. "What's to know? You feed them and watch them run around."

"Dogs aren't goldfish. They need training. And that goes double for their owners."

"So *I* need training?"

"Dogs are like children. They require rules and limits. Without them, they can make life hell for their owners."

"Are you a dog psychologist or something?"

"I used to teach dog training. You should take a class."

"Sounds like a good idea, but I don't have time to run around taking classes."

"Maybe you don't have to. Where do you live?"

"Studio city."

"Tell you what, I'll come to your home for private lessons. A hundred bucks a pop. If after the third lesson you don't feel it was worth it, you'll get your money back."

Kamal thought it over a moment. Why not? "Okay, you've got a deal."

CHAPTER 69

The guy's face ended in a point like the bottom half of the ace of diamonds. A cowboy hat sat low on his forehead, and he gave it a tug. He dropped his head low enough for his eyelashes to brush the spots off his cards. His gnarly hands reached down, cupped his two cards, and his right thumb lifted both corners. He sucked air between his teeth and released the cards with a snap. Looking at Heather, he pulled back his lips in a sly grin. "Raise." With that, he tossed a stack of chips into the pot. "That's a mighty big pot, young lady."

Heather was feeling pleased—super pleased. "I'm happy you did that, cowboy." She threw in a stack of chips. "Call." Her eyes flashed as she threw him a daring Irish smile.

The guy flipped over his cards. "Two pair."

"Sevens over fours," the dealer announced.

Heather shook her head. "Tsk, tsk, tsk." She turned over jacks and eights. "Not enough."

This was Heather's second day at the Commerce Casino, warming up for the Vegas tournament, and she was totally hyped. She was winning so much, it was hard not to get up and do a happy dance right there.

While raking in her chips, Chief Foley's voice came up from behind her. "Hello, Heather."

"Oh, hi, Chief." She was surprised, but kind of glad to see him. A familiar face was always welcome…well, almost always.

"When that cowboy turned over his low two pair, I knew you had him. Low pairs usually lose."

"That's what I had him on," Heather said.

"I'm heading to the steakhouse for dinner. Care to join me?"

Having come straight here from work, Heather liked the idea of eating at a nice restaurant. Plus, she liked Chief Foley's fatherly, gentle eyes. She had grown up without a dad and had a sense that the chief would have been a good one. "Sure, but we split the check."

They sat down, and the chief removed his Yankee cap, revealing a shiny head that reflected the bright lights. The waitress brought water and left menus.

Chief Foley stared into his glass and stirred an ice cube with his finger. "You read players very well."

Heather lowered her head and peered up into his eyes with a wily smile. "Including you?"

He flashed a wry smile back. "When you beat me with your tens full—that was good."

She sipped her water and nodded.

"What'd you put me on?"

She set down her glass. "Nines. Maybe eights."

Heather knew how to read tells—unconscious clues a lot of poker players gave off, despite trying to hide behind dark glasses, big hats, smiles, and frowns.

The waitress appeared, pen and pad in hand. "Give us a minute," Chief Foley said. He grabbed his water, downed a gulp, and ran the back of his hand across his lips. He leaned in. "Nines. How'd you know?"

Heather blushed and tried to cover her embarrassment with a cough. "Let's just say, I knew you knew I had you beat, and that you were bluffing."

Chief Foley rubbed his chin. "But you won't tell me how you knew?"

"Maybe someday."

"Fair enough," he said with a grin. "You really should enter the Vegas tournament. I think a gold bracelet would go nicely with that pretty diamond one." The chief nodded toward her wrist.

Heather glanced at Jim's birthday gift, and sadness stabbed

her heart. She forced a smile. "Diamonds *and* gold are a girl's best friend."

⋯

After dinner, Heather found a phone booth in the lobby and called Sam.

"Sam, it's Heather. What's going on?"

"How come you don't answer your phone?"

"I still don't have my charger. Did Ernie buy the story about Marcus and Clarence?"

"That's why I've been trying to reach you."

Sam stopped talking, and Heather heard muffled sounds. A drawling voice dripped over the line. "Heather, this is Ernie. I think we can work this out so nobody gets hurt—" He must have caught the sound of Heather's quick intake of breath. "Heather, are you listening?"

"I'm here."

"Good. I want you to know that no harm will come to either you or Sam." His tone was syrupy. "But you need to get on a plane, right now, bring me the drive, and we'll forget this whole thing ever happened."

"And if I don't?"

"I'll let Sam tell you."

More muffled sounds, then Sam came back on the line. "Heather," he began, his voice weak. "If Ernie doesn't get the drive before—" He whimpered like a sick dog.

"Go on, Sam, before what?"

"Before tomorrow morning—"

Heather listened as Sam took in a series of ragged breaths.

"He'll—he'll kill my sister's children." The line filled with clatter.

"Sam? Sam!"

The phone clicked. Heather dropped the receiver, and it dangled by its cord. "Oh, God, what have I done?"

CHAPTER 70

It was half-past five, and Kamal was thirty minutes late when he pulled into his driveway. With Misha being off somewhere, Kamal not only had his own fieldwork to do—collecting credit card information, and such, from gardeners and hospital workers—but was expected to supervise the office staff who sorted and logged the material.

Linda was sitting on his front porch smoking a cigarette, her crappy looking car parked in front.

"Sorry I'm late," he said, coming up the walk and mounting the porch. "Was hung up at the office."

With all the jewelry hanging from her body, she looked like a round-faced gypsy carrying extra pounds. Back home, gypsies sold needles and broomsticks on the corner.

"No problem," she said and stood up holding a cigarette and paper bag.

He unlocked the door and opened it. "No smoking in the house."

She flicked the cigarette onto the sidewalk, and they went inside. He tapped a code into the alarm pad on the wall. Lucky came charging up to them and slid on the hardwood floor. A rear leg was bandaged.

Kamal got on his knees and ruffled the dog's fur.

Linda took out a leash and collar from her bag. She handed Kamal the collar. "Here, he needs this."

He examined it. "Cool. Says his name." He put it on the dog.

"That and the leash cost twenty bucks. You can pay me later. Let's get to work."

They went out to the back yard, and Linda taught Kamal

how to hold the leash and walk the dog. Kamal padded around, stopping and starting with Lucky at his left side. Eventually, the dog learned to walk when Kamal walked, and sit when Kamal stopped.

"Practice doing that twice a day," Linda said. "Next time you'll learn some off-leash commands. Mind if I use your bathroom before I go?"

They all went inside, and Kamal felt good about what he had accomplished with Lucky. He placed a hundred and twenty bucks on the kitchen counter, and when Linda came out of the bathroom, she picked it up. "I like your taste in music."

"Oh, yeah, my Eminem poster."

"I saw him at the Rose Bowl. Front row, actually."

"No shit!"

"Interesting story, but some other time." She put the money in her purse. "You've got my number for when you're ready for another lesson. She picked up a business card from a stack on the counter. *Redistributions Unlimited.* "Is this yours?"

"Yeah, take it. I'm usually out on calls, so the cell number's the one to use."

She left, and, a couple minutes later, a knock came at the door. It was her again.

"My damn battery's dead. I've got a charger in the trunk. If you have an extension cord, and wouldn't mind, I'd like to give it a quick boost."

"No problem." They hooked everything up and headed back up the walk.

"I can wait out here on the porch," she said.

It would be rude to make her do that. Besides, she's not so bad after all. "No, come in and be comfortable."

They went into the living room. "Have a seat," he said. "Care for a brew—some wine?"

She sat on the couch. "My grandmother always said, develop good habits and stick with them. I've applied that principal to wine. Red if you've got it."

He left, and when he returned, Linda was opening a window. "I hope you don't mind," she said, "but the place is stuffy."

"I like it stuffy, but that's okay." It wasn't the stuffiness he liked, but the security that came with it. Having Misha's briefcase around, he couldn't be too careful. He handed over her wine, and they sat down, Kamal in a chair, holding a Heineken.

She scanned the room. "Nice place you've got. Nice set of wheels, too. You're a young guy. What do you do in the office to rake in the big bucks?"

He straightened in his chair. "Like my card says, redistribution. It's technical shit no one understands." The real answer was that he was a criminal, and although he felt ashamed of it, the money was good, and he would retire soon and return to school. Then do something respectable and make his father happy. He took a guzzle of beer. "So, tell me how you got front row Eminem tickets."

She began clawing through her purse. "I was living in the Bay Area and had a client who knew the stage manager of the show." She pulled out a joint and, ignoring the house rule about no smoking inside, she lit up. "I might as well tell you," her voice was low while holding in smoke, "I was going to Berkeley at the time and doing phone sex on the side." She jabbed her finger toward Lucky. "And dog training." She exhaled.

"What the hell is phone sex?" he said, chuckling, and dashed for an ashtray. He set it on the table, and she offered him the reefer. He thought a minute. He hadn't smoked marijuana in years. Why not? He took a drag.

"Professional phone sex is when girls talk dirty to guys while the guys do their thing. And incidentally, it goes on in India, too. Love that place."

Kamal let out a blast of smoke and took a swig of beer. This was getting interesting. "Go on."

"One time, while talking to a client, I had Eminem playing in the background, and the client asked if I was a fan. I said I was, and he offered to exchange two front row tickets for one hour of my time."

That sounded reasonable, but Kamal really didn't know.

"That's not the end of it." She took the joint back and

sucked on it, held her breath a few seconds, then continued talking. Smoke churned among her words. "When we hooked up at the concert, he tried to give me tickets for like, thirty rows back. I told him either he gives me the tickets he promised, or the stage manager was going to hear a recording of our last session." She lifted her glass and emptied it.

"Did you really have a recording?"

She took a final hit of the marijuana and closed one eye against the smoke. "Two things my grandmother taught me that her mother taught her. How to pop a goddamn clutch and to never trust anyone you don't know." She crushed the roach in the ashtray and stood. "My battery should be charged by now."

When she left, Kamal went back inside, and feeling paranoid from the pot, he checked on Misha's briefcase up in the hall closet. Was that the safest place for it? Maybe under his mattress. No, too thick for that. Damn! He wished Misha would hurry up and take it away. He crammed a few more towels around it.

CHAPTER 71

Heather got off the plane in Atlantic City and hurried through the terminal. She stopped short when she passed a newsstand outside a gift shop and saw the headline: *TWO NEW JERSEY CASINO EMPLOYEES FOUND SHOT DEAD IN LA MOTEL.*

A tingling chill ran down her back. A reminder that even if she gave Ernie the drive, he'd kill her, just like Marcus and Clarence had tried to do in the motel. She had to find The Man and give him the drive, let him deal with Ernie and prevent the murder of Sam's nieces. She rushed outside to the taxi stand and cut her way up the queue.

"Excuse me, pardon me. Hospital. Hospital." She reached the front taxi and jumped in. The driver turned on the meter and pulled from the curb. Heather buried her head in her hands and tried to think. She had to find The Man.

The driver, an African American with her hair tied back in a red bow, glanced in the mirror. "If you're sending telepathically, I'm not receiving."

Heather shook her head. "Please, just drive." She couldn't remember if Sam had said The Man's name. "The Man, The Man," she muttered to herself.

The driver looked in the mirror with an easy laugh. "If you've got man problems, you'd best not be thinking of going back to him." She laughed again. "You've got to think of yourself, sugar. You're not the first woman to escape to Atlantic City with only a purse and a prayer."

Heather raised her head and caught the driver's friendly face in the mirror. "I was saying *The* Man, not my man." She leaned back against the seat.

The driver's reflective eyes widened. "Ooh. What do you mean, the man?"

"I'm trying to think of someone's name." She bit her lower lip.

"You mean that mob guy they call The Man?"

Heather lurched forward. "Yes! That's who. Do you know his name?"

The driver rubbed her chin. "Can't say that I do."

Heather sank back in the seat.

The driver honked her horn. "Asshole!" She looked at Heather in the mirror. "I once dropped a lift at his house. I know because he told someone on his cell phone that's who he was going to see."

Heather threw her arms across the backrest. "You went to his house?"

"All the way in Short Hills Estates."

"That's—that's wonderful. Do you remember which house?"

"You don't forget no gangster's house."

"Let's go."

"I don't think he accepts visitors, ma'am."

"That's okay. Hurry, please."

"You sure? It's nearly a hundred miles."

"I'm sure."

"Okay, it's going to cost you, and you'll have to find your own way back."

"Just get there as fast as you can."

"Okay, it'll take a while, so relax."

Heather leaned back a moment then bent forward again. "You dropped a fare there. Tell me about it."

The driver tore open a pack of Juicy Fruit gum and held it up.

Heather shook her head. "Oh, no, thanks."

The woman unwrapped a stick and rolled it into her mouth. "It was about a year ago. The fare got out, told me to wait, said he wouldn't be long." She folded the wrapper into a neat little square and tossed it out the window. "Five minutes later a guy comes out of the house, not the passenger, another guy, tall with a long face and dent in his chin." She glanced back and tapped her chin. "He hands me five hundred, says my passenger will be detained. Said I'm to take off and forget I was ever there."

Heather took a deep breath and fell back against the seat. There was no retreating. She had to save Sam's family.

CHAPTER 72

It was a good, dark night when Heather's taxi slipped into New Jersey's Short Hills Estates. Streetlights glowed, and only the soft purr of tires on asphalt could be heard. Fancy homes dated the quiet community from the stodgy 1900s. Heather guessed the owners spent fortunes remodeling their plantation-size estates, transforming drab kitchens into bright smart ones with Feng Shui alignment and Internet refrigerators.

The taxi slipped around the corner onto Woodfield Drive and stopped. The driver pointed down the block. "That's the house, on the left." It was one of the older homes. Historic colonial, all brick. In front was a bronze statue of a golfer.

"Drive by slowly." Heather put her nose to the window and thought of Jim. It was May. Every May that little spot in her heart fluttered with longing. The Global was this month. She pushed the thought from her mind. "Turn around and drive by once more."

The driver glared into her mirror.

"Please." Heather slid across the seat, rolled down her window and inhaled the sweet scent of jasmine. The taxi eased by the house again. Bordering an iron fence, a low hedge ran across the front, square as a set of dice, as though the barber came every day. The two-story house sat back about fifty feet from the street. On the left, a driveway snaked up alongside the manicured lawn with an electric gate and communications system. Large front doors of cut glass bathed in yellow light centered the house.

"I've seen enough. You can pull over."

Heather paid the cabbie, climbed out, and crossed her arms. The air felt cold and cruel. She considered using the callbox at the gate, but quickly abandoned the thought. The Man wouldn't answer, someone else would, someone who might be friends with Ernie. Someone who might *be* Ernie.

A light shone in the downstairs back corner. Maybe that was The Man's office. She padded to the darkest end of the iron fence and hesitated. Motion sensors might give her away when she jumped over and hit the ground. Or dogs could charge out. Convinced she had to get off the street and out of sight, she wrapped her hands around the cold iron bars and climbed. Positioning her feet on the upper crossbar, she jumped. She landed and crouched, still as a fear-frozen rabbit. No floodlights, no alarms, no dogs. She remained motionless, scarcely breathing. It was easy to stop breathing when you were afraid of dying. A minute passed. Everything stayed quiet except her thumping heart.

Staying low, she dashed to the corner near the lit window and pressed her back against the house. Floodlights fanned the rear patio and swimming pool. She squatted under the window and cocked an ear. Muffled men's voices were heard, then the crack of pool balls. She inched her head up and saw two men.

"Freeze!"

She flinched, and something hard nested against her spine. Blood sped through her veins like missiles.

"Hands up and turn around."

She obeyed and found herself looking at a thin, pinched-face black man holding a gun that appeared too heavy in his spindly hand. His other hand held a cell phone, and his dark watery eyes looked nervous. "Mr. Chauffeur, I caught a woman snooping outside the game room. You want me to…okay, I'll wait here."

꿍

Upstairs in The Man's office, Chauffeur hung up and signaled to him that he'd be right back. He jerked his head for Gonzo to come along.

The two lumbered down the stairs. Chauffeur said through the corner of his mouth, "It's probably the Morrison girl. A fucking bad penny if I ever saw one. Probably wants The Man to save her ass. He doesn't trust her, and I want her gone—permanently." They passed through the game room and Chauffeur quipped, "It smells like a dog's ass in here. Someone forget to put on deodorant?"

Outside, Gonzo said, "That's her. He took out his gun.

Chauffeur nodded to the guard. "Good job, Harold. Gonzo and I will take over."

"Yes, sir, Mr. Chauffeur."

Heather lowered her hands. "Please, Mr. Chauffeur, I came here—"

"Put your fucking hands back up," Gonzo said. He thrust the gun toward her.

Her hands snapped high, and she pleaded, "I have to see The Man and explain—"

"There's nothing to explain," Chauffeur said. "The money you took is going to rot because you're never going to see it again."

She gulped.

Chauffeur tossed his head for Gonzo to take her away. "I'll go tell The Man."

"Should I use the Lincoln?"

"Take the Toyota. The trunk's big enough."

❧

Heather's knees half buckled. She turned to Gonzo. "Wait! Please, let me explain. Ernie's been stealing from the casino. I have proof." Gonzo pushed her along the drive toward the back. She twisted around. "But I—I—" She wanted to yell. In fact, she had been yelling.

Gonzo told her to stop talkin' and keep walkin'. The gun stabbed painfully against her spine, which still smarted from the earlier bludgeoning in the motel. "Just follow your nose or you won't have a head to wear it on."

Her heart pounded like that of a scared kid, locked in a

closet. She stumbled toward the garage at the end of the drive. It housed several cars, including a Toyota. She had to act now or be killed. She stopped at the Toyota, whirled, and swung her purse, knocking Gonzo's gun. A shot exploded, and her purse fell to the ground. She pushed Gonzo before he could recover. He stumbled, and she dashed to the back of the Toyota.

"You little bitch," he spat. Heather weaved and bobbed, trying to stay out of Gonzo's line of fire.

"Hold up, Gonzo," Chauffeur yelled, trotting up to him.

Gonzo lowered his gun.

"Come out, Twinkle Toes," Chauffeur called. "You get your chance to talk to The Man."

Heather hesitated. Maybe it was a trick to lure her out. Still, she wouldn't survive long trying to dodge bullets either. Trembling, she stepped out of the car's shield. Chauffeur said to Gonzo, "The Man wants to find out how much she got from Ernie."

Desperate to tell her story, Heather opened her mouth to speak.

"Keep it canned!" Chauffeur ordered. "Anything you say is noise in the wrong place."

She picked up her purse and let the thugs escort her inside the house. Her mind spun. This was her one chance. She had to convince The Man of the truth. She trudged up the stairs, palms sweaty, heartbeat pounding in her ears. Gonzo opened a door, and Chauffeur shoved her inside. She caught her balance. "Listen to me. You people don't—"

"Shut up," Chauffeur ordered.

Four men rose from chairs before a large desk. Her eyes focused on the one who remained seated behind it. The others left the room, and she was pushed down onto a vacated chair. The Man's glare forced her to look away and scan the room— big and dark with table lamps and dark wood paneling, pictures of football players, golfers and—my God! Jim! She shook her head. *This can't be real.* She glanced back at The Man and tried to swallow, but her throat was parched.

The Man folded his arms. His eyes studied her with a cold stare. "I'm listening."

Heather took a breath and rubbed her hands down her thighs, smoothing her skirt. "Thank you, Mister…" What's his real name? "Um…Thank you. I've brought proof that Ernie was skimming from your casino." She reached into her purse. What she felt made her cold as an ice bucket. She pulled out a smashed thumb drive. "Oh no!" She turned her purse upside down. Among the items tumbling to the floor were one hundred dollar Commerce Casino chips, and one bullet.

The Man bounced his fingertips together. "I'm still listening."

Heather searched his face, an open book of cruelty. Holding back tears, and with several stammers, she told him about the safe, the photograph she'd taken, and the thumb drives. She explained that Ernie had told her to return the drive to him that night or he would murder Sam's nieces.

Chauffeur, sitting off to the side, smirked. "It seems you're pretty sharp with a gun."

She straightened. "Sharp with a gun?"

"Shooting people."

"What about that?" The Man said. "Those two you shot in the motel?"

"I didn't shoot them."

Chauffeur shook his head. "They didn't die from natural causes."

"They attacked me and tried to take—" She held up the smashed drive. "—and tried to take this. They were going to shoot me until…"

"Until what?" Chauffeur asked out of a crooked mouth.

"Until someone shot them."

"Who the fuck was this someone?" Chauffeur demanded.

"Never mind that," The Man said. He got up, walked around his desk, and sat with one leg draped over the corner. "Ernie gives a different version. He says you stole casino money and skipped to LA, that he sent his men there to catch you, but you shot them."

Heather jumped to her feet. "That's *not* what happened."

"Sit down!" Chauffeur spat. He turned to The Man. "Ernie wouldn't dare skim from you. He's not that fucking dumb."

"Maybe he is, maybe he isn't," The Man said and returned to his chair. He picked up a pencil and scratched his cheek with it thoughtfully. "And maybe there's a way to find out." He leveled his eyes on Heather. "You said Ernie knows you have something showing money in a secret safe in his office?"

She nodded.

"And he's expecting you to show up at the casino tonight and deliver it to him?"

She swallowed hard. "That's right."

"Chauffeur, get Ernie's ass over here. Don't say why, just make sure it's on the fucking double."

Chauffeur left the room to make the call. Twice Heather took a deep breath, about to plead her case once more to The Man, but his silence and motionless face discouraged that.

Chauffeur returned. "Ernie said he was expecting the girl to arrive any minute with his money and wanted to wait for her."

The Man smiled. "And you told him…"

"To put a fuckin' rocket in his ass and get over here."

The Man pointed at Heather then tossed his thumb toward the door. "Out."

Chauffeur led her downstairs, shoved her into a basement closet, and slammed the door. With the crisp click of the lock, she stood in total blackness. A shiver ran down the length of her body. She lurched for the door and shook the knob, gave up, and groped around until her hands found a light switch. A loud click echoed, but cold darkness remained. *Stay calm and feel around. Maybe find something to bash the door with.* She bumped into a rug rolled up and propped against a wall, then tripped over a box of what felt like ceramic tiles. There was nothing else in the room. She was doomed.

The Man was going to kill her, and all she could do was collapse to the floor. Even if he believed her, and Ernie confessed, why should he let her live? How naïve of her to expect gratitude from someone like him. She sat against the back wall, arms tight around her drawn up knees. She rocked and sobbed. Images of her family in Ireland ran through her mind. How would they ever know what happened to her? Why the hell did she have to get involved with Ernie's skimming? *My*

God! A fist-like ball of panic slammed against her chest. Sam's nieces! If she died, so would they.

A light streamed from under the door, and a fuzzy pinpoint shone through the door lock. She got to her feet, dashed to the door, and dropped to her knees. In the keyhole was a key. It was an old-fashion door lock. Her heart surged with hope. There must be a way to get that key. After desperate moments, an idea surfaced.

She felt her way over to the box of tiles, tore off the cardboard top, took it to the door, and slid it under, thankful it was thin enough to fit. She would try to push the key out of the lock and onto the cardboard. She dug into her purse's inner pocket and found a pen, but it was too thick for the keyhole. Determined, she opened the pen and removed the ink cartridge. She prodded the key gently, but the pen's point kept slipping off the key's narrow end. She pushed harder. The key flew from the lock, clinking onto the hard floor. She peered under the door. The key lay just beyond the cardboard.

"Shit!"

CHAPTER 73

Chauffeur escorted Ernie into The Man's office, right up to his desk. He pushed a wooden chair against his calves, and Ernie fell into it. Chauffeur and Gonzo sat a little behind and to each side of him.

The desk was free of clutter, except for a new thumb drive, right there near the edge.

"So, Ernie," The Man began with a faint smile that tugged at the shadowed corners of his mouth. "We haven't had a chance to discuss the problem you've been having with the help. Tell me about it?"

"Sure, Mr. Costanzo," Ernie started, his words falling over themselves. "That woman I hired, Heather Morrison, the one Chauffeur—" He nodded toward him. "—wanted me to hire. She stole money and took off to LA. But she's returning tonight with the money, and—"

"How much money?" The Man asked.

Ernie's gaze landed on the drive. His face tightened, and he flushed a little high on the cheekbones. "I don't know exactly. We haven't figured out the—" His eyes fluttered. "—the exact figure yet." He shot a look over at Chauffeur then at The Man and loosened his tie.

"About how much?" Chauffeur asked, standing behind Ernie. *What a stupid fuck.*

Ernie scraped a knuckle under his chin and spread his hands. "It's nothin', fifty—sixty grand." Trying to speak to both Chauffeur and The Man, he swiveled his head back and forth. "But don't worry," he said, his eyes settling on The Man. "It wouldn't be fair to you to—"

"I'll take care of the being-fair-to-me department," The Man said coolly.

Ernie ran a finger under his collar. "I meant I'd cover it, that's all."

The Man rose from his chair, came around the desk, picked up the drive, and pressed his butt against the desk. He loomed over Ernie and rubbed the drive between his fingers. Nothing changed in his expression. "Fifty or sixty grand, you say?"

Ernie's face was strained, and his shoes squeaked as he squirmed in his seat. "Right, fifty or sixty grand."

Gonzo and Chauffeur got up, moved to either side of The Man and leaned against the desk facing Ernie. Ernie's shoulders twitched, and the only sound was his rugged breathing.

Suddenly, his eyes went wild.

It was beautiful. They flitted from the drive to the face of each man towering over him. He gulped like he was choking down puke and began breathing in fits and starts. He leaped from his chair, spun, and charged for the door. He flung it open and ran into Harold, the guard.

"Wait, wait! Let me explain. Let me fuckin' explain—"

Gonzo and the guard each took an arm and led him out the door. His toes bounced on the floor.

"Better use the Lincoln," Chauffeur yelled. "It'll hold Ernie and the girl."

CHAPTER 74

Heather sat in the closet next to the door, back against the wall, legs stretched out, a tile from the box in her lap. She heard a door open down the hall, gripped the tile, and clambered to her feet. Footsteps approached, and she raised her only weapon above her head.

The footsteps stopped outside her door. "What the fuck should we get, cabernet or merlot?" a voice said.

"Grab one of each," another voice said.

She heard a key go into a lock across the hall and a door open.

She peeked through the keyhole, recognizing the pool players she'd seen earlier in the game room. One of them emerged from the room holding two bottles. She straightened and readied herself, heard the door lock and a brief shuffle of feet.

"You do smell like a fuckin' dog's ass."

"Fuck you. Hey, what's this key on the floor?"

Heather tensed.

"Who cares, just leave it."

Please, kick it this way, Heather prayed.

"It probably goes in that closet door over there." Footsteps approached, the key slipped into the lock, and the footsteps moved off.

Heather got to her knees. Her heart raced. She slid the cardboard back under the door and began prodding the key with her ink cartridge until it dropped with a soft thud. She withdrew the cardboard carefully from under the door, picked up the key, and unlocked her prison.

She dashed to the stairs and up to the first floor, tiptoed

along a hallway to another set of stairs leading to The Man's office, and stopped. She peeked up the staircase. The guard stood listening at The Man's door, his back to her. The foyer and front door were only a few feet ahead. The Man's door flew open with a bang. Ernie slammed into the guard and wailed. They scuffled, and she darted to the foyer. At the front door, she reached for the knob, but items on a side table caught her eye. A comb, a wallet with the Lucky Star logo, a gun, and—*car keys*. They must have made Ernie empty his pockets. She snatched the keys then slipped out the door and ran to Ernie's Cadillac.

♧♧♧

She ditched Ernie's car at the Atlantic City Airport and caught a flight back to LA, where she felt safe holing up at her hotel. She had considered going to the police, but she worried that The Man might have them in his pocket. How would she know which ones weren't dirty? In two days, she'd be leaving for the big Vegas tournament, and, in the meantime, she'd play in a small tournament at the hotel's casino.

PART IV

CHAPTER 75

The Global was less than a week away when Grayson and Jim returned to D'Raymond's. Joe greeted them with his usual hug, and they slid into their usual booth.

"I'll have my usual," Jim said to the waitress. "Beer and lasagna."

"Same here," Grayson said, "but make it scotch and soda with a twist."

They got their drinks, and Grayson rubbed the lemon along the rim of his glass, rehearsing what he wanted to say to Jim about his sullenness. There was no time left to screw around. Jim had to start facing his problems.

"I'll be straight with you, Jim. The tournament's next week, and I'm worried about your mental state."

"What the hell's wrong with it?" Jim shot back, taking a swig of beer.

"Don't get defensive. I'm just saying, your concentration isn't always there. You sometimes—"

"Don't worry about it, okay? My concentration's fine."

Grayson pursed his lips, afraid to say more. Yet, dammit, if Jim was to win the tournament, he had to focus one hundred percent. "Jim," he said. "Remember that time we went ice fishing with your mom and Troy up in Canada?"

"What about it?"

"You got upset about something."

"You mean about the fish eggs?"

Grayson nodded.

Jim took another gulp of beer. "That was silly. I was a little kid."

"You asked what those slimy things were that gushed out of the fish. I told you, and you got upset, but didn't tell me why. It turned out you felt sorry for the fish."

Jim laughed. "I was sorry for the eggs that would never become fish."

"And you were sad all afternoon. That evening you finally talked to me about it, got your feelings out and felt better."

"I hear you, Dad. Now you hear me. When I have the need to talk, I'll come to you. Okay?"

Blood rushed up Grayson's neck. He wanted to grab Jim by the shoulders, shake him, yell at him. *Your life's on the line, goddammit!* He raised his hands in surrender. "Okay. I'll leave it to you to make it out of the rough."

CHAPTER 76

Kamal stood in his kitchen preparing a meal of Naan bread, Mango Chutney, spicy chickpeas, and curry chicken to share with one of his gardeners for lunch. Kamal had always kidded Diego about his lunches that consisted of burritos, rice, and beans, but today he'd get a taste of healthy Indian food. Kamal had just bagged everything when three hard knocks came at the door.

That must be Misha. Finally! Kamal looked through the front door's peephole, and a chill went straight up his spine. Two men with the hard-bitten look of feds. Misha's briefcase! He stepped back from the door. He wouldn't answer, and they'd go away.

"Open up, Datar. We know you're in there. Your curry's stinking up the neighborhood."

Damn! He'd forgotten to close the window that Linda had opened. He unbolted the door and swung it wide. "Hey, boys. What's the occasion?"

Looking spiffy in their suits, ties, and spit-shined shoes, they flashed their FBI badges. "Grab your coat. You're taking a ride."

"Where to?"

"Don't they have movies in India?" asked a big-eared guy with a bald top. "We're going downtown."

Twenty-five minutes later, the car bounded onto the lot at 11000 Wilshire Boulevard. FBI headquarters. Fearful of saying the wrong thing and getting locked up, Kamal would admit nothing and give no information.

The agents took him into a basement office with gray walls

and a linoleum floor old enough to have had Al Capone's scuff marks.

A hand pressed him down into a metal chair in front of a gray desk with a nameplate that said *Special Agent Specter*. The man behind the nameplate had a flat broad look and a bent nose. "Mr. Datar," he said, "your boss is Misha Abramson, is he not?"

"What if he is?"

"Well, he seems to have disappeared, and we'd like to know where to."

"I can't help you." And that was the truth. Kamal stood up. "Can I go now?"

"Sit down." Specter leaned back in his squeaky government gray chair. "Ever hear of a guy in your outfit named Snake?"

Kamal knew of him. Worked for Misha years ago. Had a wife with a wonderful singing voice. Poor Snake. "Never heard of him."

"He'd still be enjoying a long life in Hawaii right now if he'd cooperated with us. Do you know how he died?"

"Since I never heard of him, I guess not."

"He was shot between the eyes. Know what happened to his wife?"

Kamal shrugged. "Never heard of her, either." And he really hadn't.

"She was stripped naked, tied, and force-fed fire ants through her facial orifices. She died when they chewed on her brain. But that's not all. The family plot included their five-year-old-daughter."

Bile crept into Kamal's throat.

"All Snake had to do to prevent that was answer the same questions I'll ask you."

"I have nothing to say. Either charge me with something, or drive me back home."

Specter's phone buzzed. He picked up. "Yeah?…I'll be right there." He got up and tossed an envelope into Kamal's lap. "Sit tight and enjoy the pictures."

This was Kamal's chance in case Specter came up with a search warrant of his house. Misha didn't trust any of the office staff with his briefcase, and neither would he. He pulled out his cell phone and dialed. It rang several times. *Come on, come on. Answer!*

"Hello?"

"Linda, this is Kamal. Say, I wonder if you could do me a big favor. My mother's in the hospital. It's not serious—well, it might be serious. The doctors don't know yet. The thing is, I can't get away, and I'd like for you to pick up Lucky and take him to your house."

"I'm delivering some luggage right now and have a job interview in Santa Monica this afternoon, but—sure. How do I get in?"

"A key is under the stone next to the water faucet by the porch. Now listen, when you open the door, you have one minute to disable the alarm."

"I know where it is. What's the code?"

"Nine-one-one." The code Misha had told him to use.

"I hope your mother's okay. Don't worry about Lucky. I'm close by. Be there in ten minutes."

"What's your address for when I pick him up?"

She gave it to him, and he repeated it silently several times. "Say, just thought of something. You live close to the hospital where my mother is. I wonder if you could do me one more favor. In my house is a briefcase crammed full of family mementos that I know my mother would love to have one last look at. You know, just in case—"

"Sure, you want me to bring it?"

"That would be great. I'll get it when I pick up Lucky then give it to Mom in the hospital." He told her where it was and hung up. He took a deep breath, then looked inside the envelope he was holding. Gruesome pictures of Snake and his family.

Specter came back into the room. "On your feet. Your boss is back in town, so you get to go home. Too bad you didn't deal when you had the chance."

On the ride home, Kamal wondered how Specter knew Misha was back in town. He also wondered when Misha would be dropping by for his briefcase. It was almost noon, and Linda would have already picked it up by the time he got home. She lived opposite from where he worked, and he had people waiting for him. He'd see her when he got off.

CHAPTER 77

Linda punched nine-one-one into Kamal's security pad, while Lucky romped at her feet. Patting his head, she said, "Not now, Lucky." She went to the closet and opened it, stood on her tiptoes, pulled out the heavy briefcase, and almost dropped it.

What did Kamal say was in it? Family mementos? Maybe books, but who calls books mementos? She lugged it to the dining room table and hoisted it up. She drummed her purple fingernails on the silver case and wondered what was inside. While she was here, she'd look around the place. In the second bedroom she found a locked file cabinet and a desk.

Shuffling through the desk drawers, she found a checkbook with deposit entries. One, sometimes two a month. Always large, always cash. What kind of distribution was this guy into? Drugs?

She put Lucky and the briefcase in her car, then went back and set the alarm, locked up, replaced the key, and drove off.

With her heartbeat ticking fast, she couldn't stop wondering what was inside the briefcase. But how could she open it without breaking it? Wait! She was on her way to see just the person who would know.

She pulled off the 405 freeway at Roscoe, turned onto Van Nuys Boulevard, and into the Lexus parking lot. She hauled out the briefcase and Heather's suitcase that the airline had delivered to her house.

"I'm here to see Heather Morrison," she told the first salesperson she saw inside the door.

"Right this way." The woman led her down a hallway to a

door that said *Accounts Manager*. "Here you go," the woman said and left.

Heather looked up in surprise. "My suitcase! The airline finally delivered it." She pointed to the briefcase. "But that's not mine."

"I know." Linda muscled it onto the credenza against the wall. "It belongs to a guy I know who's so ditzy, he forgot the combination. I told him I knew just the person who could figure it out."

Heather got up and looked at it closely. "I can't do that."

"Sure you can. Anyone who could do those crypto-whatchamacallits and crack safes, can certainly figure out the correct alignment of three little disks."

"And each with ten numbers. Do you know how many possible combinations there are?"

"How would I know?"

"It's ten times ten times ten."

Linda thought a minute. "A thousand?"

"Here's a better idea. Tell your friend to toss it off a tall building. And if that doesn't work—" She pointed to Linda's purse. "—shoot it with your gun."

Linda glanced at her watch. "Look, I've got to drop off a dog, and then go over the hill for a job interview for a physical therapist position. I'll leave the briefcase here and pick it up afterward. Meanwhile, work that big brain of yours. You might surprise yourself."

"You can leave it here if you want, but I'm not looking at it, and I have to take off at four for a tournament at the Commerce."

Linda dashed off, confident that Heather would not resist the challenge of cracking open the briefcase. Suppose it did contain drugs? There'd be so much of it, Linda could surely skim a little, get back in touch with Brad, and make a big score. She hoped Heather wouldn't freak out.

❧❧❧

Linda left, and Heather went back to her desk, thinking it

would be a waste of time trying to open the briefcase. As she went about her work, she found herself glancing at the dazzling silver case and began wondering what was in it. If the case belonged to a friend of Linda's, it could be anything. *My God! What if it's drugs?* Now feeling nervous, she got up and locked the door. Maybe she should hide it somewhere. She glanced around the room as her fingers fiddled with the locks.

Then she peered down at them.

What the hell? Her experience with safes had taught her that people liked to use numbers easy to remember, so she tried sequencing sets of three, even and odd numbers, area codes, times of day, even famous dates. After several more attempts, she looked at the clock in surprise. She'd been at it over a half-hour and decided to give up.

She moved the briefcase under the credenza, unlocked the door, and turned around. On the wall hung a cityscape picture of New York, still displaying the Twin Towers. Inspiration struck. She hadn't thought of the emergency service number. She again locked the door and hoisted the briefcase back onto the credenza. She set the locks to nine-one-one, placed her thumbs on the latches, raced her tongue across her bottom lip, and pulled. The locks sprang open. With unsteady hands, she grasped the lid and lifted. She stared with a look usually reserved for UFO sightings.

Holy Mary and Josephine!

∽∾∽

Four o'clock, and no Linda! Why did Heather let her leave that damn thing in her office? Linda wasn't answering her phone, and Heather had to take off for her tournament. No way could she leave a million dollars in her office, where janitors come and go. She had no choice but to take the briefcase with her and lock it in her car.

CHAPTER 78

Kamal was unable to reach Linda after work, only her voice mail, and he didn't want to drive all the way to her house if she wasn't there. He'd call again when he got home.

And going home was a good decision, because Misha's car was parked out front.

Ah, shit! Kamal jumped from his car and ran inside. Misha stood in the hallway among strewn towels and linens, his shriveled little face red as Kamal's spilled blood if he didn't talk fast. "Don't worry, Misha. It's not here, but it's safe."

"What!" Misha pulled out his gun and seemed to grow taller. He started toward Kamal, murder gleaming in his eyes.

Kamal raised his hands and backed up. "Easy, Misha. Everything's all right. The feds picked me up, so I had someone hold it for me—er—for you."

Misha's forehead gained a few wrinkles. "Feds?"

"Yeah, this morning. They wanted me to tell them where you were. Then they found out you had returned to town, so they let me go." Kamal had back-stepped into the living room.

Misha waved his gun toward a chair. "Sit down." Kamal toppled into it.

"You had no business giving my property away."

"But I thought—"

"Shut up!"

Kamal's eyes crossed while focusing on the trigger of the gun pressed against his damp forehead.

"Maybe I should make an opening in your head for brains to leak in."

"Please—" Kamal's heart sank, fear pushing in on him. "We'll go get it, right now. There's no problem, honest."

"Where is it?"

"At a woman's house. I know her."

Misha's face loosened, and he lowered his gun. "For your sake, it fucking better be there."

⁢ᴏᴈᴇᴏ⁢

Kamal's sweaty hands kneaded the steering wheel. Linda had said she was going to a job interview in Santa Monica. That was probably why he kept getting her voice mail. He glanced at his watch. Five o'clock. Hopefully she'd be home by now.

Kamal's cell phone GPS had directed them off the 405 freeway at Roxford and west for two miles, then right on Linda's street to the second block.

Thank God! Linda's blue Honda was parked out front. Kamal pulled up behind it, and Misha slipped on a pair of black leather gloves and screwed a silencer onto his gun. "If that briefcase isn't there, you both are gonna catch a bullet where it hurts. He put the gun in his pocket. Let's go." They paced up to the porch as Barney watched them from the window.

"Keep your mouth shut," Misha said. "I'll handle this. Hold the screen door open."

Misha didn't bother knocking and didn't care if the door was locked or not. He raised his foot and kicked the bottom of his shoe against the door once, and it popped open like it was surprised. It smacked against the wall and bounced back to Misha's outstretched hand. He stepped inside, followed by Kamal. Lucky stood barking in the living room, and Linda lay on a couch trapped by cushions and covered with what looked like red wine. Her arms and legs flailed like a flipped cockroach's.

Misha's eyes locked onto her. "Anybody else in the house?"

Linda had scrambled free from the cushions and sat up. "Who the fuck are you, you little shit?"

"Answer my question." He whirled toward Lucky, still barking. "Shut the fuck up!"

"Sit, Lucky," Linda yelled. Lucky sat and stopped barking. "No one else is here." She turned to Kamal. "Who is this joker?"

Misha pulled out his gun. "Your worst nightmare if you don't hand over my property."

"Give him the briefcase," Kamal said, "and we'll go."

"I—I don't have it," she said, her face a spasm of fright.

Misha pressed the gun to her forehead. "Where is it?"

"Kamal asked me to pick it up for his mother, but then I had an appointment in Santa Monica and didn't want to leave it in my car, so I had a friend hold it."

Misha turned to Kamal. "Your mother?"

"I'll explain later. Linda, where does your friend live?"

Linda swallowed hard. "She's not home."

"Then where the fuck is she?" Misha snarled.

"Playing in a poker tournament. I don't know where."

Misha pressed the gun hard against her forehead. "You've got five seconds to find out."

Her face froze with terror. Then suddenly, she nodded. "Co…co…commer…commercial…commerce! That's it, commerce!"

"Where the fuck's that?"

"She means the Commerce Casino," Kamal said. "I know where it is. Let's go."

Misha turned to Linda and narrowed his eyes. Guessing his thoughts, Kamal sidled up to him. "Don't kill her, Misha. We need her to identify the girl."

Misha seemed to chew on the thought. "All right. Let's all take a field trip."

છાજી

At six-fifteen, Kamal spun into the Commerce Casino parking lot, tires squealing. Misha pointed to the red curb. "Stop there!" Everyone tumbled out under the bright lights, and Misha slapped twenty bucks in the attendant's hand. "We'll be right back."

Linda led them, scurrying through a large gaming room and into another. She stopped abruptly. "That's her at the table on the right."

"Holy shit!" Kamal shook his finger like an old lady whose handbag had been snatched. "That's Heather, the woman who ripped off the Jersey guys."

Heather looked up, and chips flew. She grabbed her purse and dashed into the next room. Misha shoved Linda aside and took off after Heather. She reached a man wearing a Yankee baseball cap and whispered to him. The guy stood and raised a badge to the charging trio. "Hold up! I'm Chief Foley. What's the rumpus about?" He jerked his head for everyone to step aside.

"I need to speak to that woman, right now," Misha spat, his mouth twisted. "She's got a briefcase of mine."

"A briefcase?" Chief Foley said.

Everybody's eyes searched for the woman. Misha pushed past the chief, and they all ran.

తిఇత

Heather reached the outside of the casino, where a horde of people stood bunched together in a circular drive, waiting for transportation. She squeezed through to the front.

A dark blue sedan pulled up and stopped so hard it rocked on its springs. A man's arm reached from behind her and opened the rear door. Then the hand pushed against her back. "Get in," the man said. He slipped in after her, and the car shot away.

తిఇత

Kamal, Linda, and Chief Foley followed Misha out of the casino and into the night. While Misha clawed his way through the crowd, trying to reach the front, Heather and a man got into a sedan. Both the sedan and a yellow taxi took off from the curb. Misha finally reached the front of the line, turned to the crowd, and yelled, "Did a woman get into that taxi?" A few shrugged. A taxi arrived, and a couple stepped out. Misha shoved them aside, jumped in, and the taxi took off.

"Let's go," Kamal said to Linda.

Foley grabbed Kamal's arm. "What's this about a brief-case?"

"That woman stole it from the guy." Not quite the truth but good enough for an old cop.

"There must be some mistake. I know the woman. Leave me your phone number, and if she has that man's briefcase, I'll see that it's returned."

Kamal thought about it. No reason why not. He scribbled his number on a piece of paper and gave it to him, then he and Linda hurried off.

ल৯ल৯

Chief Foley stuffed Kamal's phone number into his pocket and headed to the casino coffee shop to think about what the hell just happened. As he trudged in, his phone rang.

"Foley here."

"This is Grayson. Can you talk?"

The chief headed toward a table in the rear. "What's up?"

"I…uh…" There was a catch in his voice. "I saw the psy-chiatrist you referred me to after the funeral. He said you'd called and were worried about me."

"Yeah, how'd it go?"

A waitress passed by and left a menu and glass of water.

"I wanted to ask him about Jim. See if there was any hope for him emotionally. Instead, I poured everything out. We talked a few times, and I learned that—that I didn't always have my head screwed on right."

"Like insisting on Heather's abortion? Like shooting Stockard? Like dealing with Costanzo?"

"Yeah, yeah, all of that. I think I told you—God spoke to me when I was a boy. He said I would someday win the Global. But in time, I came to learn that was a false prophecy."

The chief sipped his water. "Because of your nervous stomach?"

"Something I blamed on God. He gave me the skills and the will, but also a fucked up stomach that prevented the way. Then…um…well, Troy came along with his natural talent, and I believed God meant for him to win it. After he died, I made the deal with Costanzo to save Jim's life if he won it."

"How will you get Jim off the firing line if he loses?"

"He won't be on the firing line. I guarantee it. I never told you this, but Costanzo had my mother murdered."

"Jesus Christ!"

"It was his way of getting back at me for disobeying one of his orders."

The chief sipped some more. "You have proof?"

"No, but I know the night attendant at the nursing home quit the next day. If anything happens to me, I want you to go to the police and tell them everything. I'm sure they'll investigate."

The chief rubbed the rim of his water glass and thought a minute. "Why didn't you tell the police and avoid this fiasco with Jim?"

"I couldn't. I needed Costanzo's help to handle Stockard."

"What about after that?"

"I doubt Costanzo would have appreciated that. And he had just as much evidence on me as I had on him."

"Well, you've fucked yourself royally."

"Just remember what to do if anything happens to me."

The phone clicked dead in the chief's ear.

CHAPTER 79

Kamal tromped the gas and squealed from the red curb. "That was exciting," Linda said. "You son of a bitch!" Kamal looked at her and laughed. "If it weren't for me, you'd be home wondering how your brains got on the floor. You were supposed to take the briefcase to your house, not give it to someone, who, by the fucking way, stole money from her employer back in New Jersey."

"That's not true. But what's this bullshit about your *mother's* mementos? You stole the briefcase from that little shit friend of yours and got caught."

"He's my boss. And, besides, you don't know shit."

"More than you think. You're the guy who tried to kidnap Heather from LAX, that's why you recognized her in the casino. I also know that your friends, Marcus and Clarence, tried to killed her."

"How do you know about them?"

"Never mind. What's in the briefcase that's so important?"

"I don't know for sure. Probably cash. But I'm not a killer."

"Of course not. Apu's a Hindu who wouldn't hurt a fly. He's into *redistribution*."

"Be honest," he said. "Why did you give the briefcase to Heather? Was she going to bust it open?"

"You want honesty? Okay, we'll play let's be honest. I'll go first." She brushed back her hair onto her shoulders, while making the usual jewelry racket. "I gave it to her, because she's good at cracking safes, and I was hoping she could apply her skills."

"Then what?"

"If the case had drugs in it—" A little smile crossed her lips. "—maybe some would have stuck to my fingers."

"And if it was money?"

"I hadn't thought about that yet."

Kamal threw his head back. "Ha! *Yet*, she says. You would have disappeared, and so would I, once Misha got a hold of me."

"Spare me the poor Apu sentiment. It was me who had a cold silencer pressed to my forehead. I'd be in never-never land if I wasn't needed to identify Heather." She shuddered. "Now it's you're turn. What kind of scam are you and your little sidekick into?"

"You know I can't tell you that."

"But you admit you're involved in some shady operation."

Kamal turned off the freeway at Rinaldi Street. "Not much longer. Soon, I'll have enough green to retire and live a respectable life."

"Then what?"

"Return to college and start a legitimate career. But first, spend some time back home in India."

They pulled up in front of Linda's house. She ran inside and brought out Lucky.

"Say, how did you teach him to sit and stop barking?"

She handed him Lucky's leash. "That comes with the next lesson."

೧෨೧

Chief Foley left the casino coffee shop and shuffled outside to the unattended valet station. He figured there were three places Heather could be hiding the briefcase: at work, her hotel room, or her car. He would check the easiest of those three.

Heather's key ring had a fuzzy bear attached that she always kept on the poker table by her chips. His eyes swept the many rows of keys on the pegboard until he spotted the fuzzy bear. He grabbed the keys as the attendant approached. "That's okay, Mike." He held up the keys. "I'll get it. I can use the exercise." The chief slipped him five dollars.

The lot had cars stretching to the horizon. He paced down the main aisle, clicking the remote button on the key until he heard a chirp. The car was backed against a wall. He searched the front and rear seats, then started the car and moved it up a few feet, enabling him to open the trunk. He removed the briefcase, placed it on the floor of the front seat, closed the door, ambled back to the valet station, and exchanged Heather's keys for his own. "Mike," he said to the valet, who was handing someone a ticket. "I don't know where my head was. You get a bad beat on a hand and your mind goes screwy." He held up his keys and ambled off again.

He got into his car, drove to Heather's, and retrieved the briefcase. He started to close the door, paused, opened his wallet, removed a card and placed it on the console. He closed the door and left.

❧

The dark blue sedan squealed out from the casino onto Telegraph Road with Heather in the backseat, wondering if she was being rescued or again kidnapped. She peered out the rear window and saw the little mean-faced man at the curb. He must work for The Man. The other guy was the kidnapper from the airport. There was also a woman, but Heather never saw her face.

Heather turned to the man beside her with a rumpled suit and pink lips. "Who are you?"

"Someone who just saved you from a bunch of trouble."

Her chest tightened at his tone. "That doesn't answer my question." She glanced at the door handle and thought of jumping out.

"Don't waste your time." He slipped a hand into his breast pocket, and out came a worn ostrich-skin wallet. He flipped it open.

Oh, my God! FBI. She pictured the bodies of Marcus and Clarence, and her skin crawled.

He closed his wallet, and his pink lips pulled back into a sly smile. "Have you always had the boys chasing after you, or just the last few days?"

With a scratchy voice, she asked, "What's this all about?"

The driver looked up into the mirror. He had a bald crown and floppy ears. "We want to ask you some questions."

"What kind of questions?"

"You'll find out."

Her fear swelled into defiance. "You have no right. I've done nothing wrong."

"Hey, Kevin," Pink Lips said to Big Ears behind the wheel. "Doesn't the manual say it's a no-no to shoot people in motel rooms?" He laughed, a hard, ringing laugh.

"Wait a minute! I never killed anybody."

"We'll refresh your memory at the office," Big Ears said.

The car pulled into FBI headquarters on Wilshire Boulevard. The agents led Heather into a depressing basement office, where a man sat behind a desk. He had expressionless eyes and folded hands.

Pink Lips offered her a metal chair and introduced her to Special Agent Specter. He studied her, and she studied him back. The other two agents stood nearby, each with one foot flat against the wall.

"Ms. Morrison, we need to know some things," Specter said, his voice politely casual but with a dry, stiff crackle.

"What things? I already told your agents I didn't kill anybody."

"We'll get to that later," Specter said. "But those chasing you in the casino. Kamal Datar, Misha Abramson, aka the midget, and…" He peered down at a paper on his desk. "…and Linda Meyers." He looked up. "Why were they chasing you?"

Heather gulped and, all at once, it was as if a window shade had sprung open and the light blasted her. Linda! First, she and Marcus and Clarence show up at the motel. Then she comes around with a million dollars in a briefcase that she can't open. Then she shows up at the casino with Kamal, the kidnapper.

Heather inhaled deeply. "Maybe they're after the briefcase."

Specter's eyebrows took a ride up. "Keep talking."

She didn't like getting Linda in trouble, but enough was enough. "Linda Meyers gave it to me to hold. That's all I know." She hoped to end it there. She was going to Vegas the next morning and didn't want to be held up with endless questions.

"Where is this briefcase, and what's in it?" Specter asked.

"I don't know what's in it, but it's in the trunk of my car."

He jabbed his finger up and down. "You mean right now?"

"It's parked at the casino." She handed over the claim check, and the other two agents rushed out.

Specter smiled. "Ms. Morrison, why don't you tell me about the dead thugs in your motel room?"

She felt a deep hard thud in her heart. She might not get out of there yet. "How do you know about the motel?"

"Ever since you hooked up with Kamal Datar at the airport, we've been keeping track of you."

"Then you know everything."

"Only that you were at the motel. We weren't there at the time of the killing."

Heather wouldn't protect Linda in connection with the briefcase, but she had to shield her from a murder charge, no matter how often Linda betrayed her in the past. Besides, Linda did save her life. "Two men attacked me. Then someone, maybe someone from another room, came in and shot them. I have no idea who my attackers were."

He got up and strode to the door. "Wait here."

She considered making a mad dash out of there, but that would get her in even more trouble. She had to clear herself, or she'd never be able to bring her family over from Ireland. She should never have returned to the U.S.

An hour later, Specter came back in, dangling Heather's keys. "There's no briefcase in the trunk or anywhere else in your car."

Heather's breath caught in her throat. "But—"

He handed her the keys. "That will be all for now, Ms. Morrison. Your car's outside. Please don't leave town. We'll likely want to have another word with you."

Confused, Heather hurried to her car and checked the trunk. Where the hell'd it go? She slipped behind the wheel and caught sight of a business card resting on the console.

Chief J. Edgar Foley.

☙❧

Back at his apartment, the chief placed the briefcase on the marble kitchen counter and ran his hand across its cold metallic surface. No way was this thing crammed with cooking recipes. Maybe drugs, but more likely cash. And from its weight, lots of it.

The next morning he dressed, ate breakfast, and packed his suitcase. He threw it and the briefcase into his car and drove east on Wilshire Boulevard. After making a quick stop at the Commerce Casino, he swung north into the Valley and to the Bob Hope airport.

☙❧

Specter had told Heather not to leave town, but she had an airplane ticket and a packed suitcase. She couldn't miss playing in the Vegas tournament, not at this point, not after all she'd been through. She looked out her hotel window toward the airport. To hell with Specter. Let him arrest her when she returned.

She had just unplugged her phone from its charger when it rang. "Hello?"

"Heather, I'm so glad I finally reached you."

"Linda! How could you have done that to me?"

"That was one hell of a three ring circus."

"Don't be cute. And I have no interest in even talking to you anymore."

"But you're okay, right?" She actually sounded concerned.

"I'm alive. But no thanks to you." Heather glanced at her watch. "Look, I have to go."

"Okay, we'll talk later. But first, did you get the briefcase open?"

"Wouldn't you like to know?"

"Come on, Heather, please."

"Money. Lots of money."

"*No!*"

Heather could almost hear her panting. "A million dollars. Happy?"

"Where—where is it now?"

"Chief Foley from the casino has it. I've got to go. Good-bye." She hung up. *And good riddance!* She grabbed her suit-case, checked out of the hotel, and jumped into a taxi. "Bob Hope Airport, please."

An hour later she boarded her flight and shuffled past Chief Foley, already seated. "Thanks for swiping you-know-what," she hissed. "And I didn't think your business card was very funny."

CHAPTER 80

Eight ball, right there." Chauffeur tapped the side pocket with his cue stick. He struck the cue ball with a weighted touch, and it banked once, twice, then kissed the eight ball into the pocket.

The Man yanked a thick roll of hundreds from his pocket, peeled one off, and threw it on the table. "Fuck you." He stepped to the bar and mixed a drink.

The corners of Chauffeur's lips curled, but not too much. Losing always dampened The Man's spirits. "Getting the Bolts back together was an act of genius, boss. A three-cushion bank shot."

"You fucken' better believe it." He plopped into a chair. "I'm going to make millions off that kid this weekend."

Chauffeur cruised over to the bar, poured a drink, and settled in on the sofa. "To think this all started in the jury room when Bolt put the word *not* before the word guilty."

"Before that. It was that smirk when he turned me down. Wouldn't take my case. No one makes me fuckin' grovel."

The Man always said, never forget a favor, never forgive an insult. He took a slug of his drink and smacked his lips. "It's a real three-for-one deal: the kid loses, I make a ton of money, and I fuck Bolt by knocking off his kid, like I said."

"Me and Gonzo whispered in all the right ears that you're in the kid's corner all the way."

The Man put down his drink and ran a finger across his lips. "The press is covering the kid's return to golf like flies on shit. With so much hype, you'd think fucking Michael Jackson had returned." He chuckled, and his shoulders shook.

Chauffeur returned the chuckle. "It's like a fever. One person thinks the kid's God's gift to golf and can't be beat, and the whole fucking world catches it."

"Betting against Bolt will get me sweet odds. The kid'll be lucky to finish in the top ten. Only three months of practice after years in some fucking Benghazi rat hole? Give me a fucking break."

Chauffeur drew in a deep breath. Even so, The Man was taking a hell of a gamble. No way could he afford to lose.

ℂℂℂ

While Jim warmed up on the putting green, Grayson sipped coffee in the clubhouse near the TV.

"Hello everyone, Howie Collins here. Welcome to our CBS coverage of this year's first round of the Global Championship, held right here in Summerville, South Carolina. A record forty-one million viewers will be watching golf's best players, including four-time Global champion, Bat Brady, and former US Amateur titleholder, Jim Bolt. I'm here with three-time winner Nick Nelson. Nick, does Jim Bolt stand a chance of toppling number one ranked Bat?"

"It's hard to say. Jim recently returned from three years in Benghazi, so capturing this title would be a monumental achievement. I joined him on the driving range this morning, and he's hitting the ball rust-free, looking every bit as good as when he made that record setting round, three years ago. The army has given him more muscle, and he's hitting the ball farther. We'll have to see if he still has that classic Jim Bolt touch around the greens."

"Let's talk about his abrupt withdrawal after that fabulous round," Howie said. "It was widely reported that he had a major falling out with his father."

"They've mended their differences, but their reasons for parting remain one of sport's great mysteries."

Grayson finished his coffee and sighed. *If they only knew.*

ℂℂℂ

Grayson stood behind the ropes on the eighteenth green and watched Jim put a smooth stroke on a long birdy putt. The ball had perfect speed and floated in the side door of the hole. The crowd jumped to their feet and roared all the way to Georgia, knocking over plastic cups and toppling a lawn chair.

Grayson greeted Jim with a hug and waited while he turned in his scorecard. The long weeks of practice had left him in top form, but today's course conditions had been tough. Dry winds had sucked the greens dry, leaving them hard as pool tables. Grayson glanced over at the leaderboard. Surge Michaelson was on top with one under par. Bat was holding even, while Jim was one over. Purple thunderclouds were stirring over the mountains. Nighttime rain would soften the greens for tomorrow's round. Grayson smiled. Perfect conditions for Jim.

ოჯო

Linda hung up from talking to Heather and dove into her purse for Kamal's business card. Time for a chat with his boss. She chewed her lower lip rehearsing what to say, then dialed. Kamal had said he'd usually be out making calls. Hopefully, the little shit was in.

"Hello!"

Her skin went cold at the sound of the runt's whiny high-pitched voice. "Hello, Misha."

"Who's this?"

"It's Linda. Before you reach for your gun, I know who has your briefcase."

Misha didn't say anything for a minute. "Oh, yeah! Who?"

"You have a pleasant voice when you're not yelling. Still a little high. Maybe a diaphragm thing."

"What do you want?"

"For you to get your property back. Isn't that what you call it?"

More silence. Then, "I'm listening."

"We meet someplace, you give me, say, one hundred thousand dollars, and then—"

"Excuse me, I just fell off my chair laughing. That's more

than ten times the value of what's in the fucking case. Get real, lady."

"All right. Will you agree to a ten percent finder's fee?"

"Now you're being realistic. Who has it, and where is he?"

"Not so fast, little man. You deliver my fee, then I give you the person's name and where to find him."

"How can I trust you?"

"You know where I live. By the way, I should charge you for some serious front door repair. But since you're going to be paying that hundred thousand, I'll let you off the hook. You see, Tiny Tim, I took a peek inside your little treasure chest. So no more bullshit."

He didn't say anything for a while. "Is the case intact, and the contents still inside?"

"I guarantee it." After all, Heather didn't take anything out, and Chief Foley said he wanted to return the briefcase.

"Here's what we'll do. You come to my office, and I'll give you fifty thousand. That's it. No arguments! Then together, we go get the briefcase."

She thought a moment. The casino should know where to find the chief. "Okay. But realize this. I'm recording this conversation and leaving it with a friend. So if I should suffer any mishap, even so much as a stubbed toe, he'll know what to do. Deal?"

"Deal."

☙❧☙

Chief Foley checked into the Rio Hotel and Casino, took the elevator to Room 407, and threw his suitcase onto the bed. He stood at the window and tugged an earlobe, reached into his pocket and withdrew the scrap of paper with Kamal's number. He looked at it a long time. The only way to protect Heather was to return the briefcase to its owners—rightful or otherwise. He picked up the phone and dialed. It rang once.

"Kamal here."

"This is Chief Foley. I have something to tell you, so listen carefully. Your friend's briefcase is with Anthony, head of security at the Commerce Casino. I'm sure its contents must be important. If you tell Anthony a certain something, he'll give it to you. But before I tell you what that something is, you need to understand that crossing me brings on fatal consequences. Is that clear?"

"Yes, sir. Crystal clear."

"You and your friends are to lay off Heather. She has nothing you people could possibly want. Do we have a deal?"

"Absolutely. You can count on it."

"Tell Anthony your name, and he'll give you the briefcase. Just remember what I said. Your health depends on it." Foley hung up.

Time to go downstairs for dinner and to check out tomorrow's competition.

CHAPTER 81

It was a hot, dry day in the city. The Santa Ana winds whistled in from the Valley, and Kamal's bushy hair filled with static. He just had a lovely visit with Anthony at the Commerce Casino and was driving south on La Brea. He dialed Misha's cell phone.

"Hello?"

"Put a little cheer in your voice, Misha. I've got it."

"You've got what?"

"Your briefcase. What the hell else?"

"Wait a minute. How the fuck did you—" He yelled, "I'll be right there! Kamal?"

"Yeah?"

"You've got it with you?"

"That's what I've been sayin'."

"I'll be damned. Get your ass over here right now."

Twenty minutes later, Kamal climbed the stairs to the office. Finding the door unlocked, he entered the outer workplace. Cigar smoke clogged the air. Misha shouted from his back office, "Come in, Kamal, and join the party."

Confused by what he meant, Kamal trudged down the mud-colored hallway. His shoulders drooped unevenly from the weight of the briefcase pulling on one arm. He stepped into the room.

Kamal locked eyes with Linda sitting in front of the desk. Both their jaws dropped, and so did the briefcase, with a thud.

"Surprise!" Misha yelled. His face held a sly smile, but not one to fear. He peered at the briefcase, and his smile widened like a Mexican Federale's about to reclaim the treasure of Sierra Madre. "Sit down, Kamal." He got up from his desk, closed and locked the door, then strong-armed the briefcase onto the desk. He climbed back into his chair. "You two should be happy to see one another." He pulled out a gun from a drawer and laid it on the desk.

Kamal slipped into a chair next to Linda and glanced at her, her eyes fearful. "What's goin' on, Misha? How come she's here?"

"I invited her over," he said and pulled the briefcase nearer. He turned the combination locks. Latches sprang open with sharp clicks. He lifted the lid and looked inside, then closed it as quietly as falling snow. He snapped shut the clasps, spun the numbered rings, and placed the briefcase on the floor beside him.

Kamal stretched his neck up over the desktop to see three more identical briefcases.

"Well, everything appears in order." Misha sat back. "Kamal, pick up the gun."

Kamal swallowed hard.

"Go ahead, it won't bite." Misha nodded toward the weapon.

Kamal looked at Linda, who didn't seem to breathe.

"Do it," Misha said, his face hard.

Kamal grabbed the gun by its chamber and placed it in his lap.

"Ever shoot one of those?"

Kamal nodded.

"Good. Then you should know to hold it by the grip." Misha's lips had a downward bend.

Linda's fingers clawed at her palm, purse at her side.

"Do it now."

Kamal held the gun's grip.

"Shoot Linda," Misha said, leaning on the words.

She jerked back in her chair and raised her arms. "Wait! My friend with the recording. Remember? If I'm not back, he knows where to come."

Misha chuckled. "You mean to this soon-to-be vacated office?"

Her eyes blazed with fear against the dead white of her face.

Kamal kept silent for about the time it takes to count to ten. His hands trembled and the skin around his cheeks tightened. He half smiled. His eyes flitted around the room without focusing. Then a little laugh squeaked out. "M—Misha, you're—you're kidding."

"Pretend I'm not."

A hand seemed to squeeze Kamal's chest from inside. He let out a little cough.

Linda fell to her knees before Kamal, her hands in prayer. "No, Kamal. *Please.*"

He fixed his eyes hard on her, ignoring the sweat dripping into them, stinging. Heat pumped a strange violence inside his veins. He swung the gun around to Misha and jerked the trigger three times.

Click click click.

CHAPTER 82

The explosion, the roar of flames, the mournful groans. The lieutenant holding him back. No! No! He had to save Jessie.

Jim's eyes opened wide, his shirt wet, heart pounding. It was Friday morning, day two of the Global. He lumbered to his feet and tried to rub the torture from behind his eyes. Dropping to the floor, he did ninety pushups, followed by fifty squats. He collapsed into a chair, ate a banana, and thumbed through a newspaper without comprehension. He stepped to the window and stared at the vivid blue sky and fluffy clouds. Today's course was ideal for scoring low.

He took out his laptop and googled combat stress. Christ! There were a million sites. He picked one.

Combat Stress: Restless sleep, fatigue, inability to focus. Often short-term. Helpful to talk with professional or supportive friend.

Short-term. *That means it won't last long*, he told himself. *Well, it's lasted goddamn long enough. Time to move on.*

He showered and ate breakfast—cereal and another banana. *Gotta stay focused. Think only of today's round. No more playing cautious.* The rain saw to that. Aim for the flagstick every hole.

∽∾∽

"This has been quite a Day Two here at the Global," Howie Collins commented cheerfully. "Bat Brady changed to his three-wood off the tee and has split the middle of every fairway. He's racked up six birdies, four in a row, and only one bogey. Surge Michaelson has hit sixteen greens but can't get his putter to fire. Yet the biggest shock is Jim Bolt."

"You said it," Nick Nelson agreed. "He can't get anything to work. He's not focused. He takes his stance, then appears to lose concentration and steps away from the ball. The gallery sees his pain. He's their darling who should have won three years ago. Now he's on stage and forgetting his lines. It's only because of raw talent, conditioning, and a perfect swing that Jim is only five shots behind Bat, and not more.

"He has a lot of catching up to do," Howie chimed. "Not only to Bat, but Michaelson and eight others. To win this one, he'll need to pull more than clubs from his bag. He'll need a very lucky rabbit."

૏

Jim clomped up the final fairway and three-putted the hole. He tossed the putter to his caddy, the shaft bopping his head, then turned in his scorecard and left.

Jim and Grayson rode in silence to their hotel. Jim stared out the window. The demon in his nightmares had now become a part of him. Hell, maybe *he* was the demon.

They got out of the car, and Grayson said, "I'll be in my room, son. Remember, I'm ready when you are."

"I'll never be ready, Dad. But let's talk now."

CHAPTER 83

Chauffeur grinned as The Man jumped from his cushy chair before the TV and pumped his fists, as if he was suddenly ten million dollars richer. "How fucking good does it get?"

"The kid's down the tubes," Chauffeur said from the bar.

"To win this one, he'd have to make the greatest Hail Mary golf shots in history. He was so pissed, he almost took out his caddy with his putter. Whoa. It was beautiful."

The Man was right. Three years of shell-shock did him in. "Think anybody's dumb enough to press his bet on Bolt?"

The Man laughed so loud his bones rattled. He'd predicted correctly. Jim's return from Benghazi had caught the wave of interest he'd generated three years before, making him the favorite to win. The Man had not only bet heavily on Bat, but had hedged his bet by laying odds on the field, which included everyone but Jim. That way, if anybody other than Jim won, he stood to make millions.

Costanzo hoisted his drink. "Here's to the kid and a happy afterlife."

CHAPTER 84

K amal, you forgot to say bang." Misha leaned back in his chair, opened his mouth wide, and let loose with a high-pitched sound that slightly resembled a laugh.

Kamal stared in shock at the gun, then dropped it like someone with a two-dollar ticket on a horse that tripped at the finish line.

Misha stopped laughing, opened a drawer, and came out with another gun. A Glock .45 with enough punch to blast his guests against the wall hard enough to stick.

Linda gasped.

Misha ordered her off her knees and into her chair. He fixed his eyes on Kamal. "If I killed you now, it would be self-defense."

Anger knotted around Kamal's fear. "What the hell did you expect?"

"Nothing personal, is that it?"

Kamal's jaw clenched, and he glanced at Linda, who was gripping her purse like a life raft.

"Too bad about this whole rotten business." Misha rocked in his chair, waving his gun. "We had a good operation."

Kamal stared at his boss's cold, tiny eyes. Their only chance was for him to dive over the desk and go for the gun.

"Prick-face Chauffeur," Misha went on, "and The Man screwed themselves by stickin' their noses where they didn't need to. Dumb-fuck Ernie rips them off, and they want to check *my* books. And to top it off, the feds are on our asses." He put his gun down and opened a desk drawer, but kept his eyes on Kamal.

He took out a shot glass and a pint of whiskey and poured four fingers.

Kamal sat coiled, ready to spring. *Come on, Misha, look away.*

"I'm taking an early retirement and clearing out." He glanced over his shoulder at the four briefcases, and Kamal missed his chance. "You could've gotten out of here clean if you hadn't been sloppy with my property. Goodbye, Kamal." He picked up the gun.

Boom! Boom! Boom! Shots exploded like cannons. Misha's chair whirled halfway around, slowed, then came full circle. The midget looked surprised to be dead. Three red splotches formed a triangle. One on his neck, two on his chest.

Linda let out a semi-laugh, sounding like a bark. Kamal looked at her purse, her hand buried inside. Smoke oozed out. Her laughter became high, hysterical. She took out the gun, and Kamal released his own small bark, surprised to be alive.

They got up, reached for each other, and hugged.

"Come on," Kamal said, "let's get outta here."

They trailed down the stairs, each carrying two briefcases. Kamal felt about as happy as a guy like him could feel.

CHAPTER 85

Grayson took Jim to his suite, hopeful that he'd finally talk about his problems. It was bound to happen eventually, and it had to be now, or winning the Global would be more than just a lost dream.

Jim collapsed into a stuffed chair. Grayson took out two bottles of water from the mini-bar, tossed one to Jim, and sat on the couch.

"You know, Dad, a few nights back I sat on my practice putting green, planning to down a bottle of scotch. I'd gotten to the point where I didn't give a shit about the tournament. I wanted oblivion. Total oblivion. But I never opened the bottle. I got pissed at myself, told myself I would stop drinking and tough it out."

"But it hasn't been working, has it?"

"I can't stay focused. Thoughts get into my head, the worst kind of thoughts you could think of. Used to be just nightmares. But now—" He threw his head back and stared at the ceiling.

"What sort of thoughts?"

Jim opened his water bottle and took a slug. He opened his mouth, closed it with a grimace, took a breath, and tried again. He kept his eyes closed, as if trying to shield himself from the memory. "A child's mutilated body." When his voice finally came out, it was ragged. His eyes snapped open, full of horror. "And I *caused* it. I *caused* it, Dad!"

Grayson breathed deeply though his nose.

"Now you know why I've never told anyone. How could I tell anyone that? I'm a monster."

"I—I wasn't—"

"I know." Jim gulped more water. His voice took on a dull quality, like he was reciting lines from a play, as he stared into a corner of the ceiling. "We were on foot. It was dark. We took on gunfire from a building. One of our guys got it in the face, and the rest of us hit the ground. You don't want to look at your friend who'd just had his head blown off. We threw grenades at windows and stormed the building. We got the sniper upstairs, but my grenade had gone through a downstairs window where a family slept. We found a mother dead and a little girl wearing one pink sandal and missing an arm." Jim put his fist to his mouth. "She was screaming, but she screamed even louder when we came in. She was terrified of us. She wouldn't let us near her, even when we tried to help. She just cowered in the corner as blood gushed out of the stump where her arm had been. And—oh *God*!" Jim took a ragged breath, tears filling his eyes. "Her *screams*!"

Grayson's throat constricted, and he stayed silent.

"Another time, we were looking for IEDs when a woman ran toward me, yelling and holding something in a white blanket. I yelled at her to stop and pointed my rifle at her, but she kept running at me. I had a split second to decide what was in that blanket: a baby or a bomb."

Jim picked up his water bottle and took a swig. Grayson reached for his and gulped a mouthful.

"I couldn't pull the trigger." Jim held out a quivering hand. "I shake thinking how close I came." He took a long drink from his bottle and ran his wrist across his lips. "She was running from rebels who were trying to take her baby. I couldn't shoot her. I no longer wanted to shoot anyone, even a soldier I caught raping a little girl. It's the look in their eyes, the terror, the despair. They sucked the want to kill out of me." Jim looked quizzically at his dad. "Did Stockard's eyes do that to you before you stabbed him?"

Grayson closed his eyes and nodded as painful memories returned. "Yes. But in my case, it didn't stop me."

Jim was quiet a long time. The tears flowed, harder and harder, until his body shook with sobs. Grayson's heart broke for him. He stood and walked over to his son, enfolding him in his arms. The two men wept together.

"I'm sorry for hating you," Jim finally said, his voice coming out in a whisper.

Grayson stroked his head. "You had every reason to hate me." He thought about Heather and ached deeply for coercing her into killing his own grandchild.

Jim looked up. "Since Mom and Troy died, everything you've done has been for me. I never thanked you."

Grayson shook his head. "I've put you through too much. Even your being in Benghazi was because of me. I worried for your safety every day."

"Am I safe now, Dad?"

"Jim, please believe me, if you lose tomorrow, you'll have nothing to worry about."

A smile made its way across Jim's face. "When have we ever talked about losing?"

CHAPTER 86

owie Collins nearly sprang from his chair. "Jim Bolt sets a new course record for the front nine—a staggering twenty-nine! Recapping this miraculous ninth hole, Jim, off the green and pin high, reached for his utility club and struck the ball with exactly the right touch. It crawled across the green, painfully slow at first but gathered speed, taking the precise line of the break and turning toward the hole, diving sharply at the end." Howie turned to Nick Nelson. "Nick, this has to be one of the most astounding charges in golf history."

"The change that has come over Jim Bolt in the last twenty-four hours is beyond description. Something has turned his head around."

"He appears unstoppable," Howie said. "By Bat Brady *or* the blistering heat. Golf fans, as well as fans of great theater, can't get enough. Every hole has been the same. Jim tees his ball, swings with unbounded confidence, and the ball goes exactly where he wants."

"And I don't think he spent ten minutes on the practice range," Nick added.

Howie nodded. "Forty-three of the forty-four golfers out here today would call the weather perfect if it were thirty degrees cooler. Given the chance, they'd call time out—unfair conditions. Even the azaleas are bending for cover. This is practically a replay of the US Amateur when Jim taught Richie Kelly that there's no mercy rule in golf."

"The rest of the field may as well stack their clubs and go home," Nick concluded with a grin. "It'll take a relay team to catch Jim."

ᴄᴈᴇᴐ

Grayson watched Jim's steady march through the back nine: par, par, par, eagle, par, birdie, par, par. He finished the final eighteenth hole with a birdie, completing the most dominant performance in Global history. Jim started the round five shots down when he went for his holster and fired back to score an incredible sixty-one, beating the course record he'd set three years earlier. Euphoria rattled every fiber in Grayson's body. "Go get'em, Jim!" he yelled, pumping his fist. Finally, destiny would be fulfilled. God's promise would be realized.

ᴄᴈᴇᴐ

Jim paraded off the eighteenth green, looking like he could do it on his hands. He carried with him that incredible vitality, an aura that made every eye turn. He slapped sweaty palms and high-fived people in the gallery, one fan after another. After stopping for autographs, Grayson led him from the course, overflowing with pride. The air was still raw, and a rusty sun hung low over the landscape. In the car, Grayson patted Jim's leg excitedly.

Jim winked. "One more round, Dad. Just one more."

CHAPTER 87

Chauffeur had ducked for cover. Chairs were upended, lamps broken, sofa cushions scattered to all corners of the room. An oak end table lay upside down, partway through a broken window. The plasma television bled scarlet rivulets from a Chianti bottle impaled into its shattered screen.

Wormy red veins zigzagged The Man's face. "This can't be happening," he bellowed, spinning wildly in search of something more to mangle.

"We've got to do something, boss," Chauffeur said. He needed to channel The Man's rage into more productive thoughts before the house fell apart. "There's no way that kid's gonna fuck you over." If so, Chauffeur would spend the rest of his life caring for a broken man. He had to think of something.

"You bet your sweet ass," The Man said." That son-of-a-bitch is *not* going to win that tournament. I'd be ruined."

With a good deal of labored breathing, The Man uprighted a chair and slumped heavily into it. He appeared to finally begin pondering his options. "I can hold my dick and hope the kid starts playing like he's *goddamn supposed to* and gets his ass kicked. But if the kid continues his own ass kicking, I'm finished. And *that's* not going to happen." He got up and paced back and forth through the room. "The kid needs to be eliminated—and I mean permanently."

There has to be a better way than that. "But, boss, that won't look so good. He can't just be taken out. With all the bets you've laid down, other families would look at whacking in very unfriendly ways." He lit a cigarette and hung an arm over the back of his chair. He had an idea. "On the other hand,

I don't think a blind man has ever won a golf tournament."

The Man scrunched his eyebrows into a thick bar. "What are you jabbering about?"

Chauffeur studied the burning cylinder in his hand. "Last night, I was cleaning my gun with nitric acid. Now, if that acid got into the kid's eyes by chance…"

The Man's eyebrows hiked up. He kicked aside a lamp and stomped to the window. A moment later, a smile crept across his face, and he lit up like an angel. "Yeah," he said and laughed. A joyous, bubbly laugh. "The kid lives, and Bolt becomes his dog. His seeing-eye dog."

CHAPTER 88

Jim lay sprawled on the sofa in his hotel room, feeling like his old self. Even winning the tournament tomorrow wouldn't beat his current excitement. The ease he'd felt today on the course. His body and mind a unit, merging with his environment. Every blade of grass, every dip in the green—

The phone rang and jerked him out of his reverie.

"Jim, I've made reservations at Long Horns. They have the best steaks anywhere. We'll have a quiet table, so you won't be mobbed for autographs. You're the buzz of the town. See you in thirty minutes."

It was that time of South Carolina evening when the Earth seemed to catch its breath and sigh, and Jim felt as calm as the still damp air. At the restaurant's entrance, a young couple on their way out recognized him. With a friendly smile, he signed a scrap of paper the woman dug from her purse.

"Our whole family's rooting for you," she said.

Jim and Grayson took seats in an out-of-the-way booth and were looking at menus when the maitre d' handed Jim a note: *Sergeant Bolt, excuse yourself from the table without saying why and meet me outside. It's important. Colonel Green.*

"What is it, Jim?"

"It's—it's someone I know. Excuse me. I'll be right back."

Outside, Jim heard a sharp whistle and saw the colonel standing in the rear of the parking lot. He signaled Jim over. Was there something the colonel had forgotten to tell him? Was his life again in danger? The colonel had on the same dark suit he'd worn in the mess hall, the same black gloves, same long stern face. Despite the dimming light of dusk, sunglasses covered his eyes and he held a coffee cup in his hand.

The colonel's grim face worried Jim. He gave a perfunctory salute. The colonel's lips curved up and he extended his free hand. Jim relaxed and gave a firm grip. The colonel thrust the contents of his cup into Jim's face.

Jim's hands flew to his eyes. A burning pain engulfed them, as if they were melting from their sockets. Jim screamed in agony, knees buckling. He hit the ground as his world went black.

༺༻

Grayson had just started his drink when the maitre d' rushed over, grabbed his arm, and whisked him into the kitchen, where Jim stood bent over a sink.

"Jim, what the hell happened?"

"The colonel—he threw hot coffee in my eyes and they burn like hell."

The maitre d' wrung his hands. "The kitchen boy heard the young man's screams and brought him in. I am so sorry."

The hostess came dashing in. "We've called nine-one-one."

"It'll be okay, son," Grayson assured him, his arm around Jim's shoulders protectively. But in the back of his mind, his fear grew.

༺༻

In the ambulance, the paramedics tended to Jim's eyes while Grayson talked with the hospital on the phone. "Listen," he said, his tone calm. "My son is Jim Bolt, who's playing in the Global. The paramedics think acid was thrown in his eyes, and it's imperative that an ophthalmologist be there when he arrives."

Grayson sat in the waiting room for nearly an hour before the doors swung open and a doctor approached him. Grayson jumped to his feet. "Let's hear it."

"We can't tell yet how severely his eyes were damaged."

"For Christ's sake, is he blind?"

"We don't know. His eyelids are burned. He may have seen the acid coming and closed his eyes, in which case his prognosis could be positive. He'll have to wear eye patches for a few days, then we'll examine his eyes. I'm giving you salve for his face and medication to keep his eyes from burning. Here's a prescription for pain medication if he needs it. You should meet with the police."

Grayson pushed Jim in a wheelchair from the hospital to a waiting car. On the way out, he tossed the prescription into the trash. Jim would not be taking brain-numbing medication beyond aspirin. Now when his life was on the line.

On the way back to their hotel, Jim explained what happened with Colonel Green, including their previous encounter at Fort Drum.

"There is no Colonel Green, son." He had to be one of Costanzo's henchmen.

"I just told you, goddammit. The bastard came to the fort and told me about Costanzo wanting to kill me."

"What did he look like?"

"Tall, gravelly voiced with a long face. Oh, and he had a dent in his chin."

"His name's Chauffeur. He works for Costanzo."

Jim touched his bandaged face and flinched. "How d'you know?"

"Costanzo wanted us back together. That's why Chauffeur told you that army intelligence story. It was Costanzo's way for you to learn about the past. He assumed we'd make up and you'd play in the Global."

"Then why the fuck did he throw acid in my face? Huh? Tell me that."

"Because he's obviously bet against you."

"He's got a sure bet on that one."

"The hell he does."

Jim touched his bandages again restlessly. "What do you mean? I'm blind, for Christ's sake."

"You're *temporarily* blind. The doctor said your eyelids were burned. Your sight and face will return to normal."

"That's a big help. I'm still out of the fucking tournament."

"The hell you are. You'll play, and you'll win—without your sight."

"But—"

"No buts!"

Jim needed to get that woe-is-me crap out of his head right now. Get back to thinking of winning. For whatever reason, Costanzo couldn't kill Jim before the tournament, but he'd do it soon enough—no matter if Jim scored a win or not. "Listen, Jim, think of the course. I want you to describe where you want to hit your first shot."

"What's the point? Besides, I've got a killer headache and can't think straight. I need to lie down."

"Damn it! Just do it."

Jim rubbed his temples. "The hole is four hundred fifty-five yards. I'd hit long and stay clear of the trees left and the bunker right."

"What would you use for your second shot?"

"Assuming I'm on the upslope, with only a partial flagstick in view, I'd hit anything from a six iron to a wedge, depending on wind and course conditions."

"Good. Now you're on the green. The rest is easy."

"You think because I sometimes putt with my eyes closed, I don't need to make calculations beforehand?"

"You know the slope and speed of every green on the course—hell, the green of every hole you've ever played. With your ability, and my eyes to line you up, you're not only going to sink putts, but you're going to win the goddamn tournament."

"*Your* eyes?"

"As of this moment, you have a new caddy."

Jim touched an eye patch and moaned.

☙❧

When they arrived back at the hotel, Grayson fed Jim warm soup and put him to bed. He left him with the eye medication in case his eyes began burning, then slogged to his room, trying not to think about his hatred for Costanzo—or his guilt at not having him killed by the assassin. Unfortunately, the assassin was now nowhere to be found. Probably dead or in jail. But this wasn't the time for regrets. He had to meet with Howler Stemps, chairman of the Global Committee. He found the chairman's name on the Internet, scanned his bio, and learned where he lived. His phone rang as he reached the door. He picked up.

"Grayson. I just heard," said Chief Foley. "What can I do?"

"Stay where you are. Jim's fine. He's going to continue playing."

"He is?"

"It's been worked out. But remember, if anything happens to me you're to tell the police what I told you about Costanzo."

"Okay, but if Jim loses, Costanzo *will* carry out his threat."

"No, he won't. I have a guaranteed plan to prevent it. Costanzo's only reason to kill Jim is to hurt me. If Jim loses, I'll tell Costanzo that I have proof of him ordering my mother's killing, but I won't tell him what it is. If he let's Jim live, that proof will go with me to my grave."

"He might dig it for you."

"I'm willing to accept that likelihood. And if he does, again, he'll have no reason to kill Jim."

"What's the proof you have over him?"

"That he ordered my mother killed and paid off a night attendant. I know because detective Wilson talked to the guy."

"And he admitted it?"

"For five thousand dollars. And it's recorded. He had nothing to worry about because the death was deemed natural. So long, pal." Grayson hung up and hurried downstairs. Passing through the lobby, he spotted a stack of extra editions of the *Summerville Chronicle*.

JIM BOLT AGAIN WITHDRAWS FROM GLOBAL. Acid thrown in course record-holder's face.

Grayson snatched a paper and stormed off to the South Carolina horse farm estate on Flowing Wells Road. Convincing Mr. Stemps to allow Jim to continue in the tournament would be a tough sell. Blind people played golf, even competed, but never in a PGA tournament.

Grayson knew that Stemps and his committee were, in many ways, independent of the PGA and could do what they damn well pleased. But the Global Committee had never been a progressive forerunner. Here in the twenty-first century, women were still prohibited from playing the course.

He drove up and admired the twenty-five-acre grounds of fenced pastures that he'd read about. The property boasted a pond, pool, guesthouse, tennis court, riding ring, and a barn that housed three champion Quarter horses. The house was lit up like Mount Vernon.

Grayson marched to the front door with the newspaper under his arm and rang the bell, half expecting to be greeted by the likes of Colonel Sanders.

The door opened. "Ye—es," came the southern drawl of Mr. Stemps. He stood in the doorway, stout and clean-shaven, with golden brown eyes and white hair. A gentleman of leisure in a red and blue flannel shirt, gray slacks, and two-toned suede slippers.

"Good evening, Mr. Stemps. I'm sorry to disturb you. I'm Grayson Bolt, Jim Bolt's father."

"Why, Mr. Bolt. What an unspeakable tragedy." He opened the door wide. "Come in, please."

They shook hands, and Mr. Stemps led Grayson through the foyer and into the bosom of southern comfort and hospitality. Through the spacious living room wafted the aroma of fresh coffee and the hint of a fine cigar. The fireplace mantel held candlesticks and hanging crystals. A musket hung above on brass pegs. To the side, a frayed Bible rested on a butterfly table under a painting of guns firing on Fort Sumter.

Mr. Stemps led Grayson to two overstuffed chairs. "May I offer you something, Mr. Bolt? Coffee—" He peered over his glasses. "Something a bit stronger?"

Grayson shook his head. "I'm fine, thanks." He handed the newspaper to Mr. Stemps and pointed to the headline. "Correction. Jim has *not* withdrawn from the tournament."

Mr. Stemps's head did some odd weaving. "I—why, we naturally assumed—"

"Mr. Stemps, Jim has a..." Grayson cleared his throat. "Has a bit of a vision problem, but he's quite capable of finishing the tournament."

Mr. Stemps shifted in his chair. "Mr. Bolt, I'm sorry, really I am, and please excuse me for being indelicate, but I would hardly call acid in his eyes a bit of a vision problem. I'm afraid there's no way your son can continue the competition."

"This country has thousands of blind golfers sanctioned by the US Blind Golfers Association. Furthermore, I assure you, Jim doesn't have to see to play your course. He sometimes hits with his eyes closed. It helps him stay focused."

"Oh, now, Mr. Bolt. That may be so, but—"

"Please, hear me out."

The chairman clamped his lips, raised his hands, and leaned back.

"Jim has the uncanny ability of remembering every course, every hole, every shot he's ever made since he was eight years old. He knows your course better than anyone. He knows the bounces and rolls of the fairways, the tricks of the wind. And as you know, no one has scored better in its honored seventy-plus year history."

The Chairman chewed on his cheeks awhile. "I suppose you'd expect his caddy to tell him his lie, line up his club, all that?"

Grayson nodded.

"That makes sense, but what about putting? How can he possibly putt the ball into a hole without seeing it? Does he do that with his eyes closed, too?"

Grayson smiled wryly, remembering the newspaper photo Chief Foley had seen of Jim doing just that. "Yes, as a matter of fact. Just like hundreds of other blind golfers. Mr. Stemps, Jim knows every green out there like you know your horses. Tomorrow, his caddy will tell him where the hole is, how far, and align his putter. I am not saying he won't have a three putt or two, and I am not so naïve to think he'll hold that six-stroke lead. However, he *is* capable of winning the tournament. I

hope that you and the committee won't deny him that oppor-
tunity."

Mr. Stemps chewed his cheeks some more. "You present a
convincing argument."

Grayson drew air between his lips and tried to relax.

"Please wait here. This may take a while."

Mr. Stemps left the room. Grayson closed his eyes and put
his hands together. *Please, God, please...*

CHAPTER 89

It was day one of the Las Vegas World Series of Poker Tournament, held at the Rio Hotel and Casino, and Heather played the first round old Las Vegas style—with wild abandon and cocksure brashness. The Hold'em Shootout was a deadly business, and she picked off opponents like video ninjas. She wasn't going to call a bet. When she had 'em, she raised, re-raised, and re-raised again. When she didn't have 'em, she was a sharpie, a clip-artist, a fleecer who stole the pot, leaving her opponents reaching for their hip pockets, checking whether she'd skinned their wallets. The smolder in her eyes dared anyone to risk her gaze. She was Annie Oakley, aces full, with a pair of six-shooters, just in case.

Heather was one of twenty who'd just won their respective tables and advanced to the afternoon's semifinal. At two o'clock, the round started with ten players at two tables. Heather sat at one, Chief Foley at the other. The five winners from each table would advance to the final round of ten players at one table. The winner would receive a $10,000 check and leave wearing a gold bracelet.

After four hours of play, a bell sounded for the dinner break. Heather slid from her stool and grabbed a burger in the coffee shop. Still furious with Chief Foley for taking the briefcase, she made a point of avoiding him during the tournament. His having the briefcase in itself hadn't troubled her, but because he did, she didn't. And if the gangsters came calling, she'd have nothing to give but her life.

✂✄✂

Chief Foley had just started on his steak in the casino restaurant when news of Jim's tragedy flashed on the TV.

"We now have an update on the tragic blinding of golfer Jim Bolt. Mr. Stemps, the chairman of the Global committee, has announced that Mr. Bolt will continue playing in the tournament, and his father will be caddying."

Foley watched the recap in horror then dashed to the phone and called Grayson. The line was busy. He hung up and thought a moment.

Time for Heather to learn some hard facts.

He found her sitting alone in the coffee shop. "Hello, Heather." He dragged over a chair. "We only have a short while before we're called back to the tables."

"Get away from me." She swirled a French fry in a pool of ketchup. "We have nothing to talk about."

"Yes, we do." He took off his Yankee baseball cap and set it on a chair. "I just heard news you should know about. But first you need to hear some things."

"What things? That the FBI will lock me up for skipping town? Or that people I don't know will kill me because you took their money?"

"I promise, Heather, neither of those things will happen. You need to hear the truth about your past."

"*My* past?"

"There's much you don't know."

The chief folded his hands on the table and told her about Grayson killing Stockard, about Costanzo, and the consequences of Jim losing the Global. He then related the news about Jim getting blinded by acid thrown into his face.

Heather stopped eating and tears flooded her eyes. "This is awful." She wiped her cheeks with a napkin. "What did you mean about Jim being killed if he didn't win the tournament? I can't believe that."

"It's complicated, but true. Costanzo made the threat, and he'll keep it. He'd already had Grayson's mother murdered. Grayson said there's a witness."

The public address system squawked to life. *Attention Tournament players. Two minutes to return to your tables.*

"We'd better get back," the chief said.

Heather grabbed his arm. "But—"

"I'll tell you more after this round."

CHAPTER 90

eather had become the buzz of the tournament. The crowd behind the ropes whooped and cheered, hoping to see the hot blonde with steel nerves win the gold bracelet.

After five hours of play, four of the ten players at her table were on their way out of town. One more needed to follow, and the remaining five would advance to the finals.

Heather was in a hand with one other player, whom she was hell-bent to finish off. Her turn to fold, check, or raise, but her mind couldn't focus on poker. It kept returning to Jim. To the gruesome image of acid being thrown into his dreamy blue eyes.

She turned to the dealer. "Time." She closed her eyes and remained still. *Breathe. Breathe. Clear the mind.* The only sounds came from players stacking and restacking their chips. After a minute, she took one last deep breath and opened her eyes.

She bent up the corners of her two cards and peeked again at her lowly pair of twos. A cautious player would have checked. But she had studied her opponent enough to know that he had nothing going and was counting on the next two cards dealt to make a good hand.

She counted out two neat piles of chips and pushed them into the pot. "Raise."

Her opponent, a young Asian wearing sunglasses and a hoodie, shuffled his chips awhile, then re-raised.

"You're pretty confident there, big boy." She shoved her entire stack of chips into the pot. "All in."

She had pushed the enemy to the wall. His face twisted in agonizing thought. If he called and won, Heather's dream of a gold bracelet would be lost. With sweat pouring down his face, and the tournament director standing over him, telling him he must make a decision, he reluctantly called, putting all his chips in the pot.

The final two cards were no help to either player, and Heather won with her pair.

"You bet your entire stack on a fucking pair of deuces?" her opponent screamed. "How the hell could you?"

"Sorry, lessons cost extra."

Her table finished thirty minutes before Chief Foley's, and she spent the time waiting behind the ropes, signing autographs, and watching the chief win. Both Heather and the chief had advanced to tomorrow's final shootout. She rushed over to him. They offered each other quick congratulations and retreated to a lounge.

"Tell me the rest of what you were going to say," Heather demanded.

"First, you should know that, strange as it seems, Jim's going to continue playing in the tournament."

"My God, can he do that? I mean, is it possible to play golf blind?"

"Evidently Jim and Grayson think so."

The chief ordered coffees and explained the history of the strange standoff Costanzo and Grayson were now facing.

"But how long a sentence would Grayson have got? I mean, for cripe's sake, Stockard killed his wife and son."

"With a good lawyer, he'd have gotten off light." The chief fell silent when the waitress set down their coffees.

"That's what I'm saying. Costanzo gets locked up and Jim's free. End of story."

The chief slurped his coffee. "Winning the Global has always been an obsession with Grayson."

"At the risk of Jim's life?"

"Grayson doesn't see it that way. He said he has a guaranteed plan to keep Jim from getting killed if he loses."

"What plan?"

"He has proof that Costanzo ordered the murder of his mother. He'll threaten him with it."

"He's still fucking nuts."

"I can't argue that. But imagine having a wife and son murdered, then stabbing someone to death. That would screw with anyone's head."

"Why didn't you see that he got help?"

The chief took another slurp of coffee. "I sent him to a psychiatrist."

She puffed air between her lips. "Some help that was."

"Grayson's always been obsessive. That's what makes him such a good lawyer."

"Oh, please, don't talk to me about his lawyering. You knew he kept Jim's life in danger for a fucking golf tournament and did nothing."

"There wasn't a lot I could do."

"How about having him institutionalized, where he belonged?"

"Not without proof he was a danger to himself or others."

Heather sipped her coffee. "Why'd they throw acid in Jim's face?"

"Costanzo's a heavy sports better. I'm talking millions. So it's obvious he's bet against Jim."

"Why didn't he just kill him and be done with it?"

"Outright killing wouldn't go down well. Not with all the bets he'd made."

Heather started to pick up her coffee, stopped, and looked around. "I need a fucking whiskey."

Chief Foley ordered two shots. She thought about Jim. If Costanzo wanted him to lose the tournament so badly, and blinding him didn't work, what was next?

"Listen, Chief, if Jim's life is in danger, he has to withdraw from the tournament. As slim as his chances are of winning, Costanzo can't let that happen."

The chief shook his head. "Grayson won't let him quit."

"Screw Grayson. I'll go there and talk to Jim, tell him everything, and convince him to withdraw. Then tell the police about Costanzo. Jim can play the goddamn tournament next year while Costanzo's rotting in hell." She got up. "Good luck with the poker tournament, Chief."

He grabbed her arm. "No. You stay here and finish the tournament. I'll go." He patted his breast pocket. "I've already got plane and tournament tickets."

She sat back down. "What?"

"If I didn't make it to the finals, I was going to go see Jim play."

Heather looked over the chief's shoulder and let out a yelp. The two feds from LA had bounded into the lounge like wolves seeking out a wounded animal.

Pink Lips saw her and gave Big Ears a nudge. They approached the table. "If it isn't our pretty fugitive."

Foley got to his feet and whipped out his badge. "What's this about?"

Pink Lips glanced at the chief's badge and the accompanying ID He scoffed and whipped out his own badge, flashing the word *Federal*, not *Retired*. "Your friend here is a material witness to a double homicide in LA. She needs to come with us."

"She's not being charged?"

"No, but we've got questions that need answering."

The chief asked him if she could have twenty-four hours to finish the poker tournament.

"That's a no-can-do, Chief. We're on a tight schedule."

Heather jumped to her feet. "I've got news for all of you. I'm not staying here or going to California." She nodded to the feds. "You both know I didn't kill anyone or you would've arrested me in LA."

"We also know," Big Ears said, "that your friends chasing you around the casino will soon be taken into custody, putting their identity-theft enterprise kaput."

"They're not my friends."

"You looked pretty chummy with Kamal Datar there at LAX," Pink Lips said.

"You mean my kidnapper. You've got nothing on me and you know it." She turned to Chief Foley. "Hand over the tickets, Chief."

"Hold on there," Pink Lips said. "You're coming with us. We'll cuff you if necessary."

"Listen, dimwits," she said. "I'll make you an offer you can't refuse. Let me go and I'll give you Costanzo."

"What're you talking about?" Big Ears asked.

"She's right," the chief said. "Here's a chance you guys have been drooling for."

Big Ears frowned like a wrestler trying to remember who was supposed to win this bout. "She can't give him up. No one's ever touched the guy."

"But you and the New Jersey locals can," Chief Foley said. "And not for simply spitting in the street."

"Busting Costanzo will give you more than a plaque," Heather said. "They'll name a building after you."

"What do you have on him?" Pink Ears asked, puffing out his lower lip.

"Murder," Heather answered, remembering what the chief said about Costanzo ordering the murder of Grayson's mother. "And Chief Foley here will give you a witness."

She looked into Chief Foley's soft eyes, gave him a firm little smile, and extended her hand. "Tickets, please."

The chief handed them over. "I'll deal with the airline about the change."

"Good luck, tomorrow. And, Chief, one more thing. Remember when I beat you with my full house?"

"How could I forget?"

"Your tell was your hands."

He gave her a blank look.

"It was how you held the cards that told me you believed I had you beat. Your cards were in your right hand. When you're confident, they're in your left, keeping your right free to grab chips. So long, Chief. I'll be rooting for you."

CHAPTER 91

Heather arrived in muggy springtime South Carolina late at night and checked into a motel. After five hours of sleep, she got up and ate breakfast in a coffee shop across the street. She wished she could've talked to Jim when she arrived, but hadn't thought to ask Chief Foley for his phone number or where he was staying. When she'd tried to reach the chief, she only got voice mail.

She took a taxi to the golf course. It was early but already hot and sticky. Play had begun, but Jim would be teeing off last. Her pulse raced, while she tried to enjoy all the blooming flowers. The course was crowded with people. Not only spectators, but the whole Summerville police department appeared to be out in force. She scurried to the driving range, hoping to find Jim.

It was thick with spectators, making it hard to recognize the players, though she did recognize Surge Michaelson and Bat Brady. All at once, the crowd roared, and she managed to squeeze through enough people to see Jim shuffle to a practice tee holding his dad's arm like…like a blind man. White bandages showed behind his sunglasses. He waved to supporters as if he could see.

She clenched her jaw to stifle the sob in her throat. Memories flooded back. Eating at Jim's favorite vegetarian restaurant, playing strip poker, their lovemaking. She held a knuckle to her lips.

With the size of the crowd and all the security, she'd need help to contact Jim. "Excuse me," she said to a man in a gold jacket. "Where would I find the head of security?"

"There's security offices at both gates."

She hurried to the front gate and, after talking with several people, found herself in a small room with drab walls and a gray metal desk. She told a heavyset man and a young woman in gold jackets that Jim was in danger and that she needed to speak to someone in charge. The woman left and returned with another man with captain's bars and a nametag that said Snodgrass. He was short, with a square, red face. A face not at ease. Heather repeated her story, while two Summerville police officers came in and hovered in the back of the room.

She wasn't getting through to the captain, dammit! More police came in, whispered among themselves, and left. *Oh, my God!* They thought she was a nut case. "Look," she said to the captain, "I've told you, Jim Bolt's life is in danger. He's already had acid thrown in his face. Does he have to get killed before you'll listen to me?"

The captain's face remained expressionless. "Ms. Morrison, may I see your identification?"

"For Christ's sake. Go find Jim Bolt's father. Tell him Heather Morrison has to talk to him immediately."

"Please, your identification?"

"I don't believe this." She dug into her purse, fished out her wallet, and flashed her driver's license. "Here, see."

"Take it out, please."

She drew in a breath, removed her license, and extended her arm. "Will you hurry, *please*?"

"I'll return this when I come back." On the way out, the captain ordered one of the officers to remain. When the door closed, the officer stood with his back against it, his face expressionless as dough.

Heather sat straight in her chair, heart thumping like mad.

Thirty minutes later, the captain returned and handed back her license. "Ms. Morrison, we're going to have to detain you until after the tournament."

Heather jumped to her feet. "You can't be serious."

"I'm quite serious. Mr. Bolt senior informed us that you stalked his son three years ago in California. He said he wants to talk to you after the tournament. If you need something to eat or drink, or to go to the restroom, let Officer Clemens know." The man at the door squared his shoulders.

"You can't force me to stay here."

"Yes, Ms. Morrison, I can and I will." He turned and left the room.

CHAPTER 92

The air was thick enough to slice and fry, wet enough to sizzle. Just the way Jim liked it. He had been yesterday's top attraction and today's superstar. Whispers whipped among the gallery like ghosts. Could he really play blind? He'd been on the course more than five hours and the gallery kept getting larger and louder. The greens were soft, allowing Jim to land approaches close to every hole, eliminating long putts. He managed to play seventeen holes in only four over par. He was paired with Surge Michaelson and stood one stroke ahead of him. Bat Brady, the usual crowd favorite and four-time winner, was in the group ahead and had never played such a lonely round. Everyone wanted to see the blind man play. With Jim's every shot, the ground rumbled with thundering shouts and applause.

Jim was now tied with Bat. A total score of three under par. Bat had just finished the round and was in the clubhouse. Jim prepared to hit his tee shot down the eighteenth fairway. He took a big swing and the ball took off like a rocket.

Grayson watched the ball soar and thought about what to say to Heather. He had a lot to apologize for.

Howie Collins addressed the television viewers. "The ball's high and heading toward the left side bunkers. Will it cut around the dogleg? Yes. It's fading…fading…not too much. We can't tell up here if it rolled into the rough. Let's go to Vin McKay, down on the fairway."

"It did roll into the rough, Howie. Jim must get the ball onto the green by hitting a tricky bump-and-run shot, while avoiding hanging tree branches."

"And if successful," Howie said, "it'll take a one-putt birdie to win. Two putts, and he ties with Bat, forcing a sudden death playoff that he could easily lose. We now see Jim's ball, but can't make out the lie. What about it, Vin?"

"It's not a bad lie, but the ball is resting on pine needles, so it's going to fly out fast. It's a hundred and fifty-three yards to the front of the green. His caddy will coach him to aim precisely, and he must strike down perfectly on the ball. It'd be a tough shot for anyone. It'll take a miracle for him to pull it off."

CHAPTER 93

Heather heard the action on the course, coming from a TV in an adjacent room. With mounting fear, she worried that a killer would be waiting at the eighteenth hole if Jim had a chance of winning. And with scores this close…

She had worked out a plan of escape. Earlier, Officer Clemens had escorted her to a restroom in another building with a window large enough to crawl through. Back in her detention room, she studied the course layout posted on a wall. She would dash to the tenth fairway, cut across to the eighteenth, elbow through the gallery, sprint past security, grab Jim, and beg him to leave the course or be killed.

She listened as the announcer said, "Jim is now walking up to his ball. He'll need to get the ball onto the green in one shot." Heather had to get out there. Now! "Officer Clemens, I have to go to the bathroom," she pleaded, with a face to match.

They paced across the grounds to the bathroom. Heather dashed inside and, a minute later, sprinted across the fairway. The gallery was more than thirty deep. All she could see were heads and sweaty backs. She wormed her way closer to the front, taking in curses and more than a few elbows. She gained some ground but was still far from the ropes. She stood on her toes. Security had Jim and Grayson surrounded as they stood by the ball under a tangle of tree branches. Grayson consulted a notepad.

She clawed her way close enough to hear him. "You're going to punch a six iron with a three-quarter swing. The ball will come out hot and land one hundred and forty yards out.

It'll skip onto the green and stop below the upper tier, near the hole. I'm going to position your feet a tad forward. Let's see some practice swings."

Grayson handed Jim his club, and the sounds of the gallery melted to nothing. Heather found it impossible to believe so many people could make this much silence. After Jim took his shot, everybody would start to move, and so would she.

Jim took three practice swings, then addressed the ball. His dad reached down, adjusted the club-head, and stepped back. "You're good to go."

Jim had once told Heather that when he stood over the ball, the world around him ceased to exist. Now, the same thing happened to Heather as she watched him. The crowd, including Heather, stood stock still, as if afraid to breathe.

Jim took a graceful three-quarter swing and hit the ball solidly. It took off under the trees, bounced twice, landed on the green, but rolled too far, about eight feet above the hole. The crowd whooped and hollered. The marshals began wedging a path through the fans. Grayson shouted, "You did it, Jim, you're going to…"

His voice suddenly trailed off as something caught his attention in the woods behind the crowds. Heather twisted to see what he was looking at. Horror flooded over her as she caught sight of a man leaning out from behind a tree—aiming a sniper rifle at Jim.

"*Jim!*" she shrieked, desperately clawing her way forward. Jim's head whipped toward her, pulled by her voice.

"*No!*" Grayson yelled at the same time and pushed Jim backward.

A faint pop sounded, muffled by the cheering, and Grayson collapsed to the ground.

"His caddy!" someone yelled. "He's having a heart attack!" A moment later a woman shrieked, "His head! It's bleeding!"

Heather watched in horror as a marshal rushed over and knelt beside Grayson. "He's been shot!" The marshal reached for his walkie-talkie. People ran in all directions, shrieking.

Jim knelt down, felt around for his dad, and found his bloody head. "Dad, what the hell happened?"

Heather was only a few feet away, but marshals had formed a protective barrier. Carts skidded up to the scene and more security people poured out, including the captain. "Tape off the crime scene and move everyone out." An ambulance arrived, and medics tended to Grayson. Another cart came skidding up with a sign on the windshield: Howler Stemps. The man jumped out.

Jim was on his knees, weeping. Stemps took his arm. "Come on, son, let's go."

Pop! Pop! Two more distant shots. People all around hit the ground, except Heather, who ran to Jim. Walkie-talkies croaked to life. "The shooter is down. Repeat, the shooter is down and in custody."

Heather reached Jim, who was now in the cart with Stemps. "Oh, Jim." She threw her arms around him.

"H—Heather?"

"It's me." A sob caught in her throat. "I'll explain later."

Heather's thinking had suddenly taken a hundred-eighty-degree turn. Jim was no longer in danger. The assassin was captured, and Costanzo would soon be in FBI custody. She couldn't let Jim quit. He spent his whole life dreaming of winning the Global, and here he was at victory's doorstep.

Stemps was trying to clear the crowd from around the cart. "Move aside, folks. The tournament's over."

"No!" Heather cried. "Jim, the tournament's not over." She gripped his shoulders. "You've got to continue."

"Ma'am, you must get off the cart," Stemps said.

"Jim, you can't quit." Her fingers gripped his shoulders as a marshal tugged her arm.

Jim shook his head, his face red and slick with tears.

The marshal yanked her from the cart. "Wait, please." She wrenched free and leaped back aboard. She grasped Jim's head. "Jim, I know a terrible thing just happened. But listen to me. This is your chance to destroy Costanzo forever." She felt Jim stiffen. "He'll be in jail, but he'll still have money. This is your chance to wipe him out financially, to hurl all his filth right back at him, back in his evil face."

Stemps raised a hand for the marshal to hold up.

"Come on, Jim, *snap out of it*! Go up there and sink that goddamn winning putt."

Jim swiped a knuckle across his cheeks, then reached for Heather, and cradled her head. His thumbs wiped tears from under her eyes. He put his forehead against hers and held it there a long time, taking deep breaths. He drew back. "Mr. Stemps—"

"Hold on, Jim," Stemps said. "I think I know what you're going to say." He got out of the cart and treaded to Captain Snodgrass. They spoke a minute, then he returned. "Yes, Jim, what is it?"

"I want to continue. Heather will be my caddy."

CHAPTER 94

This is the most unusual and historic event in golf history," Howie Collins told the world. "To recap. Yesterday, Jim Bolt broke the course record for the second time with a blistering sixty-one. Then double tragedy struck the twenty-one-year old. Last evening, an unknown assailant threw acid in his face, blinding him, we hope, temporarily. Today, he's been playing blind with his father caddying and coaching until a half-hour ago, when again, tragedy struck. After Jim hit onto the eighteenth green, an assassin shot and killed his father. We have reason to believe that the assassin was aiming for Jim, but his father deliberately took the bullet. We've also just learned from Captain Snodgrass of the Summerville police that spectators overpowered a second shooter, whom we believe was taking aim at Jim. It appears both father and son were targets for assassination.

"With all that's happened," Howie went on, "it's hardly conceivable that Jim could continue to play. But that's exactly what this valiant young man is about to do. Now back down to Vin on the eighteenth green."

"Events here are astonishing," Vin said. "Michaelson has already putted out. Jim and his new caddy, an unknown woman, are being driven up to the green. If Jim makes this putt, it's over. He wins the championship."

"Nick, what kind of a putt does Jim have?" Howie asked.

"A very hard one, and for two reasons. First, the man hitting it is blind. Second, the ball is above the hole, making for a curving downhill eight-footer—a putt a sighted man would miss more than half the time. If struck too hard, the ball will roll thirty feet down the rise. Jim could possibly putt till sundown and never find the hole."

"Players have been missing that putt all day," Vin said.

◌◌◌

Mr. Stemps let Jim and Heather out of the cart, and Jim took Heather's arm. "Take me to the front of the green."

"Jim, we should get someone else to help you. I'm not a caddy."

"We're going to win this together. You told me once in Berkeley that people thought you'd make a good caddy. Remember? We were having veggie burgers. Now's your chance to prove it."

Heather guided him up a few yards and stopped. "We're standing before the green between two sand traps."

"Look behind the green, and a little to the right. There should be a massive oak tree and, behind that, the clubhouse."

"That's right."

"We're at the lower of two tiers. Tell me where the hole is, and my ball in relation to it."

"The hole's just under the top tier, and the ball's up on the tier's edge."

"Oh, boy," Jim said. "This won't be easy." He took a deep breath. "Okay, I've got it pictured. Take me to my ball."

Standing before the ball, Jim pulled from his pocket the lucky peso Heather had given him while eating that same veggie burger. He showed it to her. "Bet you didn't know I still had this."

Warmth spread from her stomach, but she couldn't get emotional. Not now. She guided his hand behind the ball where he placed the peso. He picked up the ball and handed it to her. "Make sure you clean this. How many feet away is the hole?"

Heather paced it off. "Eight-and-a-half feet."

He nodded. "The question is, how big's the break?"

"It's big. I would say, um—"

"Never mind. I can visualize it. It breaks two feet, three

inches, left to right. I want you to squat down and look carefully at the line the ball must take. Then go around and check
from the other side of the hole and see if you agree with me."

Heather checked from both directions. "It breaks more than
you think. I'd say three feet."

"Three? Are you sure about that?"

Heather tried to swallow, but couldn't. Suppose she was
wrong? Jim ought to stick with his instinct. Why the hell did
she ever tell him she'd make a good caddy?

"Come on, Heather. You really think it's that much?"

She bit her lip. "It's three feet." She handed him his putter.

He took some practice strokes.

"Jim, you're swinging too hard. If you hit the ball like that
and miss the hole, it'll roll way off the green."

"I'm just releasing tension. Give me the ball and line me
up."

∽∾∽

"It looks like Jim's almost ready," Howie said. "We've got
the mic on him. He's placed his ball back down and is taking
more practice strokes. Now he turns to his caddy and calls her
over. Let's listen: 'I want you to know that I've never stopped
loving you.' Whoa. How's that for romance? He's now leaning
over his ball. She bends over and is aligning the putter-head.
She steps away. Jim adjusts his feet. 'Here goes, Dad. This is
for you and Troy.' He draws the putter back and barely taps it.
It's on the way. It might be too hard, maybe, maybe—it catches the rim, circles the clock…it drops!"

The silence held for a moment. One momentous beat to let
it sink in. It was done. The crowd's astonishment rose to a
piercing crescendo. Heather screamed and ran into Jim's arms.

"We have a new Global champion! Jim Bolt!"

CHAPTER 95

Chauffeur had serious worries about his boss's health—and his own. Costanzo looked like he'd just been grilled by a senate investigating committee. His face was drawn and gray from the strain, his voice dry and raspy from yelling. When Jim tapped in that last putt, Costanzo didn't appear to breathe. He sat perched on the edge of his chair with eyes so intense, Chauffeur thought they might make the ball skid and back up. Instead, Costanzo turned white as the ball that had just swirled down the hole, costing him ten million dollars. He staggered to the bar and poured a stiff one.

Chauffeur's cell phone rang. He switched off the TV and grabbed the phone. It was their Miami man, Tony—the ant—Spilotro. He had set up the two assassins to take out the Bolts. The Man had wanted them both killed if the kid might win it on the last hole. The ant had also been ordered to investigate the disappearance of the midget.

"Yeah," Chauffeur said. "Uh-huh…Uh-huh…Misha's *what*?…When?"

The Man shot him a look.

Chauffeur held up his hand. "Get rid of the fucking body. I'll get back to you." He hung up and turned to The Man. "You're not going to believe this, boss, but you've been ripped off for four million bucks. You're cleaned out."

Costanzo dropped his drink. He was looking over Chauffeur's shoulder. Chauffeur turned and saw a stream of men in FBI jackets dash by the window.

The door burst open. "Hands up, Costanzo. You have the right to remain silent. Anything you say…"

CHAPTER 96

The first-class flight stewardess came by with a warm smile and a cold bottle of champagne. "My, what lovely bracelets," she said.

Linda raised an arm, and the jewelry jingled "Why, thank you. I just picked them up at a gift shop in the terminal."

"Real silver," Kamal added.

The flight attendant raised the bottle. "More champagne?"

"I'll finish this," Linda said, "then switch to red. My system's still adjusting to all this luxury."

Kamal held out his glass. "Mine's already adjusted."

The attendant poured. "We'll be taking off in ten minutes."

Kamal looked at Linda and held up his glass. "What shall we toast to?"

"How about…respectability?"

"Hear, hear. And to Lucky, who like us, almost made it to the next life."

The stewardess breezed by, and Linda caught her arm. "Oh, miss, where do we pick up our pets after landing?"

"An attendant will be with them in the first-class waiting area, along with your luggage."

Linda leaned close to Kamal. "Something I've been wondering about. Why didn't you shoot me when Misha ordered you to?"

He looked at her and grinned. "Because you had promised me another lesson."

She took his hand and gave it a squeeze.

A voice filtered over the intercom. "This is your captain speaking. Welcome aboard American Airlines Flight 137, non-stop to New Delhi."

CHAPTER 97

Heather reached into her purse for sunglasses. "Oh, my gosh." She retrieved a crumpled piece of paper. "It's been two weeks and I forgot all about Chief Foley's telegram. Here, I'll read it."

"Give it to me," Jim said. "You drive, I'll read.

"'Congratulations to you, Jim, on your outstanding achievement at the Global. You are a champion of the highest order. Your dad was always justifiably proud of you. He was a rare man, and I'm honored to have been his friend. Take good care of that girl of yours. They don't come any better. Chief Foley. P.S. Thank Heather for me. I would not have won the tournament without her tip. She'll know what I mean.'"

Jim looked at her. "What's he talking about?"

"Nothing, really." With a wry smile she added, "Let's just say, I taught him everything he knows about poker."

After Grayson's funeral and memorial in New York, they spent time getting reacquainted by driving across New England and reliving their sexual experiences with romantic stays in old-world inns.

The red blotches on Jim's face were fading, and the doctor declared minimal damage in one eye, and none in the other. His eyes were healing, just like his relationship with Heather.

In time, both would be as strong as they had ever been.

They drove east on New York's Jackie Robinson Parkway, fringed with a forest of trees and blooming shrubs. The air was warm and clear with unusual spring stillness, as though everyone was indoors taking a siesta.

Heather glanced at Jim. A tear filled the corner of his eye. She reached for his hand. "Thinking of your dad?"

"I miss him." He turned to Heather. "You think you could've forgiven him?"

Her heart dropped. She smiled and stroked his cheek. "Oh, honey, I have forgiven him. He devoted his life to you. He died for you."

They crossed a bridge, and a sign read, *JFK Airport south on 678.*

"Airport?" Jim said. "Are we going somewhere?"

"Keep your pants on, you'll see." She rolled into the airport terminal and pulled into short-term parking. "Come on."

Inside the terminal, Heather checked the flight monitor. "This way." They snaked through baggage claim and stood along a chrome rail. Heather tingled with anticipation.

Jim glanced at her wrist. "Nice bracelet."

From around a corner, a horde of overseas passengers poured into the area. She clutched his arm, her heart fluttering like bird wings. Heather's mother appeared holding the hand of a young boy. "Mommy!"

Heather scooped the child up. "Troy, say hello to your daddy."

"Wha—what?" Jim said.

"Would you like to hold your son?"

"Well, sure. He's mine—er—ours?"

"He's got your nose." She handed him the child and then embraced her mother.

Her mother reached out and included Jim and Troy. "I'm so happy to finally meet you, Jim. And your father, such a generous man, and to die so tragically." She shuddered. "He literally saved my life."

Heather put her arm around Jim's waist, as he carried Troy on their way to the car. "Sweetheart," he said, "I was told that, well, you know, you had gotten—"

"I put in a ringer," she said, proud of herself. "Paid a girl to use my name when she had her own abortion. Your dad had already left town."

"You really are something. I'm only sorry you had to sacrifice your poker tournament."

"That's okay," she said with a wide smile. "There's always next year. But first, you owe me a cruise to Mexico."

THE END

Author's Note

Hi, I'm Bill A. Brier. A few years ago I put aside Hollywood movie making and took up racecar driving and mystery writing. It's been a blast. Thanks for joining the ride.

Go to billbrier.com and check out one of my mystery contests and perhaps win $1,000. Also, click on the book trailer for my second mystery, *The Killer Who Hated Soup*.

One last thing…If you liked this story, I'd consider it a personal favor if you'd spread the word to your friends, and also give your book seller an honest review.

Following is a brief preview of *The Killer Who Hated Soup*.

PROLOGUE

Defiance, Oklahoma, December 1956:

The girl tore through the woods with her baby.

Ignoring her bleeding feet, she raced until she slipped on loose leaves and crashed into a shrub, dropping the newborn. Stunned, she lay still in the biting cold and heard her father yelling and bursting through the brush behind her. She snatched up the wailing baby and held her hand to its mouth. Dashing through undergrowth that tore at her bare legs, she broke through onto the road leading to the highway, hesitated, turned, and threw herself across the open stretch and into the shrubbery.

She clawed through thick, thorny blackberry bushes, trying to protect the baby as she moved through the brush. She came out onto a narrow path that she knew would lead back to her hiding place in the burnt-out hollow of an oak tree.

Weakening now, she sucked in air with a loud, rasping noise. Her muscles ached, her legs trembled. She heard her father fighting through the blackberry bushes, and with her remaining strength, she flung herself forward.

She reached the oak and scrambled inside. Pulled up her nightshirt, pressed her baby's mouth to her nipple, and tried to quiet her own breathing. Minutes later, her heart still pounding, the crunching sound of footsteps approached, then stopped.

"Come on out, Marybeth. I know you're in there." His voice softened. "Everything's okay."

She peered through tangled branches into the starry sky. "You'll take my baby."

Darkness swept across like a curtain. Hands reached in and wrenched the infant from her grasp. "No. *You'll* give it away."

She scrambled from the tree and clawed at her father's shirt, reaching for her baby held beyond her grasp.

"God will forgive you, my daughter."

About the Author

Bill A. Brier grew up in California and went to Hollywood High School. After serving in the air force as a combat cameraman, he hired on at Disney Studios as a film loader and advanced from there.

He earned a master's degree in psychology—a big help when working with *Trumpish* Hollywood producers—you're fired! During his more-than-twenty-five years in the movie business as a cameraman, film editor, and general manager, Brier worked on everything from the hilarious, *The Love Bug,* to the creepy, *The Exorcist,* to the far out, *Star Trek* and *Battle Star Galactica.*

Eight years ago, Brier switched from reading scripts to writing mysteries and driving racecars. After completing three award-winning novels, he signed with Black Opal Books. His first novel, *The Devil Orders Takeout,* is a standalone mystery/thriller about a devoted father and husband who makes a deal with a real-life devil to protect his golf-prodigy son—after his wife and older son are killed in a mysterious accident—and pays hell for it.

Brier's second mystery, *The Killer Who Hated Soup,* launches in July, 2017: The Internet? Never heard of it. Smart phones? Who you kiddin'? It's the 1950s. Energetic and eager to make his mark on what *Time Magazine* called the next great boom town, Bucky Ontario leaves his daddy and little sister in Louisiana and rides a bus to Defiance, Oklahoma, a town not particularly adverse to murders, just the embarrassment of them when committed by high officials.

Brier lives in Southern California with his wife, dogs and chickens. He writes every day and golfs infrequently (that damn right knee!). His five children and eight grandchildren keep him busy going to birthday parties, and he never misses a one!

The Brier Patch, Brier's humorous and engaging blog about his wild and woolly early days in Hollywood, is on his website, billbrier.com, along with contests, which will award grand prizewinners $1,000.

www.ingramcontent.com/pod-product-compliance
Lightning Source LLC
Chambersburg PA
CBHW070802120726
47910CB00001B/263